lovestruck

Laura Jane Williams (she/her) is known as the queen of the meet-cute. She is the author of six novels and a novella. The rights to Laura's international bestseller *Our Stop* have been sold for television, and her books have been translated into languages all over the world. She loves romance, being a parent, and lifting really heavy weights.

Find out more about Laura on www.laurajaneauthor.com, or on Instagram as @laurajaneauthor.

Also by Laura Jane Williams

Our Stop

The Love Square

The Lucky Escape

One Night With You

The Wrong Suitcase

Just for December

LAURA JANE WILLIAMS

love struck

PENGUIN BOOKS

PENGUIN BOOKS

UK | USA | Canada | Ireland | Australia
India | New Zealand | South Africa

Penguin Books is part of the Penguin Random House group of companies
whose addresses can be found at global.penguinrandomhouse.com

Penguin
Random House
UK

First published in Penguin Books 2023
001

Typeset in 10.4/15 pt Palatino LT Pro
by Integra Software Services Pvt. Ltd, Pondicherry

Printed and bound in Great Britain by Clays Ltd, Elcograf S.p.A.

The authorised representative in the EEA is Penguin Random House Ireland,
Morrison Chambers, 32 Nassau Street, Dublin D02 YH68

A CIP catalogue record for this book is available from the British Library

ISBN: 978-1-529-15985-1

www.greenpenguin.co.uk

MIX
Paper from
responsible sources
FSC
www.fsc.org FSC® C018179

Penguin Random House is committed to a
sustainable future for our business, our readers
and our planet. This book is made from Forest
Stewardship Council® certified paper.

This one is for the four women who got on a train,
said endless encouraging things,
paid for lunch
and had me get back on the book-writing horse.
Thank you. Like, seriously.

1

'All I'm saying is, we're all going to die. Eventually, I mean. It's the only certainty. Things before then can be crappy or good – and I'm only interested in manifesting a good time. A *lovely* time, in fact. Do you know what I mean?'

As she speaks, Becca Calloway can feel scepticism oozing from her best friend Jia Li's pores. Jia Li isn't about surrender to what she calls 'the woo-woo' – she's distinctly science over faith, the founding member of life's got-to-see-it-to-believe-it society . . . but unfortunately for her, this is about to be Woo-Woo City.

'Don't look at me like that,' Becca insists with a self-deprecating chuckle. 'I know what you're thinking when you look at me like that.'

'That no single person can bend the universe to their will with their *thoughts*?' Jia Li asks, a similar smile playing across her lipstick-covered mouth. 'That if *good vibes* were all that was necessary in life, we'd have no poverty? No cancer or car crashes or paediatric wards in hospitals? That we could simply *meditate* our way out of a bad situation? Or that you look too cute in that dress and I'm going to have to steal it from you at some point?'

Becca kicks up her left heel in a showgirl-style acknowledgement of the compliment and tells her, 'Free People. In the sale. And don't change the subject. All I mean is that, exactly like you say, so much is out of our control. At the end of the day, all we can do is have an attitude of gratitude for what is good. And it's surely basic physics that what we focus on expands. Think *car parking space* and you'll get a car parking space. Think *Oh crap, I'm going to have a terrible day* and sure enough, bad things will happen to you. That's manifestation.'

'Becca,' Jia Li says, taking a big gulp of her Prosecco. 'That's not manifestation. That's confirmation bias. Also, I cannot believe you just said *attitude of gratitude* without a single trace of irony.'

'Oh, for crying out loud, you're impossible.' Becca tuts, shaking her head good-naturedly. 'And willingly obtuse. How do we manage to work together so harmoniously when we're so different?'

'I actually know the answer to that one,' Jia Li declares proudly, holding up a hand which she then proceeds to touch the fingers of as she lists her response. 'One, I'm the only woman you know who can match you drink for drink, which I think you appreciate the challenge of. Two, you enjoy living vicariously through my sex life, you butter-wouldn't-melt degenerate. You get your kicks listening to my exploits whilst still committing to this nun-like "I'd rather go without than do it just because" routine. And three—'

'Christ, Jia Li, why are you orating as if you're commanding the troops at Normandy?'

Jia Li doesn't miss a beat as she ignores her. 'I make you laugh. Sometimes I don't even mean to, and you still end up cackling like a witch.'

'The witch and the bitch, what a gruesome twosome.'

Jia Li chuckles. Becca is apparently good at making her laugh, too. 'And to think we really are single. Who could resist?'

Becca empties a nearby bottle into their glasses and surveys the room. Everything is perfect – the salon buzzing, the nibbles and drinks free-flowing, good hair everywhere.

'Look,' Becca tells her friend, lowering her voice, wanting a conclusion to this conversation before they get underway. 'The only way I can keep believing that my person is out there is by looking out for the evidence that life is, essentially, kind to me. That life loves me enough to gift me my man any minute now. I need to keep feeding my hope, and this ceremony tonight is as good a way as any. You've got to give me that. *Please* give me that!' She shakes her fist dramatically, as if she's giving a Shakespearean speech. It's easier to self-mock her desire for the One than it is to be earnest, otherwise the longing for it could kill her.

Jia Li sucks in her cheeks, her amusement obvious. 'Can I have evidence that this thing is going to get started soon? Are we still waiting for anyone to arrive?'

Becca grabs a clipboard from behind the front desk and scans down the list of attendees. Most hair salons don't run monthly events for their clientele of business owners and glossy stay-at-home mums, local DJs and media personalities, let alone auspicious manifestation rituals to bare hearts and souls on a sticky, mid-heatwave summer solstice. But then, most hair salons aren't Trim. Trim does hair, true, but it is also the beating heart of King's Heath, the little wedge of Birmingham that Becca, Jia Li and everyone else here tonight calls home. Regular clients always turn up to support Trim's after-hours events – from still-life drawing to cocktail making, sourdough baking to essential-oils blending – and judging from the number of ticks next to the names on Becca's list, the turnout for tonight's manifestation ritual isn't going to be any different.

'I think we're good to go. I'm going to find Coco and invite her to get started,' Becca pronounces. She tilts her chin towards Carlos, Trim's co-owner, who is making his way over. 'Carlos, pal, can you do something about the AC? We need to make sure it doesn't click off the timer like normal otherwise we're going to melt in this heat.'

Carlos heads out to the back room to access the salon's temperature controls, giving Becca a thumbs up as he passes. 'On it,' he says, efficiently, and Becca gives him a grateful thumbs up in return.

'Right then,' intones Jia Li, plonking down her empty glass and clapping her hands together. 'Let's go and positive-mental-attitude our way out of eternal spinsterhood by dry humping some rose quartz and howling at the moon, shall we?'

'Bloody well get in the spirit of this, or you're out on your ear,' Becca hisses under her breath. She's half joking and – actually – half dead serious. 'You can be sarky with me but don't let the clients hear you. Put on a good show. Pretend to be into this for the morale of the group, capeesh?'

Jia Li pulls a solemn face, apparently understanding that her friend – and boss – needs her to at least *feign* maturity. Becca duly notes her efforts.

'Capeesh,' Jia Li echoes, and to be fair to her, she does a pretty decent job of suspending her cynicism – right up until the chanting, anyway.

'Just let the sounds come,' instructs Coco, their pink-haired and pierced host for the evening. She has a snake tattooed from her left wrist all the way up her arm, curling around the back of her shoulders, culminating in its head over on her right bicep, which is, incidentally, chiselled like Madonna's. Becca had been totally floored by her when she'd walked in earlier, this person in full possession of themselves. She likes it. Trusts it. Wants a bit of that for herself. 'Let what is within you be drawn out instinctively, without thought,' Coco presses from her side of the 'welcome circle'. 'Inhabit your body, move out of your mind.'

Even with her eyes closed in concentration Becca knows – before the words have a chance to be spoken – exactly what Jia Li is going to say.

'I think some of us are already out of our minds,' she quips, right on cue. It generates a murmur of giggles from the more self-conscious attendees amongst the group, but Coco takes Jia Li's input with good humour.

'If you growl, you growl. If you howl, you howl,' Coco continues. 'If you moan, you moan,' she adds, as if doing so in a room of thirty fully clothed people one Wednesday evening in June is nothing out of the ordinary. Becca braces herself for Jia Li again.

'My kind of night.'

Becca opens her eyes to shoot her evils, but instead catches Coco smiling. Jia Li must feel Becca's gaze on her because she opens her eyes, clocking Becca's frown. She mouths *sorry* in an approximation of sincerity and closes them again. Becca watches her sway, as has been asked of them, and then casts an eye over everyone else, too.

The group are seated atop overstuffed tasselled pillows, on the patterned rug of what is normally the waiting area of the green and gold-accented salon. They are all cross-legged, and almost all mildly embarrassed in the face of a woman who, even for Becca's taste, talks about 'the universe' a *lot*. Coco comes recommended, though, through a client, and the command she has over the room is admirable, her voice a low rumble as though it's coming from her belly, some sort of energetic frequency that permeates the group and makes them collectively surrender to her matriarchal care. It's quite nice to let somebody else be in charge for a change.

A low hum sounds from Carlos then, and it encourages everyone else to start making their noises as well. The idea is to have their own vibrations meet the vibrations of the universe, as a way of opening the world up to hearing each individual's desires.

'Summer solstice – the twenty-first of June – is the longest day of the year,' Coco tells them over the din of their chants and the buzz of the air conditioning unit. It all sounds very dramatic – as if she's performing a monologue to the beat of human breath. Becca exhales and lets herself surrender.

'In Iceland, they believe that on this day animals can gain the power of speech. The Greeks enjoy summer solstice as the first day of the calendar. The Chinese use today to pay tribute to femininity and honour.'

The humming and chanting get louder.

'We humbly perform our rituals tonight alongside the rest of the globe to reflect the earth's abundance. Life is full, and ours for the taking. And so together, as you reopen your eyes, I welcome you, and say we are ready to manifest our deepest summertime desires into real, tangible things.'

'Amen,' says Jia Li, chirpily and silly, and everyone bursts out into giggles.

Coco nods with a wink. 'Something like that, yeah.'

It could just be Becca's imagination, but the air feels different after that. Stiller, somehow, imbued with a solemnity and gravity, everyone ready to get down to business. Coco gives out pieces of paper and pens, inviting the group to write down their intentions for the months ahead. As everyone quietly reflects and scribbles down what comes to mind, Coco walks around the room and lights several candles, reaching the centre of the circle as everyone finishes writing, placing flowers down beside a central candle and lighting that as the last one.

'When you're done,' Coco instructs, 'close your eyes again. Ruminate on your list. Breathe. Tap into your deep-rooted powers of manifestation. Call on your angels and spirit guides, the divine powers of the universe, to come to your aid.' Becca can telepathically hear Jia Li ask, *So is that, like, through an app? Or is there an email address we can use . . . ?*

7

She focuses. Becca imagines a swell in her belly. Her partner's hand in hers. Watching a blond-haired boy with her
nose play on a beach, running into and out of the waves. She
wants this. She wants this so, so much. She had enough fun
for ten women in her twenties, made a big choice to start the
business and opened Trim at thirty, and now, at thirty-five,
she wants the next bit. Her body yearns for it. Could she
freeze her eggs and take the pressure off? Maybe. Does she
want to? No. She's been single for half a decade, and enough
is enough. She wants the next part of her life: a proper romantic partner, the start of building her own family. This holding
place is no good.

'And repeat after me,' says Coco, focusing the group. She
coughs to clear her throat and begins: 'I gather in the power
of this day.'

They repeat her words. 'I gather in the power of this day.'

Coco presses: 'I call in the guardians to bring in what
is already mine.' That sentence is longer, and a few people
stumble over the words, but they repeat it too. 'To manifest
my desires in the coming harvest. I ask that this be done
within the greater good.'

And then they are invited to read their lists aloud, with
sincerity and significance.

'I ask for my sister to make a full recovery,' says Heidi, a
local food PR who comes in for a bi-annual balayage and a
blunt shoulder-length cut.

'I pray for the strength of self to finally leave him,' offers
Monique, a middle-aged woman who books a root touch-up
with Carlos for the last Friday of every month.

'I ask for love, in all of its forms,' says Carlos, and Becca catches his eye. She wasn't expecting that from him. He looks shyly away, a half-smile hanging in his cheeks, and Becca takes in the sight of him: all dark, clipped facial hair and tattoos on thick, tanned arms that are shown off to perfection through an *incredibly* fitted shirt. If Becca has a golden tan from her recent Majorcan vacation, Carlos is practically Tuscan leather, although it does come by way of Costa del Sunbed. He's as much of a pain in the arse as Jia Li, but they're both *her* pains in the arse. When Carlos looks up again, Becca sticks out her tongue. He crosses his eyes and sticks out his own, betraying the emotion she's just heard in his voice.

'I ask for love in all of its forms too,' says Jia Li. 'For me, and for everyone I care about.' She looks meaningfully at Becca then, her dark eyes sombre, and Becca nods in acceptance of what she's implying because Becca understands her friend is telling her: *I want you to have everything I tease you about wanting. Let us have it together.*

When it's Becca's turn, she tells the room: 'I want to be married, and pregnant.' She swallows, self-conscious about wanting something that in her younger years she would have thought was anti-feminist, too 'fifties housewife'. But sod it. It's the truth.

They collectively follow Coco in closing the ceremony by repeating: 'I affirm I am able and willing to allow these wishes to manifest and I participate in the miracle of creation with faith. So be it. And so, it is.' At the end, for comedic affect in acknowledgement of Jia Li, Coco then adds: 'Amen.'

'Amen,' repeat the group, chuckling, the tension of the previous forty minutes evaporating. They are done. They have told the universe what they want, they have let themselves hear it, feel it, acknowledge it, and now they can drink and chat and get on with their lives, their orders in the restaurant of life placed, their wishes in the hands of the gods, if such a thing really does exist as true.

3

It feels like magic that, not long after the ritual, the heatwave breaks and the heavens open, giving the salon a moody, atmospheric vibe. The sky outside the huge front window is dark, rain hitting the glass, candles and incense burning inside what has become a refuge from the elements. Sadly, though, Becca does not get refuge from Jia Li's sardonic cynicism, which continues to rage on.

'I'm just saying,' Becca tells her friend, 'surely you feel different after doing everything we just did. Even the *air* changed!'

If it was possible to *blink* sarcastically then Jia Li's chocolate-coloured eyes do it.

'Clearly not.' Becca laughs, shaking her head. She catches sight of her reflection at one of the styling stations and runs a hand over her highlighted beachy waves, smooths out a kink in her eyebrow. Jia Li watches her and then does the same before launching into her counter-attack.

'All this talk of wanting to find Mr Right.' Jia Li sighs, with more drama than the conversation necessitates, as is her MO. 'I mean, what even is that? I can tell you now: whoever your Forever Man is, he's not at a bloody summer solstice manifestation party. Can we manifest you downloading the apps and swiping, or even just going to a sports pub instead of a spa on your day off? You know – somewhere men actually *go*?'

'I don't want that kind of man,' Becca retorts.

They shift a few paces to the left so that Carlos can get to the extra booze for their guests. He does it theatrically, sighing to communicate: *Would it kill for you to give me a hand?*

'I want somebody . . . thoughtful. The kind of man who *does* go to a spa, or a book club, or a bloody manifestation evening. What does it say about me if I'm willing to pretend I like rugby or football in order to meet my future husband? It'd hardly win me the honesty award, would it?'

'Ever thought of competing in the Happy Hostess Awards?' stage whispers Carlos. They ignore him again, but with smiles this time. Winding Carlos up is a pastime Jia Li and Becca share. Basically, working at Trim means full-time hairdressing and part-time piss-taking of just about everyone and everything. It's just how they roll. You can (lovingly) join in or bugger off, is about the measure of it.

'Sorry, did you say something, Carlos?' Becca asks, once he's seen to topping up everyone's glasses and is very obviously finished. Carlos arranges his features into a bright – evidently sarcastic – grin, blinking madly.

'I said: my favourite ladies! What are we talking about?' He sidles up to them, his smile dazzling, his charm immediately warm.

'You've missed a button,' Becca points out, signalling playfully to the deep V-shape of his chest where precisely one button has been done in the middle and the rest left so that his shirt reveals dense slices of his toned torso top and bottom. 'In fact, you've missed nearly all of them,' she adds, archly.

Carlos makes his pecs dance – a strange habit left over from his Chippendales days, because yes, Carlos used to strip. That's how he paid for his hairdressing NVQ, and then later for his half of the start-up cash.

'You're ridiculous,' Becca jokes, bumping her shoulder into him. He blows her a kiss.

'And talented,' Jia Li counters. 'I wish I could do that.' She uses her forearms under her considerable boobs to make them jiggle awkwardly and, in doing so, drink sloshes over the rim of the glass and on to her hand, making the three of them peal with laughter.

'Smile!' chirrups Dana, their modelesque front of house manager cum social media queen, all long legs and smooth skin, her braided hair swooshing over one shoulder. Dana catches the moment on her DSLR, and several clicking sounds follow as Jia Li makes a show of licking her wrist and then winking to camera. Carlos grabs her and pretends to lick her too, making Jia Li shriek in disgusted delight, and Becca throws up her hands in affable despair at their performance. A few of the regulars glance over, noting with amusement that they're all being ridiculous, as usual. Becca blinks slowly as if she's above it all, then feels a tickle on her upper arm.

'Hey!' Coco says. 'I just wanted to say thank you for having me tonight. I have to get off, but it's been really great energy. This is a lovely group of people.'

'I was just about to come find you to say the same!' Becca replies. 'We're so grateful you could come. Thank you so, so much. I know there were a few cynics here tonight, but I don't know how anyone could have sat there and not felt *something* shift inside of them. You're really good.'

'Aww,' coos Coco. Her make-up-free skin glows, and Becca thinks to herself, *I wonder what moisturiser she uses.* 'Thank you. And you know, cynicism is just fear in different clothes. Earnestness takes a certain amount of bravery, I always think.'

'Very wise.'

Coco doesn't reply, then, but rather looks at Becca as if she's assessing her, somehow, or taking in the measure of her, the cut of her jib.

'What?' Becca asks, suddenly self-conscious, reaching up to her face as though there might be remnants of something on it, or she's insecure not to have the Earth Mother glow that Coco does, even though she tries.

'I just wanted to say . . .' Coco starts, and Becca holds her breath, waiting for the testimony and verdict of this stranger who knows her deepest desires. 'You're going to get everything you want, Becca. I see it so clearly for you. So don't worry about that. Your job is to just enjoy it, throw yourself into it. You're right on the cusp of your wildest dreams. We're talking any day now. The wait is over. He's here.'

'Thanks,' says Becca, not knowing how else to respond. Jia Li would ask for proof, evidence that what Coco's saying is true, a written report with facts and figures, dates and times, but the longer Becca stares into Coco's sparkling eyes, the

less she feels inclined to say anything at all. It's as if Coco
has cast a spell for her.

'No worries.' They hug, and Becca watches her walk away,
the bell above the salon door tinkling as it opens and closes.
Coco opens up a small umbrella and heads off into the evening,
and Becca replays the sentences they've just exchanged back in
her head, mining them for more clues. *Your job is to just enjoy
it, throw yourself into it.* If it's that simple, Becca thinks, she can
do that. What is it one of the mugs in the staff kitchen says, the
one Jia Li brought in as a joke? *Your vibe attracts your tribe.* Becca
can't properly explain, but excitement brews in her belly, an
anticipation of what's in store. It's almost like now that Coco's
said it, that everything will be OK – it will be.

And then her phone buzzes in her hand, lighting up with
a text message.

'Oh my God,' she says, looking at it.

'What?' asks Jia Li, approaching Becca with as much of a
furrow as her Botoxed brow allows, craning her neck to see
what's happened.

Becca shakes her head, trying to process it all. Really? It's
him? Becca doesn't have the number saved to her contacts,
but she immediately knows who it's from, because there's
only one person it *could* be from.

It's a photo of a piece of art by one of Becca's favourite
artists, which hangs in the Met. She's only been to New York
once, only seen it in real life once. It's a neon sign that says: *I
was so young, and you were so beautiful.* The person she stood
beside when she saw it, the person she took that trip with six
years ago, was Mike. Her Mike.

'Woah,' Becca says out loud again, her head swimming in disbelief. People around her mill about as if everything is totally normal. But standing there, frozen, with her past in the palm of her hand, Becca doesn't understand how anyone can talk about sage bundles and *Selling Sunset*, not when Mike-freaking-Henry has just reappeared back in her life with absolutely no warning. Jia Li squints at the screen too, and then lets out a little gasp.

The message underneath the photo says, *I couldn't not tell you I'm thinking of you, Bec. Saw this again and had to text x.*

'Becca? That's not . . . ?' asks Jia Li. When Becca replies her voice wavers in the way that people do when sense has suspended itself.

'Yeah,' she says. 'I just got a text from my ex.'

'Woah,' replies Jia Li, succinctly. 'As in Mike? The one who—'

'Got away,' Becca supplies, looking at her, trying to see if her face might have the answers she needs. 'Kind of, anyway.'

Surely this is a sign. A sign that she already knows her Mr Right – that he's there, in her phone? Bloody hell. It's been *years*. And now he's texting her? God, Coco is good.

Or no, wait.

Maybe this is a test, higher powers warning her that if she really does want to find her Mr Right, she must stop being held back by the past. She hasn't been serious with anyone since Mike. That's not a coincidence. Has she ever really let him go?

Becca looks up, checking that Coco actually has left for the night, that she hasn't magically returned. Surely she'd know what to do.

'Should I text back?' Becca asks Jia Li, panicked, her veins on fire with adrenaline and memories. Her cheeks are hot, her throat dry. This feels urgent, arresting, as though she has a split second to decide on her fate. 'Or not?'

Jia Li opens her mouth to answer, but before she can say anything the lights in the salon flicker and then cut out entirely.

Nobody speaks.

They are plunged into darkness.

And then there's a scream.

4

She Doesn't Text Back

'Sorry!' follows the voice of Monique, the older woman who declared in the manifestation ritual earlier that she wanted to leave her husband. 'It was the shock, everyone. I didn't mean to sound so intense!'

A confused hush descends across the salon before Carlos's voice comes out of the shadows cast by the flickering candles almost burned down to their stubs: 'And now begins the murder mystery portion of the evening,' he intones, putting on a silly, vampiric voice.

There are a few polite giggles, as though folks aren't entirely sure if he's genuine or not, but almost immediately after the lights come back on in all their glory there's a second murmur of appreciation that it's a joke. Becca's eyes readjust to the accidental on-off disco right as Carlos throws up his hands in mock despair.

'My murder mystery twist has been foiled!' he cries, affectedly.

'Carlos!' squeals Becca, across the salon. 'Watch out!'

Becca sees Carlos step back, narrowly missing a tray of empty champagne flutes teetering perilously close to the edge on one of the styling stations. He spins on his heel just in time to steady it, flushing pink down the back of his neck at the near miss of it all.

'Oh my God,' he says, picking up the tray and heading towards the staff room at the back of the salon to take the glasses out of the way. 'That could have been a disaster.'

'Dramatic much?' Jia Li teases him, but she follows it with a wide-eyed look of horror in Becca's direction, a silent acknowledgement of how much of a mess it could have been, and at great expense, too – the glasses are hired, from the pub.

Jia Li sighs as they both take gulps from the last of their fizz, a preamble to delivering unpalatable truths. Becca has heard it many times before.

'So, your ex,' she says to Becca. 'The one you've been getting over the whole time I've known you, ever since I started working here. He's texted?'

'I'm thinking it's a sign . . .' Becca starts, but immediately Jia Li screws up her face in protest, shaking her head furiously.

'No,' she insists. 'I disagree. If anything, I think it's a sign to ignore him. Here, give me your phone and I'll delete and block.'

'For real? No discussion, no considered thought, just the nuclear option?'

Jia Li shrugs as Carlos rejoins them.

'Ooooh,' he says. 'I love the nuclear option!'

'Carlos,' Becca warns. 'You don't even know what we're talking about.'

'So tell me,' he shoots back.

Becca takes a breath, but before she can explain Jia Li interrupts: 'She got a text from her ex and she's acting like it's the mystical summoning from the gods that she's been praying for because she's spirit-drunk on affirmations and deep breathing.'

'Oh,' says Carlos, chewing the specifics of the situation over. 'Well, a relit cigarette never tastes the same, and that's all I'll preach on rekindling old flames.'

Jia Li hoots a laugh. 'You stole that line, didn't you?' she accuses.

''Course I did.' Carlos laughs back. 'You think a man can be this handsome *and* that insightful?'

'Good point,' Jia Li replies. 'Although, you're not even that handsome, so . . .'

Carlos gives a histrionic guffaw, as if he can't believe Jia Li would be so disrespectful, but Jia Li has already noticed Becca scowling, waiting for somebody to get back to her problem.

'OK, OK. So. Obviously I've never met the man. I only know what you've told me, which is basically that it felt like you'd never get over him, because there was no big bang, just a dying whimper at the end when he moved to New York. That he left you behind because you wanted to set up the business here. So, you never really got closure?'

'Basically, yes,' says Becca.

'But you've been doing so well! When I first started working here you were really sad about him. I know the break-up had just happened and everything, but you've really turned a corner since then. I don't know. I just think getting back with your ex is like taking a shower and putting your dirty underwear back on.'

Becca scrunches up her nose. 'I'm not saying I want to get back with him—' she begins, but Jia Li cuts her off.

'So delete and block,' she says with a shrug. 'I actually think it's pretty shady behaviour to message out of the blue that way. I know he didn't *say*, "Hey, you up?" but it's like Casanova 101, isn't it, to send a photo like that and say he's thinking of you? What does he expect from that?'

'Speaking as a recovering Casanova,' Carlos offers, 'I am inclined to agree.'

Becca looks back and forth between her friends, taking in their concerned, defiant expressions. Nobody speaks.

'Fine,' she sighs, their point made. She opens the message again and clicks on the icon to block his number. 'There,' she announces, holding up her phone. 'The path is officially paved for forward-motion only. No going back. Message deleted; number blocked.'

'Good girl,' says Jia Li with a wink. 'You won't regret it.'

'Or maybe you will,' chimes in Carlos, helpfully. 'But it's too late now.'

The next morning the sun is as strong as ever, even after last night's storm. Becca is twenty-five minutes into a graduated bob, snipping and chatting, chatting and snipping, sitting on a black leather stool with wheels so she can move with ease and save her heat-swollen feet. She doesn't look up from her client Kaylee's left-hand side, where she's cutting into the shortest layer so it sits within the other layers instead of heavy, like a step, as she says, 'I'm glad I deleted the text. On my way in I stopped for an iced latte at the café that's just opened down the road—'

'Clemants,' interrupts Kaylee, and Becca nods.

'Clemants. Yeah! I like it there. All that light wood and those Scandinavian pastries.'

'Oh my God, yes!' says Kaylee as Becca moves behind her and pulls at her hair, either side, to check everything is even. It is. 'I said to my friend Lauren when we went, I can't believe I ever used to go and get those big sticky iced things from Starbucks. Now I've had that bun with the cardamom, it's like I've been eating squirty cream out of a can my whole life and now I've finally tried proper Cornish clotted. What a difference!'

'So good,' agrees Becca. She's done a great job on the hair. Carlos's colour is a masterclass in buttery sun-kissed blonde, too. 'Well, I was in there this morning for my coffee, and the bloke behind me started chatting to me – about nothing in particular. Just rubbish, really. But I started flirting with him. Trying to, anyway. Literally caught myself twirling my hair around my finger as I laughed at his jokes, which honestly weren't really that funny.'

Becca looks up, sensing behind her that they are being listened to.

'You're a very hit-and-miss flirt,' Carlos observes, tidying his colour tray. 'So I'm excited to hear how this turned out . . .'

Becca rolls her eyes and Kaylee giggles.

'No offence,' Carlos adds, as people do when they've been rude but want a get-out-of-jail-free card.

'Did you get his number?' Kaylee asks, and Carlos stifles a snort. 'What?' Kaylee adds. 'Why is that funny?'

Carlos is laughing because Becca cannot, despite her best efforts, despite her declarations of putting herself out there, ever find the confidence to actually make the first move on a guy. This morning she knew the man in the queue was flirting too, and she went above and beyond by giggling and being coy and trying to hold on to eye contact. But then it was her turn to order, and by the time he'd ordered, her coffee had been made. So unless Becca stopped very obviously, very deliberately, and somehow struck up conversation again, there was no way for her to make it clear that the lady was for courting. So she'd walked off.

'I'm not great at sealing the deal,' Becca explains. 'For lack of a better phrase. But – in my defence – by the time I opened up here I'd realised that that is something I can work on. I can fix that. And I'm stupid if I don't because there are *loads* of men out there. I just need to get better at making it clear that, if we laugh after striking up a bit of banter in a random public place, you can totally ask for my number.'

'Or you can ask for theirs . . .' Kaylee suggests, an eyebrow raised.

Carlos laughs again. 'One step at a time,' he warns, pushing his trolley back through to the colour station by the toilet. Over his shoulder he yells, 'We call her backwards in coming forwards!'

Becca scrunches up her nose. 'You're being mean now!' she shouts after him, before lowering her voice and confiding to Kaylee: 'He's right though. In my head I want to be swept off my feet by Prince Charming, but in reality I just think nobody is ever actually interested and so I get shy and stand-offish and run away. It's pretty pathetic.'

Becca runs product through the ends of Kaylee's new hairstyle, and then grabs a mirror to hold up at the back to show her what's been done.

'I LOVE it!' Kaylee squeals. 'Yes! Very *Sliding Doors* Gwyneth Paltrow, exactly like I said. God, you're so good Becca. And you, Carlos – this colour is *everything*.'

As Carlos reappears, he says, 'Chic. Very, very chic. Well done us, Bec.'

They high five as Becca helps Kaylee out of her cover gown, and then claps approvingly as she starts to snap a series of selfies.

'So it's a no on the ex,' Kaylee says once she's got the shot. She makes her way over to Dana to pay. 'But what's the plan? You've manifested it and so the One is just going to walk into Trim one day, out of the blue, and that's it? Or are you going to get brave like you say and seek him out . . . ?'

Becca considers it. 'Well, after this morning I'm thinking I should be more proactive, get some numbers, approach men and be direct. I've tried everything else.' She half wonders if the good-looking man might be at the coffee shop tomorrow morning, too. She'll have to ask Jia Li for some tips on how to be more obvious, just in case, although the inevitable self-satisfaction on Jia-Li's face doesn't bear thinking about. She's been trying to coach Becca's 'flirting' (because it is *always* said in inverted commas) for *years*.

'You know,' says Kaylee, looking at herself one last time in one of the salon's many mirrors, 'we should throw a singles' party. Get everyone we know mingling a bit. *Maybe* you'll find your man that way.'

'Really?' says Becca, unconvinced. 'That sounds . . . vaguely pimp-like?'

'Nooooo!' insists Kaylee as she hands over her card to Dana. 'It's cute! Have you heard of a friend-of-a-friend party? A group of women all bring a single, *eligible* male friend, so that all the men there have been vetted by someone you trust. The men all know the women there are up for a flirt, the women all know the men are cool, and poof! You wait for the magic to happen!'

Dana hands Kaylee back her card and says she'll email her the receipt. 'I've been to a couple of those,' she offers to them both. 'I actually know somebody who got engaged after meeting their partner that way.'

'Really?' says Becca. 'I mean, it makes sense. God, imagine all the heartache we could save the world if we only went out with somebody who'd been vouched for. Now I'm getting used to the idea . . . Kaylee, it's genius! We could even do it here, if you want.'

Kaylee bites her lower lip. 'Nah,' she says, looking around. 'At a bar. I know some people who know some people. Leave it with me? I'll text you?'

'Absolutely,' replies Becca. 'Although, God, now I'm thinking who I could bring. If I know an eligible man, why aren't *I* dating him?'

There's a pointed cough behind them. Carlos pipes up: 'Because he's like your brother and so you forget about him?' he asks, doing his pec dance again.

Becca smiles in spite of herself and then looks Kaylee in the eye. 'I suppose I have my guest sorted,' she says, gesturing to

Carlos and his unsubtlety. 'Text me when you have a venue and I'll put the word out.'

'Superb,' says Kaylee. 'Oh yay! I love a summer party! This is going to be so good. We'll find you a man, too,' she adds with a suggestive smile. 'I can already think of, like, three guys who should come. I can't believe I didn't think of this before! I am ninety-eight per cent sure we can realise this manifestation sooner rather than later. By this time next week, you'll have met your guy, I swear.'

Becca goes to speak, to say something self-deprecating, but stops herself. Manifestation is all about believing it's already happening for you, and in that case, Becca thinks about what to wear when she meets the man of her dreams (or manifestations) instead.

'I've got just the outfit,' she announces, waving her client goodbye, imagining wearing her red dress with the thigh split, meeting kind eyes from across a room.

'Stop it,' Carlos tells her as he tidies her station for her.

'What?' Becca asks.

'Writing the movie of how you'll meet your person, the potential romance of it all being scripted in your head before reality even has a chance to take hold. In fact, when you do that, reality doesn't even stand a chance.' He waves his hand with a flourish, and Becca narrows her eyes.

'Shut up!' she tells him. 'I hate you!'

'No you don't,' he replies, coolly, throwing a dirty towel at her that she fails to catch.

5

She Doesn't Text Back

'Perfect night for a rooftop party, isn't it?' Carlos says, just over a week later. Becca grips his arm and they walk through the park. It's a beautiful summer's evening, the last week of June, and the pavement is still warm from the day as they meander up to Jia Li's so they can share a cab into town. There are people lolling about on picnic blankets, cheersing cans of G & T or lager, some topless blokes kicking a ball around, a group of teens playing hacky-sack.

'I feel weirdly nervous,' Becca admits, her tummy gurgling slightly. 'What if tonight is the night that changes my life? My future husband could be at the bar, right now, ordering a glass of wine, chatting to whoever brought him about the view. No idea that we're about to meet. Isn't that romantic?'

'Your guy is at a dating event drinking rosé by the glass?' Carlos asks. 'I don't buy it. Your guy drinks spirits, neat, end of.'

'Do you think so?' marvels Becca. 'Because if he does, I'm going to have to learn to love whisky.'

'You can do better than that. Sake, that's the new "in" thing, isn't it?' Carlos says as they reach Jia Li's house. 'I'll teach you about it sometime. I've got a nose for it.'

'A nose for trouble more like,' Becca shoots back. 'And for the record, I didn't say he'd be drinking rosé, I said wine in general. I think it's very attractive to see a man with an iced white wine, condensation dripping down the stem on to his fingers . . .'

Carlos laughs. 'Spare me. You know, I'm pretty sure the cure for your romanticism would be a good shag.'

'I don't want a good shag.'

'It would be an awful state of affairs to be cured by a crap shag, but whatever floats your boat.'

'Pervert.'

'Prude.'

They eye each other, each refusing to be the one who laughs first. Becca can't help it – Carlos's face, the way he can communicate so much with the slightest quiver of an eyebrow – she purses her lips, close enough to a concession for Carlos to look victorious.

'Sake and Trouble could be the name of my blues band, you know,' he suggests, as if he's really been giving it some thought. 'Now you mention it, I could sing songs about my male prowess being a cover for a heart that's been bruised too many times to be brave.'

Becca looks at him. 'Carlos! Is that true?'

He looks away from her. 'Nah,' he decides. 'I'm just messing.'

'I've known you for five years and you're still a mystery to me, Mr Raverra.'

'Not all still waters run deep, love, don't worry.'

'I didn't say I was worried.'

'Your puppy-dog eyes did. You just focus on your own life and leave the rest of us to focus on ours.'

'Yes, boss.' She gives him a captain's salute. In all the time she's known him, Carlos has never had a girlfriend who has lasted more than a month or two, but there *has* been a steady enough stream of them. Becca has never been able to figure out why no one sticks.

They get to Jia Li's across the green and order a cab. The driver has his radio tuned to an old R & B station that plays classics Becca remembers from school and it makes her nostalgic and playful, and so by the time they stop to pick up Jia Li's plus one – Dave, the owner of the Fox and Hound, a pub just along the road from the salon – the collective mood is merry and bright.

'What do you reckon to all this then, Dave?' Carlos enquires once everyone is settled in. 'Are we being stitched up or what?'

Dave, a tall beanpole of a man with locks piled high on his head, looks at Jia Li. 'I bloody hope not.'

'You're not!' reassures Jia Li, reaching a hand out to Dave's knee. 'Every person there tonight is single, and every person there knows, by two degrees of separation or less, Kaylee, and you know Kaylee! I've drunk with Kaylee loads of times in the Fox!'

'Yeah,' Dave says, his voice low. 'Funny. Not as funny as you lot, but chatty. Always has a lot to say. We always get loads of bookings after she's been in as well. I think she tags us on social.'

'Exactly. Well, imagine twenty of Kaylee. And we get twenty of you! It's going to be lovely!'

'Lovely, is it?' Becca repeats, looking at her friend with, she realises too late, incredibly wide, and thus patronising, eyes. But Jia Li *is* sounding very optimistic for a self-declared man-eater.

'Oh, stop it.' Jia Li tuts. 'I'm as capable of being excited as anyone else. I'd love to find someone to put a baby in me!'

'Just not any of us,' Carlos observes. 'By definition of the party, you both have to bring somebody you're categorically *not* interested in.'

'That's what you get for missing the boat, pal,' Jia Li says simply, and Becca braces for impact. This occasionally gets brought up – the fact that one night, many, many moons ago, something happened after hours at the salon that resulted in Jia Li calling in sick for a week and avoiding eye contact with Carlos for two more. And Carlos might be a lot of things – crass, caustically sarcastic, always improbably dressed in three too few layers – but he is, all things considered, a gentleman. And as such Becca has never fully got the details of what exactly transpired. He's never let the cat out of the bag, and Jia Li has always made it very clear it's absolutely off-limits so Becca has never directly brought it up with her, either. Becca can fill in the blanks enough to know egos got bruised, but she doesn't know if they hooked up, or what. Carlos really did use to be a Casanova. The only trace of it having ever occurred is an occasional barb – but always from Jia Li, never from Carlos.

Carlos opens his mouth to speak and then thinks better of it.

'Well,' decides Becca. 'You're both fine specimens, and I'd put money on a line forming for each of you.'

'No need to take the piss,' deadpans Dave.

Carlos tuts. 'Speak for yourself.'

Inside, Kaylee has come good on her promise of knowing people who know people: they're in the centre of town, at a place Becca didn't even know existed. The exterior is all shiny glass and chrome, and it's six floors up, giving them a nice view over Birmingham, the Bullring in the distance, pub-goers spilling out on to the streets with their pints, gangs of colleagues making the most of the longer days. They get offered a flute of fizz on the way in, and as Kaylee clocks them she heads from a roped-off VIP area to say hello.

'You came!' she says, looking sensational in a skin-tight dress that skims her bum and heels that Becca can only think of as stripper shoes.

'Of course!' exclaims Becca as Kaylee kisses everyone hello on the cheek. 'I'm so excited. This is a tremendously good idea. And what a gorgeous venue.'

'Isn't it? I have the same personal trainer as the owner, and I see her between sessions sometimes. First drink is on her, bar is over there for anything else, and Meghan didn't say as much, but if you snap a photo, please do tag it. Social media followers are a currency, after all.'

She claps her manicured hands together animatedly and then waves a hand to usher them further into the space. 'Go forth and mingle!' she exclaims. 'There aren't any rules. I was going to have a sheet where everyone puts their number on it, so people could just take what they needed if there's a spark and you want to follow up or whatever, but—'

'Yeah,' agrees Jia Li. 'You just never know.'

'Exactly,' Kaylee nods, knowingly. 'You don't. Safety first. If you like somebody, you gotta tell them, and what I've been saying to everyone is that let's not take anything personally. If you get on with someone, you can ask for their number or a social media handle, and if somebody doesn't want to give it, that's totally fine too. We all just want a nice, fun night, don't we?'

'Amen,' says Dave, already heading for the bar. 'Catch you later?' he adds in Kaylee's direction, and she nods shyly.

'I've always kind of fancied Dave, you know,' Kaylee says, quietly. Becca and Jia Li look at her. Carlos presses his hands together in a prayer-like stance, says good luck, and heads inside too.

'My work here is done, then,' says Jia Li, following the lead of the men and breaking off into the crowd. 'Since I'm the one who brought Dave, I mean. I've got it on good authority he's hung like a tractor exhaust,' she adds over her shoulder. 'Godspeed, ladies!'

Kaylee toddles back over to the VIP area too, but Becca loiters, cradling her glass and sending a cursory glance out across the thin sea of people. To make herself look somewhat less self-conscious than she feels, she silently counts how many heads are in her eyeline, hoping that should anybody look in her direction, she comes across as searching somebody out rather than taking a moment to find her sea-legs. Then she feels him – not the physicality of him, but his presence, his energy. As she inhales she gets a woody, musky hint, and the hairs prickle on the back of her neck, her body standing to full attention. *Something is about to happen.*

'Wondering where to start?' he asks.

Becca turns. It's a man. A man with brown shaggy hair and a short salt-and-pepper beard cropped close to his face. Thoughtful eyes. He's in an open-necked shirt and dress trousers, effortlessly chic, with a peek of chest hair. Becca notices his hands – huge – with long, elegant fingers laced around his champagne flute. Every part of her screams THIS IS A VERY HANDSOME MAN! And so her brain launches into 'helpful' mode at this information, coaching her: FOCUS! YOU ONLY GET ONE FIRST IMPRESSION! She swallows, full of anticipation, and dares to smile at him.

'Something like that, yeah,' she admits, remembering at the last moment to try and not just make eye contact, but to hold it flirtatiously. His eyes are wide green pools, and locking into them makes Becca's heart beat triple time, *thud thud thud*.

I wonder if this is how Meg Ryan feels in all those movies, she marvels, sparkles of hope fluttering in her stomach. He briefly looks at her smiling mouth, and the forwardness of it makes her blush.

'I like your earrings,' Salt and Pepper Beard says, vaguely reaching out a hand. She can't place his accent – he's not posh, but he's not local. Certainly confident. 'May I?'

'Sure.'

Becca lifts a hand up to move her hair – except it's the hand holding her drink, and he's already closer than she thought, and so they inadvertently fist bump in the air, forcing the liquid in her glass to spill all over her shoulder before the rim then hits her cheek with a muffled *thunk*.

'Ow!' Becca squeals, right as the attractive stranger leaps back, concern bleeding out over his soft, sympathetic features.

'Are you OK?' he asks, worriedly running his gaze all over her face and, just fleetingly – but not so fleeting that Becca doesn't notice – her body. She's dripping, looking for a napkin, but there it is again: the eye contact.

'Let me get you something,' he tells her, striding purposefully over to the bar, all manly hero and all the more attractive for it, returning with a wad of paper towels.

'Here. In fact, let me take your glass and find you another drink whilst you dry off. I'm such an idiot, I'm so sorry. I'm nervous. These things . . .' He trails off, shaking his head, full of self-admonishment. So maybe he's not as confident as Becca first assumed.

'I know,' Becca replies, dabbing at herself. 'Me too. It's OK. I practically poured it over myself. If my friend Jia Li was here I'm sure she'd make a very off-colour joke about getting all wet . . .'

'But you're a lady, and so will refrain?' he supplies, a twinkle in his eye.

'Exactly.' She straightens up and runs a hand over her damp neck, inadvertently provocative, she realises too late. He gives a lop-sided grin. 'Or I try to be.'

As meet-cutes go, Becca currently feels like she's in a Nancy Meyers movie.

'Don't go anywhere,' Salt and Pepper Beard instructs, and she swears he flushes as he ascertains whether she is about to do a runner. 'OK?'

'OK,' she repeats. Becca finds somewhere to deposit the wet paper towel and briefly checks her reflection in the mirror over near the toilets, feeling Salt and Pepper Beard approaching, exactly as she did five minutes ago. Her breathing shallows as she looks up just in time to see Salt and Pepper Beard make his way back over to her from the bar. He lifts up two cocktail glasses triumphantly, and there's a swelling in her lower pelvis, a somersault of *frisson*, of recognising attraction. He's broad and manly, with the kind of face that lets every feeling ripple across – the opposite of 'hard-nosed' or 'cool'. Salt and Pepper Beard is less leather jacket and more favourite soft jumper, and it's not until this exact moment that Becca understands favourite soft jumper is exactly what she needs.

All of this goes through Becca's head as she continues to watch him, before she realises she looks like a tarsier, all wide unblinking eyes and dilated pupils.

Bloody hell, babe, her brain admonishes her. *Dial it back, would ya?*

35

'Permission to try hitting on you, Take Two?' Salt and Pepper Beard asks as he reaches her and hands over a fresh glass.

Becca doesn't know how to respond and gulps her cocktail.

'You *are* here with the friend-of-a-friend party, right?' he clarifies. 'Because if you're not, I swear to God I would never be that presumptuous.'

Becca takes another sip. *He thinks you're fit,* her brain narrates. *He thinks you're fit! Do something!*

'What's a friend-of-a-friend party?' she jokes, straight-faced, but she can't keep up the façade because immediately Salt and Pepper Beard's face falls as though he's just found out Santa isn't real. 'Oh my God, I'm kidding,' she says, before he can speak. 'Sorry, you left that one wide open.'

'Christ!' he exclaims. 'I mean, I still would have cracked on, like, but God! In those five seconds I was suddenly replaying everything we've said to one another in case I'd overstepped or been a creep!'

'Are you a creep?'

He laughs. 'Never on purpose!'

It feels nice to be there, then, with that man and that drink, wearing that red dress. Becca isn't sure what to say next, but she knows she shouldn't walk away or make an excuse to move on. She promised herself she'd show up fully tonight. She likes this man's vibe.

'Do you . . .' the man starts, and Becca decides to answer in the affirmative no matter what comes out of his mouth next. '. . . wanna go see the view? We're not very high up, but it's nice out on the balcony?'

'Cool,' Becca tells him. 'If you promise not to lunge at me again . . .'

'Only if you promise not to throw drink over yourself again. Although, if that was a tactic to get me to buzz off . . . Oh God,' he says, as if it's only just dawning on him. 'I'm so sorry. It was a tactic, wasn't it? Oh wow. I'm an even bigger prat than I thought. Wow, this is all going horribly, horribly wrong.'

It's Becca's turn to laugh now. 'It wasn't a tactic,' she says. 'Come on. Where's this rooftop?'

Salt and Pepper Beard narrows his eyes, his mouth in a thin line, as though he's choosing to believe despite all evidence to the contrary. Becca follows him as he weaves through the guests milling about and can't help but notice how incredibly good his arse looks.

'Right this way,' he tells her as they reach the glass doors to the outside. He steps back, holding out an arm, and they look at each other again, smiling, nervous, and then she takes a step, crossing over the threshold.

Half an hour later, Becca and Salt and Pepper Beard are still happily making charming small talk about chocolate pots on the balcony when Kaylee appears and forces them to circulate.

'You two are monopolising each other! If it's meant to be you'll find your way back to one another!'

Two hours later and no such luck. Becca has to accept, disappointingly, that his head was likely turned elsewhere. Dammit. She'd really thought there was a vibe. Her interest, meanwhile, was not piqued by any others, despite the fact she chatted with more men than she can count on two hands: tall ones, creepy ones, funny ones, drunk ones, Dave, and Carlos . . .

'There was just this one guy,' Becca tells Jia Li, who has just given her number to bloke number four. 'Tallish. Beard?'

'Oh yeah,' Jia Li says, her eyes sleepy from booze and banter. 'I saw you talking to him at the start, I think.'

Becca nods. 'Yeah. Good chat. Made me throw my drink over myself, but good chat. *Great* chat, actually. Everyone else though . . .' She waves a despondent hand.

'Hey,' states Jia Li, emphatically. 'This is just one night. The only objective was to have fun, was it not?'

Becca mumbles something approximating agreement, even though between eight and eight twenty-five she'd been convinced she'd met somebody special.

'And you practised talking to strangers, no?' Jia Li presses.

'I did,' says Becca. 'We can agree that much. I've only had two drinks, so it wasn't even drunk-talking. I'm practically sober. Where's my medal?'

'Sober?' Jia Li repeats. 'Well, that simply will not do.' She squints in dissatisfaction. 'Let's have one for the road downstairs. Cheers to loving *ourselves*.' She says *ourselves* with loaded irony.

'I'm every woman,' Becca hoots. 'It's all in me. Come on. You can buy.'

The friends swing by the loo together and don't stop talking even as they pee, right until they walk down the three flights of stairs to the bar and dining area and pull up a stool and look at the snacks menu.

They order skinny fries to share and a glass of Moët each, and Becca hears all about who Jia Li spoke to, who she's going to call, and who she thinks she saw Carlos leaving with about an hour and a half into the night.

'I think Dave and Kaylee left together too,' says Jia Li, 'so I expect free drinks for life at the pub.'

'You and Dave get on so well I assumed that was the deal anyway.'

Jia Li arches an eyebrow. 'He's got a good heart, that man, but an even better business brain. I've never been offered a free drink yet.'

Becca is mid-sip and mid-laugh as she tips her head back and sees him – Salt and Pepper Beard. The alarm she feels in her chest must register on her face because Jia Li immediately says, 'What?' as she looks in the same direction towards where he is talking to two women Becca recognises from the party. He feels her eyes on him and turns, smiling and holding up his glass of wine, and Becca keeps staring, uncertain of how to play it, as Jia Li waves and shouts out, 'Hi!'

Hi! he mouths back, and then one of the women he is with says something, pulling back his attention, and when he responds he looks up to Becca to smile again, forcing the woman to whip her head around to shoot Becca particularly vicious daggers.

'Well,' notes Jia Li. 'She's marking her territory, isn't she?'

Becca shrugs, nabbing the last of the fries. 'That's OK.' Her tone doesn't quite match the sentiment, but over her dead body is she going toe-to-toe with another woman for a bloke. That really would be retro. 'I said he had all right banter, not that you can start planning the playlist for the wedding reception.'

'Go give him your number!' Jia Li hisses excitedly, prodding her in the arm. 'He's not queuing up dance-floor classics himself yet, is he? They're just talking. And he keeps looking over here.'

Becca feels a pull in her stomach but doesn't know if it is bad or good. When she looks at him this time, he doesn't look back.

'He looks pretty interested in what the shorter one has to say,' Becca notes. 'And what? I'm going to just walk up to him and say, *Hey, gimme your phone*, and then save my number for him under *Busty Becca*?'

'I would have gone for *A Bit High Maintenance But Up For It*, but yours works too,' Jia Li quips archly. 'Go on!'

Becca considers it. She said she was going to be braver, to go after what she wants and put herself out there so that the universe can respond in kind. Lucky people are the ones who take the most chances, after all. She stands up and smooths down her skirt.

'Oh my God' says Jia Li, her voice high with delight. 'Becca! Yes!'

'Ready for this?' Becca asks, pulling her phone out of her bag and unlocking it.

'So ready. I'm so impressed!'

Becca opens an app on her screen. 'Uber,' she narrates. 'Order car.'

Jia Li tuts and rolls her eyes.

'Oh! Three minutes!' states Becca with fake enthusiasm. No way is she going up to a man to give him her number. Absolutely not. Jia Li is screwed in the head if she thinks she will, good vibes or not.

Jia Li tuts and downs the last of her champagne. 'Fine,' she says, hopping down off the bar stool. Becca blinks slowly and sadly, scrunching up her face, as though she understands how hard it must be to bear witness to her lack of flirtatious backbone.

'I know I've disappointed you,' Becca says consolingly. 'But look on the bright side – if we go home now, you can spend the rest of the night – the *week* – mocking me for continuing to have no game, OK?'

'Becca?' Jia Li says, sliding her handbag on to her shoulder and making her face as stern as Becca ever sees it get.

'Jia Li.'

'I'm going to go give him your number on your behalf. You can run away, or you can watch, but it's happening.'

And before Becca can stop her, Jia Li is gone. Becca makes a bolt for the exit. There is absolutely no way in hell she wants to bear witness to this – he could laugh in Jia Li's face, or reveal some awful truth about why he never circled back around to talk to her: bad breath, terrible taste in chocolate pots, pure boredom at her inane and misguidedly uncharming chat. Becca stands out on the street, the evening air having turned just cold enough to make her wish she'd brought a jacket, willing the Uber to come ASAP.

'Done,' says Jia Li, emerging behind her.

'You!' squeals Becca.

Jia Li bats her eyes. 'The only thing is, he didn't want to accept your number off me.'

Becca feels her face get hot. Of course he didn't. Well, the only thing worse than a worry of dented confidence is a confirmed case of dented confidence.

'Because . . .' Jia Li continues, 'he wanted you to have his. I just forwarded it to you.'

Becca looks down at her phone. Sure enough, Jia Li has sent a number for a Noah Brooks.

'He didn't believe he should use a number that you, yourself, didn't give him. But he said he hopes you call now you have his.'

Their Uber pulls up. Becca looks at her friend. 'Get in the car,' she instructs, fighting back a huge smile. 'You're a nightmare.'

'A nightmare who calls dibs on maid of honour though!' Jia Li laughs, clambering into the waiting taxi. 'And also, mate: he's proper fit. If it doesn't work out with him let me know because I would tap that like a maple tree.'

Becca giggles. 'A compliment of the highest order.'

6

She Texts Back

Back on the night of the manifestation party . . .

'Carlos!' Becca shouts, watching what happens in slow motion. But it's too late. He just clips the edge of a tray of dirty glasses, the angle of impact perfect for making it turn three times in the air on its way to the ground, twenty champagne flutes shattering with an ear-splitting clash.

Carlos looks up, sheepishly. 'Oops?' he offers, broken glass surrounding him.

'Oh, for God's sake.' Jia Li tuts, swiftly moving into action. 'Only Carlos could smash an *entire* tray of *hired* champagne glasses. Bec, I'll go and tidy up with him. You keep the guests happy?'

'Sure.' Becca nods, grateful, looking around with a fixed smile to let everyone know they are free to carry on enjoying themselves. Despite the phone burning in her hand, she does a circuit of the room, filling people's flutes with the dregs of the Prosecco and offering around the last of the snacks as Carlos and Jia Li dispose of the broken glass quickly and professionally.

'You OK?' asks Dana, appearing beside her once Becca is satisfied all is well. Becca looks at her exquisite, youthful face. Dana is ten years younger than them all – hence why she's in charge of their social channels – and Becca admires the quiet, thoughtful way she navigates her life. She doesn't speak often, but when she does everybody listens. She's an old soul in the tiny body of a twenty-five-year-old.

'I've just got a text from my ex,' Becca says. 'And it's thrown me for a loop.'

Dana nods. 'Hmmm,' she says. 'I see.'

Becca chews on her lip. Mike. A montage plays in her mind, as though it has been cued up and ready to go for precisely this moment: the time they went to Leeds Festival; sitting at his parents' dining-room table for Sunday lunch; skinny-dipping in Crete. Five years of happiness. Arguments that ended in laughter. Endless falling asleeps, countless sleepy wake-ups, teas drunk and hugs squeezed. Kisses had. *The sex.*

'Why did it end?' Dana enquires, adding: 'If I'm allowed to ask.'

'You can ask.' Becca keeps her voice low. She loves her clients, but she doesn't want everyone knowing her business in real time. 'Basically, he wanted to move to New York,' she explains. 'We were turning thirty and he had this whole thing about travel and adventure – I think a lot of it was about living somewhere other than where we grew up. But I wanted to set up my own business, to be *here*. And so . . . we both did our own thing. I couldn't hold him back, he didn't want to force me into anything I didn't want to do, and we've not spoken since.'

'At all?' clarifies Dana.

'A bit,' Becca says. 'At first. But it was too hard. Any time I expressed frustrations about setting up this place he took it as hope that I might jack it in and join him after all, and any time he wobbled about being so far away from home I was waiting for him to decide to come back. We'd have these chats, but never really properly communicated. So, in the end, it was easier to wish him well and cut all ties – with him, and his family, too. That sucked. I really liked his mum. All of them actually – it was a bit like breaking up with his whole family.'

'I get that,' Dana muses. 'That's a hard thing to choose, but it must have been a way to, like, protect your peace?'

Becca murmurs agreement that yes, that's exactly it. She had loved him more than she'd loved anybody and was heartbroken when it had finished. But if love is about the right person at the right time, their timing just hadn't been right . . . and because neither of them wanted to change for the other, ultimately that meant they weren't the right person in the end, either. It was a bit like a death without a body to bury, though – the relationship ended, but nobody could properly say why. It just . . . did.

'Well,' Dana says, leaning back against the marble-effect reception desk. 'I can tell you want to text him.'

'Just because I want to, doesn't mean I should,' counters Becca.

'Touché!'

Becca scrunches up her face, as if she can fight what she's thinking that way. 'But also, I have to say I'm intrigued. Then again, it could be dangerous. I wasted so much hurt hoping

45

for something to be different before. That's why we went cold turkey and decided it was best not to speak. But I mean, come on – he messages right after a manifestation ceremony where I ask for Mr Right?'

Dana smiles. 'It *was* pretty special,' she agrees. 'It was a cool thing to do. And can I tell you something?'

'What?'

'Coco slipped me her number and told me to text if I ever wanted to get a drink. I don't – I'm kind of seeing somebody already, early days — but I'm a believer right about now, too.'

Becca drops her jaw. 'What!' she says, smacking the top of Dana's arm. 'You! God! I've never known anyone to get asked out as much as you. I'm so jealous!'

'Oh, because you don't get asked out all the time too?' Dana counters. 'Or', she says, wiggling her eyebrows, 'get exes messaging you out of the blue . . .'

Cogs start whirring in Becca's head. She gets Dana's hint. 'I'm making this a bigger deal than it needs to be, aren't I?' she settles on. Dana gives her a half-smile. 'Mike is just a person – a person I have memories with. It's nice to hear from him. I can text back without it being some drama. It doesn't mean anything . . .'

Even as she's saying it, she doesn't believe it. This isn't just a text. That's not how things are with Mike. *Everything* with Mike *means* something. But then, that's what makes replying so loaded, and so exciting. Becca knows implicitly that if she does this – if she replies – she'll set something in motion that will become bigger than just a text message. She half thinks that's the point.

'What I'll say is this: conventional wisdom tells us to leave the past in the past' – Dana waves a hand – 'which is bollocks, if you ask me. Life is messy. Let's just let it be unclear, you know? Who are we to say which parts are the beginning of the story, or the middle, or the end? Nobody knows what the future holds. So, I'd text back. If it were me.'

Dana makes it seem so straightforward.

'Now?'

'*Aaj ka kaam kal par mat choro*, as my *dadi* always said.'

Becca blinks, waiting for the translation from Urdu to English.

'It basically means, better today than tomorrow.'

'So that's a yes to texting him straight back. Right. OK. Yup. I can do that. Sod it,' Becca says, pulling up his message. She looks at the photo again: *I was so young, and you were so beautiful.* It became an inside joke to them. It makes her smile, now she's allowing herself to remember him fondly, minus the fraught terror. They were so young themselves back then.

It's nice to hear from you! Becca writes back. *I hope everything out there is still great for you x.*

Then she hits send.

The world doesn't end.

It's only a text.

It's not like sending it is going to change the entire direction of her whole life, is it?

'Bec,' he says from the doorway, and everyone in the salon turns to look. There Mike stands, his short blond hair backlit by the bright midday sun, his skin caramel, like *dulce de leche*.

47

Bright blue eyes, wide chiselled shoulders, that *Mikeness* as present and obvious as it ever was. Becca doesn't speak, standing slack-jawed and mildly disbelieving instead. Is it really him? Just like that?

I'm actually at the airport on my way to visit home, he'd said when he replied to her text. *My sister had a baby!*

Jessie had a baby? she'd sent back. *Oh my gosh! Thanks for telling me! I'll send a card.*

You guys still in the same spot? he'd asked. *On York Road?*

Sure are! she'd typed. *Stop by,* she'd added, before she could regret it. *If you have time. Be great to see you x.*

She'd told herself she wouldn't actually see him – that he'd only be around for a few days and, of course, he'd be busy. She told herself that she wouldn't care if he forgot, or ran out of time, to pop into the salon before flying back. When she didn't receive a response to her last message, she resolved to think nothing more about him. Except, every time some-body walked past the window of the salon her head had whipped around so fast she'd started to get a pain down the right-hand side of her neck.

And now, it's finally him.

'Hello there,' she hears Dana say, right as her heart is busy falling out through her arse. He's almost exactly the same: same eyes, same lopsided smile. He's a smidge broader – there's more to him – and he looks a little tired. But it's him. 'Do you have an appointment?'

Mike turns his attention to Dana and it releases Becca from her freeze-frame. She smiles at her client Caroline in the mirror and says something about being right back. As Mike explains that he's not there for a haircut, but to see Becca, she slips into the back room, Jia Li following, then Carlos.

'Don't tell me that's him,' Jia Li hisses, eyes wild with excitement. 'Becca! His photos do *not* do him justice. He's aged like Brad Pitt! This puts a whole new spin on everything you've ever told us about him. All is forgiven, Mr Mike. Ding, dong!'

Becca looks at her. All she can think is *MikeIsHere-MikeIsHereMikeIsHereMikeIsHereMikeIsHere.* She needs water. And a hair wash. And six to ten more days to prepare what to say, and how to say it. Why did he have to come in on the day she'd overslept and done her make-up in a record-breaking three minutes?

'He's not *that* handsome,' Carlos dismisses, but then he looks at Becca and changes his tone slightly to say, softly: 'You're OK. Go say hi. He'll think you're a weirdo if you stay back here any longer. He's just a person.'

'A very hot person,' Jia Li corrects, peering around the door frame to get another look.

'I don't think you're helping, Jia Li.'

'Oh, what? Because the truth isn't helpful? I'm just stating facts, Carlos. The man is a god.'

Becca looks to Jia Li, blinking and struggling to know what to do next.

'Tits and teeth,' Jia Li implores her, smiling and arching her shoulders back to show more of exactly that: her tits and her teeth.

Becca nods. She opens her mouth to speak but nothing comes out.

'It's weird she's not speaking,' Carlos says to Jia Li with concern, but Becca is already moving, putting her feet one in front of the other even though she can't be sure her brain has made that request. She doesn't hear what Jia Li says in reply, but she can definitely feel them watching her as she floats towards reception. Mike has taken a seat in the waiting area, his legs set apart widely, elbows on knees, wry smile like he's not sure if he should be here. But he should, shouldn't he? She invited him. It's just, for all her head-whipping since the text, she never quite graduated to what would happen if one day it *was* him.

'I hope it's OK to stop by unannounced,' he says, his eyes crinkling with warmth, a smile playing across his face, his nerves obvious – and Becca remembers that he never did have a very good poker face. She'd always liked that about him. It makes her relax.

'Always,' replies Becca, reaching him, and it's a strange thing to say but it's what comes out.

She loiters – are they going to hug? He looks at her, raising his eyebrows in a way that in retrospect she'll understand means *are we . . .* ? but in the moment feels unreadable. He stands up and opens his arms.

'Oh,' says Becca, 'Yes, hi.'

They embrace. It's brief, with barely any physical contact. Becca had always thought hugs to be quite intimate: cheek to cheek, torsos pressed against the other. But that's not what this hug is. It's half-hearted and unsure at the last minute, their arms cooked spaghetti.

Mike pulls away and looks at the floor, then back at her, and lets out a massive sigh. Then he laughs.

'I thought I'd have more to say,' he begins, his face wide and open. 'But I don't know where to start. This place' – he gestures around the salon – 'is great. I mean, I've seen it from the car, driving past or whatever – you know, when I've been back to visit.' Becca raises her eyebrows and digests this new information. 'Jessie says it's always full. Congratulations.'

'Thank you,' she says. 'We're very proud.'

'We?' Mike asks.

Becca can feel Carlos back at his work station, his presence conspicuous by the fact he isn't talking to his client. In fact, nobody is talking. Becca could hear a pin drop: everyone is waiting to see what happens between her and the beautiful, sweet man she once loved.

'You know how I co-own it? Well, this is him, this is Carlos,' Becca says, gesturing behind her. She refuses to introduce anyone properly. God knows what they'd say.

Mike nods.

Becca grimaces.

The playlist Dana crafted especially for Trim finishes one track and starts another, low hip-hoppy beats mirroring the pounding of Becca's heart.

'I have an hour's break after this,' she offers, finally, gesturing towards Caroline, half her wet hair pinned up on top of her head, as engrossed in the soap opera playing out before her as everyone else. 'Do you have time for a coffee?'

Mike looks relieved, nodding before she's even finished her sentence. 'I'd love that,' he says. 'Yes.'

'OK.' Becca nods. 'Fifteen minutes? There's a new place round the corner. Clemants.'

'Perfect,' he tells her. 'Do you still go for iced coffee in summer, non-fat latte in winter?'

'I do,' she replies, taken aback that he remembers. 'Good memory.'

Mike shrugs nonchalantly. 'I surprise myself sometimes,' he says.

Becca watches him go, waving a hand when he glances back apprehensively before righting his expression into something once again indecipherable and heading up the road. When she turns around, she sees that everyone else has been doing the same.

'What?' she says, to no one in particular. 'What!'

Nobody says anything, but she notes the pointed look between Jia Li and Carlos. She'll have to weather their opinions later, though. For now, she's got to finish Caroline's cut, which will be quite a feat when her hands are shaking so much.

'Nerves or excitement?' Jia Li stage whispers to her. Becca looks at her client.

'Forgive me for this cussing, Caroline.' She looks at Jia Li. 'Piss off,' she tells her, and Jia Li laughs.

King's Heath is vibrant and full of life, with everything that bit better in the summer. The suburb is a couple of wide, shop-lined boulevards that peter out into residential streets, with local grocers and their striped awnings, corner shops with their broken signs, dry cleaners and a bakery, butcher, a couple of fashion stores, the odd charity shop, and a cluster of cafés. Parents push prams, older couples meander with their shoppers, schoolkids on their last days of term mess about at bus stops, playing chicken with the time or else skipping school entirely.

Becca sees Mike in the window of Clemants before he sees her. She gets the luxury of observing him for almost ten seconds, taking in the way he jiggles his leg, smooths down his hair, taps his fingers against the table. He has two iced coffees in front of him, and two small beakers of water. He feels her looking and she raises a friendly hand as she slips in through the door.

'I'm glad you sat inside,' she says, by way of greeting. 'I'd melt out there.'

She nods to the brave souls in the 4 p.m. sun, still baking hot even under the shade of an umbrella.

'It's the American in me now,' Mike replies. 'AC as standard.'

'How indulgent.' Becca smiles, taking a seat opposite him. 'Although, I dare say our little corner of this here Birmingham greenbelt has come a long way whilst you've been gone.'

Mike smiles back. 'I hear there's indoor plumbing now.' He laughs.

'And we know what oat milk is,' she says, but that forces a semblance of a frown from him.

'That's cow's milk,' he says, gesturing at the iced latte in front of her. 'Should I go and change it?'

'Oh no,' Becca says, shaking her head. 'I said we *know* of it, not that I drink the stuff. I'd rather go without than go lactose-alternative. I think they even make milk out of coconuts now.' She pulls a face that's supposed to mean *what is the world like, eh?*

'Any nut,' retorts Mike. 'And rice. They can even make milk out of rice.'

'God, if I served my mother Yorkshire Gold with *rice milk* she'd throw me out the house. Even if it was my house we were in!'

She takes the drink Mike has bought for her and takes a meaningful slurp, giving him her thanks.

'How is your mum?' he asks, mirroring her and gulping down his beverage too.

'Gay,' Becca happily tells him. 'She came out two years ago. Lives with a woman called Betty just off Blacksmith's Road and stopped shaving her armpits, but says lipstick is her choice as a woman and not a sign of patriarchal oppression, so yeah. She's as Shelley as ever!' Becca suddenly has a flashback to Mike and her mum doing karaoke one Christmas Eve, drunk on Snowballs, kicking their legs up to a Frank Sinatra song and laughing manically. Memories, bloody everywhere.

Mike nods. 'She unfriended me on Facebook,' he says, clutching his heart. 'But I've never stopped loving her, for what it's worth.'

'I'll be sure to let her know.' Becca snickers. 'Time heals all wounds,' she adds.

'I'm hoping so,' Mike says quickly – too quickly. He adds, 'Sorry. That just came out. I don't know what I even meant. Weird.'

Becca shakes her head. 'This whole thing is weird,' she says, gesturing between them. 'I'm sure I'm about three sentences away from a bizarre clanger myself.'

Mike looks at her, his eyes crinkled with fondness. 'Well, if you could get a move on with that,' he says. 'You could even up the score and make me feel better.'

'Who says I want to?' Becca doesn't *mean* to sound in any way flirtatious. And yet.

Mike bites on his bottom lip, making Becca realise that whatever she's doing – and whatever Mike is doing – she quite likes it. Huh.

There's an uncertain beat, a pause between them that makes Becca realise that she'd rather spew drivel than let it linger, heavy and full of their past.

'How's the baby?'

'Good! They've called him Sebastian. I thought babies were supposed to be tiny little things but he's a big boy! A bit like a bowling ball, you might even say. Although obviously not within earshot of my sister.'

'I'm pretty sure you were the same as a baby,' Becca says, another thing that slips out before she can assess its weight. Regina, his mother, kept walls cluttered with family photos in her house. You couldn't even go for a wee without sitting on a toilet opposite a gallery wall of moments in time from the Henry family, Regina and Paul and Jessie and Mike smiling down as their visitors wipe their arses.

'I was indeed.' Mike nods, seemingly connecting the dots that Becca is referencing said photo walls. 'I was a massive baby, and now I'm a massive adult who has to pay extra for leg room on flights and trains.'

'The hidden cost of height,' muses Becca. 'Sounds like a Channel 4 documentary.'

Another beat. More history looming over them, trying to get their attention.

'The salon is so cool,' Mike says, gesturing in the general direction of Trim. 'I know I said so before, but, like, yeah, it's proper sleek and modern, got a really nice feel.'

'My dream in action,' says Becca with a contented sigh.

'Yeah.' Mike nods. 'But for what it's worth, a lot of people have dreams that never get that far. You're in the minority. Not that I ever had any doubt.'

Becca narrows her eyes. 'You say that like you actually did have doubt,' she accuses him.

'No!' he insists. 'That is what was so . . .' He trails off.

'What?'

'No. Nothing.'

'Go on.'

It's his turn to sigh. 'I knew you'd make your dream a reality. And as a person who wasn't even sure what his dream was, back in the day, that was . . .'

Becca refuses to fill in the gap.

'Emasculating,' Mike settles on.

'Emasculating?' Becca repeats. 'You found me emasculating?'

Mike shakes his head. 'No, no, come on. I know it's bollocks. This is 2023, I get it. A woman isn't responsible for making a man feel more like a man, I just mean . . . I'm happy for you. I'm talking bollocks because I'm nervous. Sorry. I'm happy for you, the end.'

Becca nods slowly, noting his inability to meet her eye now.

'You didn't emasculate me,' he reiterates. He suddenly looks so uncomfortable, so unsure of himself, that in an instant Becca is freed from caring. It was years ago! It doesn't matter! Who cares!

She erupts into laughter.

'What?' Mike asks.

'I literally don't give two hoots.' Becca giggles. 'Like, I'm not in the business of drinking caffeinated beverages and making people feel bad about the past. We don't have to go over everything that happened. I texted you back because I wanted to say hi, see how you are, that's all. Not to sound presumptuous – I don't know if you came here wanting some big emotional reckoning or whatever.'

'No,' Mike says, shaking his head. 'Certainly not.'

'Good,' Becca says.

'Good,' he echoes.

They lift the dregs of their iced coffees and cheers, taking a moment to finish them off.

'I should get back,' Becca says then, looking at her watch. 'I have a four forty-five kid's cut booked in.'

Mike nods. 'Yeah,' he says. 'Absolutely. Sorry for dropping in unannounced. I was just out getting some stuff for Jessie and found myself nearby. Thought I'd chance it.'

Becca looks down to his feet, noting the lack of 'stuff'.

'It was a pleasant surprise,' she tells him. 'It's been nice to catch up.'

'Yeah,' Mike says. 'Cool. OK. Well. Bye, then.'

They hug, as awkward as it was before, and Becca slips out back on to the street.

'Bec?'

She turns around. 'Mike,' she replies. He scrunches his nose and tips his head to one side, nervously, as though he already regrets coming after her.

'I was just wondering what you meant when you said it was nice to catch up,' he says.

He takes a few strides towards her, his face hopeful. *He really is hot*, thinks Becca. *He always was.*

'Hmmm,' she muses. There's something about the way he's standing, boyish and full of trepidation, that's hilarious to Becca all over again. She wants to reach up and ruffle his hair, tell him not to worry so much. She's fine! She thought seeing him again would be this big, powerful thing, the ghost of boyfriends past, but it isn't. Carlos was right, too – he's just a person.

'Yes,' she says, as if she's sincerely considering his question. 'I can see how that would be open to many interpretations.'

He pushes his sunglasses back up his nose, blushing enough to be cute. 'Well,' he says, his voice sing-song in a bid to be faux-dismissive. 'You're still as obtuse and avoidant as ever, I see. Excellent.'

'Obtuse and avoidant!' Becca squeals. 'I told you it was nice to catch up, and now here I am, walking home minding my own business, getting a character assassination!'

'I didn't say obtuse and avoidant were *bad*, per se,' Mike clips back.

'No,' agrees Becca. 'You're right. They speak to an inherent mysteriousness and *je ne sais quoi*. I'll add them to my dating profiles immediately.'

And then she's said it – that she's single. It hadn't come up earlier, when it was all how's your family, how's work, what's the baby like, yes King's Heath really does have a vegan café now.

Mike spreads open his arms to show his palms, as though none of this is his fault. They both realise new information has come to pass – information that could potentially mean he's 'won' the break-up. Becca didn't ask about his relationship status. She doesn't need to know.

'*You* brought that up,' he says, and he's smirking now. No. Not smirking. Smiling. He's being his cheerful, smiling, delightful self, insecurity evaporated like smoke now they've slipped into what they were always so good at: playful repartee. 'Let the record show that wasn't my fault.'

'I'm dating,' says Becca, keeping her voice cool. 'It's not a secret.'

'No,' he says. 'I suppose not.'

This would be the natural moment at which she could say goodbye again, to tell him to have a nice evening. She doesn't want to though. The coffee wasn't enough. It was never going to be. He's just a man, and she's just a woman, but together they are still, after all this time, more than the sum of their parts.

'Do you have plans after work?' he asks.

'Oh,' says Becca, aware that her heart is expanding in her chest with every inhale and exhale. She's smiling too. She can't stop herself. In fact, she might have been smiling this whole time. 'I was just going to go home for a salad in the garden, maybe open a bottle of something.'

'Sounds nice,' he replies, patently waiting for his invitation.

'Do you want to join me?'

'Cheers for taking the hint. I'd love to.'

'Really?' she asks, before she can help it.

'Yeah. I know this is going to sound – well, I don't know. Dramatic, probably. But the older I get, the more I find myself needing the people I knew when I was younger. Does that make sense? I'd like to . . . well. Dinner would be lovely.'

Becca considers it. 'You need the people you knew when you were young? Isn't that a line from the Sunscreen Song?'

'Now I've said it, I hear myself, and yes, you're right. I am incapable of original thought and thus have stolen the words of Baz Luhrmann.'

'Mary Schmich, actually,' Becca corrects. 'Mary Schmich wrote a graduation column in a newspaper, I think in Chicago. And then Baz Luhrmann made it into a song.'

'And that,' Mike tells her with a finger point, 'is why your position as number-one pub-quiz teammate has never been filled.'

Becca takes a bow. 'Honoured,' she says. 'You're definitely still in my top six pub-quiz teammates.'

'Top six? Thrilled,' he replies, deadpan.

He clears his throat then, a sudden earnestness crossing his chiselled features. Becca braces for impact.

'Do you ever remember us talking about cost and value?' he asks, his voice faux-light and conversational, as if what he's asking is relevant to proceedings when Becca immediately knows not only where they were when they had that chat but also what they were both wearing. It isn't relevant.

It's the conversation that started the beginning of the end for them. 'When the gig in New York came up, we did a pros and cons thing?'

'Yeah.' Becca nods, copying Mike's fake bonhomie. She pauses, making out like she's slowly going through her archived memories, the ones in the dusty boxes all the way at the back of her brain: this could take a while; they've not been asked for in some time. A small lie, to protect her dignity. 'Everything has a cost, and everything has a value, right?' she clarifies. 'The value of living in New York was high for both of us, but the *cost* of living in New York was too high for me – I didn't want to be away from my family, my friends.'

'Exactly,' he says, nodding. 'And the price I paid was being away from my family and friends.'

A pause. Dare Becca ask what she wants to know? She can't help herself.

'Was it worth it?'

'That's my point,' Mike replies, quietly, blinking slowly. 'I don't think it was.'

Becca nods. What the hell is she supposed to say to that? *Goddammit.*

'Come back to the salon at half past five,' she settles on. They can have dinner, can't they? As friends, or whatever. 'We can walk to my place together.'

'Great, yeah. See you then.' Mike nods, and Becca nods back, not understanding why all this nodding is happening, as if they've both got bone-density issues and holding up their own head weight is too hard, bob, bob, bob, and then she turns away before either of them can bob up and down again.

7

She Doesn't Text Back

It takes Becca two hours to finally hit the green call button next to Noah Brooks's name. She's slept in, had a bath, drunk two cups of coffee and watched three episodes of *Love Is Blind*, texting a running commentary to Jia Li about how she really does think she could be on this show, she really does believe that she could fall in love with someone without ever seeing them, only talking to them through a wall, as the rules require. Jia Li replies, simply: *Stop being insane and text Noah.* Becca sends with a GIF of a man walking with his head down, slowly, the words *OK then* underneath. She gets a thumbs-up emoji back. That's it. Pep talk over.

Becca has mulled over all the reasons not to simply do as Jia Li – and this man (allegedly) – said and ring him. So far, she's got:

1. He didn't actually tell Jia Li he wanted a call; somehow Jia Li got his number but he was bemused, confused, an overall unwilling participant.
2. She's scared.

As such, Becca sits in the garden in her pyjamas and sunglasses, huffing and puffing and largely at a high level of unease until she recognises that it will be less painful to call him and be politely rejected than sit for a second longer wondering.

'Hello?' comes his voice down the line, smooth as oil.

'Hi,' Becca says, and it comes out at a pitch more suited to communicating with dogs than people. She coughs. 'This is, embarrassingly, the woman whose friend demanded your phone number last night at the friend-of-a-friend event Kaylee Roberts threw?' She doesn't know how else to explain it, which is why it comes out as more of a question – although perhaps her name would be useful too. 'Becca,' she adds.

It sounds like he's busy. There's clattering and movement – he could be in a café or cooking at home. Becca turns to look at the kitchen clock through the open back door: 11 a.m. The movement stops.

'Oh,' he says, curtly. God, the things Becca reads in that *oh*. Oh, why are you bothering me. Oh, I don't think I remember you. Oh, you tracked me down and now I have to report you to the authorities. 'I didn't actually think you'd call.'

'If this is a bad time . . .' Becca trails off, almost relieved to know for a fact that he isn't interested so that she can hang up and go run out into fast-moving traffic.

'It's not,' he says, but he's distracted. It definitely is a bad time. 'Hold on.' There's a vague murmur of voices and then the clattering softens and is replaced by birdsong. 'There,' he tells her. 'I can hear you properly now.'

OK. He hasn't ended the call 'by accident' and he hasn't accused her of misreading anything. This could be worse. Becca silently curses the romantic gods: she's all for equality, but shouldn't all this be the other way round? That he should be doing this nauseating legwork, tracking *her* down and asking her out? She'll happily split the bill, if only she was the one asked out instead of doing the asking.

'How are you?' he prompts when Becca doesn't speak.

'Well. Good. *Awesome*,' she replies, cringing at her word choice. Awesome? She squints her eyes closed: if she can't see the car crash, the car crash isn't happening. More words leave her mouth before she can stop them: 'Mortified to be randomly calling you, to be honest. I'm sorry if my friend left you no choice but to surrender your phone number.'

'Not at all.'

Is he smiling as he talks?

'I've never knowingly been talked into anything I didn't already want to do. I'd been looking for you, but I thought you'd left.'

'Oh. I'd been looking for you too.' Becca is doing whatever the opposite of playing-it-cool is. Playing it lukewarm?

'This worked out then,' he says.

They pause.

'I think I'm supposed to ask you out, now you've picked up and said all the right things,' Becca suggests, and it comes out breezily, almost insouciant, and so she's grateful Noah can't see down the line to where she's now found herself standing up, her balled fist at her mouth as she bites down on a knuckle. She hates this, the being-bold-and-brave thing.

She also appreciates how the manifestation gods might appreciate her showing up as fully as possible, though. And so she persists. Reluctantly – but the gods don't have to know that bit.

'I'd like it if you did,' Noah says. 'I enjoyed our chat last night, however brief – though I'm still unsure about the merits of a Cadbury chocolate pot over a Rolo yogurt. Seems a bit suspect.'

'You can't be an equal-opportunist dessert man?'

He laughs. She likes the sound of it.

'I could make an exception on this occasion,' he replies.

Another pause. How does a girl respond to something like that?

'What are you doing later?' he asks then. 'If I might be so forward.'

'One of us has to be,' Becca jokes. 'I'm . . .'

She doesn't finish the thought. What was she going to say? That she's nervous? Shy? Unsure of herself? So unabashedly idealistic that when forced to live in the real world, instead of the friction-free one in her head, she freezes like a web browser with too many tabs open?

'I know,' he says, as if he can hear inside her head. 'Me too.'

Becca isn't actually doing anything today. A day off from the salon means exactly what she's already done: a lie-in, a lazy morning, maybe a walk later. She could stop by to see her mum and Betty, or her dad at the pub if he's gone to watch the match. Something always crops up. She always bumps into somebody, finds herself doing something.

'What about a walk?' Noah asks, and Becca says that a walk sounds lovely. They agree on 2 p.m.

He's more attractive than she remembers. She'd thought him a tad geeky, a bit square, even. Yet there's an appeal to him that Becca didn't catch last night but sees as she crosses the park towards him, when he holds out his arms and casts a smile so wide it might fall off the side of his face. It feels nice that he's happy to see her, that she's the one making him grin that way: fully, unembarrassed.

'Becca,' he greets her, and as he kisses each cheek she can smell his aftershave, earthy and woody. He's in a dusty yellow polo shirt, chino shorts and Birkenstocks, with red Ray-Bans, a bit like an off-duty Jake Gyllenhaal. Becca is in a flimsy cotton sundress that ties at the shoulders, and tennis shoes. They don't look fancy, as they might on a first date. But if this was a movie, the stylist would get top marks for co-ordinating the red of his glasses with the red swoosh on her trainers, the yellow of her floral dress print being the same shade as his T-shirt. They look well matched and worn in, as if they were always a pair. Not that Becca is noticing such trivial and banal things, of course.

'Noah Brooks,' she says as she pulls away.

'Oh, we're going full name, are we?' he retorts, and she laughs.

'When Jia Li – that's my friend who accosted you – sent me your contact it was your full name. I just thought it was funny. Noah Brooks. You sound like a novelist.'

'That's because I am a novelist,' he says simply. 'Did you know that already? Are you teasing me?'

Becca's eyebrows shoot up her forehead. 'What! No, I didn't know that! I was just being ridiculous. You write books? That's fun.'

'So they tell me,' he replies. 'I would ask what you do but it seems terribly uninventive.'

'Hence why you didn't ask me the other night?' she notes aloud, and he nods. 'Well I'll tell you now. I'm a hair stylist. I have a salon just the other side of the park, actually.'

'Ah.' He smiles. 'That also sounds fun.'

Becca shrugs. 'So we're just a coupla fun people with fun jobs, hanging out on a Saturday afternoon for some . . . fun?'

'I thought we could get gelato from the new pop-up over on Doncaster Road. If you're up for it?'

'Excellent,' Becca tells him. 'I had lunch but no dessert.'

'No chocolate pots in the fridge?' he asks, gesturing in the direction they should walk and letting Becca fall in step with him.

'Can't,' Becca tells him, solemnly. 'They don't last. I told you, I don't just like them – I am *obsessed* with them.'

'The lady likes what she likes,' he says.

'The lady is obsessed with what she's obsessed with,' Becca corrects him.

'Anything else you'd like to declare up front?'

'Let me think about it . . .' muses Becca. 'I *like* a lot of stuff but *obsessed* is a special category . . .' She's nervous enough to know she's talking bollocks, but not so self-aware that she reins herself in. 'There's the chocolate pots. Jay-Z, I'd put him in that category.'

'Jay-Z? OK. Well. I wasn't expecting that.'

'Shawn Corey Carter is a modern-day prophet,' Becca explains, and she means it. He gives her a Look. 'It's true!' she insists. 'Don't fight me on it.'

'Wouldn't dream of it,' he retorts, barely concealing his amusement.

'Do you know much about him?'

'I know that he cheated on Beyoncé, which blows my mind.'

'The way he owned it, though,' marvels Becca. 'Look, I'm a die-hard romantic and I want to believe that everyone gets a happy ending, so it kills me they went through that. But there's something about how they worked through it that is even more romantic. They obviously didn't take their vows lightly. And Jay-Z, he's one of the few artists who make a true body of work – every song on every album is amazing, and every album tells a story. The *4:44* album? It's like a love letter, and it's so *sophisticated* too.'

Noah pretends to write this down on an imaginary notebook in the palm of his hand.

'A die-hard romantic . . .' he mutters theatrically, sticking his tongue out in a pronouncement of grave concentration, waggling his fingers as if he's holding a particularly unruly pen. 'Listens . . . to . . . Jay-Z . . .'

Becca cranes her neck to pretend to look at the non-existent notepad. 'You have to listen to *The Blueprint*,' she says, tapping a finger into his palm. 'Two thousand and one. That's his swansong. Whole thing is insanely lyrical. Suave. Just, *good*.' She bops his hand once more. 'Write it down,' she presses. 'It's when he started working with Kanye as his producer and it's—' She gives a chef's kiss to the air.

'Well. This is an education. And the die-hard romantic thing?'

Becca shrugs, looking up to the trees as though they're suddenly the most fascinating thing she's ever seen. She shouldn't have said that. She knows men can find it off-putting, or silly.

'I came of age in the era of Disney princesses, and then the Spice Girls,' she explains. 'It's not my fault.'

'I thought the Spice Girls were all about girl power?'

Becca smiles. 'Yes,' she agrees. 'But then they all ended up married and with kids in their mid-twenties, didn't they? Girl power with a side order of healthy fertility and nuclear family.'

'I never thought of it like that.'

Becca pulls a leaf off a particularly wild tree, shredding it in her fingers as they chat. 'Victoria Beckham was twenty-five when she got married. David Beckham was twenty-four. Can you imagine? And they already had their first kid by then, too.'

'And you just happen to know all these facts off the top of your head, do you?'

She looks at him, faux-stern. 'I have been unofficially voted King's Heath's best pub-quiz team member ever, so don't take the piss.'

'Wouldn't dream of it.'

They walk.

'Dare I ask what's on the list labelled opposite-of-obsessed? You said you're either obsessed or not interested, didn't you?' he questions.

'Ahhhh. You mean the Things That I Don't Get list?'

'I must do.'

Becca tells him, with starling clarity: 'Just two things. Soup and stairs.'

'Soup and stairs? You don't get soup and . . . stairs?'

'Nope. Food that is a liquid is actually a drink, and if you think of soup as a drink, it really makes no sense at all, what about all the bits floating in it that don't fit up straws. And stairs are just odd. Inconvenient. I think we should all live in bungalows or apartments. There's no way for stairs to be truly useful. They're . . .' She searches for the word in the sky as if it might be hanging out in the clouds, ripe for picking. 'Exhausting,' she settles on.

'Do you live in a bungalow or an apartment?' Noah bats back.

'Neither.' Becca sighs. 'I live in a very narrow three-storey townhouse. More's the pity. Stairs for days. I've got the leg strength of Lionel Messi.'

'And that's . . . a football reference . . . ?' He narrows his eyes, pulls a funny face.

She chuckles. 'So I've heard.'

Noah nods. 'I'm not much of a sports fan. I'm more of a book guy.'

'That shouldn't impress me so much, and yet . . .' Becca says, and they arrive at the ice cream shop '. . . it does?'

'I'll make a note of that too as well then.' Noah grins as he pulls open the door to let her into Gelateria Bellissima first. Her fingertips brush his as she passes. It makes every hair on the back of her neck stand to attention. There's a thought pushing for her attention, that all at once this date is nothing, and everything. *I could fall for this man,* she realises. *I could really fall hard.*

It doesn't go unnoticed by Becca that Noah laughs freely, listens closely, and always walks on the outside of the pavement, closest to the road – without making a big deal of it.

'I'm glad we did this,' she says as she hands him a wet wipe from the wicker cross-body bag on her shoulder. The weather is the hottest it's been all summer and their matching strawberry shortcake ice creams drip quickly down the cones and on to their hands and wrists, making a sticky mess of them both.

'The gelato?' Noah says, cleaning himself up. 'Me too. That place must make a killing with weather like this.'

Becca waits for the penny to drop.

'Oh,' he says, getting her point. 'You mean *this*. This-this.' He gestures between the two of them with his dirtied wipe and she takes it from him to deposit in the bin with her own.

'Same,' he tells her. 'Good call on making the call.'

'Bravery, thy name is Becca Calloway,' trills Becca, and she's not as anxious as she was – how can she be when Noah is such good company? – but she keeps surprising herself with the inane and weird things that continue to slip out.

Bravery thy name is Becca Calloway? What does that even mean? But then, the way he'd looked at her after their hands had touched, how close he stood as they ordered and paid ... is she being naïve in thinking this is actually a very good date?

Noah looks at her. They stand. They said they were going to go for a walk, and then they decided to get ice cream together, and now that's been done there's a lull. Becca wonders if he wants to say goodbye. He might have evening plans he needs to get off for. She's uncertain whether to allude to plans herself, in case she comes off as a loner or dull. He seems to be having a nice time too, but there's a chance he's just being polite. Not for the first time, she wishes she could quiet the voice in her head.

'I should let you get on with the rest of your afternoon,' Noah tells her, and her brain was right. He wants to go. She's careful not to look too disappointed, not too needy. She's had fun. It's been nice, just hanging out. But then, she has been talking a lot. He made it so easy to just natter away. Should she have asked him more questions about himself? Probably. She hasn't followed Coco's advice, hasn't leant into enjoying it; rather she's self-monitored and been a bit on edge.

'Absolutely,' says Becca, looking at her wrist for a watch she isn't wearing.

'Hair past a freckle?' he asks, noting the gesture. She goes to speak, but finds she has nothing witty to say. The wind has been rather taken from her sails.

'I have a thing, that's all,' Noah begins, and Becca is immediately mortified if he thinks he owes her an explanation. He doesn't. Of course he doesn't. It was ice cream. There's no expectation with ice cream. It's her own romanticism carrying her away, thoughts of the manifestation ritual making her put more weight on this afternoon than it needs.

'Pffft, don't worry at all,' Becca says, making a very strange noise with her lips, something between blowing a raspberry and trying not to dribble. 'You go. Do you! You go do you. Have a great evening.'

Noah raises one eyebrow. 'It's my best friend's thirtieth.'

Becca nods, digesting the information. 'I remember my thirtieth,' she muses. 'I was so young, everything seemed so beautiful . . .' Later she'll think how she's misquoted her favourite piece of art in saying this.

'Wait,' says Noah. 'You say it like it was years ago. How old are you?'

'Thirty-five.' Becca blinks. 'I mean, I'd like to think I'm a *young* thirty-five, but yes. Thirty-five.' She takes in Noah's expression, a mix of scepticism and bemusement.

'How old are *you* . . . ?' she asks, suddenly suspicious. She can feel what's coming. The man looks almost forty, with his salt-and-pepper beard and easy demeanour – the demeanour of a man who has settled into himself. But Becca's body adjusts the truth she thought she knew, because—

'Twenty-eight,' he replies. 'I thought you were too.'

'Twenty-eight!' Becca repeats, agog. 'No,' she utters. 'I don't believe you. Look at you! You can't be twenty-eight with this much . . . self-possession! No way! No.'

'It would be a weird thing to lie about,' Noah points out.

'Show me your driving licence.'

'I don't have my wallet with me,' he says. 'I pay for everything with my phone.'

'Are you Gen-Z?'

'Are you a millennial?'

Becca laughs. 'Damn. I've just had ice cream with a twenty-eight-year-old. I'm a . . . cougar! Oooooh, that makes me feel all . . . Samantha in *Sex and the City*.' She adopts a more sober face. 'Oh, right, yes, you probably don't remember when we all watched TV shows at the same time. You see, in the olden days, we had five channels and everyone had to pick one channel to watch and whatever was on we all tuned in together, at a certain time. And *Sex and the City* was on at ten p.m. on a Friday . . .'

'OK, lady, there's seven years between us, not seven decades.'

Becca shrugs. 'Sorry,' she says, not sorry at all. 'Well. In theory, it doesn't bother me.

'In theory.'

'You know what I mean. If you were the girl and I was the guy, it would be expected that I'd be older. Does it bother you?' She catches herself. 'Not that, you know . . . this was just one date, I get it . . .'

Noah laughs. 'Oh, trust me. Not only does it not bother me, but you've also just become at least twenty per cent more attractive . . . An older woman,' he reflects. 'Look at me go. I'm about to kiss an older woman . . .'

Becca flushes once again, embarrassed by his forthrightness. So he *is* having a good time.

'You're so . . .' she says, but the sentence remains unfinished. Her breathing becomes shallow, her throat dry.

'Yes?' Noah asks.

And then he takes a step towards her. In less than five seconds – four, if she leans in too – his lips are going to be on hers, on this street corner in the middle of a Saturday afternoon at the beginning of July.

'I'm so what?' he whispers, and Becca doesn't answer, because in three, two, one . . .

He tastes like chocolate flake.

8

She Texts Back

'This is a surprise,' Becca says, letting herself in through the back gate to her mum and Betty's. They're expecting her, but Becca wasn't expecting to see her dad there too. 'What are you doing here, Pops?'

Her dad goes to speak but is interrupted by Becca's mother in a kaftan and a sunhat as if she's about to take the sun on the Côte d'Azur, not baste on some olive oil whilst schlepping to the kitchen and back in a Birmingham suburb within five minutes of the M62. Betty sits in the shade, her combat shorts hiked up to mid-thigh, feet in a paddling pool.

'We're the picture of consciously uncoupling!' Shelley trills, setting down a pitcher of water ladened down with sliced lemon and sprigs of mint. 'Aren't we, Gary?'

Becca's father shrugs. 'I still love her,' he says to his daughter. 'Even if we're not in love any more.'

'Right,' says Becca, unconvinced. Her parents have been largely amicable since the split, but she wasn't aware they still saw each other socially without her. Her father lowers his voice.

'She said you'd be here,' he says. She squeezes his shoulder.

Becca removes her sunglasses to fully take in the scene. She delivers a kiss to Betty's cheek, and finally her mother's, and holds up a paper bag filled with two tubs of strawberry shortcake ice cream, picked up from the gelateria near the park. She'd felt an inexplicable urge for ice cream.

'Now, or later?' she asks her divorced parents and her mother's lover.

'Now, doll,' answers Betty. 'I'm sweating like a nun in a cucumber patch and that'll be just the ticket.'

'Darling, do you want the fan bringing out there?' Shelley shouts through from the kitchen, where a clatter of cutlery suggests she's already getting bowls and spoons. 'I think with the extension lead it should reach you!'

Betty looks up. 'Thank you, beautiful, that'd be great.'

Becca's mother comes back out, all wafting fabric and Ikea's finest crockery. 'Gary,' she says, gesturing to a fan just inside the patio door. 'Would you mind?'

Becca's dad obliges wordlessly, and the three women start scooping melting gelato into their bowls. Becca serves a portion for her father, too, and when they're all seated and fanned and shaded and quiet, her mother says: 'I saw Regina Henry the other day,' and her voice has a very specific tone to it: sympathetic and somewhat afraid. Trepidatious, you could say. Becca instantly knows where this is going. It suddenly makes sense why her dad is here: this is officially a rallying of the troops.

'I know that Mike is back,' Becca says, before her mum can continue. 'I've seen him.'

'Oh,' comments Gary, and if Becca is waiting for him to say much more she is waiting in vain.

'He texted me,' she continues. 'A little while ago now. And I told him to stop by the salon before he went home, so he did.'

Betty scrapes the last of the melted ice cream from her bowl. 'I told you, Shelley – she's fine! Look at her!' she says, gesticulating with a dirty spoon. 'She's been so worried,' Betty continues. 'But I told her – I said, you may be a sensitive soul, but you're not a fool, are you?'

'I just thought it might upset you,' Shelley says, in a way only a mother does. 'Or . . .'

'Rattle you, love,' her dad supplies, and her mum looks satisfied at his contribution.

'I'm fine,' explains Becca, somewhat bemused. Why is everyone acting like this is the time she'd fall apart? Surely Mike has been back to visit numerous times. What makes this one so special? 'I mean, when his text first came through I didn't really get it,' she adds. 'Like, we've barely spoken since he left. It's a miracle I've never bumped into him when he's been back, but I never have. I nearly didn't reply to him, to be honest, but then I just thought, well, why not?'

'Why not indeed,' Betty says. 'And your parents are a case in point. Just look at you two,' she says to Gary and Shelley. 'You're a shining example of cordiality.'

'We have a child,' says Becca's mum, slowly. 'You weren't there, Betty. It was . . .'

'Mum,' Becca says, reaching out a hand to her arm. 'It's OK. I'm OK. It was nice to see Mike, actually. We had a quick coffee together yesterday, and then I had to get back to work but he popped round for his tea as well, afterwards. It was all very low-key, very friendly.'

'Can you breathe again now, Shell?' Betty asks, reaching out to take Shelley's hand.

'My two girls,' Becca's mum says, holding on to them both. 'Oh, I've been so worried, Rebecca! You've no idea! It's such a shame what happened. You know he's back for good, don't you? Terrible stuff. Still. Regina's glad to have her only son home. You can't ever really say in the moment, can you? You can't hold your children back. I never would have pressured you to stay if you had wanted to go with him, but I'm so pleased you didn't. I don't know how she's coped.'

It takes Becca a moment to hear the most important piece of information hidden in her mother's impassioned outburst. They've already started to help themselves to seconds of the ice cream, talking about cracking open beers or white wine, maybe making an Aperol Spritz, when Becca circles back.

'Sorry Mum, I'm just catching up here. Did you say Mike is back for good?'

'That's what Regina said, yes. Has he not told you that?'

'No,' says Becca, frowning. Should he have? She hadn't asked him outright if he was back forever – she'd just assumed he was visiting. Isn't that what one of his messages had said? She pulls it up on her phone. *I'm actually at the airport on my way to visit home. My sister had a baby!* Hmmmm.

'Did he tell you about the bankruptcy?'

'Bankruptcy? No.'

'He didn't tell you much then, did he?' Betty comments, and the sound of her spoon scraping across her bowl is suddenly enough to make Becca want to knock it right out of her hands and to the floor. How odd, that a person can go from sanguine and chilled to somehow triggered in the blink of a hidden sentence.

'Like I said,' Becca says, feeling defensive – feeling *foolish*? Feeling something. It's weird to her that she's getting the actual information from her mother instead of from Mike directly. This all seems like pretty important stuff. Moving back. Bankruptcy. 'We kept it light.'

'Hmmmm,' her father says, looking at her. She knows what that means. It means she has to investigate.

'I see,' Jia Li muses when Becca tells her what she's just learned in her mother's garden. 'I think we all knew it on some level, didn't we? Like, of course he reached out now he's back for good. Seeing that art in the Met was just the excuse . . .'

'That's kind of where I'm landing too,' Becca nods. They're at the Fox and Hound, in the beer garden, Jia Li fresh from work since it was her Saturday on shift. 'If I really ask myself why he texted, maybe I sensed he must be homesick, what with his nephew being born. Just in a dusty corner of my mind, you know? But if I'd acknowledged that, I'd be acknowledging that I knew exactly what I was doing by replying, and I do *not* want to go there.'

Jia Li stirs her drink with a metal straw, shaking her head. 'I could kill Dana for letting you message back. I know it's been nice to see Mike but . . .' She pauses, as if awaiting confirmation that she's allowed to share her thoughts.

'It's funny that you're acting as though you aren't going to give me your unsolicited opinion whether I want it or not.' Becca laughs. 'Go on. Get it off your chest. Tell me what you have to say. I know you don't approve.'

'I just think you should be careful!' Jia Li counters. 'That's all. Your manifestation was Mr Right, and you should be looking towards the future for him, not searching the past. If I hadn't been on clean-up crew with Carlos that night, I would have had you delete that text and block his number. And I bet you'd have already met the *real* man of your life – some artsy type with an old soul.'

'Would I now?' Becca asks, rolling her eyes with a smile.

'If Mike's back for good, are you going to keep seeing him? Is the spark still there?'

It's Becca's turn to stir her drink with her straw. 'Hard to say, really, isn't it?'

'How so? I know you can be romantically dense but surely you can tell if he's flirting with you, or testing the waters?'

'I can't tell if that was supposed to be encouragement or admonishment.'

'Who cares! Answer the question.'

Becca considers it. Her coffee with Mike had been chatty and friendly, but she'd be lying if she said she didn't feel a tiny flame still burning for him somewhere.

'Thought so,' Jia Li nods.

'I didn't say anything!'

'You didn't have to!'

'Leave me alone!'

Jia Li drains her glass, knowing herself champion in an argument Becca didn't want to have.

'Anyway,' Becca says, changing the subject, 'you were the one who summoned me to the pub tonight, pal, so can we turn the tables of this Spanish Inquisition? What's up?'

'Get yourself another drink and I'll tell you,' Jia Li replies, and Becca can't read her face.

'OK . . .' she replies. 'What are you on?'

'Could you just get me a water?' she asks. 'I haven't drunk enough today. My last wee was the colour of Irn-Bru.'

'Charming,' says Becca, getting up.

'Did you ever hear the joke about hydration?'

Becca shakes her head.

'No,' Jia Li concludes. 'Because it's no laughing matter.'

Becca heads to the bar, half running through a mental list of what Jia Li could possibly be building up to say, and half concocting a text to Mike suggesting they meet up again. But what would she say? She wants to know why he hasn't told her the real reason he's back, or if he really plans on staying, but before she does that she wouldn't mind testing her own feelings a bit more. Could there genuinely be something still there?

'How do,' says Dave, the landlord, when she reaches the bar.

'Hey, Dave,' Becca says. 'Gin and tonic please. Just a single.' She doesn't want to down another double if Jia Li is taking it easy tonight.

'We had Mike Henry in here the other day,' Dave tells her as he finds a glass, shovels in the ice, finds a fresh piece of lemon, and then some lime, running both around the rim before he drops them in, exactly as Becca likes it.

Becca still can't get over hearing his name so much. She's heard him spoken about more today than she has in half a decade.

'I hope he knows what a fan club he's got here,' Becca says, noting the way Dave lets the measure of gin overflow in the thimble before he tips it into the glass, giving her a healthy three fingers of the stuff before the tonic is added. Single my arse, she thinks, fondly. 'His name seems to be on everyone's lips today.'

'Forewarned is forearmed,' Dave says, holding out the card machine for her to tap on with her card. 'In case you didn't already know.'

'I appreciate it,' Becca tells him, and she does. She knows it comes from a good place. 'Are you good?' she asks, politely changing the subject. 'Seeing anyone? Last time I was in here you said you were thinking of asking Kaylee for a drink. She was just in the salon last week.'

'Yeah,' Dave agrees. 'Still not done that. I think she might be a bit out of my league, to be honest. I don't know. Doesn't seem right, asking out a regular. I don't want to put her off coming in.'

'Maybe she doesn't want to ask you out because she doesn't want you to dread her coming in,' Becca offers. 'So you might be at a stalemate.'

Dave nods, opening the glasswasher under the bar, temporarily disappearing into a cloud of steam. When he reappears, he fixes Jia Li's water and passes it across the bar.

'When you put it like that,' he says, not finishing the thought.

'Thanks for the drink,' Becca replies with a wink, taking leave to get back to Jia Li. It's so much easier to encourage other people to be brave with their hearts than it is to be brave with her own.

'Cheers,' says Becca as she sits down, holding out her glass to Jia Li's. Jia Li doesn't mirror the gesture.

'Can't,' she says. 'It's bad luck to cheers with water.'

And then Becca understands. She doesn't need any more information.

'Ohmygod,' Becca says. 'Jia Li, are you . . . ?' She looks pointedly at Jia Li's stomach, then instinctively touches her own.

She waits for Jia Li to say something. She doesn't. The look on her face says it all though: she's pregnant.

'Oh, wow,' says Becca, without meaning to. She immediately puts a hand to her mouth. 'Sorry,' she self-corrects. 'Should I be saying congratulations?'

Jia Li screws up her face. 'I think so?' she says back. 'I mean, I *do* want kids. I just . . . wanted to know whose kids I was having?'

Becca nods. 'Got it,' she says. 'Do you have a shortlist?'

'Yeah.' Jia Li nods too. 'But . . . I don't want to get into it. If that's OK. I have, like, eight different emotions coursing through me right now, which is probably the hormones but also absolute terror. I can't go around telling everyone who the dad is before I tell the dad himself.'

Becca nods again. 'How far are you along?'

'This is the truly gobsmacking bit. Four months.'

'FOUR MONTHS? But . . .'

'I'm not even showing? I know. This whole thing is just . . . weird.'

Becca thinks back – four months. That was when they all had a lock-in here at the pub. Dave was here, Carlos and Becca, Cheesey, Small Leo. Is that the shortlist? Becca looks at her friend. If it was Cheesey or Small Leo, wouldn't she say? Is the reason she won't because Becca not only knows the father, but is his best friend? Is it possible that it's Carlos? Things between them have been even weirder, lately . . .

'It's not . . .' Becca starts, and Jia Li tuts.

'I said no, Bec.'

'OK.'

They sit, thoughts running away with them both. And then Becca says quietly: 'You have a baby in there?'

'That's what the stick I weed on in the salon toilet says,' Jia Li answers. 'And the doctor. I hated not telling you I was going, but telling you would have made it real? And there was a beat there where I really hoped it wasn't. But now . . . I'm happy. I'm having a baby!"

'Jia Li!' repeats Becca. 'You're having a baby!'

And she's happy for her best friend – of course she is. It's only on the short walk after they say goodbye that she feels a tingle in her throat, the threat of tears at her eyes. Somehow it feels like Jia Li has beaten her to something. Becca realises that as much as she's happy for her friend, she also feels a twinge of something else, too. Envy. If she's totally honest with herself, there at the top of her road as the twilight fades to inky blue-black, as happy as she is for her friend, Becca wishes it was her.

9

She Texts Back

Jia Li's pregnancy rearranges the mental furniture of Becca's mind. She's not allowed to tell anyone yet because Jia Li hasn't told anyone yet – and Jia Li still won't say who the dad is. Becca is terrified of giving the game away, constantly thinking to herself *don't give the game away!* to the extent that when Carlos asks her what she's thinking about one morning, it takes everything she has in her not to blurt out: *I AM THINKING ABOUT HOW I AM NOT ALLOWED TO TELL ANYONE THAT JIA LI IS HAVING A BABY FOR THE LOVE OF ALL THAT IS HOLY!*

Until Jia Li decides what to do next, Becca has to keep schtum. She can't reveal her best friend's secrets. So, since she has decided to lay low, when Mike texts her to see if it's too forward to get beers in the park she says yes, why not. He doesn't even know Jia Li – Becca met her six months after their break-up – so even if Becca did reveal it (*she won't!*) he has no context for her and her life anyway. And plus, she can get answers to the questions she has been thinking about since she last saw her mum. Is he really moving back for good? And bankrupt?

There's a sense of movement happening around her. Nothing has outwardly changed, but the shifts happening to her and the people she loves feel suddenly stronger, like a seedling you water and water and, right when you think you don't have a green thumb, up sprouts a tiny shoot to remind you that patience is a virtue and just because you can't *see* the change, doesn't mean you should give up the faith that change is indeed under way. All this to say: a huge event in her best friend's life is making Becca reassess every facet of her life by proxy, and a beer in the park sounds like a nice distraction.

'Hello, you,' Mike says to her as she finds him at the far edge of the park after work, sprawled out on a blanket, a battered paperback beside him: *Another Planet*, by Noah Brooks.

'Hello, you,' Becca says, and it's strange how not-strange it is to automatically greet each other how they always did, way back when. 'Good book?'

She plonks down next to him and he moves so that she has room.

'It's OK,' he says. 'Not his best. Beer?'

'Beer,' Becca affirms, watching him as he grabs a bottle from the small cool bag he's thought to bring, opening it with a satisfying sigh and handing it to her. She takes a long pull. It goes down quickly, easily.

'Thirsty much?' Mike asks her, noting her eagerness. She takes one last gulp and moves the bottle away from her mouth, giving a dramatic *ahhhh*.

'Apparently,' she says with a smile. 'It's the weather, isn't it? Nothing beats a cold beer on a summer day.'

87

'I'll cheers to that.' Mike smiles back, raising his bottle and taking a long sip too.

The sun is starting to get lower in the sky, providing a backlit glow to the lives being lived all around them: parents, lovers, friends, the early-evening joggers and cyclists starting to appear, everyone the leading character in their own life and the background extras to Becca and Mike's.

'How's Jessie?' Becca says, noting a set of new parents fussing over a bundle in a pushchair. 'Are you seeing her every day, or is she in a new motherhood bubble?'

'She's in a bubble,' Mike says. 'But as the prodigal brother returning, I get VIP access.'

'You get VIP access to everything,' Becca notes. 'You always have.'

'Not always,' he tells her. 'But I take your point.'

Becca wonders if he's going to tell her about his circumstances at will, or if she's going to have to open the conversational floodgates a little more. Becca was telling the truth when she told her mother that she and Mike had kept conversation light when they'd met up, but now she can't help wondering if she'd been foolish to feel content with small talk. Sometimes you have to get to the meaty stuff. That's where the truth lies.

'You never said when you're going back to New York,' she prompts, when he doesn't continue. 'Or if you did, I can't remember.'

'Becca,' Mike says, flatly. 'Your poker face is terrible. I know that you know.'

'Know what?'

88

'Becca.'

She looks at him. She didn't see it before – she saw what she wanted to: her ex, handsome and here, almost exactly as he always was, with just a few more lines around the eyes and width around his waist. But now it's clear. This is a man who is beaten. He looks tired and worn out – more so than a few years' ageing can account for.

'Mum said something about you being back for good,' Becca admits, her voice small. 'She saw Regina out and about.'

'Mum said, yeah,' Mike replies. 'I didn't deliberately with-hold anything from you, you know. I just didn't know how to bring it up, and I feel so . . . embarrassed, frankly. I think I liked that you didn't know yet. Everyone else is treating me like I might break and it's annoying, to be honest. They mean well, but . . .'

Becca tries to arrange her features to look less concerned about him when she hears that. She unknits her brow, loos-ens her jaw.

'Start at the beginning,' she instructs. 'And I promise not to feel too sorry for you, OK? But you should have said. I feel a bit miffed that my mother told me, not you.'

He sighs. 'You're right. I'm sorry.'

He looks down at the picnic blanket and reaches out a hand to the edge, picking a blade of grass, then another one, then another one, the muscles in his forearms flexing with every flick.

'God, I don't know where to start now you've asked,' he says with a hollow laugh. 'I suppose the top line is that I in-vested all my money into a company that has gone bust, and it happened right as I'd broken up with my girlfriend – or, rather, got dumped, if you want the full truth – and in the space of about six weeks I went from seemingly in control of my life, this New York high-flyer, Brit aboard, living the dream, to broke and single. And honestly, Bec, I thought I was a modern man, you know . . . none of this toxic masculinity bollocks, despite my bloody stupid comment about emasculation the other day. I've grown up. I'm in touch with my feelings, all of that, but the *shame* . . .'

He stops picking the grass, and Becca notes the tremble in his voice matches the one in his hand, as though his body is abuzz with misdirected adrenaline. He finally looks at her.

'Mum and Dad had to send the money for my plane ticket. I've got about a grand to my name. I'll be edging on forty soon, and I've lost everything, and I feel like the biggest loser . . . just so pathetic . . .'

If he's going to cry, he stops himself, curling his long, elegant fingers into a ball and pushing them to his mouth in a fist. Becca can't tell if he's biting his knuckles or pressing firmly into his face to stem an outpour.

'That sounds really shit,' she says plainly.

Unexpectedly, he laughs. 'Yeah,' he says. 'It is. It's really, really shit.'

She hears the relief in his voice, and it's a risk, but she keeps her face deadpan as she says: 'You're right though. What a loser.'

He looks at her.

'Waste of space really, aren't you?'

'Ha, ha,' he says, eyeing her suspiciously.

'I'd give up if I were you,' she presses, daring to smile as she says it. She sees the lightbulb moment in his face, that she's winding him up. 'What's the point, that's what I say. You took a risk and it didn't pay off. Good job Rockefeller gave up at his first business hurdle. And Will Smith – when he went bankrupt I heard he got a job at a local corner shop, serving Slush Puppies. Faded into obscurity.'

'OK, OK,' he says. 'I get it. You're going to come in with the tough love, are you? Because nobody else is. Got it.'

'It's a calculated gamble,' admits Becca. 'And I only half meant it.'

'Only half,' quips Mike. 'Almost as if your heart's not in it.'

'I've only ever been able to muster fifty per cent bad-bitch energy.' Becca sighs. 'I am who I am.'

Mike smiles at her.

'And you are who you are,' she tells him.

'I don't know what that means,' he says sadly. 'I was always a loser but I didn't know it?'

'Yeah, that's exactly what I meant,' Becca retorts. He rolls his eyes. She won't let him wallow – he's essentially tasked her with making sure he doesn't. But at least he's being honest. He's always known how to be truthful, never shied away from his thoughts and feelings. That's why she'd loved him as she did. Why it had felt so strange when she knew he'd been withholding.

'You're resilient. Nobody cares if you fall over – what people talk about are the ones who get back up again. That's the hard part, but you've got it in you. It might not feel like it now but when you're ready, you'll find a way to rebuild.'

'Do you think?' he asks, hopefully. 'Mum and Dad tell me to get back on the horse; Jessie is all but on suicide watch because she thinks I'm going to go and jump off a bridge – which I'm not, for the record. Just to be clear. I'm just . . . you know. Too old to be in Mum's spare room. Logically I know that when you've got nothing to lose you've got everything to play for, but then I wake up surrounded by her Peloton Bike and floral pink curtains and think, God, that's easy to say but how to hell am I even going to start?'

'I have no idea,' says Becca truthfully. 'I love me some manifestation but I don't want to insult you with notions of, like, *thinking yourself* out of the hole. Maybe you even have to be in the hole a little bit longer? Let yourself feel terrible to the point where the only other choice is action?'

'Hmmmm,' Mike says. 'You're the first person to tell me to enjoy feeling so miserable.'

'Not *enjoy*,' clarifies Becca. 'But if you accept it won't be forever – that this is a beginning, not an end – it's easier to find the good bits, isn't it? When you know this is a chapter, not the whole book, this is just a plot point before the big redemption, and when you can see that it can get . . .'

'Exciting,' provides Mike. 'God. I knew texting you was the right thing to do. All I could think about was that if I was coming home, then I'd get to see you.'

Becca feels a rush of affection for him – a warmth spreading across her chest, a tingle in her bloodstream. *That's information*, she thinks to herself.

'I know we haven't spoken,' Becca tells him. 'But I have always wished you well. From afar. I never wanted you to fail.'

Mike shakes his head. 'Mum always made sure to tell me how well you were doing, everything about the salon and the awards and stuff. And it made me want to do well too, so that you'd see, or know, or hear, that letting me go had been the right thing to do. Does that make sense?'

Becca finishes her drink. Mike motions for another, and she doesn't hesitate: she'd love one.

'You know what Jay-Z says about life, don't you?' Becca says, adjusting her position to get more comfortable.

Mike chuckles good-naturedly. 'She still loves Jay-Z, then,' he teases.

'She does,' Becca replies. 'And he says only two things can get you through this: patience and persistence.'

'Persistence I feel like I'm good at,' Mike muses. 'Patience? Not so much.'

'Oh, how could I forget that?' Becca laughs. 'At one point me and your mum were even thinking of printing you off a certificate, qualifying you with the Most Accomplished Least Patient Person in the World award. In the end we didn't know if you'd see the funny side. But I think she even sourced a fake gold frame.'

'Back in the day I probably wouldn't have seen the funny side,' concedes Mike. A stray frisbee heads right for them from a bunch of twentysomethings playing across the way. Mike reaches up, saving Becca from getting a face full of it, and as he stands up to whizz it back, he yells, 'Careful!'

'Sorry!' a girl in a backwards-facing cap yells as she catches it.

As Mike sits back down he rotates his throwing arm at the shoulder. 'I . . . am not as limber as I used to be,' he says with a grimace. 'I think I just dislocated something.'

'Oh come on,' Becca bats back. 'You're only a year older than me, and I am still *young*, my friend. Don't make out like you're an old man.'

'Oh, I don't say it as a badge of honour,' Mike insists. 'I should be in better shape than I am. I just remember being twenty-eight and, like, running five miles before work and playing hockey three nights a week. Drinking until three a.m. and still making a match the next morning, you know?'

'I swear if you say youth is wasted on the young, I'm going to have to leave.'

'It is though! What I wouldn't give to be twenty-eight again!'

Becca scowls and pretends to gather her things. 'Nope!' she says. 'I won't hear of it. Absolutely not. There's life in the old dog yet!'

'OK, OK!' Mike laughs. 'I'm thirty-six, not ninety-eight. I just miss my old metabolism, that's all. I have to work harder these days.' He pats his stomach lightly.

'Do you still play hockey?' asks Becca.

'A bit.' Mike nods. 'Not as much. I used to make it once a week, if I was lucky. I was working crazy hours – before the business went under. It's one of the reasons I got dumped – never around, prioritising my work. The usual suspects.'

'I love hairdressing,' says Becca. 'But I have to have a week off every three or four months to make sure I *stay* in love with it.'

'Is that like an absence-makes-the-heart-grow-fonder kind of thing?'

Becca shrugs. 'I guess,' she says. 'Yeah. A bit of distance never hurt anybody, did it?'

She doesn't mean it like that – she really was only talking about her job – but this keeps happening; they both keep saying things that kind of allude to their relationship.

Mike laughs. 'I love how we keep dancing around the fact that we're exes.'

'Do we?' says Becca, as if butter wouldn't melt. But she smiles as she sips her drink again, letting him know she is more than fully aware of it too.

'Look,' Mike says then, as though he's been holding something in and now is the time to say it. 'I don't suppose you fancy coming to my sister's barbeque next weekend, do you? She's having a sort of summer slash baby slash new house celebration, and they all know we had dinner last week, and that I'm seeing you today, and I've basically been told that if I don't corral you into seeing the family again I'm going to be ex-communicated. No pressure or anything.'

'No pressure but your whole sense of familial self rests on whether I accept an invitation you're only giving because of said worry?'

'And obviously I want you to come too.'

'Obviously.'

'I mean it! I do! This is nice. You've not changed, you know.'

Becca sucks in her cheeks, amused.

'Fine. You're not *exactly* the same. But you're definitely . . . more yourself . . . You're more Becca than you've ever been, and it suits you.'

'Thank you,' Becca says. 'I'm . . . happy. Proud of myself. It's not easy to build a life. I actually think it is way harder than anybody is willing to admit. But I'm doing it.'

Mike smiles. 'Yeah, you are.'

She looks at him through her sunglasses and drains her second beer. Being with him is easy. Shooting the breeze, letting the conversation ramble on, from one topic to the next: the past, the future, now, then, Jay-Z. They've been in the park for two hours and it feels like only five minutes. It always was that way: his mum Regina teased that they could talk the stars out of the sky. Mike realises she's looking at him and turns to face her, his eyes big and expectant. He reaches out a hand towards her face.

'Your beer has smudged your lipstick,' he says, running a thumb over skin perilously close to her mouth. Something shifts inside her, a slow hum in the base of her pelvis.

'Thanks,' she just about manages to mutter, and he nods, still looking at her as if he could, if he wanted to, come even closer.

'Where did we land on the barbeque?' he asks, voice low.

Becca nods. 'Yeah,' she says, swallowing hard. 'I'll come.'

'Good,' Mike replies, and Becca wonders if he's licking his lips that way on purpose. 'That makes me very happy.'

10

She Doesn't Text Back

Noah Brooks stands at the window of the salon, holding up a hand in an awkward wave. Becca doesn't see him at first, and only turns when Carlos says to her, 'Bec. I think that's for you.'

They lock eyes. She does a similarly self-conscious wave back and they grin. It's been less than a week since their first date, and she hasn't stopped thinking about him. About his kiss.

Remember this feeling, she thinks. Noah makes a ridiculously over-the-top gesture with his fingers pointing at the door and mouths, *Should I come in?* It makes her laugh, her giggle a high tinkle, and she smiles and mouths *yes*. He pushes through the door and they stand and look at each other some more.

'This is the salon, is it?' Noah says, not looking at the salon, but continuing to stare at Becca.

'Welcome, welcome,' she greets, and she steps towards him, knowing that they should somehow embrace but realising at the last minute that a kiss hello feels too forward. She forgot this part – the part where you see somebody after the first kiss, and nobody knows when the second first kiss is appropriate, when that seal should be broken. God, she could kiss him now. She won't. But she *could*.

'Hi,' he says into her hair, softly, and she says hi back, into his T-shirt.

'Hey, man,' Carlos says to Noah from across the salon; he's at the sink removing foils from half a head of highlights. 'This water a good temperature for you?' he looks down and asks his client Katie, who says it is and continues to close her eyes and enjoy her massage chair.

'Hey,' Noah says back. 'I think we met briefly at the drinks thing the other night. Noah.'

'Carlos,' says Carlos. 'And yeah, I remember.'

'Me too,' says Jia Li as she emerges from the back room. She was supposed to be leaving early this afternoon since she didn't have anyone booked in, but when Noah said he'd be in the neighbourhood she offered to do Katie's cut so Becca could go and enjoy him – Jia Li's words, not Becca's, although the sentiment is shared.

'How could I forget,' Noah quips. 'You're Cupid!'

Jia Li laughs. 'Happy to help,' she says, and when Noah finally takes in the salon, gazing at the wall hangings and local awards, the row of sleek mirrors and soft leather seats, Jia Li looks at Becca with glee and holds up the 'OK' sign which, when combined with a leery wink, seems to add up to mean *hubba hubba*.

'I just need to grab my stuff and then we can go,' Becca says. 'Give me five?'

'Sure,' says Noah, taking a seat. 'I'll just sit here and read—' He picks up a magazine from the selection on the coffee table in front of him. 'Italian *Vogue*. Excellent. Pasta, pizza, *Mamma Mia!* I'm sure I'll understand every word.'

'The pictures help!' Becca laughs, and she catches herself as she turns for the back room, her eyes twinkling, her skin bright. When she re-emerges, she says, 'I hope it's OK to wear this? I've been in it all day but don't have a change of clothes here.'

'Your outfit is perfect,' he says as they start to leave, noting her high-waisted linen chinos and racer-back vest. He holds the door open for her and she passes through in front of him, turning briefly to wave goodbye to everyone. 'You,' he says, slipping a hand into hers, 'are pretty perfect too.'

In another circumstance Becca might push him away at that, too embarrassed to accept that he means it. But she doesn't – she makes a choice, in that split second, to believe that she is here, with a kind man, saying kind things, and feeling great about it. That's pretty much what she manifested, isn't it? So now it's here, she feels duty-bound to believe it's real – she won't look a gift horse in the mouth. With one hand in his and pulling her sunglasses off her head to put them on with the other, she lets herself enjoy this tiny moment.

'Charmer,' she says, but she's grinning. She's into it.

'I do my best,' he replies. 'I once met a woman at a party who accused me of being a flirt, if you can believe it.'

She enjoys how her hand feels in his, his wide flat palms covering the whole of hers. Oh God, what he could do with those hands. When they kissed, his hard body had pressed against hers and it's all she's been able to think about since – the tenderness of his lips and the firmness of his touch on a loop in her mind.

'She sounds wise,' Becca bats back, and he chortles.

As they wait to cross the road, Becca watches a black BMW pass by, and for the strangest split-second thinks she sees her ex, Mike, behind the wheel. She shakes her head, knowing that she is only thinking of him because she is moving forward. Her thoughts must be expunging themselves, memories expelling to make room for new ones. Why would Mike be driving a BMW through King's Heath? The last she heard, he was happily living the high life in New York.

'Where are we going, anyway, Noah Brooks?' Becca asks as they cross over and hit the top of the road.

'We're going', he says, mysteriously, 'to a place where you'll need comfortable shoes you can walk a few miles in . . .'

'Check,' she says, throwing up her leg in front of her to demonstrate her Nikes.

'And, actually, maybe I should have asked this before, but how do you feel about animals?'

'Animals?' Becca repeats. 'Can you be more specific?'

'Animals with four legs,' he says. 'Bigger than a shoe but smaller than a coffee table.'

'Are we talking cats, dogs or pigs?'

'Dogs,' Noah says, slowing his walk, squinting to look around at the street signs, and then pointing across the road. 'We're going there.' He gestures to the local dog shelter.

Becca blinks twice and then double checks she's understood. 'We're going to the rescue centre?' she asks, and Noah nods.

'I volunteer here. And it's dog-walking day.'

Becca's face lights up. 'We get to walk the dogs?' she asks, hoping and praying she's getting this right. 'The little doggy-woggies who don't have anybody?'

Noah sticks his nose in the air, insulted. 'They get affronted if you call them doggy-woggies,' he says, his face the perfect arrangement of solemnity. 'Save them their dignity, please.'

'Right-o, sir.' Becca nods. 'Any other words of advice?' She likes taking instruction from him. It's masculine and reassuring that he's made the plan for their date, and is taking charge.

'No baby talk,' Noah instructs. 'Normal human voices only. And always keep treats nearby.'

'*Lead* the way, then,' Becca trills, delighted with her own wit.

'Who knew dog-walking puns existed?' Noah laughs, and as he buzzes in and announces himself Becca can't help but notice the fit of his trousers, the way they fall across his backside and sit on his hips. He's wearing them with leather sandals that have a closed toe, in a way that Becca can only think to describe as *European*. The back of his polo shirt spreads across generous shoulders, the upside-down V-shape of a swimmer. He hid all that very well at the party, and even the other day in his shorts. There's something about the smart-casualness of him that feels most quintessentially Noah, as if he's relaxed enough, now, to be more himself, even if that self is pretty formally dressed. In the reflection of the glass Becca checks her hair, braided and tucked under so she looks like a *Little House on the Prairie*-style milkmaid. This is an approximation of her most authentic self, too.

'Here we go,' Noah says as they are buzzed through another door and into a central concreted courtyard, cages all around them in a horseshoe shape that's only broken by one small corridor that seems to lead to a grassy area.

'Noah!' an older man, maybe in his sixties, opens his arms and exclaims.

'I wish I could get a greeting like that,' Becca wisecracks, right before Noah goes in for a hug, laughing and tapping the man's back and saying,

'Brian! How are you?'

Brian pulls away and lifts a hand. 'I'm still here,' he says, 'so I can't complain. And who is this?' He looks at Becca.

'My friend Becca,' Noah announces, letting a hand find its way to the small of her back protectively, and she smiles, the patch of skin in contact with his touch pulsating.

'Pleased to meet you,' Becca says.

Noah adds, 'She's going to help me with Sparkles and Captain today, if that's all right.'

'Long as the little toads get walked, that's all I care about,' says Brian, and with that he paddles off to one of the cages marked 'FOXY', telling the small bulldog inside, 'All right, all right. I've got your lead here, darlin', don't get on at me. I'm coming.'

Becca smiles and looks at Noah.

'This way,' he says.

Sparkles, it turns out, is an Alsatian bigger than a coffee table. And Captain is some sort of retriever-mix, all slobber and boundless energy. They head on up to the hilly park around the back of the rescue centre, Becca with Captain and Noah with Sparkles.

'How long have you been volunteering here?' she asks him, struggling to rein in Captain's enthusiasm for the acres of green open space up ahead.

'You can give him a tug, if you need to,' Noah says, noting her tense arm and clipped speed. 'Like this,' he adds, leaning over and putting a hand over hers, helping her to keep the dog in check. Then he answers, 'Not long. Eight or nine months?'

'It's so nice,' Becca says. 'You must see a lot of dogs moving through the system?'

Noah shrugs, and as they reach the edge of the hills he says to the dogs, 'Sit. Good,' and the dogs do as they're told so he can take off their leads, staying that way until he commands: 'And . . . go!' and they dash off together, making a break for it, right to the top of the nearest mound where they stop and turn around to check that Noah and Becca are actually following, before heading off again.

'They know the way,' Noah tells her. 'They'll be OK.'

She drops behind him as they navigate a gravelly path that demands a single-file ascent. She watches the long stride of his legs, his purposefulness. At the top they see an expanse of woody area, the evening sun demonstrating the precise meaning of the word *dappled* as it plays hide and seek behind.

'Woah,' Becca says. 'How did I not know this was here?' she marvels. 'I don't think I have ever been here in my life – and I've lived around here since I was born!'

'Gorgeous, isn't it?' Noah says, beckoning her to keep following him. 'I love it here. And to answer your question: yes, I've seen a lot of dogs pass through, even in eight months, but the bigger dogs – people are frightened of them. So Sparkles has been with me almost every day of that.'

'You come every day?'

'Most days, yeah. It helps with the writing, as you might expect. Walking, the meditation of it, nature and all that.'

Becca nods. 'Makes sense. And are you working on anything right now?'

'Trying to,' he says. 'I do sci-fi/fantasy crossover. I'm into the string theory of physics? That there's several dimensions all happening at the same time.'

'So in another dimension I'm an archaeologist in the desert?'

'And in another dimension *I'm* an Olympic athlete. I'm a chocolatier in a third dimension, too.'

'Do dimensions ever collide?'

'They do in my books.'

'That's awesome. How did you even get into that?'

He shrugs, as though he doesn't really want to be drawn on it. 'Gave it a bash, sent it off, got a book deal. I was a very confident twenty-four-year-old. Now I'm getting older, even by only a few years, I'm not sure I'd be so blasé about it. Maybe I just know too much now.'

The mention of him being twenty-four only a few years ago lingers in Becca's mind. He's younger, yes, but, God, his ambition is attractive. He's more driven and self-aware than most thirty-somethings she knows. They trudge up the hill to where the dogs are waiting for them, reassuring the dogs that it's okay to carry on up ahead.

'Nice spot, hey?' He gestures to the trees. Becca looks at him, his breadth, his presence. She thinks of their kiss again. She needs another one. Craves it.

'I'll say,' Becca agrees as they reach the edge. There are several winding, well-worn paths to choose from and Noah leads them up to the right.

'You good?' he asks her, signalling ahead. 'I normally like to go up here, and down through the middle. You see all sorts that way.'

'Sounds great,' Becca tells him. 'I trust you,' she adds.

He turns back to look at her, but he doesn't smile. She looks right back at him. It's an unspoken agreement; something passes between them. Becca can't quite put her finger on it, but as they go deeper into the forest, she has no doubt that it was there. She doesn't think of his age again. She decides to simply enjoy the date.

After dropping Sparkles and Captain back at the dog shelter, Becca and Noah go to the Fox and Hound, passing Dave and Kaylee on the way.

'Well, look what the cat dragged in!' Kaylee squeals as she sees Becca, reaching out for a hug.

'Kaylee!' cries Becca. 'Hi!'

They hug, aware they both have a gentleman of the species either side of them, hovering and waiting.

'Kaylee, this is Noah,' Becca says. 'Noah, this is Kaylee, and this is Dave. It's Dave's pub, actually.'

'Hey, man,' says Dave.

'Hey,' replies Noah.

'You two heading in for a drink?' Kaylee asks. 'We're just . . .'

Dave looks at her, struggling to supress a smile.

'I can pretend I haven't seen you, if you prefer,' Becca offers. 'Or assume you're about to go and meet friends of some description?'

Kaylee looks at her, barely containing her excitement. She sucks in her cheeks and says everything without saying anything at all. Well, thinks Becca. Bloody good for Kaylee and Dave.

'Let's leave these two to it, shall we?' Noah interrupts then, reading the mood. 'We don't want to keep you.' He smiles, and Becca feels a rush of something for him that he has the emotional intellect to know everyone needs to go their separate ways. Fair play if Kaylee and Dave don't want the world knowing what they are just yet. Better to keep it discreet – or as discreet as something can be in a place where everybody knows everybody.

Inside the pub Becca finds a table outside the back door just as another couple are leaving, where fairy lights glimmer in amongst ivy expertly trailed around a wooden pergola; each table has a couple of tea lights in a big jar, and citronella sticks are placed strategically around the gardens to ward off the creepy crawlies.

'Fun fact,' says Noah as he delivers her a white wine, and himself a neat whisky. 'I don't get bitten by mosquitos.'

'What,' asks Becca, incredulously. 'Not ever?'

'Not ever,' replies Noah. 'They just don't find me sweet,' he says with a nonchalant shrug.

'Imagine that,' quips Becca.

'Exactly what my Auntie Pat says,' he shoots back and they laugh.

'So you write books, you walk rescue dogs, you get a round in,' observes Becca as he settles into his seat. 'I think you should cut to the chase and tell me exactly what's *not* right about you.'

Noah nods solemnly, as if he was waiting for this. Of course, there's the age difference. She hopes he doesn't think that's what she's getting at.

'I'm crap in bed,' he replies, earnestly. 'So I've been told that's a turn-off.'

'Understandably,' agrees Becca, delighted by his humour. 'Although, in your defence, a bad teacher always blames the pupil.'

'That's true!' he exclaims, as if she's the cleverest person alive. She likes sparring with him this way, likes how she never knows which conversational alleyway they're going to turn down next.

'What about you?' he asks then, swilling whisky around his glass and holding it inches from his mouth.

'What, am I terrible in bed?' Becca asks.

'No,' he replies. 'What are you like as a teacher?'

She lowers her eyes to look at the table, and then bites her lip as she finds the bravery to look at him.

'Well, put it this way,' she replies. 'I haven't failed anyone yet.'

He tips his head back and laughs throatily, pleased by her answer. It makes her laugh, too, and as she catches his eye they grin knowingly. Becca finds she can't look away.

'Spider-Man?' Becca repeats, three drinks later. 'Sorry, I feel like I'm misunderstanding here.'

Noah's face is nonplussed. 'You're not.'

'Right.' Becca nods. 'So you heard the question, didn't you? I asked what your biggest passion is.'

'And I said Spider-Man.'

'OK then,' Becca says, and she's laughing now, and he's laughing, and really, for the past two hours, they haven't stopped laughing.

'Look,' he says. 'I was a bookish child. No surprises there, hey?'

Becca takes him in, his hair, his sharp jaw, the charisma of him. He's wearing glasses, having slipped them out as the night wears on. 'My eyes get tired now I'm an old man,' he says, the joke being that they both know twenty-eight is practically foetal.

'No,' Becca concedes. 'I'll bet you were very cute, though. I imagine you sat under your duvet with a torch after you were supposed to go to sleep, your parents downstairs fully aware of it, but letting you think it was a huge break of the rules so that reading felt rebellious and cool.'

'Two things,' he says, and he's switched seats now. They're side by side, and he's leaning in, tentatively, the air between them crackling with promise. 'One,' he says, and Becca is pleasantly surprised to find his fingertips on the underside of her forearm, lightly caressing so that suddenly, her nipples ping to attention and her skin is alert. 'I was raised by my dad, and he worked nights, so I read because I was afraid to be home alone in the dark, if you want the facts of the matter.'

'Oh,' says Becca, his admission coming more of a surprise because it's sandwiched in between breathy approximations of flirting, and that's how she knows it really hurts: he won't dwell; he makes a joke of it. It's the definition of a truth bomb, coming out of nowhere, a drive-by revelation.

'And two,' he continues, 'the cute child grew into an angry, gawky, pimply teenager who felt all alone in the world. Spoiler alert: Peter Parker was the only friend I had.'

'Noah . . .' begins Becca. She wants to pull him in for a hug, find that angry teenager and make him a sandwich, tell him he's loved.

'Peter Parker had to learn everything on his own after he got bitten,' Noah presses on, and Becca has a running mental list currently at 253 questions about his life, where is mum was, how he managed, where his parents are now, how he's (seemingly) so well adjusted. 'And I felt like that. He was vulnerable, too. In the comics there are all these speech bubbles coming from him where he talks about his feelings and difficulties. It was like being inside his head. Spider-Man made me feel like I'd be OK.'

'I get that,' Becca says. 'It's like I said about Jay-Z, about somebody else owning their vulnerabilities.'

'Exactly.' He nods. 'And Spider-Man is funny, too. Sharp and witty, distracting his enemies with these zingy one-liners. Plus, he quits. He gets tired, can't cope with the responsibility of it and so walks away. But he always steels himself again. Never gives up. And you know, the whole time he's a kid. He's thirteen or fourteen but everyone thinks he's grown up because of the mask. He hides it. But he was never really Spider "Man" at all. I had to grow up too soon too. There were plenty of times I wanted to quit. But I didn't. Because of Spider-Man, in a lot of ways. Even after my dad died, I was eighteen, but I still thought of Spider-Man. He lost his parents too.'

'That's . . .' says Becca softly. 'Sad, Noah. I'm sad for teenage you.'

He busies himself with a dog-eared beermat, his jaw clenched. 'I don't know where all that came from,' he says. 'Sorry.'

'Thank you for understanding the assignment,' Becca says softly. He dares to look up. 'I mean, I'm not *excellent* at date getting-to-know-yous or whatever, but I do want to get to know you. All of you.'

'You might change your mind when you see this,' he says, taking off his watch. It's a tiny spider-web tattoo that has been hidden by the strap. 'When I commit to something, I commit,' he says, and it's Becca's turn to reach out and rub a finger over the delicate skin on the underside of his arm.

'I like it,' she declares. 'I've always been too scared to get a tattoo.'

'Imagine when I tell you I did it myself. I'm surprised I didn't get sepsis and have my arm fall off.'

'This piercing?' Becca moves her hair from her neck and points at the second hole up in her left ear. 'Was done with a needle by my best friend at school when we were fourteen. I passed out. Mum found us on the bathroom floor, me unconscious with blood coming from my ear and my friend Christy hovering over me flapping her hands and saying, "I didn't mean to! I didn't mean to!" Mum thought she'd killed me!'

'Oh my God,' Noah chuckles. 'Jesus! And yet here you are, ear still intact.'

'And friend still intact,' Becca reflects. 'Although she lives in Weston-super-Mare now. But yeah, her continued existence is surprising because the way my mother tells the story she was ready to bury her alive. And you know what? Christy never told her that it was my idea, that I begged her to do it.'

'Stoic loyalty.' Noah nods. 'I'm a fan.'

'I could have been a little bit more loyal in return,' admits Becca. 'I didn't exactly speak up and explain that I'd pestered her every day for a month until she finally gave in.'

Noah looks at her. 'Naughty, naughty,' he says, and it's a comment that doesn't suit the conversation, but absolutely does suit the mood. Somebody has to nudge them in the direction that Becca has certainly been hoping they'll go ever since he arrived at the salon. The wait is killing her.

'Provocative words,' she says, quietly, daringly, and he leans in even further, tipping his head backwards so that the closest part of him is his mouth.

It's odd, but the other side of the age-difference coin with Noah is that Becca feels a tiny bit less afraid to experiment with being more forward, just as she's been telling everyone she'd try. Not that she's the grown-up – twenty-eight makes them as grown as each other – but there's a freedom to it, a sort of role she can slip into as the older woman that means she does things like lower her voice until it rasps, or linger with her gaze. All the things Jia Li has tried to coach her on before now feel easier, more fluid.

'Dare you,' he intones, and she reddens. But he doesn't. And so, intently, bravely, Becca holds his chin and rubs a thumb over his lips. He issues an *mmmm* and she looks at him. Properly, deliberately. How strange that two weeks ago she didn't even know he existed. It doesn't make sense how a person can do that – pop up out of nowhere and alter every-thing that happens next.

She kisses him the way she drank her beer – a long, hard pull, a full appreciation. She lets the feeling of power wash over her.

'Would you like to come home with me?' she asks, and Noah stands up immediately.

'I haven't done this in a while,' he tells her on the way up to her bedroom.

'How long is a while?' she says.

'Almost a year,' he tells her. 'I've been focusing on work. God, that's lame. I might need to . . .'

He doesn't finish the thought.

'It's OK,' Becca tells him. 'It's been a while for me too.'

Becca isn't sure anybody has ever looked at her body the way Noah does. It's as if he is committing her to memory, making sure he knows every part, every inch, getting familiar with the landscape before daring to set off without a map.

He pulls at the cotton of her vest, kissing her shoulder hungrily before deciding the whole thing needs to come off. Becca stands in her sheer lace bra looking at him and he looks at her chest. He pointedly pops the top button of his trousers.

'Just need to make some room,' he notes with a smile.

'I can help with that.' She smiles back, letting him look at her some more before she pushes him on to the bed, and gets to her knees.

'I'm going to make a suggestion,' she says, as she lowers one leg of his chinos, and then the other.

'I'm feeling particularly receptive to your ideas.' He bites his lip as he watches her.

'May I?' she asks, once she's dispensed with his trousers and socks, the only thing still on his lower half his boxers: bright white, Calvin Klein, promising bulge.

'You may.'

'My suggestion is this.' Noah's penis is at an admirable angle beside her face, and she gives it the side eye, in on the joke. He swallows, not quite allowing himself to joke back. He is in a bit of an exposed position, Becca thinks. Fair play.

'I'm going to make you come,' she declares, 'and once I've done that, we're going to . . . play.'

He nods hungrily. She swears she sees him gulp.

'I think that's very generous of you,' Noah says, and he is short of breath now, Becca notes, with something adjacent to pride. Good. It makes her feel sexy, seeing that he wants her. Desire is a potent aphrodisiac.

She takes him in her mouth.

It takes her forty-three seconds before he calls her name.

She gives him exactly forty-three more seconds before taking off her knickers and straddling him.

It's not long before she calls his name, too.

11

She Texts Back

Jia Li has questions about Becca's decision to go to Jessie's barbeque, as per Mike's invitation. She has questions mostly because Becca has begged – *pleaded* – for Jia Li to come along for moral support, which has made it obvious that Becca is trepidatious about whatever is happening with Mike, because once bitten, twice shy and all that.

'Just for an hour?' Becca asks. 'Whilst you're still a free agent.' She looks pointedly at Jia Li's stomach, which even two weeks after her pregnancy revelation has suddenly bloomed, making it very obvious that there's a baby in there. 'Who knows what your schedule will be next summer, it'll all be so different . . .'

Jia Li narrows her eyes.

'And Jessie has a teeny tiny baby who will melt your heart, apparently . . .'

Jia Li gives a half-smile. 'Get me where it hurts, why don't you?'

'Is that a yes?'

Jia Li sighs. 'Can't you ask Carlos?'

'He has a date.'

Jia Li hoots with indignation. 'I'm your second choice?'

Becca grimaces comically. 'Well, you *are* growing life. I promise I'm using my favours up wisely . . .'

'Fine. But only because I want to meet him properly, this man who dented your heart before I knew you. I've got questions.'

'Excellent,' Becca exclaims. 'I appreciate you.'

When Mike had briefly mentioned in passing that Jessie's kitchen was good for entertaining, he'd failed to mention the whole house was good for entertaining. It's a mansion, essentially. When Becca and Jia Li had given the address Mike had sent to the cab driver, he'd whistled between his teeth. Becca didn't ask for elaboration because she was too busy faffing with windows opening and seatbelts clicking and Jia Li saying, 'God, sorry about that, the wind I've been getting lately really is criminal,' but now they've pulled up she can see, retrospectively, exactly what the driver meant.

'Is she loaded then?' Jia Li asks, admiring the wrought-iron gate with buzzer intercom to get in, then the long, pebbled driveway, the looming white house with black metal window frames, oversized planters with bushes the size of people dramatically framing the double-height doorway.

'She *wasn't*,' Becca marvels, wondering how a person comes to be in possession of enough money for something so grand. There are nice houses and then there are houses like *this*. 'I suppose girl came good. Mike never said, though, and I've not heard any village gossip or anything like that.'

'You mean Mike never mentioned it in your brief chats about nothing?' Jia Li says, wryly, as the door opens and Becca is saved from having to decide between defence or attack. Trust Jia Li to be fully aware that whatever Becca has said about *just a catch-up, all a bunch of nothing really*, she knows that anything willingly described as *nothing* is seldom, in fact, ever that. Sod eyes being the window to the soul: try best friends.

'Hello!' chirrups a tall, spiky-haired blond with an Aussie accent, casually dressed in jeans, flip-flops and loose vest. 'Niall,' he tells them. He looks at Becca with a smile. 'I think we met, way back when? Right?'

'Niall! Yes! Hi, how are you?' Becca says, turning to Jia Li to explain: 'Niall had just started seeing Jessie right before Mike and I broke up.' She turns back to him. 'I suppose your year abroad turned out to be more than just a taster event, then? You decided to stay?'

'What can I say?' Niall shrugs, ushering them through as Becca tries not to outwardly *gasp* at the tasteful marble floor and a piece of art so expensive it has a proper spotlight on it, like in a gallery. There're acres of space, fresh flowers in vases like fish tanks, little frames of family life dotted in amongst Diptyque candles with multiple wicks. 'When a woman like Jessie tells you she's fallen in love, you stay in the country.'

Niall laughs and Becca feels Jia Li slip a hand into hers, knowing that whilst it's lovely for Niall and Jessie that they've found love by staying in the same country, it wasn't the same for Becca and Mike. God bless Jia Li for understanding that.

After walking for forty days and forty nights, they arrive at the 'informal barbeque' happening 'just off the kitchen', which is, in fact, a fully catered event with waiters and waitresses for a group of about fifty people, taking place in an industrial restaurant-like space with several low-backed linen sofas and a splattering of brass bar tables. There's a children's entertainer in one corner of the field-like garden, blowing up balloons as kids chant, and an older man Becca presumes to be the father-in-law isn't grilling pink burgers on a rusty rack outside, but rather roasting a full hog at a *second kitchen* outside. It's like a Real Housewife lives here.

'Needless to say,' Jia Li whispers into Becca's ear, before she lets go of her hand, 'I am rather pleased to have come after all.'

Becca raises her eyebrows in agreement. What a way to spend an early Saturday evening. They give a drinks order to one of the staff and wander to the back lawn, smiling at folks as they pass – mostly parents of babies and toddlers who look thrilled to have handed over responsibility to a woman dressed as a mermaid as they sit, talk, drink. A labradoodle runs up and down the garden, playing frisbee with a teenager who keeps yelling, 'Barbara! Barbara!' Interesting name for a dog, Becca thinks.

'Rebecca Calloway, as I live and breathe!' comes a voice, and Becca welcomes the enthusiastic embrace of Mike's mum, Regina, flanked by his dad, Paul. They've come from where Jessie and Niall are changing Sebastian's nappy, and in her line of sight Jessie waves and yells, 'I'll come say hi in a minute!' pointing to the baby's bare bum and then wafts the air under her nose to demonstrate that it's dirty work, but somebody has to do it. Becca half shifts her gaze to search out Mike but Regina demands her attention with a barrage of questions. Becca focuses.

'You're even more beautiful than when I saw you last,' she says, reaching out a hand to Becca's hair, fingering it with an intimacy even her own mother wouldn't venture. 'Your skin, your hair, your eyes – you glow, bab! *Glow!* Doesn't she glow, Paul!'

'Hiya, love,' Paul says, a tank of a man with a heart of gold. 'We heard you were coming.'

'Yeah.' She smiles.

Regina reaches out and squeezes her arm, pleased.

'And this is my friend Jia Li.'

Regina opens her arms to pull Jia Li into a hug, as she does everyone. That's what Becca remembers about the Henry family most of all: the easy physical affection, their readiness to treat anyone as one of them.

'You're pregnant!' Regina says, and bemused Jia Li says, 'Yes!' and then everyone laughs.

'I hear you've reconnected with Mikey since he's been back,' Regina says then, and Paul warns her by saying '*Regina!*' in a low tone.

'What?' Regina says, looking at him and then looking skyward as if God might help her. 'I can't ask my son's favourite ex if she's single now he's home? Is it a *crime* to say how *pleased* we are that they've been meeting up? Hmmmm?'

'And with that, we're going to check on our grandchild again, aren't we, Reggie?'

Paul takes Regina by the elbow, nodding politely at Jia Li and Becca, who watch the pair go before turning their backs to howl with laughter.

'Subtle.' Jia Li giggles again. 'Christ alive. I wouldn't be surprised if she's not got a petition going amongst the guests to lobby for the reunification of your relationship through parliamentary law. Are you sure you weren't shagging *her*?'

Becca chuckles. 'I appreciate your faith in my lovemaking prowess, but no. We just really got on. They're one of those lovely friendly families who like hanging out with each other as much as they like other people. They're great to be around.'

'How odd,' quips Jia Li. 'I must say, though, I can't wait to get a proper look at your man now. His dad is silver fox material. If it doesn't work out with Regina at any given point in the future . . .'

'I'll be sure to pass along that information should the situation arise,' Becca says, and she's done it again, reflexively, without realising it: she's searching out Mike. And then she clocks him. She nods in his direction and Jia Li looks over to where he is in the kids' corner, a toddler on each arm, and two on each leg, walking like a robot and dragging them all along as he says, 'I. AM. RO-BOT. I. AM. RO-BOT.'

'Showy-off bastard,' Jia Li says, after they've both absorbed the scene.

'He always was good with kids,' Becca reflects. 'And I always found it hot, to be honest.'

'I'm *already* pregnant and seeing that sort of behaviour makes me want a baby in me.'

'Yeah,' marvels Becca, smiling. 'I know what you mean.'

Mike continues to play robot as he somehow manages to deposit children back on to the grass in a way that is fun and has them laughing instead of crying that he's pulled the plug on their playtime together.

'I'll be back!' he tells them. 'As soon as you find me five green things! That's your challenge!' He checks the handful of kids within his orbit have understood and then jogs away, finally looking up directly to Becca, a smile as wide as the moon pasted across his face.

'You came,' he says, reaching them. 'Hello.'

'Hello,' Becca repeats. He's caught the sun; his T-shirt is sitting snugly across his chest. He looks well. He looks . . . fit. And the way he is looking at her – how pleased he is that she's here. The space between them feels charged in a way that, truly, it has only ever done with him. There have been men these past few years. Some have lasted a month or two, one almost eight months, but this feeling – this exact feeling – is Mike's and Mike's alone. The truth of it feels freeing, and inconvenient.

'Well, if you'll excuse me, this level of eye-contact is very not-my-vibe, so I'm going to check out the food station,' Jia Li announces, and she's gone before Becca can compute what she's said.

'Funny girl,' Mike says as Becca cringes. 'I can see why you're friends.'

'Yeah,' Becca agrees. 'She's . . . well. She's Jia Li.'

'And you're Becca.'

'I am,' Becca says.

A twenty-something woman in black uniform passes by, collecting the odd empty glass from the veranda.

'Claudia, when you've got a moment, could we get a couple more drinks here, please? Maybe some nibbles?'

'Absolutely,' Claudia says, her ponytail swishing. 'Just gimme five.'

Becca can't believe, once again, that this is Jessie's life. Mike gestures to a small outdoor sofa, brown wicker with thick cream cushions.

Becca lowers her voice as they sit. 'I've got to ask . . .' she says, eyes bright with gossip. She doesn't need to fill in the blanks.

'They won the lottery,' says Mike. 'Like, the actual lottery. Isn't that crazy?'

Becca's jaw slackens. 'Noooo,' she says, somehow feeling as if the extraordinary notion of a lottery win makes it more OK to outwardly appraise what she can see. 'The *lottery*? And you didn't think to mention it?'

'They're exactly the same people for it,' Mike explains. 'But they have this knock-off big house and people to help them with it. This is the first time they've had a party or anything like that. I think they want to share their spoils, you know? But it's their business, not mine.'

'I get that,' Becca says. 'That's very Jessie.'

'For sure. Last night we still had Pizza Express.'

'Hey – dough balls are *life*.'

'Oh, I agree entirely. It hasn't changed them, is my point. I think they'll probably have more kids now, because they can afford it, but Niall still works. Says it keeps him busy, keeps him young. It means Jessie can rest more, hiring help. Her MS has been pretty bad since her pregnancy. It helps that she's got the means to go slower, to do less.'

Becca nods. 'It's awesome they panned out. That she and Niall have gone the distance.'

Claudia reappears with a tray balancing two flutes of champagne already dripping with condensation and a bread basket lined with a thick starched napkin, filled with warm focaccia and salted nuts.

'This is perfect,' Mike says. 'Thank you so much.'

'I aim to please,' replies Claudia, and it could just be Becca's imagination but she swears Claudia's eyes flicker with something as she looks at her.

'It's weird – I'll admit that much,' Mike says, taking a gulp of champagne and helping himself to a handful of pistachios. It's only 6 p.m. but tiny little lights have started to show up in the foliage generously dotted around, as if solar powered and understanding now is literally their time to shine. The kids are all snuggled down in the kids' corner where a huge screen is showing a movie about singing animals, and tiki lamps have been lit at a safe distance, the naked flames dancing in the late sun, keeping the mosquitos away. Jia Li is just inside the house, sprawled on a sofa where a very attentive forty-something in board shorts and no top is massaging her feet. Becca shakes her head. Unbelievable. They've been here less than an hour and Jia Li is getting her feet rubbed by a fit bloke. If Becca ever thought pregnancy could dial down her best friend's sex appeal, she'd been wrong.

'Weird having a lottery win in the family?' Becca clarifies, and she can feel herself sinking further into the plush seats. She hadn't realised quite how anxious she'd been until

123

now – anxious at being here, with him – but the first taste of bubbles on her tongue is helping her relax.

'Whilst being broke and hopeless, yeah,' he says, and he's not self-pitying. He can see the edge of wickedness to the universe's sense of humour. 'It's a hell of a contrast.'

'You feeling any better about all that?'

'What, in the ten minutes since I last saw you?' he says, and again, he's joking – it's just with this joke there is obviously wounded pride underneath.

She winks at him. 'Did you miss me?' she asks, and Mike hoots in surprise.

'Ha!' he says. 'You have no idea.'

They look at each other and then Mike peals with laughter, Becca following his lead, the tension dispersed.

'Changing the subject . . .' he suggests, laughing, and Becca drinks with a smile. She tears a piece of bread in half and stuffs part of it into her mouth.

'What the hell am I eating?' she says as she chews. It is divine. Warm, buttery but not heavy, flavoursome but oddly simple. She chews exaggeratedly, making noises to signal appreciation.

'Better than dough balls with garlic butter?' Mike clarifies.

Becca swallows. 'That's the best thing I've ever put in my mouth. I would say try it but the rest of that bread basket is mine,' she says, reaching over to pull it towards herself.

'Never get between a woman and her bread. I think I read that in the rules somewhere.'

Becca helps herself to another piece. 'The rules to dating?' she says, distracted right up until the words come out of her mouth, and then acutely aware that she just cannot be cool with this man and if the last of the sentence is hanging in the air she'd like to pull it by the tail and push it back down her throat.

'Something like that, yeah,' he says.

They sit, the sky changing around them, rich colours melding into one another like a watercolour.

'I'm glad you came, anyway,' Mike says, playing with the stem of his empty glass.

'Yeah,' she agrees. 'Like I say, I think it's nice that you're back. But what was it like out there? We haven't really talked about you living in the States,' she asks. 'Do you miss it?'

He considers it. 'I don't know.' He narrows his eyes as if that might help his perspective on the matter. 'I really got used to it, but being an expat – even in an English-speaking country – always made me feel one step removed at the strangest times. Like here, if I need something from the pharmacy I go into Boots and instinctively know which aisle it's in. The knowledge is just in me, in my body from growing up here, years and years of navigating the place without realising. And in New York I can go into a CVS and you'd *think* it would be straightforward, but it takes a beat extra to find the lotion or vitamins or whatever. It's less instinctual. But there's stuff I loved, too. I liked the sort of spirit of convenience and the built-in storage even in a rental – have you ever noticed that? British houses don't have built-in storage? – but yeah. I guess there's no place like home.'

'So you'll stay?'

'Who the hell knows? I've begun to think about my next steps and starting a new business, although there are rules around that with how the last one worked out . . . but for now . . .'

'Exhaling,' provides Becca.

'Exactly.' He smiles. 'Finding the good stuff where I can.'

'Look at you two!'

Becca looks around to see Regina approaching and Mike positively *sinks* into his seat at the sound of his mother's voice.

He whispers: 'I am going to do the best I can with this.' He nods in his mother's direction. 'But I'm sorry in advance.'

'It's so nice to see you chatting,' Regina says, cheeks pink with drink and fun. 'I just said to Paul, imagine if you got back together. You're so good for each other. I know I'm an old bat and I shouldn't be sticking my nose in, but six different people have asked me who my beautiful son is talking to with such rapt attention.'

She hugs him from behind, wrapping her arms around his neck and kissing his cheek before extending her arms to include Becca, making an incredibly awkward threesome.

'Mum,' Mike says, his tone a warning.

'I know, I know!' she exclaims. 'I get it! Back off! But I couldn't not say just one tiny little thing. If it kick-starts the conversation for you . . .'

'Look at Becca's face,' Mike says. 'You're embarrassing her, Mum.'

He's creased up his nose, cross, but Regina is just so damned charming it's tough, Becca acknowledges, to be properly annoyed.

'I think your vested interest is absolutely natural,' Becca tells her, patting her hand. 'But let's give Mike a moment to regroup before we marry him off, hey?'

Regina looks at her, pulling in her chin to her neck and pursing her lips, the picture of pondering.

'Spoken very sensibly,' she says, putting her hand over Becca's.

Mike is quiet once Regina begins to shift herself off, before she turns on her heel and claps her hands together as if delivering the closing line of her very own TED talk.

'Just to say . . .' she starts, and Mike sets his mouth in a firm line and looks at Becca, who smiles, because what else can she do? 'It really would make me so very happy if you found a way to make this' – she gestures between them – 'work. It felt like losing a daughter when you broke up. And I'd just hate for pride or wounded egos to get in the way of happiness. Because that's all life is about: finding the happiness where you can, then holding on to it tighter than tight.'

'Jesus, Mum, you're not on your deathbed. It's like you're issuing dying wishes!'

'No!' she says, turning away properly now. 'I'm not! Just some motherly advice! I'm gone,' she says from over her shoulder. 'Look, I'm gone!'

Mike opens his mouth as though he's going to say something but then thinks better of it, and Becca finds that she can't fill the space between them now. The ease they had five minutes ago has evaporated: Regina's comments have had the opposite effect of what she intended. Becca isn't so stupid that she doesn't know *something* is happening between them, but for as much as that's exciting, what they really need to do – despite what she said when they had that first coffee together – is have it out about why it didn't work last time. It's boring, and uncomfortable, though, to dredge up the past, however important it might be, and Mike certainly isn't jumping to dissect precisely what happened. And so they sit, quietly, until Mike says, 'We're probably being rude. Off in a corner like this. Shall we . . . ?'

He gestures to the patio directly off the kitchen, where most people have gathered now. There's some sort of hot food being served, and a two-piece band has appeared as if from nowhere, a woman setting up a mic and a man behind her perched with his acoustic guitar.

'Oh. Yes,' says Becca, taking the hint. 'I should check on Jia Li, you're right.'

Music plays and food is eaten and a few couples even dance, swaying to covers of 'Dancing in the Moonlight' and 'Perfect Day'. Jia Li comments how handsome Mike is, how nice his family are, how she's got Jessie's phone number to hang out once the baby comes, her first mother-and-baby friend, if Becca doesn't mind. Becca says she doesn't, of course she doesn't, and they sit, leaning on each other, people-watching until one of them suggests heading home.

Becca seeks out Jessie and Niall to thank them for the invitation, hugs Regina and Paul goodbye with promises to see them soon. Mid-embrace, Becca opens her eyes to see, across from the kids' corner, Mike watching her, expressionless. She raises a hand, not sure whether to smile herself, and they suspend themselves in time that way, like a long-distance, rather un-fun high-five.

'I have so many questions to ask you about Mike,' Jia Li says as they start to leave, accepting a doggy bag of leftover food for the next day. 'So many questions.'

Becca gives a non-committal murmur, thinking to herself: *But I don't have any answers.* She's got just as many questions herself. It's about finding the courage to ask them.

'Bec,' she hears then, right as Jia Li opens the front door. Mike.

'We were just talking about you,' says Jia Li. 'Thanks so much for letting me tag along tonight.'

'Sure, no worries,' he says. 'Any friend of Becca's.'

Jia Li looks between them and says, 'Well, thanks again. I'm just going to wait at the end of the drive so our cabbie doesn't miss us. That OK, Becca?'

'Sure,' Becca replies. She turns back to Mike. 'Did things get awkward before?' she asks. 'I really didn't think anything of your mum saying what she did. I know what she's like. I'm Regina-proof, remember?'

Mike nods. 'No,' he says. 'I know. It's actually more that I think she has a point? And . . .'

'Oh,' Becca says.

'Yeah,' Mike agrees.

'You're thinking this might be . . .' Becca starts, letting the question hang.

'Maybe?' Mike says. 'Or am I mad?'

Becca weighs it up.

'Sod it,' she says. 'No. You're not mad. But listen, I'm not for messing about, OK? I'm happy, and I want to settle down and, you know, I'm not saying if we got back together it would have to be marriage, but I'm saying . . .'

'Don't suggest getting back together if I'm not sticking around?'

Becca shrugs. 'Exactly,' she says. 'Yeah.'

'Got it.' Mike nods. 'Consider this my pledge, then.'

'Yeah?'

'Yeah.'

Becca looks at him. 'So . . . what? Are we going to . . . Well, what . . . what's happening here?'

'A date?' Mike asks. 'A day-one, start-over, let's-take-this-slowly-but-let-me-be-deliberate-about-it date?'

Becca smiles. Headlights of a car backlight Jia Li from the end of the winding drive.

'Cab's here!' Jia Li yells.

'Coming!' Becca shouts back.

'I'll text you, yeah?' Mike says.

'OK then,' says Becca, and as she walks away she can feel him watching her, and it takes everything she's got in her not to turn back around.

12

She Texts Back

How about Sunday lunch?

Mike's text comes through as Becca is waiting for her 2 p.m. to arrive – a new client with an extra fifteen minutes' consultation time booked in, which is something Becca likes to do with people she hasn't worked with before, especially if they're having colour as well, just so she can get the measure of them well enough to give them almost exactly what they want. It's always an almost and never an *exactly*, because quite frankly some clients think she's more of a plastic surgeon than a hairdresser, so there's often a tiny element of disappointment when she's done, if only because she can't make them magically become somebody else. She only has the powers to make them themselves – but with infinitely better hair.

Becca feels Carlos looking at her. They're on the back steps in companionable silence where he's smoking a rare cigarette and they're both scrolling on their phones. At the sight of Mike's words Becca flushes with excitement – and trepidation. She knows what's coming. Carlos has *opinions*, and now they're going to have The Chat. The are-you-really-sure-about-the-ex chat, the I'm-only-concerned-for-you chat.

'Sunday, aye?' Carlos asks, pulling her from her thoughts. He's not hiding the fact he's looking at her screen and he's read what it says. 'I assume that's Mike,' he adds.

'Nosy,' Becca replies, clicking her phone on to the lock screen.

'Jia Li filled me in anyway.' He waves. 'It's heading in that direction, is it? Getting back together? You've been hanging out a lot. Got that look on your face.'

Becca looks at him. 'There's no look on my face.'

'Yes, there is. I can see it right now.'

Becca furrows her brow, screwing up her features. 'Please be supportive,' she says. 'Come on. I'm not doing this lightly. It's still there – this *thing*, this feeling.'

'Hmmmm.'

Becca can hear the tone to his *hmmmm.* She's heard that tone before. It's judgement. 'What?' she asks.

'I'm not getting involved,' Carlos insists, holding up his hands.

'You've already got involved!' Becca counters. 'Bloody hell, between you and Jia Li . . .'

'If I did, I'd want you to actually listen, not just brace for impact because you think I'm saying it for the sake of being devil's advocate. Your happiness isn't a game to me, for what it's worth. OK?'

'I'm listening.'

Carlos shrugs. 'You've been in a really good place,' he says. 'And the summer solstice night – I know you said you wanted to settle down asap, but are you sure it's the right thing to start things back up with him again? You can't *force* a happy ending . . .'

'Is that what you think I'm doing?'

'I don't think anything, I'm merely inviting discussion. But from that defensive attitude I can tell I've hit a nerve.'

Becca hates that he's right – that he's got a point. It's just his expression as he says it: it makes her actively not want to listen.

'Get your own love life,' she settles on.

'*Love* life?' he says, his eyebrows shooting up to his hair-line in dramatic reflex. 'Duly noted. And I have, for what it's worth.' He stands up and pulls a chiselled arm across his chest to stretch. Hairdressing can be surprisingly hard on the body, all that hunching over and twisting and being on your feet. 'Got my own love life, I mean.'

'*Love*, I said,' Becca reiterates him teasingly. 'Not *lust*.'

Carlos switches arms. He shrugs. 'Can't have one without the other.'

'You would say that, wouldn't you?'

He finishes what he's doing and looks at the clock on the wall. After a beat he says: 'Don't do that.'

'What?'

'Act like I'm just one big swinging dick. I know I play up to it a bit but you are actually supposed to be kind to your friends, all witty bants aside.'

He looks at her. She looks at him.

'Sorry,' Becca tells him, defensively. 'I didn't mean anything by it.'

'Hmmm,' replies Carlos, in the same way as before.

'Carlos!' She raises her voice in the way that being called out on your bull makes a person do. She's trying to be cool, but she's being defensive because she's been told off. 'Don't be like that! I was only messing!'

She waits for him to crack a smile, to tell her he's just playing with her. When he doesn't, it brings a hot shame to Becca's cheeks, leaving her slightly agog at the strange turn of events. If Carlos yells at her, she can get indignant too – he was looking at her phone, after all, and that's what started this whole exchange. But he doesn't. He actually looks kind of sad.

'Carlos,' Becca says again, half-smiling.

'Sorry,' Carlos says. 'It's just – well, I've wanted to say for ages to be honest.'

'OK.' Becca nods. 'I hear you. Thank you for saying something. I'll go gentle, now.

'There's a joke in there somewhere.'

'I'm not allowed to make jokes any more.'

Carlos cocks an eyebrow. 'Proper jokes include everyone in on the laugh; they don't exclude somebody for a punchline.'

'Did you see that printed on a mug?'

'You're a twat. You know that, don't you?' He looks up to the heavens, as if the answer for Becca's behaviour might be up there.

'Let me take you to the pub tonight,' Becca says. 'I can be a twat with a tab open? We'll ask Jia Li too?'

'Fine,' Carlos says, and he's sucking in his cheeks to prevent himself from smiling. 'Although if that's how you apologise I might have to have hurt feelings more often.'

Becca goes to speak.

'Ah!' interrupts Carlos, holding a finger to her lips. 'I swear to God if you make a joke about only just discovering I have feelings, I will *not* be giving you an apology do-over.'

Becca nods, biting her lip. 'Mmmmm,' she says. 'Uh-huh.' When Carlos removes his hand and she's able to speak, Becca adds: 'Of course.'

Before the client arrives, she texts Mike back: *Just tell me when and where*, she says. *I can't wait.*

It takes exactly three and a half minutes for Jia Li's pregnancy cover to be blown as they settle at their favourite summer table in the courtyard of the Fox and Hound. When Becca says it's her round, Jia Li asks for half a pint of lemonade and Carlos quips, like somebody's unfunny uncle, 'Half a lemonade? What are you, pregnant?' And instead of everyone laughing the air gets thick and the pause – pregnant – inadvertently reveals that exact truth.

'Whaaaaat?' Carlos breathes from his seat by the brick wall covered with the fairy lights. 'Jia Li? Are you up the duff?' He looks from where Jia Li sits opposite him up to Becca, who is standing, one foot turned towards the bar inside and the other foot turned – stuck! – resolutely to her friends.

'Is she?' asks Carlos, staring at Becca now. Nobody speaks. Carlos looks briefly panicked, and Becca finds herself wondering if there's any conceivable way that it could be his.

As if reading her mind, Jia Li says, 'It's not his, Becca. Don't look so worried.'

Becca goes to say something about how she never thought it was, anyway, but Jia Li rolls her eyes and shakes her head, her patience for idiocy at zero. Becca looks at Carlos, who seems as relaxed and insouciant as ever. He's very obviously not worried one bit that it could be his, so Becca is clearly wide off the mark. But then why can't she shake this feeling that she knows something she shouldn't? That she's closing in on the secret they share?

'Woah,' Carlos says, shaking his head as though he needs to dissolve the information into his brain matter with a gentle swill. He leans across the table and loudly whispers, 'Does Dave know?'

'Shhhh!' Jia Li hisses, and Becca stands closer to the table, somehow reasoning that her body mass will muffle the chat. 'What the hell do *you* know about Dave?'

Becca really would go and get that round in, except: Yeah, what the hell *does* Carlos know about Dave? Jia Li and Dave have never hooked up, at least to Becca's knowledge.

Carlos inhales affectedly, like a man who couldn't possibly reveal his source. 'I didn't know anything about Dave until you just confirmed it,' he says with a wave. 'You might want to sort your face out,' he adds, nodding towards Jia Li. 'It's a walking billboard.'

Becca squints at Jia Li. 'You and Dave?'

Jia Li rolls her eyes once again – her new default state now pregnancy has drained her of every last bit of her already limited patience. 'No,' she says. 'Don't be ridiculous. The man is nearly fifty years old. Now. Drinks?'

'Drinks,' says Becca. 'I'll be back.'

She gets Jia Li's lemonade, a pint for Carlos, and upgrades from a small rosé to a large at Dave's suggestion. It's so weird, talking to him whilst she's trying to piece together any evidence she might unwittingly have for Jia Li and him hooking up. They've always been nice to each other, but then Dave is nice to everyone. She remembers the lock-in at the pub a few months ago. Had Jia Li left when Becca did? Becca can't remember.

'Yeah, it's been proper mad hot this summer, hasn't it?' Dave says as he charges her card. 'Rather that than rain though, hey?'

'Yeah,' says Becca, eyeing him as if she'll be able to see through to his skin and ascertain if he really has ever been with Jia Li. She can be crafty, her friend, never fully filling in the picture of her love life – or her sex life. There hasn't been a proper boyfriend in a while, and last Becca heard she'd been seeing Cheesey a couple of nights a week. But then, why wouldn't Jia Li just say it's Cheesey's baby if, indeed, it is? Becca could all but promise not to make any *Are you going to call it Cheddar then?* jokes. Although if it's a girl, maybe Brie would be nice.

'Oh, hey, how's it going with Kaylee?' Becca asks.

'It isn't,' Dave says with a shrug, and Becca understands that she shouldn't push it any further.

'Oh, sorry to hear that,' she says, vaguely remembering how she had pushed him to ask her out a few weeks ago. So he *is* single then, she notes.

By the time Becca gets back to the table, evidently the pregnancy news has lost its gossipy lustre, because instead of rapt and eager conversation Becca finds her friends playing a competitive game of beer-mat flipping, all semblance of sensible or meaningful conversation on hold, or forgotten.

'Here you go,' announces Becca, proud of herself for managing to hold all three glasses at once. She waits for Jia Li to rest her beer mat on the edge of the table, flick it up, and almost catch it.

'Dammit,' Jia Li says.

Carlos follows her lead, only he catches his.

'Maybe your centre of gravity is off now,' he notes in Jia Li's direction, as if being pregnant is the reason she didn't catch her mat.

'Yes, I'll bet that's exactly right.' Jia Li rolls her eyes as she accepts her drink from Becca, who settles in beside Carlos. Becca smiles back.

'OK, who thinks I can get up to flipping five?' Carlos ponders, taking a big sip from his pint glass and getting froth all over his top lip.

'Look at you, mucky pup,' Becca says, reaching out a finger towards him. Carlos jerks away.

'Don't play mother,' he says, going in for another glug and then using his tongue to defoam his moustache area, like a toddler, or a St Bernard. 'Save that role for her,' he adds, using his eyebrows to gesture towards Jia Li.

'What did I say?' Jia Li warns, continuing to flip a mat. She'll keep going until she catches it, Becca knows that much.

'You said I'm a clever little shit for outing the pregnancy, but re talking about the situation further, you said read this, and then you put your middle finger up at me.'

'Good boy.' Jia Li flips another beet mat up and finally catches it. 'Yes!' she celebrates, waving it in victory. Carlos piles up five beer mats, one on top of the other, flicks his wrist so they spin up, and knocks them at an angle that spills them all over the place.

'I meant to do that,' he says, going back in for the rest of his drink.

It's all entirely usual for them. They have a favourite table outside for summer, and a favourite table for inside when it's cold. They drink, they play silly bar games, they swap mindless chat and rubbish jokes, and it's nice. A comfort. Family. Carlos rummages in the condiments tray that's on every table, locating a box of toothpicks and saying, '*Bingo!*'

'Dave will kill you if he sees you,' Jia Li admonishes, watching him take off the lid to the plastic container and press his palm into the top of them all. He lifts it away, some stuck into the fleshy part of his hand.

'Six,' he says, brushing them out and returning them. 'Beat that.'

Jia Li sighs, shaking her head and flicking her eyes to the door. Becca goes in for her turn, collecting only two.

'What have I told you guys about playing pick-up with my *very expensive* cocktail sticks?' a voice looms from behind Becca's shoulder.

'Speak of the devil.' Carlos turns his attention to the looming figure at their table. 'All right, Dave?'

'I mean it!' Dave warns. 'It's fifty-five pence a pack. If everyone was doing it, I'd lose what? Twenty quid a night? A hundred pounds a week? Five grand *a year*?'

'I wish I was as good at maths as you.' Becca grins, fluttering her eyelashes. Carlos laughs. Jia Li looks up.

'Jia Li,' Dave says, all eyes and heart. Could Jia Li be the reason it didn't pan out with Kaylee?

'Dave,' replies Jia Li, unreadable.

Becca dares look sideways at Carlos, who has his chin in his hand and his elbow on the table, looking dreamily between Jia Li and Dave in a display of the exact opposite of minding your own business.

'Well,' says Dave, seemingly unnerved. Carlos blinks heavily. Becca can feel herself begin to spill over into laughter. Jia Li is practically holding her breath. The whole thing is all incredibly unkind, but that doesn't make it any less funny. Dave leans over and takes the cocktail sticks.

'Hey!' says Carlos.

'Children!' bats back Dave.

Jia Li issues a double kick under the table, one to Carlos and one to Becca.

'Ouch!' the pair say in unison, and Dave leaves with a grateful smile in Jia Li's direction. It could just be Becca's imagination, but she swears she sees Jia Li flush. How is it possible she missed the fact that they sleep together sometimes? Jia Li has done a grand job of throwing her off the scent.

'Very mature,' says Jia Li, once Dave has gone. 'Really golden of you, that. Thanks so much.'

'It wasn't me,' Becca says in a small voice.

'It was both of us,' says Carlos, plainly. 'But really, it was Dave!' he adds, making a terrible defence. 'He doesn't care about the sticks. He just comes over to be near you, Jia Li!'

Jia Li holds up her middle finger again. Carlos holds up his hands in surrender. She finishes her drink.

'Well,' she announces. 'I know I've only been here fifteen minutes, but I'm tired already, and it's crap that I can't have a rosé, and Dave is, I'll admit, looking at me all weird and funny, and so if it's OK with you two, I'm going to go.'

'Oh,' says Becca. 'I was just thinking how nice this was. We've not been to the pub together in ages.'

Jia Li stands up and moves around the table to kiss the top of Becca's head, and then Carlos.

'Goodnight, my babies,' she says, yawning as if to prove her point. 'Don't stay out too late.'

Becca and Carlos watch her go, and because it's now just the two of them Becca angles her body so she's facing Carlos at the side of her.

'I'm shook,' he says. 'Like, a baby is cool, but . . . is it just me she doesn't want to name Daddy to?'

Becca purses her lips in thought. 'No,' she tells him. 'I think she's shell-shocked. I know she's the ultimate cool-and-collected go-with-the-flow one of us, but it's almost like her total refusal to discuss it *at all* is a sort of . . . I don't know. Method of denial? Now that it's happening I think she's excited to be a mum, but I'm just reading in between the lines.'

'Got it,' muses Carlos. 'So we've got to be extra nice and look after her now, I suppose?'

'I hear that's how it goes.'

'I always thought you'd be the first one of us to cross over into parenthood. It feels strange that it isn't.'

Becca looks at him. 'Are you teasing me? Because—'

'No!' Carlos insists. 'No, honestly. I just know how much you want it. That's all.'

'Yeah.' Becca is surprised that she's surprised by his emotional intelligence on this one. But then, Carlos often knows her better than she knows herself. 'I suppose I feel a bit . . . not jealous, but . . . well. I do want it. You're right.'

'You'll get it,' Carlos tells her. 'I can feel it in my waters.'

'Yeah?' says Becca. She can feel something pushing its way up from her throat, her eyes getting hot. Goddammit. She blinks rapidly to prevent tears from forming.

'Oh no, wait,' Carlos says, holding up a hand. 'It's piss. What I feel in my waters is that my bladder is full and I need a piss.'

He stands up and it gives Becca a beat to collect herself. Urgh. That was a near-miss. She thinks Carlos is gone, but then he puts a hand on her shoulder. She looks up at him and he bends to kiss her forehead, just as Jia Li did, and when he pulls away he says, 'Becca?'

'Yes?' She waits for some kind words.

'You did say drinks are on you tonight, didn't you? I'll take another when you're ready.'

She takes a breath and smiles, relieved he's purposely changed the subject and lightened the mood. She further chooses the distraction of the bar to shake off whatever it was she was just feeling. Between Mike being back and Jia Li's baby, the world feels off kilter.

'Diamond,' declares Carlos as she delivers him another pint, along with tequila for good measure. 'Shots?' he says, as she pops the two thimbles down too. 'Are we turning this into a sesh?'

'No,' says Becca, raising her glass to him. He does the same. 'But here's to taking the edge off,' she declares, and they clink and drink.

'Oh, that was quite smooth actually,' notes Carlos.

'I got the good stuff. If I'm going to be thirty-five and shotting hard liquor, I need it to not be lighter fuel.'

'See, I'm almost thirty-eight and still go for the lighter fuel every time.'

'How did I end up in business with a man so resolutely committed to such low standards?'

'How did I end up in business with a woman so uppity about things that have absolutely no effect on her whatsoever?' Carlos winks. 'Another?'

Becca can't think of a reason why not, apart from the fact that hangovers linger far worse and far longer than they did in her twenties, that she has to work tomorrow, that her drunkenness is a gamble between high jinks ensuing and crying in a bathroom stall . . .

'Sure,' she says. 'Sod it.'

Three large wines and four tequila shots later, and Becca is *drunk*. It feels glorious. It's fun, being with Carlos, talking about Trim in the same breath as making jokes about badgers or bringing up an old memory from one of the other eleventy million times they've been pissed at the Fox and Hound.

'Oh my God, remember when Jia Li did the Coyote Ugly routine on the bar that New Year?' Becca giggles. 'And she got that massive bruise from falling on the Old Abbot beer tap?'

'That bruise!' hoots Carlos. 'It was like a map of Brazil all down her thigh!'

'And didn't you once have sex in the ladies' toilet here?'

'Bec,' he says, and she can tell he's about to issue a punchline. 'Not *once*.'

It makes Becca burst into hysterics, her wild friends and their wild times. In fact, she's so busy laughing and recalling fragments of a night that was so messy it took all three of them forty-eight hours and a recce mission to piece together what had happened (a Halloween party with a case of mixed identities, too much apple cider and a traffic cone) that she didn't realise her phone had buzzed.

'Persistent, isn't he?' Carlos notes.

Becca looks down.

2pm, Baked in Brick at the Custard Factory – they've got a Sunday roast pop-up happening. Take a cab so we can drink?

She instantly pulls her phone to her chest to shield it from prying eyes. 'What did I say about being a nosy bastard?' she asks, pretending to scowl.

'No idea,' sing-songs Carlos. 'I've got the memory of a fish.'

'My arse you have,' quips Becca. She slips the phone into her bag. Carlos pretends he's misheard.

'What are we saying about your arse?' he asks, as though butter wouldn't melt, pretending to crane and look.

'Ha, ha.'

It's water off a duck's back.

'You're tighter-lipped about this business with your ex than Jia Li is about her private life. I'm your friend and you can talk to me about stuff. If you ever need an ear . . .'

'Thanks,' says Becca, almost earnestly. They both smile, and Carlos laughs, and then Becca laughs. 'What's so funny?'

'I have no idea. Life. All of it.'

'I'll say.'

'You're right that me and Mike have been seeing quite a bit of each other. And he's asked to try again, and I think we should. I'm nervous, because I've built a life without him here. I don't want to open up a spot in my life for him just like that, but then – I don't want to punish him for the decisions we both made in the past. He says he's back.'

Carlos raises his eyebrows. 'I see.'

'I know you think I put too much weight on him texting right after the manifestations we did at summer solstice, but—'

'Jesus, Becca! Yeah! You do put too much weight on that night! Come on. It was just a bit of fun . . .'

'So maybe I'll date Mike as a bit of fun?'

Carlos clucks, knowing she is incapable of doing that. 'Becca Calloway isn't known for keeping matters of the heart light,' he says, his voice low. 'You're making a choice here, Bec . . .'

'Mine to make.' She shrugs. 'But I'm going to need my friends.'

Carlos inhales forcefully, as if he's making a decision not to push it any further, and Becca watches as his eyes linger on something across the courtyard. She looks where his gaze is fixed. It's a gaggle of girlfriends sharing wine from an ice bucket.

'Which one are you after?' asks Becca, glad of the subject change.

'Oh. No. No one. Go on.'

Becca shakes her head. 'I'm done.'

Carlos nods at one of the women as she walks by. 'Hey, Amy. How's it going?'

A leggy redhead pauses to issue Carlos with a coy smile and then carries on. Becca knows what *Hey, Amy* means. She knows what *How's it going?* means. She's seen this particular look on Carlos's face, heard this exact tone in his voice, at far too many pub sessions to count. She looks at her watch: 9.55 p.m. She gives it until ten fifteen, when she knows he'll excuse himself to 'head off', not adding the part that, miraculously, it's with Amy.

'What?' he says to Becca when he sees her shaking her head. 'Man's gotta eat.'

'You're insatiable.'

'I like a good time . . .' he defends himself.

'Well. Thank you for your two and a half minutes of wisdom and shoulder-to-cry-on. That was really helpful.'

'You didn't want to cry on my shoulder,' Carlos says, one eye on the door for, presumably, the return of Amy. 'You wanted me to say it's OK to want to get back with your ex. But I don't know the bloke, so I don't have a positive opinion, I'm afraid. I just know you're worth more than you think you are, and if he screws you over, I'll . . .'

'You'll what? Beat him up for me?'

'Yeah, to be honest.'

She winks. 'I knew you cared really.'

Becca excuses herself for the loo, and when she's back Carlos is standing at Amy's table, charming her and her friends. It's not even 10 p.m. It took him four minutes. She drums her fingertips on the table and watches Carlos make his new audience laugh, pulling up Mike's number on her phone.

'Oi!' she hollers across the beer garden. Carlos turns to her. 'I'm off!'

Carlos raises his glass to her, cheersing her exit. She hits the green button against Mike's name, waving goodbye to Dave behind the bar as she goes.

'Evening,' Mike's voice comes down the line. 'To what do I owe this pleasure?'

Becca takes in the dusky view of King's Heath, almost dark but still balmy, like the weather on holiday.

'I just wanted to hear your voice,' she tells him, which is as simple a truth as they come. It's nice to have somebody texting her throughout the day. Comforting to have somebody to call on her way home, to say good-night to. A joy to have plans for the weekend, too. He keeps her company all the way home, until she hops in the shower.

I am NOT seeing Mike just because of the bloody manifestation ceremony, she texts Carlos before plugging her phone in to charge before bed. *OK?*

She sees three dots on the screen, indicating he's texting back. Then they disappear, and Becca is left having a conversation only with herself.

I'm glad you called, Mike texts then. *I feel like I'm getting a second chance,* he adds.

You are, Becca replies. *Lucky bugger xx.*

She falls asleep wondering what it would be like to sleep with Mike again. If he still moves slowly. Knowingly. Is still generous about ladies first. She imagines kissing him, pressing her body against his, her nipple in his mouth.

She turns on the light and gets a small bullet vibrator from her nightstand. She flicks it on to the medium setting, puts the light out again, and lets her imagination run wild.

13

She Doesn't Text Back

'Sorry, can I just clarify,' Becca says, holding up a copy of Noah's latest book from where she has found it on the shelf of Waterstones. 'You wrote this.'

Noah blinks slowly, like a teenager embarrassed by his mum. 'Yes. Now stop it. Come on. We came, we saw, now we can go eat. I'm starving.'

'I'm starving too, but that was before I realised dinner was with a person who typed all of these words out, from his brain, and put them in a book that *people can buy in the shops*.'

He raises his eyebrows. 'This isn't new information to you,' he reminds her.

'But *knowing* and *understanding* are two different skill sets,' argues Becca. 'I *knew* you wrote books, but I didn't truly understand what that meant.'

'Right. Well. I didn't know I was hanging out with a doctor of philosophy, either, so I suppose we're both learning things, aren't we?'

'How am I a doctor of philosophy?'

'The difference between knowing and understanding? Never mind. Becca, I *know* I am hungry, I *understand* I am hungry, can we make like a tree now?'

'And leaf?' asks Becca, amused. 'OK, fine. But first I'm going to buy this, and have you sign it.'

They head to the checkout of Birmingham Waterstones and Becca proudly hands over her purchase.

'He wrote it,' Becca says to the salesperson as they scan it and charge her card. 'Isn't that cool?'

The salesperson looks up at them, and then down at the book. 'Oh, wicked,' he says. 'Do you have a minute to sign any stock we've got? People love it.'

Noah gives a sanguine smile and says of course he doesn't mind, it would be an honour.

'I'll just hunt out a Sharpie that works,' they're told. 'I won't be a minute. I'll go get your books, too.'

Noah looks at Becca. 'So your middle name is definitely not *stealth*. Or covert. Or modest.'

'What do I have to be modest about? They're not my books. *You* might have to be modest as the author, but as the woman who is . . .'

She falters on her words then. She was going to say *dating you*. Then, inexplicably, she thinks *as the woman who is sleeping with you*. What are they? This is only their third date, but where they're headed seems obvious. And that's thrilling – and terrifying. He's so intoxicatingly straightforward, it's seductive.

Noah looks at her, obviously amused. She juts her lip playfully and doesn't bother hiding the predicament of describing what they are to each other. A small expectant smile plays on his lips. He's so gorgeous. His eyes twinkle in mischief.

'As the woman who is about to have dinner with you,' Becca settles on, wrinkling her nose impishly, 'I think I am very much allowed to show off on your behalf. I think it's cool!'

He shakes his head, and dutifully signs the dozen or so paperbacks the salesperson has dug out. As they leave, Noah says thank you, and Becca holds up the book she bought to a man in the queue to pay and says, 'My friend here wrote this. Isn't that wicked?'

The man nods. 'Yeah, it is,' he says, and Noah mutters thanks and then slips his hand in hers to tug her away.

The bad news is: he genuinely seems a bit ruffled by her enthusiasm.

The good news is: he doesn't let go, all the way to the restaurant.

Becca's phone buzzes as she sips her champagne at the table of the bijou restaurant Noah says comes recommended, waiting for him to get back from the loo. It's Jia Li, with a link to an article.

I promise I wasn't just googling third dates and what they mean, she's texted. *But this came up on my news app and I thought of you! Hope you're having fun!!*

It's an article called *You've Made It to the Third Date! It's Make or Break Time!* Becca furrows her brow. Make or break? She thought it was just dinner.

'Whatcha reading?' asks Noah, settling back into his seat. He picks up the flute that has been deposited in his absence and says, 'Cheers.'

'Cheers,' echoes Becca, adding: 'Although I did start without you. Sorry.'

He shrugs. 'I would have done the same. Erm. Excuse me – are you . . . Becca? Are these dating tips?'

Becca has her phone in her hand, sort of waving it about as she chats, and didn't realise the screen was still unlocked, still open on whatever rubbish Jia Li has sent.

'Am I flattered or terrified?' Noah presses, reaching out to take her phone from her so he can see better. She lets him. She sees him note her good humour.

'"You've Made It to the Third Date! It's Make or Break Time!"' he reads, and then, looking at her, waits for further information.

'Jia Li just sent it,' Becca tells him. 'I think she's trolling me.'

'If my best mate was sending me dating advice it'd probably be to an article called "If You Didn't Already Marry Your High School Girlfriend You Are Probably Going To Die Alone".'

'Did your best mate actually meet his wife at school?' Becca questions.

Noah grimaces and nods.

'Awww!' says Becca. 'That's cute!'

'And do you want to know the really perverted thing?'

Becca widens her eyes. 'Desperately.'

'They're actually happy.'

'Urgh.' She laughs. 'A romantic's wet dream!'

'Yup. Right up your street.'

'Hashtag not sorry.'

Noah narrows his deep brown eyes, sizing her up.

'What?' she questions.

'I suppose it just surprises me, in a way,' Noah admits. 'It's not very fashionable, is it?'

'I don't know,' muses Becca. 'Doesn't everyone want a happy ending?'

'Are we talking in or out of a massage parlour?'

'Out. I actually got offered a happy ending after a massage once and, no judgement, but it freaked me out.'

'No!'

'Yup. I was on holiday and had a massage booked in at the hotel, and I came from the pool so was in a one-piece, you know – just a swimsuit? And so I just took the whole thing off, because what else could I do, but I suppose that was some kind of code for, like . . . an *extra* area to be massaged?'

Noah is agog. A middle-aged waiter comes over and asks if they're ready to order and Noah tells him that unfortunately they're going to need at least ten more minutes because he's currently chewing over the best story he's ever heard. Becca rolls her eyes.

'So did you . . .' he starts, his eyes like saucers as he waits for the juicy details.

'No!' squeals Becca, covering her face with her hands. 'Nooooo. I didn't notice what was happening, really, because I was zonked out, but then became super aware that the masseuse was spending ages on the tops of my legs. I must have been about half an hour into it, and it was only going to be fifty minutes so she should have been on my back already, or asking me to turn over, but she hadn't, she was just rubbing my legs and my bum and I sort of clamped my legs together and waited for the moment to pass but it didn't. And there was maybe a teeny tiny part of me that thought, *Ahhhh, you're on holiday! Roll with it!* But I just couldn't do it. In the end – and we're talking after a solid five to seven minutes here – I asked to go to the toilet and when I came back told her my neck hurt and could she focus there.'

'Well,' marvels Noah. 'Now I know the code . . .'

Becca laughs. 'Yes, do try it out and let me know how it goes.'

'Will do,' he says, grinning.

They order their food – a warm goat's cheese salad and a terrine to split, pasta alla Norma for him, seafood risotto for her – and Noah asks to see Becca's phone again.

'I'm still thinking about that article,' he explains. 'This is date three, Becca. It could all go tits up if we're not well versed enough.'

'True.' Becca nods. 'Left to our own devices we might have no idea where to go from here. We could say goodnight and never see each other again.'

'So you see my point,' Noah bats back. It's easy, being with him. It has been right from that night they first met. 'I think we'd better prepare ourselves.'

Becca unlocks her phone, opens the link again, and they both lean forward so they can see. As they do their shoulders touch – God, Becca loves a side-by-side seating arrangement over an opposite-ends-of-the-table one. It's so much more sexy. She glances at him, his stubbled face and long eyelashes lit up by the screen, his eyes scanning for the information he wants. He looks up and instinctively, so as not to be caught staring, Becca looks down at the phone too. She can *feel* him smile.

'Right,' Becca says, reading aloud:

'Arriving at a third date is no small deal. In modern dating, it's too easy for people to ghost, or decide to keep swiping for the dopamine rush of somebody new instead of becoming known by somebody else. Dating is, without a doubt, a minefield. This isn't news. According to a recent study, only 34 per cent of daters get to the third date. We know that first dates are stressful, and there's a level of expectation attached to second dates, but third dates, if they're done right ... third dates are the gateway to glory.'

Becca giggles at this. 'No pressure!'

Noah gives a cheerful smile. 'I'm up for the challenge.'

Becca keeps reading:

'So if you've made it this far: well done. You're both enjoying your time together, maybe you've kissed or even slept together, and the third date is the moment you more or less decide: are we in this?

'This isn't about finding the One. A good third date doesn't mean sending out save-the-date cards. But if you're dating because you want to find a life partner over something a lot more casual, a lot can depend on how the date goes. Sex and relationships expert Grant Garby says: "By the third date we know if there's chemistry, and by this point it's wise to be clear about what you're looking for. Before now, it should have been fun, light, and exciting. But at this point, you can afford to test the waters now with any of your non-negotiables or deal-breakers, gently bringing up anything that might be considered impolite dinner-guest talk: sex, religion, and politics.

'"This is the time to actually listen to what your date says, don't just project on to them what you hope they'll be. If you want six kids and your date is adamant they will never have any, or you want to live in the city forever and your date has just bought a farm in the country, it's stuff you want to know now, before you get in any deeper.

'"Getting this far means you're both having a good time, and the third date is the test point where you can both establish if you want to keep having a good time, armed with the knowledge you're both broadly on the same page about what you need from a partner. Could you introduce this person to your friends? Do you have the same general priorities for your life? Is this a fit?"'

Becca stops reading and bites her lip in thought.

'Woah,' says Noah. 'I don't think I've ever read a women's magazine before. Is that what they're all like?'

'Hey,' retorts Becca. 'I'll bet if I google it, I'll find just as many "third date" pieces in men's media, in *GQ* or whatever.'

'Actually, yeah,' agrees Noah. 'And it is quite instructive . . .'

Their starters arrive and they busy themselves with tasting and refilling glasses and mopping up dressings with crusty bread.

'So,' says Noah. 'Go on then. Sex, politics, religion . . .'

'You mean what are my values?' asks Becca. She says *values* as though she's taking the piss, but quickly sees that Noah is genuinely asking. 'Well, I don't really practise a religion. I was christened but I don't go to church or anything. I went to a midnight mass with Jia Li and Carlos once, but we came from the pub and thought it actually started at midnight, when – in case you didn't know – that is false advertising and midnight mass starts at half past eleven. We were asked never to come back.'

'Wait,' says Noah, his face lighting up. 'That wasn't at St Thomas's was it? Maybe . . . God, maybe four or five years ago?'

'Three,' clarifies Becca. 'Don't tell me you were there. In fact – wouldn't you have been too young?'

'Too young for Christmas?'

'I meant . . . you know. Actually, forget it. I don't know what I meant.'

'You *do* want to talk about the age difference!' he accuses.

Becca shrugs with one shoulder. 'No,' she settles on. 'I don't. Continue.'

'Well,' he says. 'I was there. And speaking of false advertising, if that really was you – and I'm starting to remember the details now: three people, one clutching an empty bottle, lots of laughing and shushing until the organist went and ushered you out? In fact . . . and God, imagine what useful knowledge I might have room for in my head if I wasn't, apparently, holding on to these random details . . .'

Becca holds her head in her hands, mortified that all of this lines up with what happened.

'I'm pretty sure one of you shouted, "*GOOD WILL TO ALL MEN EXCEPT FOR YOU MISERABLE ARSES!*" as a parting shot.'

Becca cringes. That last gem had been Jia Li, for reference, but it had been Becca's one attempt at something grown up over the festive period and she'd been *ejected* from it, and in a cloud of profanity too. The organist, now she thinks about it, told them to kindly do one as she shut the heavy church door behind them, and that only made them all laugh harder. It was the most hungover Christmas Day of Becca's life. She spent most of it asleep on the sofa and threw up when she tried to eat Christmas lunch.

'OK, I think we can establish you were there. Does that mean you're religious?'

'Kinda. I'd want my kids christened, I think.'

'So the devil doesn't take them?'

'Exactly.'

Becca smiles. 'You want kids, plural?'

He pushes the last mouthful of terrine across his plate to signal it's all hers. 'Yeah,' he says. 'I always thought I was too modern for all that, too . . . I don't know. I thought it was stupid, to be frank. I had a rubbish childhood, really – and

158

then with Dad having his heart attack before I'd even left secondary school – I guess I didn't want to inflict anything like that on another kid who didn't ask to be born. But then, what's the point, otherwise?'

'That's the spirit!' jokes Becca, helping herself to the last of the terrine starter.

'Sometimes I wonder if it's because of Mum, more than anything else. What if I didn't love my kids enough to stay?'

'Noah,' Becca says. 'I didn't know she left. I'm sorry.'

'She's the one who should be sorry. But – whatever.' He shakes his head and forces a smile. 'Abandonment issues 101. Boring. Anyway,' he says, with a big breath. 'Did you always know you wanted kids?'

'Yeah,' she says, making a mental note to eventually circle back to his mum. No way can he be as OK with it as he is pretending to be. 'I maybe wobbled in my twenties but . . . yeah, I do. I can't wait, actually.'

'How do you feel about marriage?' Noah proceeds to ask.

'Oh well, if you're asking, sure. Why not?' Becca jokes.

'Ha, ha. Don't make me call your bluff, Ms Calloway.'

Becca's heart does a funny double beat and she keeps her eyes down, playing with her fork and making patterns in the gloopy remains of what's on her plate. It's not lost on her that right after the age difference being brought up, they're now talking about such grown-up things. She's never even jokingly broached the m-word on a date. She knows it's only in jest, and yet . . .

'Yeah,' she says. 'Going back to what you said about it not being fashionable to be romantic, I don't think I agree. There

159

are all these books and movies and TV shows about sisters doing it for themselves or whatever, but I've *been* doing it for myself for a while now and, honestly, I don't want a relationship for the sake of a relationship but I do think it's nice. Proper partnership is hard, and not for the faint-hearted, and I know of plenty of couples who seem to be together because any port in a storm will do, you know? And no judgement, because being alone is rough, sometimes. There was this whole debate that went viral a while ago about women learning to settle – we've been told for a while now that we're worth it, to date aspirationally in terms of a guy who is just as clever, makes just as much money, does just as many household chores . . .' She pauses here, to note the look on his face.

'I'm listening,' he says. 'Go on. I'm enjoying learning how your brain works. What makes Becca, Becca.'

Becca pretends to do a little sick, sticking out her tongue and pointing her finger to the back of her throat, but secretly she's a tiny bit in love with what he's just said. She's enjoying learning what makes Noah, Noah.

'Some psychologist or social scientist said if women only married the perfect guy who checked every box, we'd all die single. So it's about compromising and understanding that not every box does get ticked, and near enough is good enough if you want companionship. I think that's what she meant, anyway.'

Noah considers what she's said. 'Am I horrified, or am I on board with this?' he muses. 'I suppose if I think about my friends who are married – Nate and Sarah met at church, got married at *nineteen*, if you can believe that . . . yeah, neither of them is perfect. She can nag and doesn't cook, I know for a fact he has to be told when to put the bins out and doesn't know the exact date of his kids' birthdays, but those things don't exclude either of them from the race. I guess that together they're worth more than the sum of their imperfect parts.'

'Yeah!' Becca nods. 'That's a nice way to look at it, Noah Brooks. That they're more than the sum of their imperfect parts.'

He chuckles. 'I've impressed myself there, truth be told.'

Becca smiles, amused. 'What would Nate and Sarah say about you if they were here?'

Noah guffaws.'Too self-contained. Not open enough. Must smile more.'

'What! That is not the Noah I've met. Not at all.'

'I know,' he agrees. 'Isn't that the darndest thing?'

Becca smiles at him, suddenly shy. The implication of what he's saying isn't lost on her: he likes who he is when he's with her.

'I kind of feel like I'm the best version of myself when I'm with you.'

She nods as he speaks. She figured that's what he was getting at. 'I accept the compliment,' she tells him, and they hold eye contact then, smiling and looking, and he reaches out a hand and gently strokes her cheek.

'What?' he asks her, suddenly.

'What?' she says back.

'You've gone somewhere. I can see it in your eyes.'

Becca goes to protest, screwing her face up as though he's insane, but the way he looks at her, holding her gaze, opening up space for her to really be honest, she settles on the truth.

'I really don't want to spoil the moment by saying this,' she starts. 'But . . . I suppose I was thinking of my ex.'

Noah raises his eyebrows, but it's less in outrage and more in shock, she thinks.

'It's not what you think! It's just . . .'

'We can have the ex talk if you want to have the ex talk. We're both going to have pasts, aren't we?'

'How's your past?' she asks.

Noah holds open his hands as though he has nothing to hide. 'I had a girlfriend in secondary school, messed about a bit at uni but nothing really proper, and a year ago broke up with somebody I'd been seeing on and off for about two years. It was kind of toxic, to be honest – one of those can't-live-with-you, can't-live-without-you situations where I kept going back for more, just to see if it could be different next time.'

'So you ended it?'

'Not exactly. She's South African, lives in Cape Town, so it's not like we just bump into each other on the street. But she's a novelist too, same genre, so at conferences and literary festivals we cross paths – that's how we first met, actually. Last time it happened she'd brought somebody else with her, so that was the end of that, really. I guess I was dumped, but only because I'd been too cowardly to do the dumping myself.'

Becca nods. 'Got it,' she says. 'And how do you feel now?'

'About her?'

Becca lifts a shoulder, trying to be cool.

'I feel like . . . I'm moving on with my life, and I'm happy about it,' he says, and then he smiles, tentatively, waiting for Becca to understand that he means with her.

'Uh-huh,' she says, smiling back. She has the sensation of being on a moving train, whizzing through the countryside: everything in front of her is crystal clear but the sheer velocity of movement makes everything else a blur. 'I see.'

'And you?' he asks.

Becca nods. 'I was with a guy for most of my twenties, but we broke up five years ago when he moved away and I wanted to stay. We don't speak or anything. I don't even have his phone number any more,' she says, not adding that it's only because Jia Li made her delete it at the manifestation ceremony.

'Does he live around here?' Noah asks.

'No,' Becca replies. 'He's in New York still, far as I know.'

Noah lifts his eyebrows, surprised, and then seems to run a sum in his head, nodding at the conclusion. 'So . . . have I got competition?' he clarifies, half smiling and half terribly solemn.

'No,' Becca replies, quickly. 'It's ancient history. I'm moving on with my life and happy about it too,' she adds, echoing his earlier sentiment. The tiniest part of her wonders if she really does mean what she says, but she knows it isn't real. If Mike hadn't texted, and she hadn't caught a glimpse of him – or someone she thought could be him – from a distance, in the car the other day, she wouldn't be thinking twice about her ability to move on. In fact, she's *been* moving on. Mike isn't going to stop that. No way.

'Good,' Noah says, and his face is closer now, his head tipped to one side, their noses almost touching. 'Because if anyone was going to change my mind about settling down, Becca Calloway, it would be you. If I may be so blunt.'

It's so strange, getting to know somebody new: he has been inside her, and yet she has waited for his kiss on this date like a child too shy to ask for more milk from the babysitter. They've kissed before, but each new kiss feels as if it needs permission, a build-up. They're getting to know one another in every way it is possible to get to know another person, but they don't know each other yet. They're an onion, peeling back layers. Kisses aren't given freely, they're calculated and considered. And this kiss, now, given over dirty plates in a tiny restaurant off the main street, is as intoxicating as the first. How strange, that not so long ago they didn't know each other at all. And now, Noah's tongue in her mouth and her hand on the back of his neck, Becca has the smallest flicker of this being not just a maybe, but a definite. She kisses him back, any lingering thoughts of the past melting away as she surrenders to this newness, to this discovery.

'I want to meet your friends,' Noah says as they temporarily part. 'And have you meet mine. Can we do that? Like the article says?'

'We can do that.' Becca grins, going back in for more kisses. 'I'd like that. And I'm afraid you're going to have to meet my mother soon enough, too. She's . . . involved – that's the polite turn of phrase.'

'Do I have to impress her in order to move up to the next level?' Noah teases.

Becca laughs. 'Yes,' she teases back. 'I can't be your girlfriend until Mother gives her blessing.'

'That's a shame.'

Becca squints, trying to figure out what he means.

'I just mean . . . well, sod it. This,' Noah says, gesturing between them. 'It's a thing, isn't it?'

'You mean an exclusive thing?'

'Yeah.'

'I don't want to date anybody else, if that's what you're asking,' she tells him.

'Same,' he replies. 'So we're . . .'

'Together?' asks Becca, with trepidation. The whizzing train sensation happens again: she likes this man and has nothing to lose, but *whoosh, whoosh, whoosh*: everything else is whizzing past in a haze.

'Girlfriend and boyfriend?' clarifies Noah. 'I know it's not been long, but I don't want to mess around. I could really see myself falling for you, Becca . . .'

Becca looks at him. Of course she wants to be his girlfriend. Of course she wants this to be official. Yes! This is exactly how she always thought it would work: living her life, minding her own business, and then poof! Out of nowhere comes the love of her life, and within days everything is different. That's basically the story of her own parents' meeting, not to mention every book and movie in which she's ever wistfully imagined herself as the main character.

'Come here,' she says, going in for another kiss. 'Boyfriend.'

'Yes, girlfriend,' he says back to her, and they're both grinning like fools.

*

There's something about how they make love that night, the night they decide to become boyfriend and girlfriend. It's slow and passionate, with long, lingering looks that feel weighted and important.

'God, you're good at this,' Noah pants as Becca wraps her legs around him and holds on to the headboard. 'So . . . so . . . good . . .'

She responds to the praise, feels sexy and powerful when she feels how much he wants her, how much he enjoys her body.

He moves her, flipping her off him so he's on top, arms above her head, held by his hand. He really looks at her now, pushing into her with all his length, rocking his hips, making sure she feels every movement. It's everything she likes sex to be: two bodies becoming one, in tune, a melting together so she doesn't know where she ends and he begins.

'I could very easily fall in love with you,' he tells her afterwards, as they lie in the dark, naked and sweaty.

Becca smiles. She'd been thinking the same thing. Girlfriend and boyfriend, *making love* . . . it's fast – she knows that – but she can't help it. That's why it's called falling in love, isn't it? Because once you're on your way it's very difficult to stop. Being his girlfriend makes her feel safe and secure: it's a sign they both want to move in the same direction, even after three dates. What is time, though, when she knows herself as well as she does? It's not like this with every Tom, Dick or Harry; this – *them* – is special. That he feels it too is confirmation.

'Same,' she says, sleepily. 'Same.'

14

She Doesn't Text Back

Noah walks Becca to work the next morning. He's in last night's shirt, crumpled from her bedroom floor, and he hasn't showered because he said he wanted to smell like her for a little while longer. It thrilled Becca to hear that. It was disgusting, but she knew exactly what he meant.

He loops an arm around her as they walk – or, in Becca's case, *floats*, as she basks in the romanticism of last night, of throwing caution to the wind and deciding to really go for it. They're in step, and they don't talk. The silence is a contented one. The early-morning July sun is already beating overhead, and Becca is lazily thinking about her day. She's got four clients booked in, and likes them all. Jia Li, Carlos and Dana are in, too, so it's a full house. Noah joked about her calling in sick for the day, and considering he was still inside her when he suggested it Becca almost agreed. But she's not like that. She could happily stay in bed with him all day, but not at the cost of Trim.

God, it was hard to finally leave the house, though.

'I'm going to get coffee for the guys,' Becca says as Clemants comes into view.

'Cool.' Noah nods, and they step behind a bloke totally unaware of them trying to get to the door, his labradoodle pulling a lead across the pavement, the man talking loudly into his AirPods about his day rate and availability.

Becca tuts, 'Pardon *you*.' He doesn't hear her; he's in his own little world.

As they wait in line Becca relishes how it feels to be there as a two. She fits perfectly in the space under Noah's arm and finds the back pocket of his chinos with her hand easily, as if it belongs there. He rests his chin on top of her head as they look at the menu on the board behind the counter, absent-mindedly running his thumb on her forearm. Becca looks up as the person in front of them collects their order. She recognises him but can't figure out from where.

'Hey,' he says to her in an Aussie accent as he clocks her as well. 'How's it going?' He doesn't stop walking because he doesn't actually want the answer. It's only friendly acknowledgement. Does he recognise her as well? Is he a client? The friend of somebody she's dated, maybe?

'Hey,' Becca replies, still struggling to place him.

Noah has stepped forward and is saying to the woman behind the counter that he wants a long black. Becca just catches the barista eyeing him up as Noah turns to Becca. 'What're you having?' he says, iPhone in hand ready to use Apple Pay. Becca feels a thrill that somebody else thinks Noah is cute. *But he's mine!* She happily grins, slipping a hand back into that chino pocket.

She glances back quickly – it's bugging her that she can't think where she knows that guy from. Everyone knows everyone around here, and she's normally so good with faces. She watches him hand a coffee to another bloke outside who, now he has turned around, she can see clear as day. It's Mike.

Her body runs cold.

Through the open coffee shop door, she hears the Aussie man say, 'I'll take Barbara back,' as Mike hands over the lead to him.

'Becca?' Noah is looking at her expectantly. 'What do you want, babe?'

She drags her attention back to the task at hand.

'Babe?' she says, trying to joke her way out of the low-level terror she's feeling. Has Mike seen her? If he has, he's chosen to ignore her, which is fair enough when she ignored his text. But still.

'Yeah,' Noah says, self-consciously grabbing a look at the waiting barista. 'Babe. Come on, there's a queue forming.'

'I'll pay,' Becca insists, outlining the four different drinks orders for herself and everyone at the salon, as well as Noah's long black.

'Nah,' Noah insists, batting her wrist away as she tries to hold her card up to the reader. 'Tell them it's on me.'

'Getting them onside early?' Becca teases. She sounds so light, so jovial, but she's overrun with thoughts of Mike. She thought she'd seen him the other day, too, but had written it off. What's he doing in town? Just back for a visit?

'Oh yes,' Noah bats back. 'I'm taking no chances.'

They head on out of the door, and Becca finds herself looking up and down the road to see if they're still about. And then it hits her: the Aussie guy she recognised – he was dating Jessie, Mike's sister, right as Mike and Becca broke up. They must still be together. Huh. It's funny to her to think of everyone else's life trucking on, even when she's no longer part of it. Not bad, or even sad, just . . . bittersweet, in a way.

'I am going to leave you here,' Noah announces on the corner. 'If that's all right. I smell like your vagina and haven't shaved, so you'll have to be delivery woman.'

Becca squints in the direction of the hair salon, her tummy lurching. She doesn't want to say goodbye. She wants to keep her hand where it is, and feel his across her back. It doesn't seem right that they should be parting after the night they've shared. Plus, he feels like protection, somehow. Protection from Mike, from what could have been. She's finally found somebody she can imagine a proper future with. It feels precious. Valuable.

'OK,' Becca says, grudgingly, and she can tell by the look on Noah's face he doesn't want to go either. He grins. She grins.

'OK,' he repeats, but neither of them moves.

'Right then.'

'Uh-huh.'

'I'll . . . be seeing you.'

'You will.'

'OK.'

'Maybe . . . tomorrow night?'

'Tomorrow night. At mine?'

'Let me take you out,' he says. 'Seven?'

'Seven,' Becca nods, and this time she's not shy about going in for a kiss goodbye, on the lips, as it is expected. Because that's what you do with a boyfriend – take and give kisses freely. She feels him watch her walk the few doors down to the salon and, before she goes in, she turns and waves. He blows her a kiss. She can't help but wonder what Mike would think if he saw.

15

She Texts Back

'No, I'm dead serious,' Becca says, spearing a roast potato and dipping it in her gravy. 'He's only just discovered *Breaking Bad*, but because I told him there's so many seasons – it's over sixty episodes, total – he tries to get three in a night so that – in his words – he doesn't meet his maker before he gets to see Walter White's fate play out.'

'That's bleak,' Mike says as Becca explains the level of her father's commitment.

'Bleak is that after my mum left he rewrote his will, and invited me over one night to tell me where to find it, who to contact, and that he's already paid for his own funeral – all I have to do is call the number on the card in the packet he's left for me in his desk drawer.'

'No!' Mike laughs, shaking his head.

'Yup.' Becca laughs back. 'I didn't sleep for a week afterwards, suddenly confronted with parental mortality. Even when Mum and Dad broke up, it was like the cracking of some sort of veneer, a peek into the fact that parents actually *don't* have all the answers.'

'Liar.'

'Sorry to break it to you.'

They eat their food sitting opposite one another, stopping periodically to look at the other and take in the magnitude of the moment: Becca and Mike, on their second first date. They've talked on the phone every night this week, sometimes until two or three in the morning. They've reminisced about when they were younger, teased each other about past mistakes, filled in the gaps of what they've missed since they've been apart. Mike has confided in her about how lost he feels right now, too, without a job. She's listened, but tried not give too much advice. She wants him to find his own way, so she can be sure he's living a life he's happy with. Nobody can do the work for him.

Mike sighs. 'I can't imagine not having my parents around. It makes me sad to think about it.'

'Our parents are still young; I think we've got time,' Becca says. 'Although . . .' She sighs, weighing up if she can bear to say what she's thinking out loud.

'What?'

'It's funny, isn't it, how we can trick ourselves? I was just thinking how I hope I've got so much time left with them – they're only in their sixties. But at the same time, I feel the ticking of my stupid biological clock, and all that tells me is that time is running out, every second of every day. I don't know. Maybe it's just a girl thing.'

Mike picks at the ring pull of an empty Coke can. 'Probably,' he says, but he's being a douchebag on purpose.

'Arsehole,' Becca says.

'What do you expect?' He chuckles. 'Talk about existential angst! Jesus. Like I've not got enough of my own.'

'Pardon me for sharing something about my *feelings*,' jokes Becca, but she's not offended. 'But fine. I get it. There's a time and a place for contemplating the ways of the universe, and maybe it's not second-first-date chat.'

'If MI6 are looking for new ways to torture terrorists, though . . .' Mike shrugs. 'What a way to get a person to break down.'

'OK, don't push it, mister.'

'Did you mean it, though? You want kids soon?'

Becca shrugs. They've danced round this on their phone calls, so it's not as if it's coming out of the blue. 'Yeah,' she admits. 'I'm ready, I think. Jia Li being pregnant really makes me feel like . . . well, this will sound awful, because obviously I know life isn't a race, but it's making me feel left behind.'

Mike nods, digesting this. 'Jessie's baby can make me feel that way too,' he says. 'I get it.'

Becca daren't look up at him.

Mike looks at his watch. 'It's eight p.m., Bec! We've been here six hours!'

'We always could talk.' Becca smiles. She adds, 'But crikey, I'm about ready for bed after all this red wine.'

'There was a time where we didn't even leave the house until eight p.m., sometimes nine p.m.'

'Imagine!' Becca laughs. 'All those nights in town at some grubby bar, listening to some piss-poor band.'

'I used to love those nights!' counters Mike.

'So much eyeliner,' Becca notes. 'And that was just you.'

'Russell Brand has a lot to answer for. Remember my collection of skinny jeans? I don't think my thighs got any blood flow for the whole of the twenty-tens.

Becca nods with a sigh. 'Feels like it was only yesterday . . .'

'Goes quick, doesn't it?'

'I know. I tell you! Time! She marches on!'

'No escape.'

They consider this fact.

'The pandemic robbed us of a couple of years, though. Messed with everyone's head.'

'What did you do during that time? In the lockdowns?'

Mike splutters a laugh. 'Got Covid, actually. And suffered with long Covid, too, before anyone knew what it was or we had proper testing. My girlfriend got it as well.'

Girlfriend, Becca notes. *Should I ask, or should I leave it?*

'Not the ex who I just broke up with – this was before. Rashida. We broke up that summer, and then I met Priya. Not that you asked me for my relationship history. I don't know why I'm telling you all this. I just want you to know, I suppose. We've talked about so much on the phone, but not who we've been with.'

Becca nods. 'I think I understand. There's still a lot to catch up on.'

'And maybe some new memories to make too?' Mike catches himself then, colour burning his cheeks as he squints in self-disgust. 'I can't believe I just said that. *Make new memories too.*'

'Dude, you need to chill out. I am aware you're a tongue-tied idiot sometimes, you know. I was in the privileged position to see it up close and in all its glory for a number of years.'

'Now who's the arsehole?'

She winks. 'Just keeping it real.'

'Is that really how you remember me? An idiot?' His tone has changed, as though he's actually quite hurt by the suggestion.

'No!' she says. 'God, I was devastated after you left. If it hadn't been for the salon, having something to get to every day, something to focus on . . .'

'Sorry,' Mike says, voice low. 'I didn't mean to be overly sensitive.'

'And I didn't mean to be a cow. Carlos says I'm a bit *too* good at crossing the line, sometimes. I have a habit of thinking that men can take it, somehow. I'm working on it.'

Mike puts his feet up on the chair across from him, stealing the extra throw cushion to stuff behind him for comfort. 'Seems like a cool guy, Carlos. From what you've said.'

'Yeah. It feels like he's always been here, you know? Always been around.'

'And it was through Facebook that you met?'

Becca nods her head and shrugs, as if to say, *Mad, isn't it?* 'In a hairdressing group. He posted about looking for a place, and I was getting tired of going into town to UpDo every day. I don't know if you remember that I'd already thought about setting up on my own, somehow?'

'I remember.'

Becca looks at him. She sighs, and it hits her all over again: *Mike. I'm sitting here with* Mike.

'I messaged him and we met up. We hit it off right away, and ten days later got the keys to Trim. It was like divine intervention or something.'

'Wow. And he's gay, isn't he?'

'Carlos?' asks Becca.

'Yeah.'

'No, he dates women.'

'Oh,' says Mike. 'I mean, whatever, obviously. Sexuality is a sliding scale, et cetera, et cetera. I just thought—'

'That the tattoos and tan on a man working in hairdressing must mean he's not straight?'

'You're doing a very good job of pointing out my prejudice here.'

'No, no,' sing-songs Becca. 'You're doing that all by yourself.' She scrunches up her nose at him, code for: *It's OK, a lot of people assume the same thing.*

'Well, it's awesome. It's obvious you both really get on and the salon is thriving. Would you ever expand it?'

'I don't know. Maybe. We've talked about it, but then it would mean both of us working in different locations, at least for a while, and part of what makes Trim so great is the team – all of us getting to work together every day. Maybe we'll get a bigger space, but where we are is so badass, right in the heart of King's Heath, so . . .'

'So, basically, you're happy.'

Becca smiles. 'Basically,' she says. 'Yeah.'

'Happy is good. I'm happy you're happy.'

'Thank you. And . . . I know you're figuring out a lot of things, but you'll be sorted soon enough too. I believe in you.'

'Yeah, thanks. I've got a chat with a guy about an eight-week contract for his business on Monday, actually. I'd have to go to London, but I think I'm going to do it. Get some money in, remind myself that I do, in fact, have skills worth paying for.'

'Oh,' says Becca, and she's immediately mad at herself for not only being disappointed by the idea of Mike leaving again, if only temporarily, but also mad at herself for letting *him* know that.

'I'll be back,' he says, quickly.

'Sure. Yeah.' She's trying to keep her cool. What's the word? *Insouciant.* Like a Frenchwoman.

'Maybe you could come and visit.'

Becca looks at him. 'Maybe,' she says. She sounds prickly. *It's not safe*, she thinks suddenly. *It's not safe to relax with him, to feel how I felt with him, because he will leave.* She didn't know she felt that way until just now, right this second. Mike Henry will never settle down where he grew up. He just won't. Of course he's already found work in London.

'Or not,' he adds, quickly.

'I don't mean to sound . . . I suppose I just don't want to get too comfortable with you being here. I know you say you might be back for good, but . . .'

'Hey,' Mike says, reaching out a hand to her arm. She looks down at where he has touched her, feels the heat of his palm on her skin, the way it makes her heart beat in double time. She feels Mike looking down, too, and for some reason it makes her afraid to catch his eye again. 'I'm not going to mess you around.'

'I feel like, if we're going to do this, maybe we need a proper talk about last time.'

'Urgh. Yes,' he says. 'Shall we set a timer, keep it to a tight ten?'

'Deal,' Becca says, and Mike reaches around to his denim jacket pocket, where he has – like a gentleman – kept his phone this whole time. In fact, Becca realises she's seldom even seen him on his phone except to take a call. He's been giving her his undivided attention.

'Oh,' he says, frowning at the screen. 'Jessie's texted. She's asking if I've spoken to Dad yet.'

'Spoken to your dad as in, like, about going golfing this week, or spoken to your dad in a family emergency kind of a way?'

'Let me ask her,' he says, his voice distracted, the words less formed than they should be. 'Sorry,' he adds, quickly. 'Can't risk it for a biscuit, you know?'

'No worries, you go ahead,' Becca tells him.

'OK, sent.' He looks up, puts his phone on the table with screen up, so they can see when the reply comes through – which it does, right away.

'She says in an emergency kind of a way . . .' Mike starts, and Becca can tell his mind is racing, that he doesn't know what to do. 'I'm just going to call her,' he says.

Becca watches him as he waits for Jessie to pick up, saying, 'Yo, what's happening? You're scaring me.'

Becca can't read his face. Mike keeps his eyes down, looking at the table, brow heavy. He doesn't even do the usual 'hmmmm' or 'OK' noises as Jessie speaks. Becca can't make out what she's saying very clearly, only that she doesn't pause for breath.

All Mike says is, 'OK.'

Becca looks at him and waits, watching as the colour drains from his face right before her eyes.

'Dad's got prostate cancer,' he says. 'They found out on Friday. Mum just told Jessie. Apparently, they were wondering whether to even tell me or not, what with everything that's happened these past few months—'

His voice breaks.

'Sorry,' he says. 'It's just, I bloody knew something was up, I knew something was happening that they weren't telling me but I didn't push it because I'm a selfish prick.' He lets out a choked sob.

'You're not a selfish prick,' Becca says. 'Not at all. You've been carrying this huge weight, and you don't love your mum or your dad any less just because you didn't press them harder than you could have done. They have each other. Parents hate worrying their kids, and they hate telling their kids stuff before they really have to.'

Mike nods.

'Remember when my dad got a new kneecap when we were in the south of France one year? They didn't tell me it was all booked, didn't tell me it had happened, didn't fill me in on anything until we were back and I saw he was walking with a stick at home.'

'I remember that, yeah.'

Becca reaches out a hand. 'Did Jessie tell you any details? Do you want to go home?'

Mike nods. 'Do you mind? All Jessie really said was that his PSA was high – you know, the blood test they do – and so he went for more screenings and it was all there, on the scan.'

'Have they caught it early?'

'I honestly don't know. Let's just pay and go. I'm so sorry.'

'Don't be sorry!' Becca exclaims. 'God! I want Paul to be OK too! Let's just go and get the details, all right?'

'Actually,' Mike says, 'do you mind if I go alone? I'll text you later?'

'Oh,' says Becca. 'No, yeah. Of course. Sorry. I don't know what I was thinking there. You go.'

'Thank you,' he says.

'No worries,' Becca tells him. 'But text me when you know more, all right?'

'Will do.'

He's gone before she knows it, and she's left sitting amongst their dirty plates, all alone.

16

She Doesn't Text Back

'Morning,' Becca trills, entering the salon. It's late July now, and she's just had a series of dreamy nights with Noah, so she's in a particularly good mood. 'Coffee!' she says, and Jia Li pokes her head out from the back room.

'One sec!' she says, and when she reappears Becca can't put her finger on it, but Jia Li seems different, somehow.

'Listen,' Jia Li says. 'I have something to tell you and it could affect future coffee orders, so I need you to pay attention.'

'You're switching to skimmed milk again?' Becca guesses, walking through to the staff room to dump her bag and open the back door for some air circulation. 'Are we the first here?'

'Carlos isn't in until later, but he already knows.'

This gets Becca's attention. What information could Carlos possibly know before Becca? How rude!

'I'm going to be drinking decaf for a little while,' Jia Li presses, following Becca as she walks. 'Because I'm pregnant.'

Becca stops in her tracks and waits for the punchline.

'I told Carlos last night, and feel bad he knows and you don't – we ended up having a bit of a heart-to-heart here after work, after you'd gone, and it just came out . . . although he says he guessed.'

'What!' squeals Becca, careful to keep her voice down in case anyone arrives. 'Pregnant with who?'

'*That* is a chat I'd like to save for another time, if that's OK.'

Becca eyes her. 'OK . . .' she says slowly. 'That's . . . totally your choice. I'm with you . . .'

Jia Li purses her lips, amused. 'Just . . . give me time,' she says. 'To tell him, I mean. I feel like he's going to need time to get used to it. I only found out myself two weeks ago, which . . . is a whole thing. I didn't even realise I'd missed my period – you know how I get crazy long cycles sometimes. I was vaguely aware it was overdue. And I know my trousers have felt tight, but . . . I never thought . . . I'm still feeling feelings about it, and I'm sure I'll need to talk about it at some point but for now . . . you know what I know. And Carlos.'

'Are you two talking about me back there?' a voice comes from down near the front desk. Becca peeks her head out to see Carlos already helping himself to coffee.

'Noah sends his regards,' Becca tells him, gesturing at his cup. 'He paid. Again!'

'Smarmy bugger continuing to try to win us all over, is he?' Carlos quips, taking the lid off to check he's picked up the right one. He has.

'Is it working?' Becca asks.

Carlos takes a big gulp of coffee.

'Tell him to send muffins next time too,' he retorts, and when Becca raises an eyebrow adds: 'But yeah, cheers.'

Jia Li comes out behind Becca and tells Carlos: 'I've just told Bec.'

Carlos looks between the two women. 'About . . .' he says, checking he's understood.

'Yeah.'

He makes a swooshing noise with his outward breath. 'Isn't it mental?' He walks over, sets his coffee down and puts a hand on each of their shoulders. 'Our Jia Li, up the duff!'

Becca still hasn't had time to process it. She's here, present, in the salon, but a slice of her brain has been left behind with Noah, and another crumb with Mike, and it makes it harder to concentrate.

'What do you need from us?' Becca asks, noting from the clock on the wall that they've got five minutes, tops, before their first clients arrive. 'And congratulations, by the way!' She catches herself. 'Congratulations!'

'Thank you. And . . . nothing.' Jia Li shrugs. 'All that stuff about a first trimester and the throwing up or feeling ill? I didn't even know. I've been fine. Like, more than fine. I feel great!'

'God, come here,' Becca says, looking at her friend. 'Really – congratulations, darling. This is amazing. I'm so happy for you.' She can feel herself getting misty-eyed. In fact, hold on, yup . . .

'You're crying?' asks Jia Li. 'Don't you cry! I had enough of that from Carlos last night!'

Becca grabs a tissue from a nearby box and dabs at her eyes. 'You cried?' she asks Carlos.

He starts prepping his work station. ''Course I cried,' he says. 'It's magic, innit? All this time we've just been living our lives, and there's an actual human growing in there.' He gestures to Jia Li's belly.

'Let me be a warning though,' she tells Becca. 'I came off the pill but hadn't had my IUD fitted yet. I hope your man is double-wrapping it.'

Carlos's eyes shoot to Becca's. 'Going well, is it?' he asks, and Becca can hear the judgement in his voice.

'He's nice,' she says. 'He bought you coffee!'

Carlos locates his trolley and starts tearing off foils. 'I'm sure he is,' he says. 'I would just like to note, though, that he does wear polo shirts. We've all seen that, haven't we, when he's picked you up?'

'What's wrong with a polo shirt?' asks Becca, all high-pitched and outraged on Noah's behalf.

'You know exactly what's wrong with a polo shirt,' he bats back.

Dana walks in with a wave and smile, taking her place behind the reception desk and getting stuck into her coffee. 'Morning, everyone!'

Everyone says morning back.

'So you don't like him. Are you going to be busy the day of the wedding too?'

'I think I am, actually,' Carlos says, but Becca frowns and it seems to do the trick. He issues a benevolent smile and says, in a tone she can't quite place, 'Of course I'd come to your wedding. But, just for the record . . . Becca . . . I think you need to take things easy. Things seem to be moving faster than usual for you and I know you really like him but he's young, right? Even if you're boyfriend and girlfriend now, he's probably not *actually* looking for anything serious.'

'You don't know him. How can you say that when you don't know him?'

Carlos shrugs. 'Because I know you, and I can just tell. Plus, you have sex hair.'

She puts a hand to the back of her head and feels a massive lumpy knot. 'Crap,' she says, as Carlos and Jia Li laugh.

They're interrupted by a shrill: 'Here she is, my newly-in-love daughter!'

Becca looks up from behind the reception desk to see her mum smiling manically, Betty just at her shoulder, behind her.

'Mum!' she says, as if she wasn't expecting them, even though literally seconds ago she told Dana that her mum and Betty were coming in for Pride makeovers before they left for Brighton the weekend after next.

Everyone hugs, and Betty tells her: 'Just seen the photos of your new man, Becca – very nice, I must say! I can't wait for our dinner next week.'

Becca acts outraged. 'Mum!' she says. 'I sent you that photo as personal reference! Sharing it is creepy!'

Shelley shrugs. 'We come as a package. Carlos, hello!'

Carlos opens his arms from across the salon and walks towards them, going in for hugs and air kisses himself.

'Shelley!' he says, smacking his lips together as he goes left and then right. 'Betty!' he cries. The women coo over him, as most women do.

Carlos steers the women into two salon chairs next to each other, making a show of slipping gowns over them, getting a coffee order, issuing compliments about jawlines and cheek-bones. Both her mother and Betty are, like everyone else in this world, totally entranced by Carlos, and Becca stands nearby, admiring his ease with them as they talk about putting a semi-permanent pink tint into her mum's blonde bob, and taking Betty's cropped hair platinum.

'And you know what? You don't like it, we change it up next week, or next month. What's a Pride celebration for if not experimentation?'

'The last thing I experimented with was chilli oil on my pizza, and I've got to say, it didn't work out so well,' Betty warns, her face deadpan, in true Betty style.

'Well, thanks for sharing,' Carlos says, equally deadpan. 'Your trauma can be my salvation. Avoid the chilli oil on the pizza. Got it. Now, I'll just let Bec give you the onceover for your cut, and Shelley, I'll start with you. Becca, if you touch up Betty I can work on fresh hair?'

'Got it,' says Becca, stepping behind the pair to take them both in through the mirrors. 'OK, Mum, how about we keep this length through the front, but I shape it a bit more to frame your face, and go just a little bit shorter through the back here to keep it the right side of modern? Sort of chic, but not too "finished"?'

Her mum waves a hand. 'I trust you with it,' she says. And then she adds, her voice lowered. 'I mean, at least I think I do.'

She meets Betty's eyes in the mirror and they smile, Betty amused at the drollness that is obviously rubbing off.

'And I'll go for a number three all over,' Betty says. 'Keep it short, keep it easy. That's my motto.'

'I can work to that,' Carlos declares.

Everyone sets to work, Dana delivering cups of coffee and water, Carlos prepping colour, Becca working on Betty's crop. They talk about the importance of older lesbians at Pride events and how Betty has never been to Brighton before, and how everyone should get involved with Birmingham Pride when it happens in September. Becca is halfway through wondering aloud if they should do a Pride evening event at the salon when a delivery woman comes through the shop door with a huge bunch of flowers, rendering everyone the sort of quiet that happens right before a shock reveal happens, when air stills and something shifts.

'Becca Calloway?' the woman asks, addressing the salon. Everyone looks at her.

'Yes, thank you,' she says, bewildered. One part of her brain is yelling, *FLOWERS FOR ME? BUT FROM WHO?!* And the other part of her brain knows exactly who they are from. He's so thoughtful. Sometimes she can't believe Noah, seven years her junior, has more manners and romantic nous that most thirty- or forty-something men she knows. The more she learns, the more she falls for him. She feels safe with him. Special. *Her boyfriend.* Her boyfriend who is about to meet her parents, too.

Becca accepts the small box of yellow roses and says thank you, and because it's her family in the salon, she gives herself a second to pull out the card right there and then. With anybody else she'd be more professional, but she can't help herself. She opens the tiny envelope and pulls out the card, already concocting the text message of thanks in her mind.

I just wanted to say, I've moved back home. Forewarned is forearmed! Yours (with no expectations) Mike.

'Becca? What is it?' her mum asks.

Becca looks up. 'From Mike,' she tells her, confused.

'Mike your ex?' Betty clarifies. 'Not – Noah? The new one?'

Becca nods, slipping the card back into the side of the flowers and perching them on an empty chair in reception. 'Yeah,' she says.

'Does he want to get back together?' her mother asks.

'Mother! Jesus! I'm going to start calling you Spliffy, bloody hell! Just give me a minute. This is so weird.'

'Spliffy?' her mum questions, mostly to Betty.

'I'm assuming she means something along the lines of you being blunt, like *a* blunt, like a joint.'

Shelley shakes her head, not comprehending.

'Marijuana, Shelley,' Betty clarifies. 'Drugs!'

Shelley tuts. 'A joke isn't funny if you have to explain it,' she insists, and Carlos chuckles, catching Becca's eye and then looking away. Why does nobody understand how awful it is that Mike has sent flowers? Becca's happy – she's moving forward! The lack of text message reply was a reply in itself!

'Do you want me to get those out of your way?' Dana asks in a quiet voice. Everyone looks at Becca as she weighs up her reply.

'Um, no, it's OK,' she settles on. She has no idea how she feels but getting rid of them probably isn't the answer. 'Just leave them in the waiting area. Could you take the card out though?' She thinks of Noah, how he asked if he had competition. 'Thank you.'

17

She Doesn't Text Back

Mike's flowers and the accompanying note – that he's back, and for good – have Becca spooked.

'It's not that I think he's a threat to anything I have now,' she tries to explain to Carlos as they lock up one night and she decides that, after five days, the flowers can go in the bin. 'But if I had a choice, I'd prefer to simply not have to think about him.'

'Are you mad he sent them?' Carlos asks, helping her dump the contents of the vase into a black bin liner, swooping in to take the vase to the back room.

When he returns, Becca answers, 'No. I *did* block his number, and at least now I haven't been seeing things – it must have been him in the car that day, ages ago, and at the café. Paths will inevitably cross. He's right about that. And it's finished business, obviously. Of course it is! Sometimes I think I want to tell Noah I love him. I know that's bonkers—'

'*Love* him?' clarifies Carlos.

'I know.' Becca smiles. 'I'm such a sap.'

'I can't wait to hear what Shelley and Betty make of him then,' he replies, and they usher themselves out, locking the front door and Becca reaches up for the metal security shutters.

'I'll be sure to report back,' Becca tells him. 'Wish me luck!'

'You don't need my luck,' Carlos waves, watching her go. 'But I hope you have fun.'

Noah is already in Betty and Shelley's front room with a beer and tiny bowl of peanuts – he lives closer, so the plan was to meet there. Becca didn't think he'd arrive first though.

'I'm so sorry,' she whispers to him as she goes in for a kiss. 'Are you OK? Have you been given the Spanish Inquisition?'

Noah uses his free hand to pull at her waist so that there's barely room for a piece of paper between them and murmurs, 'I'm fine, Bec. Hello.'

'Becca, darling!' he mother trills as she comes through from the kitchen. 'Lemon pasta tonight, love – isn't that so chic? I got the idea from one of the magazines at the salon.'

Betty follows, carrying a white wine for Becca. 'I don't think pasta is pasta without a sauce, but what do I know?' she says, handing it over. 'Lemons are for gin, sauce is for pasta, that's what I always thought. Apparently, that makes me an unadventurous heathen though, so—' She mimes zipping her lips and throwing away the key.

'Sounds lovely,' Noah says. 'Unusual,' he adds, appeasing Betty's sensibilities, 'but then they said that about salted caramel for years, didn't they, and look how that turned out.'

Betty nods, seeing his point. 'I do enjoy a salted caramel.' She throws up her hands. 'I'll get involved!' she declares, reaching out for Shelley's hand. 'For you, my beautiful, I'd try anything.'

Becca and Noah watch Shelley and Betty exchange a Look – a look filled with love and warmth and fondness. It makes them turn their attentions to each other. Meeting the parents. They both know this is a big deal.

'Do you want to take a seat at the table?' Shelley asks. 'It's ready.'

They fuss about who should sit where, unfurl napkins and pour water, and Shelley presents a steaming pile of glossy summer pasta, steaming and slick, and then a hunk of parmesan they all take turns shaving onto their dinner.

'Bon appétit,' Noah says with a grin. 'It's so nice to meet you.'

'It's so nice to meet you!' exclaims Shelley. 'It's been a long time since this one has brought a boy home.' She gestures at Becca.

'Mum—' Becca begins, but her mother cuts her off.

'It's exciting!' she defends herself, topping up her wine glass. 'And you seem so happy together – very well suited. And what a fun way you met, too, at a friend-of-a-friend party. Very clever idea, that.'

'And it's so strange,' Noah says, in between mouthfuls. 'But as soon as I was invited to that, through a bookseller I know, I had this feeling.'

'A feeling?' clarifies Betty, pasta sauce dripping down her chin. Shelley mimes wiping it across the table, but she doesn't take the hint. Shelley smiles, fondly, tutting with affection.

'Yeah,' says Noah. 'I've actually never told you this, have I, Becca?'

'I know nothing about a feeling,' she tells him. 'But I'm intrigued . . .'

'I just knew I was going to meet somebody significant. I've dated, I've been in love before, I've had my heart broken too, got back out there . . . all those normal things. But I've never set out to a party knowing I'd meet somebody special. It's normally something you hope for, isn't it?'

'But you *knew*?' Shelley is loving this – it's right up her street. Becca has to get her romanticism from somewhere, after all. 'Did *you* know?' she asks Becca.

Becca thinks. 'I wouldn't say I was *certain*, but I remember telling Carlos it was strange to think my guy could be at the bar already, drinking his drink and getting on with his life and then, boom, we were five minutes away from meeting and . . .'

She looks at Noah. This is all very heavy, very honest and open. He grins, and she knows it's OK. He really does feel it too.

'And just like that everything meant something different,' Betty supplies. 'I know the feeling.'

Becca watches the look between Betty and her mother, and gets the impression she's bearing witness to something she either didn't notice before, or hasn't been privy too. Are they being more couple-like in the presence of another couple? Becca doesn't mind it if they are. She likes being in a couple too, likes being her with her boyfriend and her mum and stepmum.

They eat – the lemon pasta is delicious, and Becca takes seconds – and it's not long before Shelley and Betty get down to the nuts and bolts of who Noah is, regard for Becca aside.

'Did you grow up in these parts, Noah? I was just thinking how you don't sound very Brummie,' Shelley says.

Noah smiles and nods. 'I grew up towards Leicester, just me and my dad. I ended up this way because my best friend Nate moved here, after he got married, and he's just about as much family as I've got left now, so . . .'

'Oh, love, I'm sorry to hear that. Your dad has passed on?'

'Yeah.' He nods, reaching for a gulp of wine. 'Happened years ago now.'

Betty supplies: 'Doesn't get any easier though, does it?'

His eyes flicker up, landing on Betty in gratitude. *She gets it*, Becca practically hears him think.

'No,' he admits, and Becca reaches out a hand to squeeze his knee. He takes her hand appreciatively, and they sit like that, fingers entwined under the table, Becca rubbing her thumb over the soft part of his skin between his thumb and forefinger, reassuringly. 'I miss him every day,' Noah says. 'He was a good man.'

'Understandably,' says Shelley, following up with a very tactless: 'And your mum?'

'Mum!' Becca squeals, outraged by the turn this simple conversation is taking, headed towards an all-out interrogation.

'It's OK.' Noah smiles, but Becca knows it's not. She's been desperate for more information about his mum – it's

one of the few things she feels she hasn't got to the nub of —
but she can tell from the way Noah's shoulders tense, how
his lower jaw locks whenever mums are brought up as a
subject in general, that it's not easy for him. 'She left,' he explains. 'Dropped me off at school one day when I was eight,
and didn't come back – like, ever. She did a complete runner.'

'No!' gasps Betty, seemingly unable to moderate her
reaction.

'I don't like to really tell people, because *pity, urgh,*' Noah
says, shuddering. 'It's her loss.'

'A huge loss,' Shelley agrees. 'I'm sorry I asked – I didn't
mean to pry. That was thoughtless of me.'

Becca is relieved her mother has shown this glimmer of
self-awareness.

Noah uses a small hunk of bread to wipe the last of the
lemon and parmesan from his plate as he says: 'You know,
I'd like to be honest with you, as Becca's family. No secrets,'
he adds, looking at Becca with a smile. 'This one', he says,
gesturing towards her, 'is a keeper.'

'We think so,' her mother agrees, thrilled to be compli-
mented on the work of raising her.

'So, wait,' Betty clarifies. 'Your mother left one day and
you've never heard from her since?'

'Nope,' says Noah. 'A few years after it happened Dad
said he had an address for her, via her brother's ex-wife or
something, but then he died and I realised I didn't want to
track her down – not if she wasn't even going to reach out to
me when I was technically orphaned. I don't hate her, but I
don't want anything to do with her, either. Not that she wants

anything to do with me. Maybe I'm just protecting myself – who can say?'

'And your best friend, you say he's like family?'

'Nate, yeah. Known him my whole life – his family looked after me when Dad was working, and invite me over at Christmas even now, have a stocking for me by the fireplace along with everybody else.'

'How sweet!'

'It's definitely taught me that you can create your family, I suppose. God – I feel like I'm babbling on as if this is paid-for therapy! I'm sorry. Let's change the subject. How did you two meet?'

Shelley and Betty launch into their duologue about their own romance story, but Becca can't hear them: she's too busy looking at her man, this empathetic, kind, great company of a man who is sitting beside her as her boyfriend, charming her parents, her heart fluttering with the simple truth of it: she loves him. It's happened. She's fallen.

'You're staring at me,' Noah tells her as Betty and Shelley insist on clearing the table and locating the strawberries and cream for pudding. 'Am I talking too much?'

Becca shakes her head. 'Nope,' she tells him. 'You're talking the perfect amount. I'm so happy you're here. They really like you.'

'Good.' He grins. 'I really like them too.'

'Good!' Becca echoes. 'So everyone likes everyone.'

'Something like that, yeah,' he whispers. He goes to say something else, but the women return victorious, fruit and bowls in hand, but Becca knows implicitly he was about to say it. I love you.

They walk home shy and quiet, their bodies doing the talking. At home, Becca locks the door and leads Noah upstairs wordlessly, where she undresses him, and he undresses her, and they look at each other the whole time. Some sex is fucking, and some sex is making love, but on the night you say those three little words for the very first time, it gets to be a delectable mix of both.

'I love you,' he tells her, simply, as she straddles him, pulling him in, deeper and deeper.

Her heart bursts with a thousand fireworks.

'I love you too,' she tells him, moving her hips.

Becca doesn't often come through penetration. She needs hands or a mouth, a vibrator even. But wrapped around Noah in a tangle of sheets, feeling him inside her, hearing those words in her ear, hot and heavy and full of meaning, she feels the build-up to an orgasm that is big, a proper crescendo of everything that hasn't just been building up tonight, but since she met him. She moves her hips faster and faster, Noah pushing back frantically, understanding the effect he's having on her.

'I love you,' he repeats. 'I love you, I love you, I love you.'

'I love you,' she echoes. 'I love you.'

'I love you.'

'I love you.'

And then she comes, hard and fast, in delicious waves, pulling Noah towards her so that close becomes closer, and he comes too, and it feels divine in its timing, that falling in love and saying it out loud and orgasming together that way, like a freaking Boys II Men song . . .

'I can't believe we found each other,' Noah pants when they're done. 'You're amazing,' he tells her.

'Jesus,' is Becca's reply. 'I could stick around for that,' and she laughs, patting his generous naked thigh.

'I fully intend to stick around.' Noah laughs back, and then they do it all again.

18

She Texts Back

'OK,' Carlos says from his position in the salon's office space in the eaves, a room big enough for shelves neatly arranged with financial files and two desks with two leather chairs, the place as sleek and modern as the salon itself, at a tenth of the square footage. 'You keep sighing like you're trying to huff and puff and blow the house down, and every time I ask if you're OK you insist that you are. But I don't think you are, are you?'

Becca looks at him.

'If it's about Mike, you *can* tell me, you know. I give you a hard time but I do actually want you to be happy. Unless it's because of him that you're unhappy, in which case give me his address because I will kick his ass, no questions asked.'

'Calm down, Rambo,' she says. 'Mike doesn't need his ass kicking. His dad is poorly.'

'How poorly?'

'Cancer. Prostate.'

Carlos screws up his face. 'Oh, no,' he says. 'Is it bad?'

'Apparently it's treatable,' she says. 'But obviously everyone is worried sick. And nobody even wanted to tell Mike because he's had his own stuff going on. So he's sort of being the perfect son right now, proving everybody wrong.'

'In what way?'

'In a nice way, I suppose,' she says. 'Asking questions, going over possible treatment plans, just being there.'

Carlos nods. 'My older brother had prostate cancer,' he says. 'Well, my half-brother from Dad's first marriage, you know, Gio?'

'Yeah.' Becca nods. 'I didn't know he's had prostate cancer though. Is he OK now?'

'Can't get a stiffy any more,' Carlos says with a wince. 'And dribbles so has to wear a nappy-type thing in his pants to soak it up. I know what I'm telling you is personal, but he'd want me to share. He didn't know about any of this when he was diagnosed. But he's alive and very grateful to be so. Do you know if Mike's dad is getting surgery, or radiotherapy . . . ?'

'Mike said he's leaning towards radiotherapy, exactly because of what you said. I think it's something about the surgery being near to the nerves that help sexual function and continence – he doesn't want to be an old man who smells like piss, apparently. Paul's words.'

'I can understand that,' says Carlos. 'I remember from when Gio was choosing, his doctor said the younger the patient the more likely they are to have surgery – get the damned thing out, even if it costs them in other ways. Gio has three kids, he just wanted to make sure he saw them get to secondary school, lived to see them graduate and get married, all that stuff. He didn't care about the—' Carlos makes a whistling sound as he raises his hand in the air, which Becca assumes means sexual function. 'Or about the adult nappies. He just wanted to be cancer-free and alive. Not that every surgery ends up that way – but for Gio it did, unfortunately.'

'I never knew any of this, Carlos. When did this happen?'

Carlos waves a hand. 'Before I met you,' he says. 'He's older than me, isn't he, so yeah, when he was fifty?'

'I'm glad he's OK,' Becca tells him. 'I like a nice hopeful story like that.'

'I'm sure Paul will be OK. It's assumed that when you're diagnosed with prostate cancer now you'll survive, I think. It's like ninety-eight per cent survival or something crazy like that. I know the journey is rough though. And hey, I know Gio benefited from talking to other dudes about it all when it was happening. Even if you have family, it's all the . . . *equipment*, isn't it? Sometimes you need another man to talk to about it all. If he wants Gio's number, I'm sure Gio will happily chat to him.'

'That's really kind.' Becca smiles. 'Thank you. I'll pass that along.'

'Sure,' he says, clicking his pen a couple of times and, apparently deciding he has nothing further to add, spinning back around on his chair to get back to balancing the books.

'But things with Mike,' Carlos says, after a few minutes of working in companionable silence. 'All that's good?'

Becca swivels back around on her chair to face him. 'Um,' she says. 'Yes? At least, I think so.'

'You *think* so.'

'Well, he's really making the effort, and he's been super forthcoming with his feelings and stuff, which is nice. It's reassuring.'

'Sure,' Carlos says. 'You want a ring on your finger and so no time-wasters allowed, correct?'

'You make it sound like I'd marry the next person that asks!' Becca squeals. 'I just want to be happy, is all. And partnership makes me happy. Did you ever see that TV show *Love Life*?'

'With Anna Kendrick?'

'No. The second season, when it was William Jackson Harper? He was this divorcé and the arc of the show was how he got over divorce in his thirties to end up where he should have been all along?'

Carlos nods. 'Yup, I'm with you. If you remember, we actually watched that series together?'

Becca narrows her eyes. 'On a hangover, in a day,' she nods. 'Yes. I remember.'

'And now I know exactly which bit you're going to quote to me.'

'No, you don't.'

'I do! Because you talked about it for weeks afterwards. There's a bit where the voiceover says that being a man isn't just stepping up to the plate, but stepping up to the plate in perpetuity. And then the guy says that actually, the meaning of life is having a plate to step up to at all.'

'OK, fine.' Becca laughs. 'That is what I was going to quote. I've just been thinking about that again lately, you know? That's not even what a *man* is, that's all humans to me. I want a plate to step up to – a family who are going to be a pain in my arse but the loves of my life.'

'As long as he's treating you right.'

Becca hesitates.

'Becca? Is he treating you right?'

She sighs. 'Technically, yes,' she says. 'But right before he got the call about his dad and left the pub, he told me he's talking about maybe taking a two-month contract in London doing some consultancy work. And that didn't feel great. It brought back all those memories of being left. And two months isn't forever, but at the moment he's here, and I like it, but then he's going to be gone again, and it gives me . . . feelings.'

Carlos closes the binder they've been working from, which Becca takes to mean they're finished.

'Are you hungry?' he asks her.

Becca nods. 'Yeah,' she says. 'Now you mention it.'

'Pizzeria Giacomo? My treat?'

Becca whistles through her teeth. 'Christ,' she teases. 'You must be about to really give me a talking-to if you're paying.'

He narrows his eyes. 'I could withdraw the offer,' he says, and Becca pouts.

'Little Carlos can't take a jokey-wokey?' she says in a baby voice. 'Awwwww!'

'Come on,' he says. 'Before I change my mind.'

It's chilly outside, the air heavy with the threat of rain.

'I can't believe I ever complained about the heat this summer,' Becca says as Carlos locks up. She looks at the ominous clouds despondently. 'It's going to chuck it down.'

'Best walk fast, then,' Carlos says, tapping her on the stomach as though they're in a game of tag and sprinting halfway down the road.

'Are you joking?' she squeals to the back of his head. 'Carlos! CARLOS!'

He disappears around the corner and Becca waits for him to reappear, expecting him to stick his head back around or something. When he doesn't, she walks a bit faster, and when she turns the same corner and doesn't see him, gets confused.

'Carlos?' she says to the air. He's gone. He's bloody well gone! What an idiot! She looks at her watch. It's only 6 p.m. She could loop back around and see if there's anyone at the pub, or stop by at her mum and Betty's. Plodding on, unsure of why Carlos would disappear, she considers going to the pizza place alone. She *is* hungry now the promise of food has been dangled.

'STICK 'EM UP!' a voice booms into her face, so loud and out of nowhere that she squeals, high-pitched and dramatic, at the intrusion of it. Her phone clatters to the floor.

'Ah!' she yells, stepping back and scrunching up her eyes. And then: laughter.

'Oh! My! God! It's just me, you daft cow!'

Becca opens her eyes. 'Carlos! What the hell, dude? That scared me!'

But he isn't looking at her, he's got his eyes closed now too, bent over double, laughing and clutching his sides.

'You pig!'

'I'm sorry,' he wheezes. 'I didn't know you'd *actually* be afraid.' He straightens up and looks at her, still at the edge of his laughter. 'Really,' he says, seeming to note her furious expression. What is he, twelve? 'I'm sorry, OK?'

Carlos reaches down to get her phone; mercifully it hasn't cracked. Becca takes it and slips it into her bag and, dropping her bag to the floor, play-slaps Carlos on the arm.

'THAT is for being a grade-A arsehole,' she tells him with a thwack, and he nurses the site of impact and says, 'Hey!'

She looks at him. She feels better now. Carlos holds her gaze. For some reason, she reaches out and hits him again.

'Ow.'

She gets closer and hits him once more, but before she can make contact he grabs her hand, pulls her towards him, and goes right for her Achilles heel: he tickles her.

'No!' she squeals from the alleyway they've ended up down. She feels a fat splosh of something wet hit her neck, and then again. 'Carlos!' she screeches, gaining purchase to tickle him back, two grown adults behaving like schoolkids.

Another splosh of water hits her. Rain.

'Carlos!'

He tugs at her arm as she tries to reach around to his back, attempting a wedgie. God, she hasn't given somebody a wedgie in years.

'I don't think so,' Carlos grunts, nimbly side-stepping her so she is forced to spin around, lest *he* give *her* a wedgie. She lunges again, and he grabs her arms, and then somehow she's not only got her arms pinned by her sides, but she's pinned up against the brick wall, too, and now it's raining properly: big heavy drops of water that she only notices because of the way they fall on Carlos's face, which she appears to be staring at, and breathing heavily into.

Neither of them speak, but his grip on her doesn't lessen. It's then that Becca realises what she's holding on to: the muscle of Carlos's thick, manly arms. Her grip is just as firm as his is, if not more so.

Time stops.

Becca would like some answers. She'd like answers to questions such as: why is he looking at me this way? Why is nobody speaking? Why does this feel like . . . *something*? He looks at her, and she looks at him, and she couldn't open her mouth and form the words even if she wanted to. This is Carlos! This all feels so weird for *Carlos*.

She can't be enjoying the way Carlos's bicep feels under her hand, or how his pupils have dilated that way. The rain has made the front of his hair slick, so it flops into his face. Becca resists the urge to wipe it away for him, to smooth it back like a lover. This is *Carlos*. The salon is the very best thing in her life; it stands for so much. He's her *business partner*. She releases her grip.

The spell is broken. Their breathing is shallow. Carlos searches her face, his own full of questions, but before they can get into it Becca grabs her bag from the ground.

'Race you there,' she says, sprinting back around the corner, away from the alleyway and him and everything, and she runs the whole way to the restaurant, so fast that she gets a stitch.

19

She Doesn't Text Back

'It's not that I'm not grateful,' Carlos effuses, smoothing down the fabric of his shirt across his taut stomach as he sits in the cab, chest pushed forward in his peacocking way. 'But doesn't this feel like introducing your in-laws? You bring your best friends, he brings his best friends . . . it's all very the merging of two dynasties.'

'No it's not,' Becca says with an eye-roll. 'It's two people dating who want to know as much as possible about each other, which is very romantic and normal. And everyone is so busy that instead of me meeting Sarah and Nate one night, and then Noah meeting you and Jia Li another, it seemed fun to just hang out together. It's been two months already and we're together almost every night of the week. I love him! I want you to know him properly!'

'Hmmm,' says Jia Li as their cab pulls up on Warstone Lane. The sleek red-brick entrance to the restaurant is flanked by leafy branches festooned with lights and two plaques: one with the restaurant's name, the Wilderness, the other with its Michelin-star status.

Carlos looks around at the chicness of their location. 'I suppose when a man says he wants to pick up the tab on a hundred-quid-a-head meal to celebrate his sales in China or wherever it was, who am I to turn him down?'

'Sweden bought his backlist all at once,' Becca corrects Carlos, before leaning towards the cab to help pull out Jia Li. 'You OK, Mama?'

'Grand,' Jia Li says, resplendent in a black robe she bought from the Buddhist temple in town, with a flower crown for added festive effect. At nearly six months pregnant now, she's displaying quite the bump – and quite the cleavage.

Inside is exquisite. The charcoal-black interior and gentle rock music make it cool and relaxed, not the uptight dining room Becca was expecting from a place with tables more in demand than Beyoncé tickets. There are exposed black brick and loft lights, huge banquette seats running the length of either side of the room with mid-century black leather and walnut-legged chairs opposite, making walking through to the table at the back a catwalk-like experience. Noah is waiting, flanked by his best friend and his wife, who beam when they clock Becca and her entourage. She can't wait to spend proper time with them. It sounds like Nate and Sarah are the exact kind of best friends a person could want for their partner: they've been together forever, but they're honest about the work a marriage takes and not arseholes about getting everybody else married off. Noah says that they laugh a lot, and are clearly in love even after a decade. Noah and Becca have been in their own little love bubble, but they're finally ready to come up for air and invite other people into their love affair.

'Hello!' Becca says, opening her arms out first for a hug from Sarah, then Nate. 'These are my friends, both of whom you've heard terrible things about, of course.'

Carlos rolls his eyes. 'Ha, ha,' he says, extending a hand.

'You must be Carlos,' Sarah says.

Becca is only half listening as she searches for Jia Li's elbow to steer her towards the group. 'And this is Jia Li, my ride or die.'

Once everyone has been introduced, Becca finally turns her attention to Noah, all bright eyes and wide smile and a particularly amorous kiss hello.

'Mmmmm,' he says into her mouth as he greets her, and it's sensual enough that Becca bats his hand away from her arse and says, 'Hey, where's the foreplay,' which makes him laugh harder than the joke warrants and makes some of the other diners turn to stare.

'Are you OK?' Becca asks, crinkling her brow. 'You seem . . . I dunno. Everything all right with work?'

'Work?' he repeats, as if he's confused for a moment, before he nods and says, 'Oh, work. No, everything's fine. I suppose I'm just a bit keen that we have a nice night, you know? That everyone gets on.'

Becca looks pointedly towards Carlos and Sarah, who appear to be bonding over a recipe she's showing him on her phone, and then at Nate with Jia Li, saying something about the books *Killing Eve* was based on.

'I think we're good. And look! This place!' she gestures around at the low lighting and glossy interior. 'You're so sweet to treat us when it's your work win. This is amazing. *You* are amazing.'

They kiss again, and this time Becca embraces the booty squeeze.

Noah issues instruction to the waiter that they'll take whatever wine pairing the barperson suggests for each course, except Jia Li, who chugs orange-lemonades like a kid out at the pub with her dad. It's nice being fancy in a fancy place, and tonight it gives her a thrill as Noah commands the room in a way she hasn't seen before. He is kind but precise with what he orders for the table and how he does it. It makes her a little horny, really, three glasses of wine in.

They eat shrimp doughnuts and celeriac tart, crab and cod and a smoked salad with caviar. There's pigeon, too, which Becca likes less, but there's so much ceremony to the evening, to the food, that she rolls with the punches. Everyone is on great form, sharing stories and laughing and toasting. It's exactly as she'd hoped it would be.

'This is nice,' Becca whispers into Noah's ear as their last savoury plate is cleared away and the waiter announces a short break before dessert.

'I'm just going to pop out for a smoke if there's a natural pause,' announces Carlos. He looks at Noah. 'I think this has been the best dining experience of my life, and it's not even over yet.' He wags a finger. He's a little buzzed on the booze and the company. 'I wasn't sure about you, dude, but this . . .' He points his finger at Becca. 'You're in good hands,' he says to her, and Becca has a rush of triumph. She knew Carlos would overlook the polo shirts in the end.

As Carlos pushes back his chair to stand up, Noah interrupts him to ask if he doesn't mind waiting a moment.

'It's just . . .' Noah adds, and there's something to the way he addresses the table that makes everyone immediately hush. *Is he going to cry?* Becca wonders. He looks emotional. Oh God. Men who get their friends together to celebrate a 'work thing' invariably have news about work that means travel, or time apart, or relocation. Becca can feel the other shoe about to drop.

'I've got something to say,' he settles on, and he holds Carlos's eye until Carlos is back in his seat, his face quizzical, his arm draped over Jia Li's chair. Becca looks at Jia Li, who is looking at Noah. Sarah is looking at Becca, though. Her eyes are misty, confusingly, as if she knows what's coming.

Noah stands. 'I wanted you all here tonight because there is something I would like to celebrate. I've led you up the garden path a bit with all the job stuff – there's no Swedish book deal. Well, there is, but that's not why we're here. We're here because . . . Becca – I love you, and I wanted the people closest to us here for this.'

And then he pulls out a ring box from his jacket pocket.

'Oh my God,' Jia Li says. Becca's jaw drops.

'Becca.' She sits, gazing up at him. 'I've been lonely my whole life. And then I met you. You're the MJ to my Peter Parker – you just *get me*. And I just *get you*. Loving you is something that happened so quickly and naturally, and it's something I feel sure I will do for the rest of my life, because we're perfect together, you and me. And it may not have been long since I met you but, like Jay-Z allegedly said: when you've got a queen, you don't reshuffle the deck.'

Becca can't stop smiling. She's being proposed to. She can't believe it. This perfect, gorgeous, beautiful man is proposing to her. It's only been two months, but it's love. There are probably a gazillion reasons why she should slow this down, but she doesn't want to. She has a gut feeling, and it's telling her . . .

'Yes,' she exclaims, simply, which makes everyone laugh.

'I'm not done yet!' Noah says back, laughing.

'Hurry up!' she tells him, banging a hand lightly on the table. Her eyes are filled with tears, about to spill over. 'Noah, oh my God!' She shakes her head and dabs at her eyes, blinking quickly to clear her vision. Sarah hands her a tissue.

'Becca Calloway, ladies and gentlemen,' Noah says, gesturing to her, and half the restaurant has paused their conversations to turn and watch the biggest moment of Becca's life play out. 'Becca, would consider doing me the utmost honour of becoming my wife? Will you marry me?'

Becca looks at him, trying to cement the moment in her memory forever: the way he's holding the ring, the hopefulness in his eyes, the feeling of bliss – heady, woozy – in her stomach.

'I'm speechless,' she says, holding out her hand so he can put the delicate studded band on her finger. She holds it up for everyone to see and says, 'Yes, I'll marry you, Noah Brooks!'

The whole place erupts into applause, and Becca thinks she could explode from the twenty thousand volts of shock and love and pure joy that have just been thrust into her system. They hug and then they kiss and she tells him she loves him. And when she pulls away to turn and hug her friends there's a split second where time slows and Carlos meets her eyes and he blinks. She has a thought she can't quite catch the tailcoats of – something she sees in him that comes as fast as it goes, before he seems to catch himself and rearrange his features into a smile, mimicking the congratulations of everybody else. And the night goes on. She is engaged.

Inside the salon the next morning, Becca is surprised to see Jia Li and Carlos are already there, sitting in the waiting area, faces long and wan.

'Oh!' she says, smiling. 'Morning!'

The pair don't really say anything back, and as Becca fusses with looping her bag off her shoulder and over her neck, sorting out her hair, the air slowly becomes thicker.

'What?' she says, when neither of them speak. 'What happened?'

Jia Li looks at Carlos, who looks at Becca, and then back at Jia Li with a shrug. Jia Li says to him: 'Fine. I'll say it.' She takes a breath and sighs. 'You're really going to get engaged to a man you've known for only a few weeks?'

Becca takes a breath, licks her lips. 'We're going to do this? Really?'

'It's quick,' Carlos reasons. 'What's the rush?'

'This coming from Mr Life-Is-Short himself.'

Jia Li interjects: 'That's his excuse when he's talking about a one-night stand, Becca, not the rest of his life.'

'You're having a surprise baby! Isn't that the same?'

Jia Li throws up her hands with a sigh – and a smile. 'Yes,' she admits. 'Worse, probably. You can't divorce your child.'

Becca turns to get some lip balm from her bag – all that post-engagement kissing has her lips chapped.

'You've got shag-fest written all over your face, anyway,' says Jia Li. 'Look at you! Although, mate, good sex is no reason to get married. *Especially* to a twenty-eight-year-old.'

Reflexively Becca looks up into one of the salon mirrors. She doesn't have a neon sign above her head that says she's been up all night doing terrifically naughty things, but she does look tired. What else are you supposed to do after getting engaged except stay up all night?

'Come on. Plenty of twenty-eight-year-olds get married. It's not *that* unusual.'

'Were you ready to get married at twenty-eight?' Carlos asks.

Becca considers it. 'I'm not Noah, am I?' she shoots back. 'Not that it's any of your business, but his family situation meant that he had to grow up very quickly. He's more mature than either of you.'

Jia Li raises an eyebrow.

'Or,' Becca corrects, 'at least *as* mature as all of us. And you met his friends – Nate and Sarah are religious, been together years. Honestly, I don't think the age gap is an issue at all. The moving-fast thing I get, but not the fact that he's twenty-eight. That's plenty old enough to settle down.'

'OK then.' Carlos nods. 'So you admit that it's crazy fast? Impulsive?'

'Yeah,' says Becca, humbly. 'Of course I do. But I also think . . . when you know, you know.'

'Urgh,' grunts Jia Li. 'Come off it.'

'Right from the night we met, we just clicked – you know that.'

'That's chemicals,' says Jia Li. 'Factually speaking. *Scientifically* speaking. I'm not against mad lust – obviously.' She rubs her belly as she says this. 'But falling in love is supposed to be a mental, hormone-fuelled buzz. I celebrate that for you! Everything he says is funny! All his little habits are still cute! Non-stop shagging!'

Becca smirks at this. 'It *is* excellent shagging,' she says, cheekily.

'Is it at least going to be a long engagement?' Carlos asks. 'Jia Li is right – just until the honeymoon period has worn off, so that you're seeing straight.'

'You're both being very patronising,' says Becca.

'Not patronising,' Carlos says. 'Prudent.'

'Prudent?'

'Prudent.'

'Since when do you use words like *prudent*?'

'Since one of my best friends got engaged to a man she barely knows.'

'I know him, Carlos.'

'Good,' he says. 'It's ... We're happy for you. Just checking in is all, OK?'

Becca's client walks through the door then, ending the apparent intervention.

'I know him,' Becca clarifies, before welcoming Kiran and whisking her to the stylist chair. 'I know what I'm doing,' she adds. And yet, strangely, Becca finds herself unable to meet her own eye in the mirror.

20

She Texts Back

'Bloody hell, Bec – you smell like a brewery. Have you showered today? Or . . . ever?'

It is a miracle that Becca is here, at her dad's house, standing before him and his wrinkled, dramatic nose. The wine, the tequila, the lack of a proper dinner – she should have eaten properly before the pub last night. She'd been trying to get the Carlos thing out of her system. Seeing him at work after their . . . *thing* in the alleyway, both of them acting so normal – *too* normal. It was weird. So after work she'd gone to the pub with Dana, who'd stayed for a bit but then left Becca with some of the Fox and Hound regulars. By the time she got home, Becca had decided to take the Incident, fold it in half in her mind, in half once more, and then in half again. Next, she'd mentally taken that folded memory and put it in a box, wrapped the box in chains, and found the darkest and least-visited corner of her mind to deposit it. The last thought she'd had before bed was a pledge to herself that she'll never get it out for further examination ever, ever again. No need. It had been the first night in two months that she hadn't texted Mike before bed.

But yes, the drink. She is paying for it now. The four slices of buttered toast this morning didn't touch the sides. Her head is throbbing. But she's here, ready to build a bloody pergola in her dad's garden, as promised. Just as soon as she's had coffee. And orange juice. And an hour or two to gather her emotionally fragmented self, because that's what a hangover does to her.

'Be nice,' Becca pouts, closing one eye as a way to demonstrate that her temples are pulsating unfairly. 'I was nice to you after Uncle Brendan's sixtieth. You have to be nice to me today.'

'This *is* me being nice,' Gary insists good-naturedly, letting her into their old family home. There's a comfort to it – there always is. The ornate silver mirrors and heart-shaped trinkets, the massive sofa that sags in the middle and the smell that could not, even with all the time and money in the world, be replicated. To Becca home smells like love. Although *The Smell of Love* sounds like it could be a sex show, now she considers it. There must be another way to phrase it.

She kicks off her shoes and plops down on to the settee, her feet under her, her head resting against the ancient pillows.

'Tea or coffee?' her dad asks, ruffling her hair as he passes through to the kitchen. It isn't lost on Becca that he is using a voice so soft it's actually sarcastic. But she'll take it. She'll take sarcastically nice over anything else right now, happily.

'Both,' Becca replies. 'Double espresso from the machine to start, and a tea to dip my four digestives in please.'

'My my,' Gary yells from beside the Lavazza. She hears him switch it on and the low hum of the machine warming itself up. As he fills the kettle with water from the kitchen tap, he adds, 'We do know how to honour what we want today, don't we?' But Becca can see his reflection in the glass of the kitchen door and she peeks at him, seeing that he's smiling as he says it. It's become a bit of an in-joke between them, because when Becca's mum left him for Betty, there was a lot of talk about how she needed to honour herself and her truth and her wants. Since then, everyone – even Shelley herself, who gets how that sounded despite her earnestness at the time – has sent themselves or each other up by using it. A new family in-joke. *I just need to honour my need for a steak dinner tonight. I just to need to honour my need for a new haircut. I need to honour my desire to ignore what you just said.*

'I'm honouring myself, and all the women who came before me,' Becca shoots back, and her coffee is delivered to her with a kiss to the forehead.

'Not to sound unkind,' her dad reiterates, 'but *did* you shower?'

'No, actually,' Becca admits. 'Maybe I'll do it here before we go? If it's that bad? I just figured we'd be getting hot and sweaty today is all.'

'We will,' he notes. 'But I think if I have to inhale the odours coming off you I'll be drunk myself. Did you have a heavy night?'

Becca looks at him. Gary's not judging, just asking. To be fair, it's pretty unusual for her to (*a*) go anywhere unwashed and (*b*) be hungover to this extent. Becca scrunches up her

219

nose and shifts her gaze from side to side, trying to decide how to respond. Her dad lowers himself to the coffee table in front of her so that he sits, and they're eye-to-eye. He waits.

'I . . .' She picks her words carefully. Her dad knows Carlos, after all. 'I feel like Carlos is mad at me,' she settles on. 'And then Mike has started this contract in London and even though he's back most weekends, I hate that he's away, as if he might choose another place or another job over me like he did last time, even though we're not . . . you know . . . Technically we're friends, but not *just* friends. I don't know. It's a whole thing. And Jia Li is pregnant,' Becca tells him, then, warming up to her theme of self-pity and All the Feelings. 'I'm a bit jealous of that, which is embarrassing. I feel . . .'

'All mushed up inside?' her dad supplies. Becca nods. 'That makes sense,' he agrees.

'Like a teenager.'

Becca's dad looks at her kindly. 'You'll always be teenage Becca to me. You were born a teenager. So independent, so determined – and so moody. You always had time for your old dad, though. Your mum? She bore the brunt of all your existential angst. But for some reason you always found kindness for me.'

Becca reaches for her espresso. It is thick and bitter, and as soon as it hits her tongue it perks her right up, a rush of energy zipping through her veins, awakening her brain. She finishes it in two gulps and she smiles at her dad gratefully.

'You like Mike, don't you?' Becca asks, surprising herself with how much she wants somebody else to tell her what to do, to reassure her that she's going to be OK. Coco said she was going to get everything her heart desired, but between Mike's London job in the week and his dad's illness, lately she's felt like she only gets scraps of him. She wants can't-live-without-you, all-in, all-consuming love. But what kind of a person gets mad at someone for having a lot on their plate?

'Hmmm,' Gary muses. 'He still a cheeky little bastard?'

'Yeah.' Bec smiles. 'Cheeky and silly and easy company, like always. He's asked me if I want to go away with him in early November. His parents have a reservation in the Lakes they can't use because of Paul's treatment. They can't make the timings work alongside his hospital appointments, and they want to send us since it's non-refundable.'

'And did you say yes?'

'Yeah.'

'Well,' he says. 'An underestimated quality if you ask me, being easy company. Fireworks are great, big laughs and huge passions – but day in and day out, it's nice to rub alongside somebody comfortably. A lot of life is just sitting beside somebody else, after all. Sitting on the sofa. On a plane somewhere. Being side by side when you drive in the car.'

'You make it sound depressing.'

'No!' Gary insists. 'It's the opposite of depressing. Good company makes even a trip to the hardware shop an adventure.'

'And just like that, he got the day back on track.' Becca says it smiling, shaking her head. Her dad looks at his watch.

'It *is* half past ten already,' he says with a wink. He gets up and disappears into the kitchen, returning with two white tablets and a glass of water. 'Take these. Shower. Decide to have a good day. And get your DIY-pants on. We can talk, but we must also build.'

Becca takes the pills and downs the water.

'OK, Napoleon,' she declares. 'Whatever you say.'

'I say: first, B&Q. And then, the world.'

'Your ambitions for this pergola are dizzying,' replies Becca, her eyebrow raised.

B&Q is a maze of men who all look alarmingly like Becca's dad: cargo shorts with pockets and round-neck T-shirts in faded shades that betray their age. Becca remembers childhood holidays with her dad in the T-shirt he is wearing today, so that must make it *at least* twenty-five years old. Boomer dads: the original slow-fashion pioneers. Although 'fashion' might be pushing it.

Becca navigates the low trolley awkwardly, trying to stop it from snapping at anyone's ankles as she pushes it down the middle aisle, and follows her dad up to where all the garden stuff is, and the materials for building.

'Oh, look,' she points out as they pass a display. 'You can *buy* a pergola set instead of building it yourself. Why don't we just do that?'

Becca's dad doesn't even turn around. She's yanking his chain, of course. Boomer dads don't do flat packs. If they did, how could they prove themselves as men? Oh no. Instead, Gary has got the back of an envelope and a Bic biro scrawl of measurements, walking with a swagger towards a young guy dressed in an orange and black T-shirt, a name tag that says he is happy to help, and is called Michael.

Michael, thinks Becca, automatically thinking of Mike.

As if on cue her phone vibrates in the back pocket of her denim shorts, and it's not lost on her that she feels a burst of excitement that Mike's name is on the screen. *That's information*, she thinks to herself. *So I am happy about him, about us.* She steps away from her dad and his measurements envelope to answer the phone with: 'I'm at B&Q being served by a Michael, and thus you were literally just on my mind.'

She can hear him smile down the line.

'Thrilled to have been thought of,' he tells her, 'but, more concerningly, B&Q? Blink three times if you need rescuing.'

Becca laughs. 'But you can't see me?'

'Right, yes,' Mike replies. 'This is why I never got into the superhero business.'

It's Becca's turn to smile. When Mike doesn't say anything else she tells him: 'Dad's building a new pergola. The old one got knocked down by the big storm we had at Easter. I think he's mad I'm hungover . . .'

'Ah, yes,' Mike acknowledges. 'The last text I got from you was at about seven p.m., saying *Yeah baby! Why not!*'

'I'm afraid I have no idea what I meant. Are you back up from London all right?'

'Yes I am! Four weeks down, four more to go . . . and I just invoiced for my first month too, so I'm finally financially solvent!'

'You sound good,' Becca tells him. 'You sound more . . . I don't know. Happy.'

'I'm getting there,' he says. 'One step at a time.'

'Good.'

'So a pergola, eh?' Mike begins, and Becca knows he is going to offer to help before he even says it. All these phone calls they've had serve to remind her that before he waltzed back into King's Heath it'd been years since they'd talked, before that it was years of getting to know one another, layer after layer after layer. And it turns out that even after five years some of that knowing isn't *un*known, a bit like forever remembering the All Saints rap on 'Never Ever' even though it's not been on the radio in aeons, or how to spell 'difficulty' after reading *Matilda*. 'If you want any help . . .'

Becca looks at her dad, waving his arms and issuing instructions to the assistant, supervising the cutting of wood, checking the back of his envelope again.

'My dad has been talking very fondly of you this morning, actually,' Becca admits, and Gary looks up and tips his chin as if to say, *Who's that?* Becca covers the mouthpiece and mouths that it is Mike.

'Ask him if he's coming to help an old man put up the pergola of dreams,' he jokes, leaning to shout a bit louder, 'Bring lunch!'

'Did you hear that?' Becca asks, shaking her head at her dad, secretly pleased. She can get her dad's take on him, and won't have to work as hard with the hammer if Mike is there to do it.

'I'll be there at about one, then,' Mike tells her. 'Lunch in hand.'

'Noooo,' Becca insists. 'You don't have to; we're both kidding. I can see you later for that coffee?'

'I'm not doing anything else,' he tells her. 'I'd love to catch up with your dad, and I'm pretty handy, if you remember. My dad wants to be left alone this weekend apparently. Sick of us all fussing and worrying.' Becca hesitates. 'But I don't want to intrude,' Mike adds.

'Um,' says Becca. 'I mean . . .' She thinks about it. 'I'm happy for you to intrude. But only if you're sure.'

'I am.'

She smiles. 'I don't know if you're my saviour, then, or Dad's.'

'I'll settle for both.' Mike chuckles. 'See you shortly.'

'There he is,' a voice comes as the side gate to the garden is flung open. 'Mr C! I'd recognise those cargo shorts anywhere!'

Becca looks up from where she's squatting, helping to lay out all the bits for one side of the wood structure they're building. They're using the base from the old pergola, which remained intact after the storm, so they can get right to assembly – thankfully.

'Mike Henry,' Becca's dad salutes. 'As I live and breathe.'

The men embrace, a friendly whack on each other's backs, like long-lost brothers reunited after the war. And then Carlos appears behind them.

'Carlos! Hello!'

Gary and Mike drop their hug, and Mike stands back to smile at Carlos and waits to be formally introduced.

'We've met at the salon,' Carlos tells him. 'But hi, I'm Carlos.' Carlos and Mike shake hands, and Becca nods at Gary, who then turns to Becca and says, 'I forgot to say, love

– Carlos called when you were in the loo and I picked up, asked him over. More the merrier, et cetera. I hope that's OK.'

'Sure,' Becca says. 'I mean, we need to talk about privacy when it comes to answering my phone, but that's not a chat for now.'

'I'll look forward to that later then!' Gary chortles, delighted to have raised such a sassy and funny girl.

'I brought beer and Soleros,' Carlos says, holding up a reusable tote that says *Hair Is EVERYTHING* on it.

'Sandwiches and Fanta lemon,' Mike says, holding up his own reusable tote, which says *Books Are My Bag*.

'Excellent,' Gary says. 'Carlos, do you mind playing chef and plating up? Mike, just come and take a look at this, would you?'

Mike and Gary busy themselves using two cut-offs of timber to measure the distance between the poles, making sure they're the same length before laying a rafter across the top.

'About two hundred mil either side?' asks Mike, squinting.

'I reckon so, yeah.' Becca's dad nods with a weightiness akin to a bomb squad choosing between the red or the blue wire.

'This looks like a giant game of Tetris,' Carlos quips, emerging from the house with plates of sandwiches and crisps. The other men wave a hand, acknowledging what he's said but not replying. They're focusing.

Carlos puts everything down on the garden table and Becca watches him note that the outdoor pillows aren't out of the storage box for the accompanying chairs. He knows his way around, though – Carlos has been treated like an extended member of the family since starting Trim with Becca, enjoying Sunday lunches and the odd beer in the garden after work if Becca was stopping by too. Carlos's mum and dad moved to Gran Canaria when he was nineteen, and he says it's nice to feel like he's got an 'England mum and dad'. In fact, he probably took her parents' divorce harder than Becca did, until he realised that Betty and Shelley wouldn't take away from anything, but add to it. He couldn't believe everyone would be so amicable, in fact.

Becca watches Carlos open the grey garden storage box by the back wall and leaves Mike and her dad to Be Normal, as she'd promised herself, and help him. Carlos pulls out the pillows, and she matches the right cushion to the right chair. She wanders to the food table when they're done, nicking a crisp from one of the bowls.

'Mike's here,' he says to her quietly, an eyebrow raised, as he fluffs up a striped cushion.

'I'm beginning to think Dad didn't reckon I'd be much help,' Becca says. 'He's getting everyone involved today.' She looks at him. 'I'm hungover. Got carried away with Dana in the Fox last night.'

'Nothing wrong with a bit of fun,' Carlos replies, nicking a crisp too.

'What did you get up to?'

There's a formality to them; they're both trying too hard to be normal.

'Saw Amy, actually. Hung out.'

Becca finds herself surprised. 'Oh. Are you sleeping with her then?'

Carlos shrugs. 'A gentleman never kisses and tells,' he says, and right as Becca is about to joke that he's not a gentleman he heads inside to get the Fanta. She takes the hint: Amy is not for discussion. She remembers the way he held her in the alleyway. She wills herself not to.

'I'll help with glasses,' Becca tells him, following and manoeuvring around him in the kitchen and pulling out four tumblers from the cupboard beside the extraction fan.

'Mike and your dad seem . . . close.' There's an edge to Carlos's voice, almost like envy. Becca puts the glasses down on the worktop and sees he's peering at them out of the window. She watches what he watches: Mike and her dad bent over the wooden frame, pointing and squinting.

'They were, yeah, back in the day.' She pulls herself back from the edge of making a joke. What was it Carlos had told her? He has feelings, too. That he's supposed to be *in* on the joke, not made fun of. 'Obvs they've not seen each other since we broke up.'

'How's his London job going?'

'Good. I think it's good for him. He seems happier.'

'That's good.'

Becca doesn't know what else to say.

Carlos raises his eyebrows. Nods. Taps his fingers on the draining board.

'You sizing him up for me?' she settles on, knocking a shoulder against him.

Carlos looks at her. 'Of course I am,' he replies, and then he floats back outside, leaving Becca to watch the three of them, chatting about the pergola together: her dad, her ex and her friend who quite clearly does not approve, the one whose grip she can still feel on her skin, even though she tries not to.

21

She Doesn't Text Back

It's mid-September when Noah asks his fiancée of less than a month if she wants to come with him to Miami.

'There's an SF convention there – SF AuthorCon Miami, it's called – and I go every year. I sit on some panels, sign some books and whatever. I don't want to be away from you for a week. What do you think?'

They're in bed together, a summer storm raging outside and breaking the heat that has come to be almost unbearable these past few weeks. Becca has lit candles, is wearing her sex nightie, and Noah has just wiped himself off with a towel after they played with massage oil and he'd . . . well. Really rather enjoyed it. They've been experimenting together, indulging in what Jia Li calls *naked play*. There's sex, and then there's everything that comes with it. The touching, the stroking, the *togetherness*, everything the Spice Girls sang about in '2 Become 1'. Becca is happy. There's a levity to her lately. Colours are brighter, smells are sweeter, love songs have been written just for her.

Falling, falling, falling. She'd thought she was in love before, but it's like every day since they got engaged she goes deeper and feels more.

'I mean,' she says, gently tickling the skin around Noah's belly button, shadows from the flames cast across his sticky, glistening body. 'I *have* always wanted to go to Miami . . .'

She wants to jump and scream that of course she'll go with him. This is exactly what she wants for herself: to be safe, secure, together, taking trips and not being self-conscious about needing the other.

'When is it?'

'Two weeks away,' he tells her. 'My American publisher is putting me up at a place called the Fontainebleau? It's really nice. Don't get me wrong, it's a box room on the first floor, but it has pools and restaurants and it's in Mid-Beach, which in my humble opinion is the best part of Miami. I've been going for a few years now.'

'Wait,' Becca says, holding up her hand. 'The Fontainebleau? I'm *sure* that's the hotel Whitney Houston stays at in *The Bodyguard*.' She reaches for her phone, frowning when it isn't where she left it on the charge station on the bedside table, and then realising it got knocked off earlier on and is, in fact, nestled on Noah's boxer shorts on the floor.

'Probably,' Noah tells her as she googles it. 'They were filming a TV show there when I went a couple of years ago too. It *is* like a movie set down in the lobby, and pretty famous. Frank Sinatra used to go there. God. I didn't realise I knew so much trivia about a random American hotel, but here we are.' Becca feels his nearness as he leans across to see her screen, peering over her shoulder. 'Anyway,' he adds, and she jabs at the screen trying to confirm her theory. 'I don't get paid for the panels I do, but the deal is that I get time off to enjoy it, make it a working holiday. It's cool.'

'Ah-ha!' exclaims Becca, showing him a webpage all about the filming locations *The Bodyguard* used. 'It is the place! Oh God – you know the film, don't you?' She looks at him, searching for confirmation. 'The bit where she's in the big ballroom in those glass earrings and that *fabulous* silver head-wrap? And her performance is just so effortless and Kevin Costner is all brooding and gorgeous and right as she goes for the key change: *poof!* At the edge of the penthouse her name comes up in fireworks – or lights, I can't remember, actually – but it's so, *so* glamorous.'

He shakes his head. 'I have to admit, I thought that *The Bodyguard* was a drama on the BBC.'

Becca blinks uncomprehendingly. He shrugs.

'Is this one of those things you're obsessed with and will now insist I need an education on?'

'If you're going to be my husband, yes. Do you know her music, even?' Becca presses, the answer to his question being obvious. *The Bodyguard* is a modern classic! 'Even this scene I'm talking about, she's singing "I Have Nothing", and *urgh.* I don't think there's a song out there that is as honest about love. Literally one of the first lines is: "Take my love, I'll never ask for too much – just all that you are and everything that you do." Isn't that genius? *Just all that you are and everything that you do.* We all pretend to be so cool and nonchalant in love, but when it comes down to it, I think that *is* what we're asking for, in a way. Like hey, no pressure, but give me your everything and I promise I'll do the same. It's a song with zero chill. You've really never seen the movie?'

Noah shakes his head, watching her so closely Becca instinctively feels a hot flush of self-consciousness and reaches a hand up to her face.

'No,' Noah says, clocking it. 'Sorry, you don't have anything there. I just . . . It's wicked, when you get like this. Excited about stuff. I love that about you.'

'I'm a geek . . .' she starts, and Noah loops an arm around her shoulders and pulls her in to press his lips to the back of her neck. He gives her a kiss, and then another one, and another, little butterflies trailing across her body, around to her front until he's at her breasts, tugging off her nightie and kissing lower, and lower, and lower, until he is between her legs and Becca isn't thinking about Whitney Houston, or being a geek, only how this is so right, how powerful it feels to not only have a boyfriend kissing her thighs this way, but her *fiancé*. Her soon-to-husband. Something about that makes what he's doing even hotter.

22

She Doesn't Text Back

Driving over the water from Miami International Airport to Miami Beach, Becca pulls off her sunglasses to take it all in properly. She hadn't been able to sit next to Noah on the flight since she was a last-minute addition, and she missed him. He passed her a note down the seven rows separating them, other passengers furrowing their brows and then smiling as they realised they were part of a love story, craning their necks to watch her open it. Echoing her thoughts, it said, simply, *I miss you!* She wants to get to the hotel to have a hot shower and then *not* get dressed again.

'Look at this place. Woah. This is the hotel?' she says as they come off the highway on to the tiny floating island they'll be staying on. The hotel is huge and imposing, a massive white thing with a thousand tiny windows, the building curved like a comma.

'My sentiments exactly.' Noah smiles, and Becca continues to marvel as he tips their taxi driver and a bell boy grabs a luggage trolley for their little hard-shell Away cases.

'I don't think I've been anywhere more glamorous,' she tells him in the white marbled lobby. It's punctuated with the odd black tile and seems to stretch on for millennia. Tasselled, glittering chandeliers twinkle overhead, but the people aren't especially glamorous, she notes. It's just folks on vacation or business – families, even, making their way out to the pool. It's relaxed, but fancy to look at.

'You see that there?' Noah asks, pointing to a winding staircase at the far wall. 'That's the staircase to nowhere. It's where the cloakroom used to be, so women could check in their coats and then walk down on display to everyone to show off their dresses.'

'My feminist sensibilities *should* be on high alert at that,' Becca tells him, 'except I kind of want to wear a nipped-in waist and be admired across the lobby myself.'

As they wait their turn at check-in, Noah leans in and whispers, 'How about you wear nothing, and get admired across our bedroom?'

She bats at his arm playfully, as if she'd put up any resistance to the idea.

It's humid. The air in Miami has no concept of personal space, pressing up against their skin, but out by the pool where they spend a few hours in a small cabana, ordering food and drinks and snoozing, it doesn't matter.

'So what's the plan, man?' Becca asks him, once they start thinking about where to go for dinner, how the week might play out for them.

'I can send you my schedule,' Noah says. 'And I don't mind telling you – despite the fact I know you'll take the piss – I have an Excel doc with places to go, stuff to do.'

'You keep a spreadsheet of where you've been?' Becca asks, stuffing the last of some cold French fries into her mouth. She's ravenous. She could order another basket, now she thinks about it.

'Only for trips I do for work – you know, when time off is of the essence and you wanna make sure you don't waste your one night of freedom or whatever on a crappy experience. I don't do it in real life.'

'Hey,' Becca tells him, holding up her hands. 'No judgement! I'll take the spreadsheet, for sure. You're engaged to *me*, so evidently you have great taste in *experiences*.'

He takes a stray cushion from their little double sunbed and chucks it at her.

'And the convention – should I come with? What's the vibe?'

'The vibe is anything and everything SF: authors talking about their books, like me, but also lectures on everything you could think of, a chance for SF fans to network and meet up or even dress up . . . it's pretty intense. I one hundred per cent do not expect you to attend *anything*. To come all the way to a place like this and spend all of it in a dark box with no natural light is criminal.'

'Well, I'd like to at least stop by at some point. I didn't come all this way to *not* see you in action, after all. You hardly ever talk about your work – I have no context for who you are when you're out there in the world doing your job. I suppose a lot of people never get to see their partner at work, but when your work is so public . . .'

'The *promotion* of my work is so public,' he clarifies.

'See,' Becca smiles. 'I don't even know the words or the nuances. You teach me so much,' she says, but with an accent, hamming it up to soften her sincerity.

'It's nothing compared to what you teach me.'

'Down, boy.'

In the end, they agree that Becca will accompany Noah to the opening of the event, where he's on a panel of science-fiction authors and she can get a sense of the occasion. She sits there, in the aisle seat of a long row in her mid-calf floaty summer dress that is perfect for the heat but terrible for weathering the high-octane air conditioning in the theatre, which she quickly realises is needed because the place fills up fast, and to the brim, body heat pulsating.

If she thought science fiction meant a particular type of person, she quickly understands she assumed incorrectly. There's every type of person here, all with matching plastic lanyards around their necks, and conversation happens easily, happily, between folks she's sure were strangers even just a moment ago. The lights go down and everyone applauds, and then a host comes out to take a seat on the chair situated farthest from her entrance, leaving four other chairs free, Becca presumes for the guests.

'Good evening,' the woman on stage says. 'This is the 24th SF AuthorCon Miami, and this is our opening night round-table event, *What can SF do that other genres can't?* I am your host, Jenny Chen, and I am proud to welcome to the stage Deepti Kaur!'

The audience issues a roaring applause.

'Charles Wachozski!'

Applause.

'Rachel White! And Noah Brooks!'

Does Becca imagine it, or is the clapping louder for Noah? People are *whooping*, even. Becca looks around. The audience is, without exception, looking towards the stage with rapt attention. Nobody has a phone out, nobody is looking down or around – well, except for her.

'Shall we get stuck in?' Jenny asks, as much for the audience as the panellists. 'I could spend ten minutes introducing you all and reading out bios, but I think it's safe to say that none of you need *any* introduction.'

More whooping from the audience. Becca finds herself beaming from ear to ear. The energy in the place is electric. She knows that she can give people a great feeling from a great haircut, but this is a whole other level. She hadn't known Noah was a literary rock star.

'I know, I know,' Jenny tells the crowd. 'I feel exactly the same way.'

Everyone laughs, including Noah, Becca sees. She watches him. The way he moves in his chair, the way he fiddles with the microphone he's been given. He's sweating a bit, and looks down a lot, but not out of shyness – it's like he looks down to focus on what's being said. It's cute. He looks beautiful up there. She's proud of him.

'We're going to do exactly what it says on the tin,' Jenny tells the authors, 'and get right to it. What *can* SF do that other genres can't? Deepti?'

Deepti has ravishing waist-length black hair so shiny Becca feels she could probably see her own face reflected in it if she got close enough. She has wide brown pools for eyes and bright red lips. When she smiles, it warms the room.

'Well,' Deepti says, 'personally, I love love. Obviously that's what I started in, straight rom-com. But in a conventional love story, as an author I felt limited to boy meets girl. Boy loses girl. Boy gets girl back. And that absolutely has merit, and I still read those stories, but I started to dabble in more speculative fiction, you know? Playing with time or more dystopian settings, and I just realised it gives me so much more room to explore my own storytelling. You can have boy meets girl, boy loses girl, girl dies, girl comes back as a vampire or robot or goddess or *anything*. And that's so freeing.'

Charles, a very short, slim man with a beard, nods beside her. 'That's so interesting,' he says, his American accent smooth like silk. 'I feel the same way. It throws up new considerations, right? If she comes back as, like you say, a vampire or robot or whatever, is it really her? Can she still love him? If she lives forever and he's human, what does that mean? Does he care that she's a vampire? Of course I do a kind of SF/Fantasy crossover, so there's even more freedom there.'

'Yes!' Deepti nods. 'And that's not to say those conditions for writing are an improvement in any quantifiable way, it's just that it gives us – well, me, anyway; I won't speak for all of us! – more to work with.'

'Cool.' The host nods. 'I suppose it must take your imagination to more extreme places than what's possible in other genres, Rachel?'

Rachel nods, pushing her thick, black-rimmed glasses further up her nose and then using a hand to smooth down her red bob. 'Yes,' she agrees, her voice merely a squeak. 'And I think SF allows us to comment on contemporary society from behind a sort of mask, the mask of future society, say, or an alternate universe. Rachel dares to look up, then, at the audience. She's a small, shy little thing.

'We love you, Rachel!' somebody shouts, inciting more laughter.

'I love you too,' she replies, quietly. 'Whoever you are.'

Rachel looks at Noah then, who must feel it because very quickly, almost imperceptibly, he looks at her, then straight back down at his lap.

'Absolutely,' he says into his mic, still looking down. 'I think it is a genre that lends itself to the possibility of new horizons, a new world.'

'Yeah,' agrees Rachel. 'And I do think SF gets a bit of a bad rep amongst more literary types but at the end of the day good books are good books, and they're all about humans, really – the human condition.'

'Also,' says Charles, pausing before he delivers the next part of his sentence, 'SF is just cool, too.'

The host chuckles. 'Fair point,' she says, nodding. 'Excellently made.'

Deepti adds: 'You say that with humour, Charles, but I feel the same. All I want is to bring light to a dark world. Who cares how? It's entertainment, you know?'

'And how do you get started with that mission?' asks Jenny. 'When you sit down at the blank page do you have the whole story planned out, or are you writing to see what will happen just as much as readers keep turning pages to find out?'

'For sure entertaining myself,' says Charles. 'That's how I know if I'm doing a good job. If I'm having fun doing it, I know my readers are going to enjoy it too.'

Noah finally looks up. 'I love that part,' he says, then he squints. 'Sorry,' he says to no one and everyone. 'These stage lights are so bright and so hot I am melting here.' Laughter. 'Um, what was I going to say? Oh, yeah. The what-if part. That's what I do it for. I love asking myself *what if?* and taking it from there.'

'Can you clarify what you mean by that?' the host presses, adding: 'And also yes, I agree about these lights. This is like interviewing you on the surface of the sun!'

The audiences love it.

'Just that, with *what if*, there are no limits as long as what you're writing is credible. What's that saying about how *you couldn't make it up?* We say that when life is wild and doesn't make sense. In fiction, to be credible, what you write has to make sense even if it is a crazy scenario or situation or world. So, asking myself *what if* in terms of *what if the world was run by trolls?* OK, well, I can write a world run by trolls, sure, but the way everyone acts and behaves around that has to be believable too.'

'Like we said about all stories being human,' Rachel chimes in. 'You could say, for example, what if she breaks up with her boyfriend? What if she regrets it? What if she got the chance to say sorry?'

For a split second, Becca thinks of her ex, Mike. There have been others, but Mike was the significant one. What if she'd gone with him to New York after all? Or even, what if she'd replied to his text back in June, when he'd reached out? What if she bumped into him here, or at home? She gets a weird sense of déjà vu or something like it: herself, in another universe somewhere, drinking wine at a party with Mike, his family all around. But no. She did the right thing. Her fiancé is up there on stage, in his element. It was supposed to be this way.

Noah looks up at Rachel again, and suddenly there's a sixth sense tapping Becca on the shoulder.

That look means something, she thinks to herself.

'And that human predicament can be set against a zombie apocalypse, medieval dragons, *anything*.'

Noah moves his microphone to speak but decides against it. What is that look on his face? Is he blushing? Flustered? Becca watches Rachel then, the noise of the auditorium fading out as Becca hones in on her expression, her body language, the smallness of her body but the largeness of something else – her presence, somehow. She's not all bells and whistles but she's got presence. That much is undeniable.

Noah sneaks another look at her, at Rachel, and Becca can see for sure that he is pink-cheeked.

And then everyone is on their feet and clapping and cheering, and the event is over and Becca cannot observe any more. *That's the ex,* she realises. *Why didn't he tell me she'd be here?*

Becca is mad. After the opening event with Noah's ex, she waits for him to explain. Becca wants to know if he knew she'd be here, and if so why didn't he warn her? She feels silly and foolish, watching Rachel bat eyes at her soon-to-be-husband that way. Does Rachel even know Noah is engaged? But when Noah came to find her afterwards he was so hyped up on adrenaline that he barely noticed Becca's hesitation. She doesn't want to spoil his work event, and doesn't want to go around throwing accusations when she's not sure, exactly, what she'd be accusing him of, but when he suggests a late lunch it seemed obvious it's so he can explain.

And yet, sitting here now at a small Greek taverna called Mandolin, back across the bay, Noah is carrying on as normal.

It's a beautiful place. From the outside it looked like a squat single-storey white box with sea-blue shutters, but the shaded courtyard at the back is spacious and welcoming, greenery hanging over them and trees actually growing up from the ground right there in the middle of the outdoor restaurant, the wooden tables and benches arranged around them.

'Are you guys ready to order?' asks an olive-skinned beauty of a man with eyebrows so impressive Becca wouldn't mind getting the name of his salon. 'Or do we need a few minutes?'

243

Noah puts his menu down. 'Shall we just get a bunch of stuff?'

'Sounds great,' Becca tells him, and Noah reels off dishes: roasted cauliflower with Aleppo-peppered garlic yogurt; mussels with white wine and garlic; Swiss chard horta; grilled octopus.

'And a small bottle of the Retsina please.' He looks at Becca. 'Unless you want the full?'

'No, no,' she says. 'A small bottle to share sounds great. Thank you.'

'You OK?' Noah asks, once the waiter has come back with their wine and poured them both a tumbler of it. 'Jet-lagged?'

'No, not jet-lagged. I'm fine,' she insists, in the way that women often do when they are anything but. 'Hungry,' she adds, doing her best to sound more upbeat. 'It all sounds so good.'

Surely he's going to bring up Rachel. Any second now, he'll do it. Surely.

'I love it here,' he says. 'A group of us came the year before last, then last year too. Just a relaxed vibe, *amazing* food done simply, you know?'

Becca sees her chance. She's not proud for needing to get to the bottom of this but there's just something in her, the most primitive, jealous part, that needs reassurance.

'Oh yeah?' she asks, taking a gulp of the wine and willing herself to sound nonchalant. 'Who came?'

'Last year?' he clarifies, and Becca nods, remembering to add in a non-threatening smile. God. Why is she like this?

Why can't she just ask him outright? It's not a big deal. She has exes too, doesn't she? And yet. *That feeling.*

'Well, you met some of them at the event – Deepti and Charles and everyone.'

Becca notices that he hasn't named Rachel out loud, despite her being there.

'My agent came last year, because he represents a couple of us, and that was wicked, schmoozing a bit. But yeah. It's the same crowd every year. I suppose that's why I do it. It's a nice excuse to have a hotel paid for.'

'Right, yes,' agrees Becca. She drinks more wine. 'Rachel seems nice,' she says, inwardly cringing by how it sounds coming out of her mouth. 'I enjoyed what she had to say.'

'She's cool.' Noah nods as a bread basket and some olives are delivered. He busies himself dipping bits into the oils on the table, saying something about the difference between good bread not needing butter, that it's better this way. Becca tries again.

'You must all get up to some mischief. You know, if you all come every year. Like a high-school reunion.'

'Be a good arc for a book, that,' he replies. 'The same group of people meeting up and how the dynamics change every year.'

'It would,' she says, seeing her 'in'. 'You must have had dalliances or whatever, then you see them the next year and circumstances have changed . . .'

He looks at her. That's got his attention. 'I suppose,' he says, slowly.

'Is there somebody like that here for you?'

245

She hates that she is asking. Hates, hates, hates.

'Well. We all have a past, don't we?'

Evasive, notes Becca. Interesting. She eats her bread and drinks her wine and looks around to see if their food is coming. They only ordered ten minutes ago. It isn't.

'Is Rachel your ex?'

'Not my *ex*, no . . .'

'Noah.'

'We've . . . sort of been together, yeah.'

Becca puts down her wine. 'And you didn't think it would be polite to forewarn me she'd be here?'

Noah shrugs. 'I didn't know she'd be here. I would have told you when I invited you if I had. I found out she was here five minutes before we went on stage.'

'But the same people come every year.'

Noah looks at her then, opens his mouth and then closes it.

'I'm not trying to trip you up or catch you out,' Becca says. 'I love you. That wouldn't be kind. But I just . . . Why wouldn't you tell me?'

'I don't know.'

Their food arrives, and it sits between them, untouched, as they sit in silence. Becca can't get a hold of it. Noah is closing down the discussion, Becca thinks. Noah, the man who talks about anything and everything, doesn't want to talk about this. *Which is more information,* she thinks. *This means something.*

Noah sighs, and Becca can tell he's annoyed. The dark cloud passing over his features, the minor scowl, the slump of his shoulders. Why isn't she letting this go? She's a dog with a bone, a kid refusing to turn off the TV for bedtime.

'What?' she asks.

'Nothing,' he says. 'You're just . . . being weird, is all.'

'I happen to think you're being weird, is all,' she shoots back. 'I don't think I'm asking anything unusual.'

'OK . . .' he tells her. 'Do you regret coming or something?'

'No!' Becca implores him. 'I mean, do you regret asking me?'

'I *didn't*,' he says, and she thinks he's half joking but it bruises her. She's tender. 'But it's supposed to be fun, Bec, being here. And I have to be honest, you don't seem to be having any.'

On the inside she's screaming, *Reassure me! Let me know it's safe to keep falling!* Yet her mouth forms different words.

'I'm having fun.' The comment would carry more weight if her tone of voice matched up. As it is, she sounds furious. She tries again, softening. 'I'm having fun, Noah. I'm sorry. Maybe I am just tired, is all. If you didn't know she was going to be here . . .'

'I'm tired too,' he says. 'Come on, let's eat.'

They eat mostly in silence, occasionally commenting on the food or a nice bird perched on a nearby branch.

'OK then,' Noah says once they've finished. 'Are you going to be all right this afternoon? If I go to the convention hall from here?'

If Becca feels a chill, it isn't from the weather. She *wants* to reach out, to hug him, to say she'll miss him whilst he's gone and to have a great time, that she'll be thinking of him but she'll enjoy herself at the hotel, by the pool, maybe take a walk down the beach or grab a drink somewhere lovely. But she doesn't. Instead, she signals for the bill and gives the waiter her card and says, 'I'm a big girl. I'm sure I'll manage.'

'I didn't mean you needed a tour guide,' he says. 'I was just asking.'

'I know,' she says, and what is this tone she's got? What's the tone *he*'s got? 'And I'm just answering. Go, enjoy the signing, stay late if you want to. I'll probably just go to bed early anyway so there's no need to rush back.'

Pushing him away. She's all but using her arms to tell him to back off.

'Oh,' he says, frowning. 'I'll text you, then, see where you've found yourself. Or if you'd rather, I can just give you some alone time.'

Becca stands up and puts on her sunglasses.

'Whatever you think,' she says, and on the kerbside of paradise, her hot new fiancé at her side and a million thoughts racing through her mind, she hails a cab and says: 'You get this one, actually. I'm going to walk.'

When he's gone, she cries. She can't say why, but she does.

23

She Doesn't Text Back

Was that our first fight? Noah texts her later. Becca took a walk after she'd seen him off, tears falling for exactly a minute and a half before she stopped and asked herself what *exactly* this was all about.

It was certainly close, she replies, and he sends a sad-face emoji. She doesn't know what to say to that. She's old enough and wise enough to know it's probably best not to try and resolve anything over text. She decides not to reply. Anything she might say could come off wrong without the context of her voice, her face. Better to make up in person, once she's decided what to say.

It's only half past one, and Noah's schedule has him blocked out until at least 8 p.m. She has a choice: slink back to the hotel and mope whilst getting a massage and a green juice, or turn the day around. What will probably help more is a walk, perhaps some shopping, pounding the pavement into meditation until she calms down and runs out of the energy it takes to lie to herself, so she's only left with how she really feels and what she really needs.

OK then, she concludes. *Option B.*

Her phone map tells her she's right beside the Miami Design District, so she googles that to see if it's worth sticking around. There's always Noah's spreadsheet to consult, but the stubborn part of her wants to discover her own version of Miami. Several articles confirm it's a high-end place to be so she circles back to the restaurant and in their loo cleans up her face, pops a mint, and takes a deep breath. She's in a cotton sundress with a deep V front and back, frills keeping it cute rather than overly revealing. It's a blue and white stripe, and she's got red lip balm and nice leather sandals. With her tote and a bit of sea air in her wavy hair, she's able to look in the mirror and not wince at a puffy, post-cry face. She's cute. She's going to spend the rest of the day on a date with herself. There.

She decides to head off on foot and goes straight to the Institute of Contemporary Art. She's not been to a gallery or museum in ages. There's always a reason not to – the pub, mostly. But she's always enjoyed how small it can make her feel in the context of the world, seeing what somebody else has made, whilst simultaneously filling up a well somewhere – a well in her soul that so often she hasn't realised needs filling.

It's an amazing collection and she's struck, as she walks, that she is halfway around the world, alone, and fine. She could be anybody to the people around her. It's thrilling. She loves King's Heath and the community it provides, but this sense of aloneness gives her a matching sense of hope, the canvases around her daring her to believe that we can make anything of this life if we have the courage to do so.

Her favourites are a Clifford Prince King called *Just the Two of Us*, a photo depicting Black male love in a small kitchen, and an Ewa Juszkiewicz painting of a woman shrouded in a silky turquoise wrap with a delicate décolletage on show, a mass of red curls in place of a face. *Ginger Locks*, it says underneath. It speaks to the hair stylist in her, that the right hair can make us feel like somebody else. She doesn't know if that's shallow, but her ex had studied art and once told her the only right way to talk about it is honestly.

It's a Vojtěch Kovařík that makes her pause. It's an acrylic, a genderless body contorted into a frame in shades of blue, all angular legs and arms. The face is impassive, and the longer she looks at it the more she thinks it's actually a contented smirk, not the sad, reflective notion she saw at first. She looks at the name of it: *Stuck in Place of His Youth*. Instantly she realises: *I can't be immature about this.* She thinks of Noah. The gallery does its job: she's calmer, more rational now. She's letting old wounds dictate how she reacts to a new love. She's worried Noah is going to leave her the way Mike left her, and that's why she has never properly been with somebody since. If she's going to trust him enough to marry him, she needs to trust him with her everything. Noah isn't Mike. They're so different, in fact. Noah is the man she wants to be with, but the notion of truly surrendering makes her feel vulnerable because sometimes things don't work out, even if you love each other and nothing is 'broken'.

Am I testing him? she wonders, knowing that she is.

She googles where to grab a cocktail. That's what she needs now. A crisp, cold drink and a moment to people watch and let herself take a breath. Her phone tells her to go to the Mia Market Miami. She obeys.

At the gift shop on the way out of the gallery she buys a handful of postcards with her favourite pieces on, and then locates the central cocktail bar in the middle of the outdoor market. Settled in with some crisps and a Mojito, she calls Jia Li on FaceTime. Sometimes you just need a piece of home, even when you're on holiday.

'Hey!' Jia Li says, and Becca immediately sees that she's at the salon, working a late finish. 'The intrepid traveller!'

'Hey, friend,' Becca says, and immediately Jia Li frowns.

'You OK?' she asks, and Becca can tell even by the tiny corner of the frame without Jia Li's hair in it that she's in the back room of Trim, away from prying ears and eyes.

'I did a freak-out,' Becca says. 'I picked a fight.'

'Right.' Jia Li nods. 'Well. I'd say that's pretty much on schedule. It's all been a bit plain sailing, hasn't it? Be weirder if you hadn't fought, to be honest.'

'Do you really think so?'

'I know so. Love isn't all hearts and flowers and friction-free. Well, maybe it is if it's a superficial love. But real love needs to exist in real life, and real life has friction. So don't look so sad, boo. It actually makes me happy if you've had a fight – adds some realism into this whirlwind romance.'

'It unnerves me when you're this nice.'

'Practising my maternal side.' Jia Li grins. 'How am I doing?'

'Scarily well,' says Becca. After a pause she says, 'I do love him, Jia Li. I know it's fast, and I know nobody approves, but I do.'

Jia Li nods, digesting the information.

'Sorry to hear that,' she eventually replies, sucking in her cheeks with amusement.

'I know.' Becca grimaces. 'Horrid, isn't it?'

'What, realising somebody else has the ability to crush your heart right there in the palm of their hand? Poof, just like that? Nah. I'd wager a bet he's off somewhere FaceTiming his best friend too, worrying how to break the news that he feels the same – scared, a bit. I actually just read somewhere that relationships are essentially a case of two people breaking each other down, and then rebuilding together. Which makes it sound horrible, but almost kind of romantic, since you're into that kind of stuff?'

Becca exhales deeply. She's so lucky to have Jia Li.

'Who you talking to?' Becca hears Carlos ask then, off camera. Jia Li tells him and he sneaks into frame.

'Bored enough to call home already?' he says whilst mixing a colour.

'I've called for a pep talk, actually.'

'Oh?'

'I'm all fixed now, though. Jia Li did the job.'

'Thrilled to hear it,' Carlos says. 'Are you having a good time? I love Miami. Go to the Design District – you'll love all the art galleries there.'

Becca smiles. 'I just came from there.'

'I hope you got me a postcard.'

'I did, actually.'

Carlos smiles too. 'Well,' he says. 'Don't waste any more time on the phone to us then. Go! Enjoy! I've got a client waiting on a full head and she's got more hair than a Bernese Mountain Dog.'

'OK, OK' – Becca laughs – 'I'm going! I love you!'

'I love you too,' Carlos says, over his shoulder, leaving Becca alone with Jia Li again.

'I just want to say, Bec – if love wasn't so scary everyone would be doing it, you know? Go and say sorry for picking a fight and peel another layer off this intimacy you're supposed to be building. You're a goddess. He'll forgive you.'

She sees Noah across the hotel lobby as she gets back. She sees him pull out his phone, squint at it, type, and then hers beeps.

I'm back, it says.

She texts back, *I know. I can see you.*

He spins around on the marble floor, searching her out, and when he sees her breaks out into a smile. She smiles back, lifting a hand to wave and watches as he uses his phone once more.

I missed you, it says. It beeps again. *I didn't like fighting.*

She looks up. He's waiting for her to read it, people milling about in their evening wear between them, checking in, checking out, heading to one of the restaurants or to a waiting car outside. But the two of them, standing there, are all that matters.

I think I've been a little crazy, she texts, and when he reads it he chuckles and then shrugs in her direction. She takes it to mean, *Well, what can you do?*

I hate to ask, she types then. *But Rachel. Is that . . . finished business? I just need to hear you say it.*

He crinkles up his face at that, and this time he doesn't look back across the lobby at her. He stays eyes down. Becca observes him for a moment, until it feels too tense. Too loaded. Urgh. She's about to get an answer she doesn't want. She can feel it.

Yes, comes his reply. *I didn't know she was going to be here. Honestly. But I told her about you and told her I'm happy. She has a boyfriend.*

He's dared to look at her again now, and so Becca nods at him, a silent *OK.* She smiles.

Can you come over here now? What I want to say next can't be typed.

Becca takes a breath, steeling herself. Jia Li is right. It's been too perfect so far, fast as it's been. And today has helped, in its own way. They'll be even closer after this.

'Hey,' she says as she reaches him, and he touches her wrist, holding it in his fingers. It feels possessive, in the best possible way. She wants to belong to him. She wants him to stake his claim.

'Hey,' he says, and she swears his smile is almost nervous. 'I love you.' He issues a peck on her lips.

'I love you too,' she replies.

'Let's not fight. I should have asked my agent if Rachel was going to be here, and I should have warned you, and I'm sorry. I've felt so nervous all afternoon. I hate fighting. When I met you that day, and we had that ice cream, do you remember?'

'I remember,' Becca tells him, reaching up to touch his cheek.

'I just knew. I absolutely, categorically knew that you would be significant to me and it's happened, Becca. I am not going to mess this up. We're going to have a life together and probably a million little fights, but let's never argue and not make up before one of us gets in a taxi or walks off, OK? I can't handle it. My mum—'

'I'm not going to walk out on you, Noah. OK?'

He swallows, eyes full of tears. 'I'm so scared,' he tells her. 'I wouldn't survive if this didn't work. I need you. I have this thing, you know? About how women leave. And you're the first person . . .'

He lets go of her arm, then, to issue a big wide-armed shrug, and he's shaking his head like he can't believe he's saying all this, that he feels this way, and it's the sweetest, most vulnerable thing she's ever seen, and her heart breaks.

'I'll never leave you,' Becca says to him. 'OK? I promise you that. I'll never leave you.'

24

She Texts Back

Becca had always enjoyed being in the passenger seat when Mike was driving, and today is no different. He picked her up at the crack of dawn so that they could get to the Lakes for lunchtime, in time for a reservation at the pub they're staying at, a beautiful crumbling place with cottages at the back facing the lake. A whole weekend to themselves, no family or friends or distractions.

'It's like you're in a *mariage blanc*,' Jia Li had commented before Becca had left. 'You talk every night, make plans together every weekend he's back from London, but you still haven't even kissed?'

'I don't think it's a bad thing,' Carlos had said. 'She said herself she's not convinced he'll really stay.'

Becca can't articulate what she and Mike are to each other, except that they're something. Between his dad's illness and his travelling, and Becca wanting to be absolutely certain getting back together is the right thing to do, this slow reacquaintance has been decadent but important.

That all said, Becca has shaved her legs and worn her good underwear for the trip, because finally being alone surely means only one thing.

The plan is a nice scenic drive, lunch, a walk around the water, and at some point a trip to the Beatrix Potter museum. In between all that, there's a hot tub on the back patio of their room, and dinner is already paid for, drinks included.

'This is so nice,' Becca says as they come off the motorway and into countryside proper. The view out of the front window is equal parts moody sky, clouds rippling in waves, five hundred shades of grey, and the looming hills up ahead, green and mossy and rugged. The road begins to weave more and more, making Mike slow down in a way that Becca enjoys: that's the point of taking a trip, after all – to slow down, to take it all in.

'I didn't realise how much I needed this,' Mike notes, hands at ten and two, elegant fingers wrapped around the leather steering wheel of his sister's new electric BMW.

'Getting away?' Becca asks.

'Yeah. I mean, obviously I wish none of what my dad is going through was happening at all, and that they could be taking this little holiday they'd planned themselves. But I won't look a gift horse in the mouth: a couple of nights in a bed that doesn't belong to a family member or crappy London hotel is a treat. Not that I'm not thrilled the contract was extended, of course.'

Becca murmurs agreement, understanding, whilst also thinking of said bed up ahead.

Something else Jia Li had wondered aloud: what if by the time they get down to it, they've lost the magic they used to have together?

'What if it's terrible?' she'd asked.

'It won't be terrible,' Becca had insisted. 'It never was.'

Becca turns over the conversation in her mind now. She's hyper-aware of Mike's hands, the way his legs part, spread wide over his seat.

'How's the mood been?' Becca asks as they approach more undulous terrain, the hills that were in front of them enveloping them now on either side. 'Or is that a silly question?'

'Not at all,' Mike tells her, chewing on a Midget Gem. His car snacks are as on point as they've ever been. He's got those, strawberry bonbons, and Dolly Mixtures too, all from the old-fashioned sweet shop on the high street. 'Everyone has been quite chipper, all things considered. I think going over all the treatment options was the hard bit, weighing up the pros and cons, because then you're really staring mortality in the eye.'

'Carlos says the younger the guy, the more likely they are to choose surgery.'

'I heard that too, yeah.' Mike nods, taking a hand off the wheel to stick a finger into his mouth, jabbing around at a tooth covered in sweets. 'But Dad is going for it – going for the surgery instead of radiotherapy or anything like that. Apparently, it's a nice round tumour and should be easy to get out, and he's in pretty good nick so the doctor says his recovery shouldn't be too bad.'

'Thank God for western medicine,' Becca says.

'I know,' Mike agrees. 'You hear cancer, you think death. I mean, at least I do. That's where my head immediately went. But it's so common. A lot of the time it doesn't develop enough to even register, so men don't die *from* prostate cancer but a lot die *with* it.'

'It's that common?'

'It's that common.'

'That's crazy,' Becca notes, reaching for the Dolly Mixtures. Then she has a thought: 'Do you have a higher chance of getting it? Is it hereditary?'

'No idea,' says Mike. 'But I think a lot of men get their bloods done as part of a screening programme now anyway – you know, when they reach a certain age. Fifty, I think.'

'A bit like smears, it sounds like.'

'Maybe,' he replies.

They're using Becca's phone as the satnav and it instructs them to make a left, where the road gets even narrower.

'Small mercies about everything going wrong in New York, though – being around as he goes through it. We've been staying up late on the weekends when I'm back, having some chats about life and stuff. It's been nice. I suppose being in America I put a distance between us emotionally, to deal with the actual distance.'

The satnav tells them to take another left and drive for two miles. Water appears to the left of them, a vast expanse of ink bleeding out against the broccoli-heads of the land.

'Do you ever wonder about divine intervention?' asks Becca.

'That everything happens for a reason?'

'Yeah,' she says. 'Not that you had to hit rock bottom to be here, but, like you say, it all worked out in a way that means you can focus on what's really important: family.'

It starts spitting then, tiny flecks of rain hitting the wind-screen haphazardly. Mike slows down even more. 'Better safe than sorry,' he says under his breath, as if he's reminding himself.

They continue to drive, the sky dark even at midday, the dramatic hills more ominous now. Becca has half a thought about what would happen if they broke down, but then shakes it from her head. They're fine. The satnav says five more minutes.

'I *have* been thinking about what would have happened if you didn't text me back,' Mike admits after a few moments, with enough trepidation to suggest he's not sure he wants to consider that reality. 'Thinking about if we would have still bumped into each other and whatnot.'

Becca reaches out a hand to his knee and squeezes. He smiles at her.

'I never did ask,' she says. 'Why *did* you text?

Mike shakes his head as if he's trying to remember. 'I don't know,' he admits. 'I saw that artwork that reminded me of you, and I knew I was coming back, and I suppose it always felt like unfinished business between us. Nobody did any-thing wrong, nobody screwed up, it's just your path went one way and mine went another. I think I just never stopped loving you, even though we weren't together any more.'

'Mike,' says Becca, touched. 'You big softie.'

'I wasn't even sure you'd message me back.'

'I'm sure that in the world where I didn't I'm not half as happy as I am now, here, with you.'

Mike smiles again as he flicks the indicator, and Becca sees a tiny wooden sign that says *Hope and Anchor* and then underneath: *Pub with Rooms*.

'Even if you're teasing me,' he says. 'That's the nicest thing I've heard all day.'

'I'm not teasing you!' she insists. 'I'm glad we've grown closer again these past two months. I mean, the elephant in the room is that it's all been very chaste . . .'

Mike hoots a laugh, surprised. 'That hadn't escaped my notice, either.'

'I'm not hinting or anything.'

'Of course you're not,' he says, laughing again. 'What was it like?' he asks then, reaching for his fancy recyclable can of water from the drinks holder and taking a long swig. 'Seeing my name on your phone that day? Did it make you happy?'

'It made me scared,' Becca tells him, plainly. 'And confused. But – oh wow . . . actually, I don't think I've told you this . . . about the manifestation ceremony?'

'God, Bec,' he says. 'You and your woo-woo . . .'

'That's what Jia Li calls it too.'

'Because that's what it is.'

Becca wags a finger. 'Let me finish the story,' she says, 'because I don't think you'll take the piss when I tell you this.'

Mike adopts a serious face, with furrowed brows and pursed lips.

'So the salon does these events, right? Book clubs, tattoo parties, cool things to get people in after hours, build community, all that. And I'd read this article somewhere about planning for the summer solstice.'

'The longest day of the year?'

'Exactly. It's supposed to be really potent and ripe for stating what you want from life and helping you get it. We burned sage and told the universe what we wanted from the year and I said I wanted to get married – not to scare you or anything – but you know, to finally find the person I'm meant to be with. And five minutes after we finished, you texted me.'

Mike narrows his eyes as though he isn't sure what to make of this information.

'I had this whole thing about, like, was that a warning from the universe not to be dragged back to my past, or divine intervention that Mr Right was . . .'

'Me.'

Becca makes a face. 'Something like that. It was Dana, at the salon, who's only twenty-five, but wise beyond her years. She basically said people deserve to be heard; that it's stupid to pull the door on the past simply because it's the past. It was like she gave me permission to reply. I know Prince William and Kate got back together after a break-up, but beyond that, who else gets back with an ex and has it work? Common wisdom is that seeing you again would have been stupid, in a way. It's not like we'd been in touch in that time. We hadn't bumped into one another at the pub or park. It had been nothing. Zero. Zilch. And then: *Hey, you up?*'

'I did not say HEY, YOU UP!' Mike laughs. 'It wasn't a booty call. It was a . . .'

'I know,' Becca says. She doesn't need him to explain. 'So, there. Take the piss if you want but to answer your question, I texted back because of a manifestation ritual on the summer solstice, and you're welcome.'

'Well.' Mike sighs. 'I take it all back. Praise be to the woo-woo. Although, let the record show', he says, and they both see the ramshackle ivy-covered pub up ahead at the same time, simultaneously gasping, 'that even if you hadn't replied, I don't think that would have been the last of me.'

The gravel of the driveway crunches under the car tyres with a satisfying sound. Becca winds a window down to get a better look.

'This is adorable,' she says.

Mike pulls into an area marked *Car Park*, written on a wooden sign like the one up by the side of the road, and turns off the engine.

'Do you think,' he says, a hand on the door as if he's about to get out, but feet resolute in the footwell as though he isn't going anywhere, 'that this might be it? Not to be too forward, but you know – even my dad asked. It feels special, Becca, to be getting a second chance with you.'

'It feels special to be getting a second chance with you, too,' she says.

Neither of them move to get out of the car. Mike reaches out to her face, pushes hair behind her ear, half smiles as his chest rises and falls. For a moment, Becca could almost cry. It's all been so right, so perfect – even his weeks in London working out in the end, forcing them into phone calls and

FaceTimes, really doing the work of reconnecting. But it's time, now. Becca bites her lip. Mike leans in.

And then they kiss.

Five and a half years since the last time their lips touched, they find each other again, forehead to forehead and then nose to nose and then his tongue in her mouth and her hand on the collar of his shirt, pulling him in closer.

'I've wanted to do that since the bloody café,' he says when they pull apart. Becca wipes a finger at the corner of her mouth and coyly smiles.

'That might have been a little *too* forward,' she says, and then she looks at him. 'Even though it kind of crossed my mind too.'

'We're like magnets, getting pulled back together,' he says.

'Poetic,' Becca teases.

'I'm serious,' he says, and something about the way he says it, the gravitas to his voice, makes her look at him once more.

'What would you say if I asked you to marry me?'

She stops fiddling with her seatbelt. 'What?' she asks. 'What did you just say?'

'We know each other, don't we? It's not that crazy. I know I want to be with you, and I think you know you want to be with me. All of this – it's for a reason, isn't it? So, what would you say?'

'If you asked me to marry you?'

'Yeah. That's what you asked for at your manifestation ceremony, is it not?'

Becca looks at the sky, as if the answer might be up there.

'If you asked, I'd say . . .' She racks her brain. Surely they're not about to get engaged after a kiss, just like that, out of the blue. It would be romantic, of course, but they only just kissed for the second first time, what, ninety seconds ago?

'I'd say, can we eat?' Becca settles on, looking at him. 'I'm starving. I can't talk to you about the rest of my life when my left bum cheek is asleep from the drive.'

'OK then.' Mike nods, and Becca smiles and shakes her head, thinking this is all rhetorical, that they're just shooting the breeze. They clamber out of the car to be greeted by a woman coming out of the pub's front door.

'Welcome!' she says. 'You must be the Henrys!'

Mike shoots Becca a look and says with a mischievous grin, 'Well, I'm a Henry. She isn't yet. Says she needs lunch before she can agree to marry me.'

The woman looks between them, not knowing what to say next. 'Well,' she settles on. 'Let's get you a table then, shall we?'

Becca thinks Mike is ribbing her, as they order Aperol Spritz and a bread basket and he looks at her, grinning stupidly. He's starting to take the joke too far.

'I didn't tell you about the manifestation stuff so that you could pretend to propose,' she says over the top of her menu. Above the fireplace – stocked with unlit logs for late summer – is a specials board boasting a surf-and-turf platter to share: scallops and lobster, fishcake and ribeye, served with a salad garnish and chips.

Mike follows where Becca's attention has gone to and says, 'We could split that if you want.'

'It's expensive,' Becca points out.

'I'm telling you,' Mike insists, 'they've pre-paid for nearly everything. I think they're just relieved to have me out of the house, to be honest. I *have* been cramping their style.'

'But you'll go to Jessie's when your contract finishes?'

'Yeah,' he says, slurping his drink. 'Which makes sense. I probably should have stayed there all along, but then with a new baby . . .'

'God, you're in the way everywhere, aren't you?' She winks at him, payback for pushing her buttons.

'Low blow,' Mike says. 'Now give me another kiss.'

Becca leans in, smiling, and they knock teeth before they can lock lips, making them both giggle.

'Ouch,' Mike says. 'Be gentle with me, will you?'

'You be gentle with *me*!' insists Becca, and before they can actually kiss the waiter comes to take their order. They settle on sharing the surf-and-turf platter, and order another Spritz.

'Hey,' Mike says, once the waiter is gone. 'That day at the pub, when I first said about the London job . . . ?'

'Yeah . . .' replies Becca. It's redundant now – he's already over halfway through the contract.

'You seemed mad at me when I brought it up.'

Becca considers it. 'Well, you can do what you want, obviously,' she begins, but Mike holds up a hand to stop her from saying any more.

'Let me finish,' he insists. 'I just want to make it clear that I needed this job, and I am glad I took it. I needed the money and, to be quite honest, I needed to feel useful, in control of *something*. I felt helpless before, but after a few weeks here, unemployed, I felt . . . impotent.'

Becca nods. She can understand that helpless feeling.

'But it's just this one contract, and this one extension to it. I get it: I left you before. So if you're nervous I'll do that again, I am saying it as plainly as I can: I won't. I'm not. This is temporary, so I can get back on my feet.'

Becca waits to make sure he's finished, or if there's more to be said.

'OK,' she says, eventually, in a small voice. That's basically it, after all. He's called it.

'OK?' he echoes.

'I'm going to make a choice to trust you,' she tells him. 'And it's up to you to honour that trust, and if you don't, in whatever way, or for whatever reason, that's not on me. That's on you. I believe you.'

Mike looks at her, blinking. 'Well, that's good then.'

Becca laughs. 'Yeah,' she says, drumming her fingertips on the table. 'I happen to think it is too.'

And they look at each other, and they laugh, and then they get back to the kissing. The delicious, long-awaited, perfect, perfect, perfect kissing.

25

She Texts Back

Lunch with Mike is a lingering affair, unrushed and enjoyed. They don't have to be anywhere or do anything, and the pub is open all day so the surf and turf is relished, and after their second Spritz they order very cold white wine served in glasses as big as their heads, and they take a full thirty minutes between their main course and deciding on pudding: chocolate torte for her, crème brûlée for him. They taste each off one another's spoons. The kissing continues.

'You're so bloody sexy,' Mike tells her by the time they have coffee – two double espressos, no sugar. Her foot is rubbing up against his calf, under the table, his hand snaked around her lower back, gently rubbing with his thumb.

Becca giggles. 'Shut up.' She's unfurled as she's been sitting at the table: shoulders more relaxed, breathing deeper. If Mike is like the lakes glistening with rain the other side of the window, she has slipped into him like the cardigan Taylor Swift sings about, reclaimed from under the bed. He still fits. With this new understanding it's exactly as good as it ever was.

*

They get the key to their cottage and Becca goes to open the front door as Mike heads out into the rain for their overnight bags. He's borrowed an umbrella but struggles to hold it as well as the bags, so he's sodden by the time his frame fills the front door, water dripping down his face, seeping out from under his shoes, bleeding wet into the welcome mat.

Becca could make a joke – could say something about home sweet home for the next two nights, or invite him to get out of those wet, wet clothes. But she doesn't. He looks at her, eyes like saucers, breathing heavily. He drops the bags with a thud, turns and closes the front door.

'Come here,' Becca says and, wet shoes and all, he does, pushing her up against the fridge of the open-plan kitchen, grabbing at the parts of her he couldn't before – her breasts, her bum, in between her legs. She wants his touch more than she has ever wanted anything. It almost hurts, how much she wants him.

His hands roam under the hem of her dress, pulling at her underwear. She undoes the button of his trousers, tugs at his boxer shorts.

'I want you inside me,' she tells him, and so it is.

They have sex on every surface it is possible to have sex on, or against, or in front of, in the whole of the small cottage, there on the edge of the lake. When it stops raining and the sky is clear they sit on the back patio in dressing gowns, the air still, the birds the only sound beyond each other's breath, sharing a vape that Mike thought to pack.

He would never smoke at home, he says, it would be disrespectful to his parents. But free for the night, he thought they might enjoy it.

'Jia Li told me we might have forgotten how to do that.' Becca grins as she takes a long pull and lets the weed permeate her bloodstream.

'Bec, I have *never* forgotten how good we are at that,' he says. 'We're *very* good at that, aren't we?'

Becca grins. 'So good,' she says. 'And your stamina is impressive.'

'Thank you.' Mike laughs. 'I think.'

That's how it goes, then, for the next forty-eight hours. They don't leave the cottage. They look at the lake from the back porch. They eat more seafood, and more steak, right there at the pub, and on the drive home, before they get to the motorway, they pull over for one last drink of the scenery, and have sex in the car, too, which Mike says Jessie would kill him for, but that it's worth it.

When they're done, they catch their breath and venture outside to sit on the bonnet, loitering, because this feeling of being together is magic.

'Becca,' Mike says when they're looking up at the clouds. 'I was serious before. You and me – I don't want to mess around. I want to do this.'

She looks at him. 'I want to do this too,' she says, reaching for a hand and kissing his knuckles.

'Yeah?' he asks, and Becca scrunches up her nose, nods, and says, 'Yeah.'

Mike smiles and takes a breath, suddenly sitting upright.

'In that case . . .' he tells her, and Becca watches as he stands up, holding out a hand for him to follow her. He walks her over to an open part of the woods by where they've parked up, with a view of a small stream, where it is cool in the shade of verdant trees. There's a light hum from the insects and Mike gets down on to one knee, taking her hand and looking up at her.

'I have spent every moment since I left for New York knowing that nothing, and no one, would ever come close to the feeling I have when I'm with you. I don't want to waste a moment more. Nothing in this life is certain or guaranteed, except for this feeling I have always had, and always will do. Talking like we do every night, I've loved it, Bec. I want it forever, with you.'

'I feel the same,' Becca says, because it's true. She does. She's scared, because love is scary. But she's never stopped loving Mike. That's why there has never been anybody else.

Becca stands up, and she holds her hands at his chest, and he looks at her and she looks at him and she says, her voice a tiny croak, 'Will you marry me?'

'I wanted to ask you!' Mike says.

She laughs. 'So ask me then.'

He nods, blinking back tears. 'Will you marry me?'

'Yes,' she says, and then they both burst out crying, sobbing happily into each other's mouth as they kiss and kiss and kiss, interrupted only by Mike needing to run back to the car to grab something – a velvet box with an antique ring inside.

'It was my grandmother's,' he tells her. 'My dad's mum. This isn't out of the blue or a rash decision, Becca. I knew I wanted to propose this weekend. I just wanted to make sure you felt this was right too.'

She looks at the ruby ring surrounded by tiny diamonds, stunned.

'Do you want to try it?' he asks, and she nods, too overwhelmed to speak. It fits like a glove.

'Everyone is going to think we're nuts,' she tells him. 'Aren't they?'

'I don't think so,' Mike replies. 'I think everyone knew this was where it was headed.'

'Even before we did?'

'I think we always knew, too, didn't we?'

Becca thinks back to the pressure she'd felt the night he texted. Yeah, she'd known. She'd known that if she replied, this is what would happen, one way or another, sooner or later.

'Yes,' she agrees. 'I think we did.'

26

She Texts Back

There's nobody at Mike's mum and dad's when they arrive after their trip to the Lakes. Initially they were stopping by to get Mike's stuff, so he could move it into Jessie's house, but about an hour from home Becca had turned to him and said, 'You're moving your stuff into mine, aren't you?'

'Oh,' he'd replied, grinning, because if they're engaged, *of course* he's moving into her place and not his sister's. 'Do you want me to?' he'd asked, obviously wanting to hear her say it.

'I *need* you to,' Becca had replied, taking her hand from where it had been resting on his knee and sliding it up his thigh teasingly.

'Message received, boss.'

In Regina and Paul's spare room, Becca helps pack up the clothes draped over the Peloton and admires the efficient packing system Mike has for his 'London case'.

'I quickly learned that I could just take the same five out-fits and call it a day,' Mike admits, moving his toiletry bag from his weekend bag to his work bag. 'Throw in shorts and trainers for the gym and a toothbrush, and I'm golden.'

'Urgh,' grunts Becca dramatically. 'It just doesn't seem fair that you have to leave so early in the morning for yet another week away. The nightly phone calls were fine as a seduction technique . . .'

'Seduction technique?' questions Mike. 'Who was doing the seducing on those calls, may I ask? Because my intentions were *very* pure.'

Becca blinks, as though butter wouldn't melt. 'Mike Henry,' she says. 'Are you telling me that on all those calls over all those nights, all the way into the small hours, you didn't have your hand in your pants? Or imagine me lying in bed with my hand in *my* pants?'

He stops folding clothes and steps towards her. Dropping his voice, he says, 'Well, now you mention it . . .'

He runs a finger down her cheek and then cups the back of her neck. He looks at her, forcing her chin up so her mouth is near his and with his free hand he searches between her legs, tickling her so lightly that it's a tease.

'God, you're good with your hands,' Becca says, enjoying the hold he has over her, how they finally get to touch whenever they want, however they want.

'Yeah?' he whispers, his touch getting firmer, his fingers tugging at the fabric of her underwear.

'Yeah,' she tells him, and it takes another half an hour for them to finally leave the house.

They call at Jessie's on the way back to Becca's, solving the mystery of where Regina and Paul are because their car is in the driveway, as is Becca's dad's Peugeot, and Betty's Mini.

'Why is everyone . . .' Becca begins, but then she stops, because *of course* everyone is here. If Regina Henry had any inclination her son was going to propose, *obviously* she's assembled the families to properly celebrate it.

'They got it out of me on the phone earlier on,' Mike says, the electronic gates closing behind them. 'But for what it's worth, your dad knew it was happening before everyone. I asked his permission last weekend.'

'You did?' Becca marvels, craning to see if she can see anyone through the front windows of the house. She can't.

'I know it's old-fashioned, but I respect him, and I wanted to give him a heads-up.'

'What would you have done if he'd said no?'

Mike tips his head and raises his eyebrows. 'Becca,' he says. 'The man loves me.'

Becca thinks of when they built the pergola the other week, how happy her dad was to see him.

'Everybody loves you,' she replies.

Inside, Jessie has decorated with silver balloons and has a tray of champagne waiting.

'Congratulations!' their assembled families squeal as they walk through the hallway after letting themselves in.

'My darling!' Becca's mother coos, arms flung open for a big mother-daughter hug. 'Oh my love, I'm beside myself.'

'Thanks, Mum,' Becca says, as Shelley turns to Mike and says, 'And you! I always knew it would be you! Come here, beautiful son-in-law!'

Everyone fusses and coos, and Becca gets to show off the engagement ring whilst waiting for somebody to ask if it's all a bit fast, because it is, and she knows it – but they don't. Regina says she's been waiting for them both to come to their senses, Paul says life is short and he's pleased they're grabbing it with two hands, and Jessie and Niall ask if they've set the date.

'It only happened today!' squeals Becca, admiring her ring yet again.

'You could have it here . . .' Jessie suggests, and Becca looks at Mike for his reaction. He shrugs amiably.

'I enjoy the economy of that,' he says, and chuckles, and Becca laughs too.

'It's more beautiful than most hospitality suites,' she concedes, which isn't quite a yes – or a no – but even so Regina seizes on it.

'How marvellous!' she exclaims, clapping her hands in little flashes of movement, like a seal at Water World. 'A nice marquee outside, a band, a DJ for later.'

Becca looks to her own mum, who she's sure will have numerous opinions on her only child's wedding day.

'Fantastic,' she says. 'Fantastic! Regina, how are you fixed for a planning session, maybe next week? I can't do Tuesday or Wednesday, but if you're free for lunch on Thursday?'

'Friday?' checks Regina.

'Friday it is. I'll book us into the garden at the Italian place. Make the most of the last of the summer sun. Gosh, we used to lunch all the time the first time around, didn't we? I'm very sorry it ever stopped. I'll really look forward to it, Regina.'

'Me too, Shelley. It'll be just like old times.'

Becca's dad inserts himself between Becca and Mike then, an arm around each of their shoulders, a ruddy cheer to his cheeks from the champagne.

'Mum's changed her tune,' Becca says to him, and Mike looks shocked.

'I beg your pardon?' he asks. 'Was she a Mike sceptic before today?'

He looks between Becca and her father, and Gary says, 'Only in the ways you'd expect,' and then he winks, letting Mike truly know all is forgiven.

'I hear you were in on the secret,' Becca says. Her dad releases his dual bear hug and leans against the back of the sofa.

'I thought it was nice he came to me,' Gary says, right as Mike gets commandeered by Betty about where she can find the loo.

'I made the grave error of the garlic green beans at lunch,' Becca hears her say. 'Big mistake.'

Gary and Becca roll their eyes good-naturedly. Betty – who would have thought her mother would fall for someone her polar opposite in so many ways?

'I didn't know it was going to be this weekend,' her dad tells her. 'Only that he had his grandmother's ring and knew he wanted to prove his commitment.'

'I know it's fast—' Becca starts.

Gary waves. 'Well, it is and it isn't. It's been a couple of months since he came home. But you've known him for years. Your mother and I knew each other for five months before we got married.'

'But you got divorced,' Becca points out.

'Does that make what we had before then any less real?' her father asks. 'I still love her. We're just not married any more. And the thirty-four years we had together weren't nothing, kid.'

Becca searches her mother out: she's standing chatting with Regina, Jessie and Niall, Paul at her shoulder, holding a bottle and offering a top-up, her new extended family.

'Paul seems in good spirits,' Becca notes. 'His surgery is next week.'

'Amazing what some good news in the family can do to get you through another day,' her dad observes. 'Mike talked about it when he came over, actually – said being home when his dad was going through cancer made him realise this is where he wants to be, wants to settle.'

'That's good,' Becca replies. 'I can't wait for this London contract to be done so he's here properly.'

Her father opens his mouth to speak, and Becca waits for what he has to say. But then he closes his mouth again and shakes his head, as if it doesn't matter.

'What?' she asks.

'It's just . . .' her dad begins.

'Dad.'

'It's none of my business, but then you're my little girl and so it is my business.'

Becca nods. 'That's why I'm asking you to actually tell me what you're thinking, instead of letting you open and close your mouth like a trout.'

'My only advice is to make sure he's settled into a job of some sort before you walk down the aisle. It's not very PC of me to say, but that doesn't mean it isn't true: a man needs a job, darling, proper work so he can feel useful and hold his own. I know he has the short-term contract but he won't feel properly settled until he's earning a living doing something stable and permanent. He was always intimidated by your determination to make the most of your life when he wasn't sure what he wanted to do with his, and I think to keep the marriage happy he has to have his own ways to shine.' Her dad holds up his hands to show he has nothing to hide. 'Just my twopence worth,' he adds. 'Disregard as you see fit.'

27

She Doesn't Text Back

After Becca and Noah get back from Miami, everything is the same – but different. Since the fight about Noah's ex and Becca's pledge to never leave him, he's showered her with even more affection and attention than before. He's still got his flat closer to town, but they stay at Becca's, mostly, since he can work from anywhere he has his laptop and she needs to be close to the salon. He makes her coffee in the mornings and walks her to work, heading to the dog shelter after. They meet for lunch, and he randomly drops pastries and maca-roons and green juice at the front desk for the whole team, saying a quick hello and goodbye. What Becca loves most is that he nearly always has dinner underway when she gets home. *This is better than I ever thought it could be,* she thinks to herself when he hands her a chilled glass of something, or a steaming plate. He cooks; she does the dishes. She vacuums; he dusts. He plans cute dates and she wears her very sexi-est underwear to them. It's him, and her, in bed. Him, and her, knocking knees at a restaurant table. Him, and her, walking the dogs from the shelter together, when they can, up through the woods in the autumn sunshine. They've gone to the local climbing wall, emboldened by their new romance to try things they wouldn't normally try. They've taken a pedalo out on the reservoir. They've eaten ice-cream cone after ice-cream cone, just as they did on their first date – it's their Thing. And it's him and her at night, when the sky has darkened and they've had dinner and maybe even had sex, on the sofa, or on the kitchen floor, or once – regrettably – on the carpeted stairs. Becca still has friction burn from last week on the bottom part of her back, and Noah's knees are still scabbed.

Weeks pass that way, time spent and memories made, which is why Becca has *insisted* he come tonight, to Trim's annual tattoo party. She's barely seen Carlos and Jia Li outside of work, preferring to reunite with Noah at every available moment. She was given a grace period, she knows, the time all friends must acquiesce to when their pals fall in love, but the odd comment about how she's never around has given way to out-and-out threats from them: she'd better start making time for them, or else.

'Bec, can we stop by the pub? Not to be crass but – I gotta drop the kids off at the pool?'

They're just at the edge of the park, about to turn down the main street, Trim up ahead.

'Woah. I don't think you've ever talked to me about needing a poo before,' Becca says, trying to decide how she feels about such a revelation.

'The magic can't last forever.' Noah shrugs, giving her a kiss on the top of her head. 'Or it can – it just needs to involve the very human trait of nervous stomachs. And to be fair, if I can hear you panting because it hurts to pee, you can assist me in finding somewhere to take a dump.'

Becca holds up a hand. 'I'm drawing the line at the phrase *taking a dump*. And', she adds, ushering him towards the Fox and Hound up on the corner, 'that panting was a water infection that was caused by too much sex, so, in a way, it was all your fault anyway.'

Noah pulls her into him, pressing her up against him right there, in the entrance to the pub. He lowers his voice and whispers into her ear, so close and low that his breath makes the hairs on her neck stand up in pleasure: 'If you don't want so much sex, you shouldn't be so bloody hot, should you, Becca?'

She feels turned on when her name is in his mouth. It feels like looping a tag around her neck, marking her out as belonging to him. He only has eyes for her, and she likes it.

'And to think I'd be going weak at the knees right now were it not for the fact that I know you're pushing cloth.'

He nods, sanguine. 'I'll be right back,' he says. 'Get me a quick whisky? I feel a bit nervous about tonight, you know. Just a single shot.'

Becca makes for the bar, waiting patiently for Lizzie, the barperson, to finish with the man she's serving and get to her.

'He's so handsome,' Lizzie says when she gets to Becca's end of the bar. 'Every time I see you two I think it. Well done.'

Becca grins. 'Well done to him more though, right?' she asks, and Lizzie laughs.

'Obviously,' she replies. 'I suppose what I mean is: well done for finding such a perfectly good-looking match.'

'Oh, well, in that case: thank you,' Becca says, and she feels what she did in their early days, at Clemants, when the barista was checking Noah out, a certain sort of suspiciously un-feminist pride at bagging a hottie. She refrains from revealing that Noah is, at this exact moment, currently expelling the contents of his large intestine into the toilet bowl, lest she spoil their overall impression of a fit, happy couple.

'You're a marvel,' Noah says, joining Becca at the bar once she's paid for his whisky and her wine. 'Thank you for this. And sorry I've been so graphic. I don't know. This feels . . . something. I'm not usually one to get nervous but I know they all think we're crazy, that's it's too fast . . .'

'Noah, I never told you that to make you worry. They know I'm happy. My parents are happy about it, Carlos and Jia Li are happy about it . . .'

'Yeah,' he says. 'You just have so many *people* on your side! I've got Nate and Sarah and that's it.'

'I know,' Becca soothes him. 'It kills me that I can't meet your dad.'

'He would have liked you though. Loved you as his daughter-in-law.'

They clink glasses to Noah's dad's memory and Noah takes a sip of whisky as he leans against the smooth wood of the bar. His dark eyes are serious and solemn.

'My friends think you're awesome because *I* think you're awesome,' Becca tells him, finding the fingers of his free hand and winding them around her own playfully. 'But even if I didn't vouch for you, you charm literally everyone that crosses your path: climbing instructors, deli owners, you name it. Just be yourself tonight. They *want* to like you. They've asked to spend more time with you.'

'Hmmmm,' he says, already draining his glass. 'If you say so.'

'I do. Feel better for the poo and the drink?'

'Practically reborn,' he retorts, understanding it's time to crack on and leave. 'To the party!' he says, slipping his arm over her shoulders once more.

'Well, well, well,' Jia Li says as Becca and Noah make their way through the salon to where she's pouring champagne for some of the earlier guests. 'Look what the cat dragged in!'

Jia Li hands out the full glasses and opens her arms to give Becca a hug, and then Noah two kisses, one on each cheek.

'You make it sound like I didn't just see you an hour ago when my last words were – and I quote – "See you at six thirty, Jia Li!"'

Jia Li sucks in her cheeks. 'You're still in the honeymoon period,' she says, plainly, before looking at Noah and saying: 'When you're in the love bubble, all bets are off.'

Noah smiles. 'I apologise if I've been keeping her from you. Although, I would say the blame is an equal fifty-fifty split.'

'Enjoy it.' Jia Li smiles. 'She called you in from the universe, you know.'

Noah looks at Becca. 'Did you pray for me? Am I the answer to your actual, literal prayers?' He's joking, but

Becca could kill Jia Li for bringing this up. At no point has Becca let the words 'manifestation ritual' pass her lips in conversation with Noah. The thought of admitting that she requested a man from the universe isn't something she thinks, even as an SF writer, she wants him to know. It's embarrassing.

'Oh,' says Jia Li, sensing that she shouldn't have teased Becca like that. 'Nothing. I'm being stupid. Hey, did you know I'm pregnant and don't know who the father is?'

Jia Li shoots Becca a look that says, *See the things I do for you? See how I know when I've overstepped?*

Noah's eyes widen and then glance down at the growing mound of Jia Li's stomach. She's eight months now, and her bump is prominent, to say the least.

'I . . . did not know that, no,' Noah says slowly, looking at Becca for how to proceed. 'I didn't know there was any . . . secrecy, to the proceedings.'

'I didn't know I was allowed to tell,' Becca says to them both with a shrug. 'Are you telling people now?'

Jia Li rubs her tummy. She looks at Noah. 'It's privileged information. I'm trying to bond with you.'

'My lips are sealed,' he tells her. 'Congratulations.'

'Do you have any children?' Jia Li asks him.

'Me? No. Not that I know of.'

'Do you want them?'

'I think so, yes.'

'Brothers or sisters?'

'Only child.'

'Most embarrassing moment?'

'Definitely this moment, right now, being under interrogation by you.'

This makes Jia Li laugh. 'Sorry,' she says. 'It's just – you're so mysterious. You come by and pick Becca up, you guys disappear off together, all we get from Becca is *Noah loves tomatoes, he says they're the fruits of the Gods,* and *Noah says that movie should be on everyone's must-watch list.* But concrete facts? She doesn't give us any of those. Oh, you're the best sex she's ever had – she did tell me that.'

Noah takes Jia Li in his stride, which is impressive, considering Becca knows how nervous he felt only fifteen minutes ago.

'Did she now?' He chuckles, and Becca hits her friend's arm playfully.

'I've also told *you* that,' Becca says, 'so don't act like it's news.'

'Oh, but I love to hear it.' Noah grins. 'Over and over again.'

'I'd love to know if I was the best sex somebody had had.' Jia Li shrugs. 'It's a right ego boost.'

The three stand, not knowing where to go from here. The conversation has escalated quickly, and it's only 6.35 p.m.

'Well,' Noah settles on, 'I'll happily oblige in filling in any gaps in my personal biography.' He smiles. 'Because it's strange you don't know anything about me. I feel like I know you and Carlos intimately. Becca talks about you both like you're a cross between strawberry shortcake gelato and Buddha reincarnate. The three musketeers.'

Jia Li shoots Becca a pleased smile. 'Right then,' she says, taking Noah's arm. 'Let's go and look at tattoos and talk about our girl then. Becca, you can take over the champagne station for ten minutes, can't you?'

Becca watches helplessly as Noah is commandeered by her best friend, Jia Li gesticulating and Noah nodding, saying something here and there that makes Jia Li laugh. It frightens her, and it thrills her. They seem to be getting on. She's proud of her friend for stepping up and making the effort.

'Tall bastard, isn't he?'

Becca looks at Carlos.

'Evening,' she says, going in for a kiss on each cheek.

'How European,' Carlos notes, making *mwah* noises back. 'Do we do this now?'

Becca touches Carlos's arm. 'I just felt like a formal greeting,' she says. 'According to you and Jia Li, I've essentially been MIA since the summer, so this is me making the effort.'

He nods –'Duly noted' – and Becca can't read the look on his face.

'I suppose I've been letting myself be MIA,' Becca continues. 'I do know that. Getting engaged doesn't happen every day. And he's good for me. We laugh a lot.'

Carlos appears to consider this as he takes a mouthful of champagne.

'Yeah,' he says. 'I get it. I want you to be happy. You deserve the world, though, so I'm not going to go easy on him just because you're doped up on serotonin. It's my job as your friend to look out for you, and it will always be that way, whether he's your husband or not.'

Becca opens her mouth to explain that technically as a friend he should simply just be there for her no matter what happens – be there for any successes or potential mistakes – but actually, when it comes to Carlos, she isn't sure she does feel that way. He has been her protector over the past few years, working so closely together at the salon and swapping as many jokes and stories as advice and unpaid-for counsel. Maybe everybody needs that one friend who'll stay cynical, be the sensible one, keep a watchful eye.

'Thank you,' she settles on, and once again he nods.

They're interrupted by an incredibly tall, Amazonian-like woman with a wild mane of creamy bronze hair that falls to her waist. She has bright blue eyes, a problematic bindi and a flower crown. Her teeth are the brightest, most white teeth Becca has seen outside of the movies or models. In fact, this woman might well be a model. She is most certainly not a regular customer of Trim.

'Baby!' she exclaims, her face creasing into a sunbeam of a smile. 'I thought I'd lost you! Come here!'

Becca wonders who on earth she's talking to, even as the woman plants a wet kiss on Carlos's mouth, pressing her nose to his and whispering something that makes Carlos – shockingly – blush.

'I missed you,' he tells her, and Becca watches, slack-jawed, at the way Carlos runs a finger up the top part of the woman's body and then bops her – *BOPS* HER! – on the nose.

'My little love bug,' she coos.

'My sexy señorita,' he fusses back.

Becca waits for them to pull apart, and as the seconds tick by feels as if she should be in a mac and rimless glasses, a pervert pressed up close against this display of intimate behaviour right in front of her. Should she leave, or at least look away?

'Sorry,' says Carlos, coming to. As he speaks he keeps staring at the woman. She giggles. Carlos scrunches up his nose, rabbit-like and terrifying as all hell. 'This is Anoushka,' he adds, finally dragging his eyes back to Becca, who looks, she assumes, as though she's just seen a zebra prepare a sliced banana sandwich. 'Noosh, this is Becca.'

'Oh my God,' Noosh squeals. 'Becca!' Becca finds herself enveloped in a bony hug. 'Carlos raves about you. *Raves!* He calls you his sister from another mister, but to be honest talks about you like you're his . . . oh gosh, I don't know, his personal Oprah! I'm so excited to finally be meeting you! This place – I can't believe I'm only just getting to see it. It's amazing. What you two have built here is so beautiful. I have friends who come here, actually. Well, you probably know that – I'm sure Carlos has told you everything!'

Becca smiles, trying to be kind in the face of all this new information. Evidently Noosh is *very* into her friend, but this is the first she's heard of her and it's quite overwhelming to try and appear incredibly happy to meet somebody you never even knew existed.

'You're just as wonderful as he said you were,' Becca settles on, smiling as warmly as possible at Noosh and then pointedly at Carlos, who doesn't seem to notice. 'I, erm . . .' At this moment Becca realises Noah is across the room in the tattooist's chair, and when he sees her he lifts his eyebrows as if to say *when in Rome!*

'Sorry,' Becca says. 'My . . . Noah appears to be getting a tattoo. Will you excuse me? I'll be right back.'

'Just having my web tidied up,' Noah says as Becca approaches. 'Jia Li persuaded me, although I don't know where she's gone now. Does she really not know who the father of her baby is?'

The tattooist – a man-bun-wearing forty-something with thick fingers and, Becca notices because it's impossible not to, dazzlingly large feet – looks up at this, from Noah to Becca and then back down at his work.

'Sorry,' Noah says, realising he's been indiscreet. 'No further questions, your honour.'

'Can I get you anything?' Becca asks him, soothed to be back in his presence. Even as he winces at the needle, he's attractive. The sudden appearance of this 'Noosh' woman has wound her up, somehow. She has never seen Carlos be so sappy in her life. 'Does it hurt?'

'Nah,' he says, squinting through one eye and gurning. 'I'm fine!' he adds, making his voice high-pitched and squeaky.

Becca laughs. 'My macho-macho man.'

Becca says hello to a few key clients as Noah finishes up, topping up glasses and nipping to the loo. By the time she comes out, she sees Noah is standing off to one side, talking with Carlos, Noosh and Jia Li. She stands for a moment, looking at them, those worlds she knew needed to collide, laughing and listening to each other. Noah must feel her eyes, that special skill lovers develop, because he looks in her direction, quickly followed by Carlos. She smiles and heads over.

'What's the goss?' she says as Noosh lifts up her T-shirt to reveal washboard abs and a tiny star tattoo.

'I thought it would hurt way more,' Noosh explains. 'Do you like it?'

Becca nods. 'It's very cute. I don't think I'm brave enough.'

'Bollocks,' Carlos hoots. 'You're the bravest person I know.'

'Careful. That almost sounds like a compliment.'

'It is,' Carlos says. 'I'm nice sometimes, you know.'

Noosh grins and pulls him in for a kiss. 'You're nice all the time, baby.'

Jia Li locks eyes with Becca, who looks to the floor in case she laughs. She steels herself, wondering if Jia Li is OK with this display of affection.

'So, how did you two meet?' asks Noah, filling the silence that has fallen.

'At a bar.' Noosh smiles shyly, sneaking a look at Carlos who nods in confirmation. Becca has honestly never seen him like this – shy and coy and playful and affectionate. She's seen him with women, sure, but always 'in character' somehow, playing a role. 'I was out for a friend's birthday at a place with gender-neutral bathrooms, so we were in the line together and it was taking so long that we got chatting, and he was just so . . . well, you guys know.' She beams, gesturing at Jia Li and Becca. 'He's . . .' She doesn't finish the sentence. She grins at him, and Carlos grins back, everyone else fading into the background of their private moment.

'Ahhh,' said Noah. 'That's lovely. Was it long ago, or . . . ?'

'About a month ago,' says Noosh, looking at Carlos to confirm. Becca begins to exclaim that she can't believe he hasn't said he's seeing somebody before she remembers Noosh doesn't know she's been his secret.

'Did *you* know?' she hisses at Jia Li later on.

'Nope,' she says. 'I guess it's been a bit of a mad few months. I've been growing a human, you've been off in dreamland with Noah of the Good Hair, and Carlos has, apparently, been living his own life too.'

'She's . . .'

'Yeah,' Jia Li agrees. 'But he seems happy?'

'I know,' whispers Becca. 'I've never seen him like this before.'

'What are you two in cahoots about?' Noah asks, sidling up to the side of them. 'Or daren't I ask?'

'Nothing.' Becca smiles, letting him slip an arm around her and enjoying the weight of it. It's felt special, tonight, ebbing and flowing with him, drifting apart and then finding each other in the crowd. 'Just Carlos's new . . . girlfriend? I don't know if it's official. We didn't know he was seeing anyone.'

'I get that,' says Noah. 'If he really likes her, he must want to protect it.'

The three of them instinctively look over to where Carlos and Noosh are standing. Carlos is whispering into her neck and she's giggling and playfully hitting his arm. Carlos looks up, raises his glass to them, and then carries on.

'Yeah,' says Becca, nodding. 'He must.'

'I'm kind of into this vibe shift,' Jia Li says. 'We should all hang out properly. It looks like Noosh is here to stay and I don't have the energy to fight it. Triple date? My date can be the baby – although I have to say, and sorry you have to hear this Noah—'

Noah waves a hand, batting away her protestations.

'—but I'm hornier than I've ever been. Like, in my life. Even my best vibrator isn't enough. I need a proper, rock-hard man to rail me, again and again. But, you know . . .' She pats her bump once more.

Noah nods sympathetically and Becca goes wide-eyed and shakes her head, letting Jia Li know that she can't believe she's going there with Noah right in front of them. It must mean she likes him, if she's going to issue the girl talk in his presence.

'Aren't there men who specifically fantasise about sex with pregnant women?' Noah muses. 'I'm sure that's a thing.'

Jia Li snorts. 'Know anyone?' she asks.

'I could do a call-out in my next author newsletter,' Noah says, deadpan.

'Ewww,' says Jia Li. 'Pregnancy fetish is one thing. Sci-fi nerd is a step too far.'

'Great.' Noah nods. 'Just my whole readership you're repulsed by then. That's humbling.'

Jia Li looks at Becca and smiles. 'I really like your fiancé,' she says, and then Noah and Becca look at each other.

'I like him too.' Becca grins, and she accepts a forehead kiss from Noah who grins too.

'I'm not going to lie,' Jia Li adds. 'Noah, I've been suspicious of the speed of things with you two, but . . . I approve. I do. Maybe the baby is making me a softie, but this love? We love to see it. It's an A plus from me.'

Becca reaches out to squeeze her hand, overjoyed that her friend is finally on board. 'Good,' she says. 'Because in just a few weeks, we're on. Town Hall, the thirtieth of November.'

Jia Li looks between them, trying to figure out if it's true.

'We'll have known each other exactly five months, yes,' Becca says. 'Will you . . . be my maid of honour?'

'Oh my gosh, Becca!' Jia Li starts crying, a rarity on par with a once-in-a-lifetime celestial movement. 'Yes!' she squeals. 'Yes!'

Carlos looks over at the sudden outburst, but doesn't come over. Becca lets herself be enveloped by Jia Li and her bump in a bear hug. Noah looks on, happily.

And yet, something doesn't feel right. But what?

28

She Doesn't Text Back

After the tattoo party, Becca goes to the Fox and Hound with Noah, Jia Li, Carlos and Noosh, who, suddenly, seems to be giving Carlos the cold shoulder.

'Your girl seems pissed off with you,' Becca says, voice lowered, as they assemble at the bar and take turns ordering drinks.

'*Sssshhh*,' Carlos replies, shaking his head. 'Shut up.'

Becca keeps her eyes on the back of Noosh's head, who is talking to Dave about what gin he's got in.

'What happened?' she asks out of the side of her mouth.

'No,' Carlos replies, waving at Dave and giving a thumbs up when Dave mouths *the usual?* 'Put it all on my tab?' Carlos adds, signalling to their small group. Dave nods efficiently.

'We'll find us a table,' Becca announces, letting Noah get her nightcap and steering Carlos by the elbow to a leather booth in the corner.

'Don't mess it up,' Becca says as they sit. 'I don't know why you didn't tell us about Noosh, but she's obviously super into you. So. Fix the cold shoulder.'

Carlos sighs. 'I don't need romantic advice from you, thankyouverymuch,' he says.

'Apparently you do,' Becca bats back. She looks up, just in time to see Noosh point at the table as she chats to Noah, who has lowered his head and is furrowing his brow at whatever he's being told. She locks eyes with him and he frowns again, and then Noosh gives her a weak smile.

'What are you talking about?' Jia Li asks, appearing beside them, having apparently just come from the loo. Jia Li looks to where Becca and Carlos are staring, at the bar towards Noah and Noosh, looking from the table to the bar, the bar to the table.

'You know, I think I'm going to go . . .' she says, and Becca glances up in surprise.

'What? No! We haven't been to the pub in ages!'

Jia Li shrugs. 'That's because I've been pregnant for ages,' she shoots back, a hand at her lower back. 'Mama is tired, I'm feeling weird in my hips, and my back, and my everything, to be honest, and this' – she gestures from Carlos and Becca to Noosh and Noah – 'is about to get toxic.'

'Toxic?' Becca asks, and Carlos shakes his head.

'Jia Li . . .' he warns, and Becca throws up her hands and says, 'Will somebody, for the love of God, tell me what is going on?'

But before anyone can answer her, her heart stops beating and her breath suspends itself, because Mike Henry has walked into the Fox and Hound.

He sees her right as she sees him, and if he's shocked it doesn't show.

'Becca!' Mike says from across the pub, and the way he moves towards her table, the size of his pupils, the unease in his body he's trying too hard to cover up, Becca can see that he's drunk. 'As I live and breathe . . .' he slurs when he gets to their table. A man follows him. Niall. Becca recognises him from the coffee shop all those months ago.

'Come on, mate,' Niall says, 'We really should be getting home . . .'

Mike shrugs him off.

'Hey,' Becca says, standing up for a hug. She doesn't know what else to do. She always thought if – when – they crossed paths, it would be polite and brief, but he's drunk and seems upset and she doesn't know how to navigate that. 'Fancy seeing you here!'

Noah and Noosh come over.

'Hey, man,' Noah says, eyes flicking between Becca and Mike.

'Hey, man,' Mike echoes, pointedly watching Noah's arm snake around Becca's waist.

'Did you get my flowers?' he asks.

Becca nods. 'I did. So you're back for good?'

'Yeah,' he says, swaying. 'Just doing some work in London, back on the weekends to see my nephew. You remember Niall.' He points to him. 'Niall and Jessie, man! They're going the distance!'

'Hi.' Niall waves. 'We've been out for dinner and I think maybe the wine we had has reacted with his medication – we've drunk the same and I'm fine.'

'Valium,' shrugs Mike. 'Thanks for telling everyone, Niall.'

'I didn't say which medication, mate, sorry – I just . . . Let's go, OK? You need some sleep.'

Nobody says anything, and it makes Becca's skin tingle with self-consciousness. This isn't her Mike. She doesn't recognise this Mike. His eyes are glassy, gaze unfocused. He hasn't shaved but his facial hair isn't manscaped in any discernible way – he doesn't look rugged so much as unkempt. His cheeks are ruddy, his complexion sallow. He looks, all in all, terribly sad.

'Don't look at me like that,' Mike says. 'God, Becca, don't look at me like that. So what if New York went tits up? So what. At least I'm here for my dad – he's got cancer, by the way. He'll be fine, but I'm here for it, you know? And I'll find another job . . . everybody acts like they're so worried for me but when have I ever not been fine?'

'I'm sorry to hear about your dad,' she says.

'No you're not.' Mike shakes his head, sadly. 'You didn't even say thank you for the flowers.'

Becca feels Noah's grip tighten at the mention of flowers, his intrigue growing.

'I . . .' she says, not knowing how to say that she doesn't even have his number any more.

'Anyway, who is the drainpipe?' He gestures to Noah.

'My fiancé,' she tells him. 'Noah.'

'Fiancé?' Mike echoes. 'Seriously?'

She shows him the ring.

'Hmmm,' he says.

Becca can't put her finger on what she was expecting, but it wasn't this. The Mike she loved was kind-hearted and fun, playful and sweet. The Mike propping up the bar has an edge, an unspoken nastiness. She's torn between feeling sorry for him and asking if he needs help.

'Come on, mate,' Carlos suddenly says, standing up. 'Let's get you in a cab. Valium and booze, man, that's a crazy mix. I've done it before myself with antibiotics – easily done. Come on.'

Becca feels a rush of gratitude for somebody intervening, helping to end this awkward, weird, uncomfortable scene she's found herself in. She wants to cry. Seeing Mike this way is heart breaking. He seems lost at sea, totally unsure of himself. She knows he is drunk, but the despondency to him, the gloom . . . that's not the drink. That's the truth rising to the surface.

'Piss off,' Mike spits as Carlos reaches for his arm. Mike goes to take a swing, but he's not in control of his limbs, of his fist, and the momentum of throwing his arm forces him off balance so he spins on the spot and then stumbles, Niall looking on, horrified, Carlos ducking and getting his weight under Mike, giving him a fireman's lift.

'Oh God,' Mike says. 'I think I'm going to be sick.'

And then they're gone, Becca and Noah, Jia Li and Noosh looking on as Carlos lifts Mike out of the pub doors, Niall issuing a small bow and apologising once again before following.

'The medication,' he repeats, before he ducks out.

'My ex,' Becca announces to the group, as they all blink madly and process what just happened. 'That was him.'

Noosh shakes her head. 'Not over you, is he?' she says, looking at the door Carlos just carried him through. 'Clearly not over you at all.'

Becca looks at her. She doesn't know how to respond.

29

She Texts Back

'Hello, hello,' Becca says as Jia Li opens her front door. She's grown bigger even over a weekend. She's eight months, now, and Becca doesn't understand how she can still have another six weeks to go.

'I know,' Jia Li says. 'I'm a house. The price of hair like Brooke Shields is the weight of twenty babies, apparently, spread all over my body. The science makes no sense: the kid can't weigh more than nine pounds and yet I've become sphere-like? That's how I know God is a man.'

'Come here,' Becca says. 'Less sarcasm, more hugging.'

They embrace, and Becca insists that Jia Li get back to her spot on the sofa so she can make tea and locate biscuits.

'Did you bring me anything back from the Lakes?' Jia Li yells through to the kitchen, and Becca pauses. She deliberately wanted to share her news face to face.

'Actually . . .' begins Becca, arranging mugs and a saucer of Hobnobs on to a tray. Becca puts down the tray and shows off her left hand, the fourth finger of which bears the ring.

'What!' Jia Li exclaims. 'Seriously? Becca! You're engaged!'

'Yup.'

'Shut up!'

'I know. Mad, isn't it?'

'You're engaged to Mike?' Jia Li clarifies, and Becca nods and Jia Li squeals and tries to get up for a hug but can't quite find her momentum, and so Becca leans over and saves her the trip.

'What! When did this happen?' Jia Li asks, eyes wide and cheeks flushed. 'Oh my God!'

'When we were away.' Becca shrugs. 'And it just seemed so obvious. We kind of proposed to each other, really. It was romantic, but there was no huge dinner or rented football stadium or anything like that. It was just the both of us having a chat and coming to the same conclusion at the same time: we're meant to be together, and once we realised that it seemed silly not to just . . . get on with it.'

'Woah,' says Jia Li. 'So me and Carlos were wrong.'

Becca tips her head, the motion serving as the question.

'About the text, when it came – in the summer. We said don't get back in touch with an ex, but here you are, marrying yours.'

'I know,' says Becca. 'It feels right. You know I've had this whole life without him – starting the salon, meeting you and Carlos, buying my house. And I thought our paths had gone in two different directions when he moved, but I get the feeling that's not it at all, they just diverged a bit, running parallel to each other. And because of what we experienced on those parallel journeys, now we're able to come back together again.'

'Hmmm,' says Jia Li. 'Either that, or it's all random chance and we've got to make the best of it.'

'Either way, I have a fiancé.' Becca smiles. 'And I suppose my little flower girl or page boy is already taken care of?' She nods at Jia Li's belly, as Jia Li shifts uncomfortably.

'Oh, you're having a long engagement? If this bean will be old enough to walk?'

'I don't know, actually,' admits Becca. 'Maybe not. There's no point waiting too long . . .'

'Does Carlos know?' Jia Li shifts uncomfortably again.

'Do you want me to rub your back?' Becca asks, and Jia Li considers it as if conceding to the pain is defeat. 'Don't be a prick, come on. Get on the floor and turn around.'

'That's what got me into this mess,' she quips.

Becca hoots a laugh. 'Trust you to be punny at a time like this.'

Becca kneads her hands against the small of Jia Li's back, and assumes that the noises it elicits mean she's doing a good job.

'We still haven't talked about a birthing plan,' Becca comments.

'Don't have one,' says Jia Li. 'Labour pains start, go to hospital, get pumped full of drugs, out it comes. I'm not making it anything more complicated than it needs to be.'

'And have you . . . bought stuff?' Becca looks around, suddenly realising she can see nothing babylike in the house. No clothes, no toys, nothing a person could reasonably expect for an impending mother.

'A bassinet,' Jia Li says, and her breathing is harder, now. Becca really must be doing something helpful. She can barely speak. 'Upstairs. I can get same-day delivery when I figure out

what's important versus what's . . . oh God, yes, thank you
. . .' Jia Li shudders in relief as Becca presses down on her hips
even harder. 'What's important versus what's a load of crap.'

'Very sensible,' says Becca, resisting the urge to ask why
she doesn't want to go mad in the kid's department of John
Lewis. Who cares if she ends up with a bunch of crap? It's a
baby! Becca understands that Jia Li thinks differently, is a bit
more practical, but no onesies? No tiny little booties or bot-
tles? 'Well,' she continues, 'you know you can always send
us to get whatever you need.'

'You and Carlos?'

'I meant me and Mike, but sure, Carlos too. You're not
short of people to run ragged after you.'

'Becca?'

'Mmm?'

'The pain is getting worse.'

Becca drops her hands from Jia Li's back in horror. 'Have
I hurt you?' she says. 'I'm so sorry – are you OK?'

'Mmmmm,' moans Jia Li. She twists so that she's sitting
on the floor instead of kneeling, her back against the sofa.
Becca studies her. Should she call an ambulance? Is this what
they call Braxton Hicks? 'Could you get me a flannel?' Jia Li
asks. 'It helps. They're upstairs in the bathroom cupboard.
Run the tap cold. Really cold.'

'Roger that.' Becca pauses at the door and looks back
before she races up the stairs. As she's running the cold tap
she hears Jia Li cry out – a low, guttural mooing sound, unlike
anything she's ever heard a person make before. She shuts
off the tap and, inexplicably, pulls three thick white towels

off the shelf where she got the flannel, too, racing back downstairs to find Jia Li on all fours, panting.

'Oh Christ,' Becca says. 'What's happening?'

'I . . . don't know . . .' Jia Li huffs and puffs. 'Take my knickers off. I feel like . . . GAH!'

Becca doesn't know if Jia Li is serious. Take her knickers off? To do what?

'Check if my waters have broken. I felt a trickle earlier, maybe it was that. My midwife said it doesn't always gush out like in the movies,' Jia Li says. 'Please, Becca. Just take my knickers off and check!'

Becca does as instructed and, regardless of the damp in Jia Lia's knickers, it's the way in which her friend is crouched that tells her it is very obvious that the baby is on the way right now, this very second.

'Is that the head?' Jia Li says, panting and sweaty.

'It looks like it might be, soon,' Becca says, frozen. This is terrifying. Surely that can't be natural, a woman's body stretching that way. 'You're like . . .' She moves towards her friend, unsure if she should be looking at something so private. She's scared.

'Becca, get to it, babe,' Jia Li tells her. 'Don't be a priss about it.' She moans again.

Becca drops to her knees, handing Jia Li the cold flannel, and faces the issue head on, holding up a hand, her thumb and forefinger a measuring stick. 'Your . . . vagina . . . is about this far apart. Dilated? You're this far dilated.' Becca holds up her fingers about seven centimetres apart.

'Buggar,' says Jia Li. 'Buggar, buggar, buggar. OK.'

She moans again. Becca feels useless.

'An ambulance!' Jia Li instructs. 'Alexa!' She has a voice activated speaker on her sideboard. 'Call 999!'

Alexa calls the emergency services and Becca explains her friend is in labour. The man at the end of the phone tells Becca she's doing a great job, which isn't true but now isn't the time to argue. He says an ambulance is on its way, but there's road-works on the A road and there's been an accident just outside of town, so he can't say how long it will be.

'You need towels, to keep Mum calm, and have her sit however is comfortable – all fours can be best. We'll be there as soon as we can.'

'Is that it?' Becca asks, panicked.

'I'm afraid so,' the man says. 'We're coming. I'll stay on the line if you need me.'

Jia Li and Becca look at each other.

'OK then,' says Becca, a sudden feeling of calm washing over her. She can do this. She has no choice. Jia Li, and this baby, are in her care. 'Let's have a baby.'

'Bec,' says Jia Li, reaching for her hand. 'I'm scared.'

'But I've got you, OK?'

'OK.'

'Now flip over on to all fours again.'

As Becca runs upstairs to get more towels, she asks her Apple Watch to call Carlos.

'Too early,' he mumbles down the line. 'Bye bye.'

'Carlos, don't hang up,' Becca implores, and she's relieved to hear he doesn't. She gets towels, more flannels and a couple of pillows off Jia Li's bed. The Moses basket is already set up, a woven thing on a wooden rocking frame, white frills and single teddy bear inside. Becca stares at it as she says, 'Come to Jia Li's. She's in labour and I am *freaking out*. The ambulance is on its way but there's an accident blocking the road. Can you run here, Carlos? I need you.'

'I'm on my way,' he says, and then the line goes dead.

Downstairs Jia Li is in a contorted yoga pose, on her knees and elbows so her head is pressed to the floor and her arse is in the air.

'Honey,' soothes Becca, rubbing Jia Li's back. 'Carlos is coming, OK? Is that all right? I can keep him outside in the hallway, or in the kitchen.'

'I don't care,' she replies. 'Call Dave, too. Tell him it's his.'

'What?' says Becca, stunned. 'It is?'

Jia Li moans again, and through more pants reveals: 'I've always known. I was just afraid.'

There's a knock. Carlos. Thank God he only lives two streets over.

'She just told me to call Dave,' Becca says, registering the waft of last night's alcohol radiating off his body. 'She said she's always known, she was just afraid.'

Carlos nods. 'Yeah,' he says. 'We have that in common.'

'What?' Becca asks, remembering there's an elastic on her wrist and so tying up her hair.

'Nothing,' says Carlos, slipping off his coat. He's sweating; panting too. Jia Li moans again and he looks at her.

'I know,' Becca tells him. 'Go and wash your hands, and then come through.'

30

She Texts Back

Carlos is incredible – far calmer than Becca.

'Right then,' he says, rubbing his hands together as he enters the room, as though he's excited about the joint he's got roasting for lunch, not about to deliver an actual baby in an actual living room with no actual qualifications. 'Jia Li, hello, my darling. Way to keep us all on our toes.'

Jia Li shoots him a look but doesn't say anything. She's breathing deeply, at Becca's instruction.

'May I?' he says, and Jia Li nods.

'Yup,' Carlos says, taking a look. 'You're having a baby all right. Has anyone googled this?'

'Oh yeah,' snipes Becca. 'We watched a YouTube video and then thought, sure, why not give it a try?'

Carlos looks at her. 'I sense your sarcasm,' he says, 'and with all due respect that's not helpful. I'm actually serious. I don't know how much this thing has to . . . you know . . . *stretch*. I don't know how we get a baby out, do you?'

A voice comes through the Alexa: 'Is Mum OK?'

Carlos eyes Becca as if to say, *Is that God, or . . . ?*

'The Alexa,' Becca tells him, and then replies: 'She's OK!'

Becca looks at Jia Li, who has her eyes closed as she breathes in, breathes out. In a vicious whisper she says, 'Hey. Don't panic, anyone. We're not delivering the baby. The ambulance will be here.'

'The ambulance is still eleven to fourteen minutes away,' the godlike voice comes from the Alexa.

Carlos pulls out his phone and punches at it with two fingers. He shakes his head. 'This says after seven centimetres it's game on, and that' – he nods towards Jia Li – 'is more than seven.'

'So what do we do?' Becca will follow Carlos's commands. Right now, he is her Jesus, her Jay-Z, her path and holy light.

Carlos nods, the information percolating in his head.

Through the Alexa they are asked: 'Is the door unlocked, or propped open if you can't take it off the latch?'

'No, but I can do that,' shouts Becca, already in the hall.

'I say we get more sheets and towels – everything she has,' Carlos muses. 'Jia Li – how are you feeling, darlin'? Can we get you anything?'

Jia Li snorts. 'Oh no,' she pants, her tone dry as white wine, despite the circumstance. 'I'm peachy.'

'Water, maybe,' he directs Becca. 'In something she can't knock over. Jia Li? I suppose asking if you want anything to eat is pointless?'

She takes a breath, and as Becca commandeers an old Evian bottle out of the recycling she braces herself for a torrent of abuse. What she isn't expecting is for Jia Li to ask for an energy bar.

'I can't do this,' Jia Li says, pushing the energy bar away after all. 'I can't do this.'

'You can, and you already are. Look at me, OK? I'm here. It's you and me. That's it. I love you, and nothing is going to go wrong.'

Jia Li nods, her bottom lip wobbling, and Becca moves to hold her hand. 'Gah, the sheets,' she remembers, releasing herself and running back upstairs.

'Here,' she says, when she's back. 'I found a mattress protector too. I'm just thinking . . .' Becca gestures to the wool of the carpet.

'Great,' says Carlos and, as Becca starts putting everything down to protect the house from as many bodily fluids as possible, he reaches out, takes her hand, and in a sweet, tender voice says: 'Becca. You're doing great too.'

It makes her inhale deeply, steadying herself.

Jia Li screams out.

The voice from the Alexa says: 'OK, Jia Li, this is all happening very fast. Try not to push. Just breathe, all right?'

'I can see the baby's head,' Carlos says. 'I think she's going to have this baby really soon!'

'Then you'll need to guide it out, OK?' the instructions come. Carlos looks at Becca. He swallows.

In response, Jia Li screams again.

Becca mops her brow as Jia Lia whimpers, 'I need to lie down.'

'Let's move you then,' Becca says, and together they shift her round so that Jia Li is sitting between Becca's legs, leaning her back against her breasts, holding each hand. Jia

Li and Becca breathe together, and Becca focuses on Carlos's face, the angular line of his jaw, his day-old stubble, his long, thick eyelashes against his cheeks as he looks down, brow furrowed.

Jia Li makes a low groan through gritted teeth and Carlos shouts, 'It's coming, Jia Li! Well done! Keep breathing!'

Jia Li takes a deep breath in, her eyes scrunched closed, breathes out, and then there's a knock at the door and a cheery, 'Hello?' It's Dave.

'Shitting hell,' he says, when he turns the corner and sees what's happening.

'You're about to be a dad,' Becca tells him, and Jia Li gives her biggest breath yet and Carlos guides the baby out as Dave hits the floor, hard and fast, so only his feet are visible from where they all are.

Becca waits for the baby to cry. Nothing comes.

'Carlos?'

'Becca.'

The way he says it makes her understand, immediately, that something has gone wrong. She slips out from under Jia Li, whose eyes are closed in exhaustion, and quickly sees that the umbilical cord is around the baby's neck.

'Operator, are you still there?' Becca cries in the direction of the Alexa. 'What do I do if the umbilical cord is around the baby's neck?' The words are out before Becca realises how alarming that will be to Jia Li. Jia Li opens her eyes and locks her gaze on to Becca's as they all listen to the emergency services voice say: 'If the umbilical cord is around your baby's neck, do not try to tie or cut the cord. The cord must stay attached until help arrives. See if you can ease it over the baby's head slowly, or loosen it enough to form a loop so their body can slip through.'

'You can do this, Carlos,' Becca says, once the person on the speaker has given his instruction. Carlos nods at her, holding the tiny, blood-covered baby so lovingly it makes Becca's breath catch in her throat. She takes a towel, and doesn't realise she's holding her breath until Carlos does it – he gets the cord off.

'OK. Thank God,' he whispers, looking at Becca, tears in his eyes.

'Is it OK?' Jia Li says, and by way of reply the baby takes its first gulp of air and lets out a shriek, and they all laugh in a strange relief.

'Let's wrap your little guy up,' Carlos says, 'and careful of the cord. Jia Li, you need to pass the placenta too. Operator: how long after birth does the placenta come?'

Even the tiny baby seems to turn to the speaker, the voice of their new commander-in-chief, as he says, 'A birthing person should deliver the placenta within thirty to sixty minutes after the baby—'

'Got it,' Carlos says, knowing how important the placenta delivery is but also knowing that, in this very moment, there's something more important he needs to focus on.

He gently passes Jia Li the bundle of towel containing her child and she says, full of love, 'It's a boy.'

Carlos nods. 'Tiniest little wiener I've ever seen, but yes,' he tells her, 'it's a boy.'

'Hello?' comes a woman's voice from the hallway. 'Ambulance service. Is there a woman in labour here?'

'In here!' Carlos and Becca trill in unison, and it's enough to make Dave come to.

'Are you all right sir?' the paramedic says as she comes through.

'Yeah,' Dave says, groggily. 'I think I fainted.'

'Did you hit your head?'

'Maybe?'

'OK,' clucks the paramedic. 'We'll check you out, sir, OK?'

The woman appears in the living room then, looks at Jia Li and the baby and the mass of towels and sheets and nods. 'Well, better late than never,' she declares. 'Could we get some room, please?'

Becca kisses Jia Li's head. 'I'm so proud of you. Congratulations, Mama,' she says.

She heads out to the front of the house with Carlos. It's only when they're both sitting on the front wall that they realise they're both sobbing.

31

She Doesn't Text Back

'Carlos!' Becca shouts as she walks into the salon. Carlos is already there with a client who Becca will style later, turning around mid-foil. 'Jia Li had the baby! Early!'

He looks at her, screwing up his face as if her joke isn't a funny one.

'I'm not kidding,' Becca says. 'Her mum just called me, like five minutes ago. Her funny feelings at the pub last night were labour pains.' She hoots a laugh of disbelief. 'I'm laughing because I know they're OK,' she says. 'Like, look at me – I'm shaking!' She holds out a trembling hand.

'What?' asks Carlos. 'Are they both OK?'

'Absolutely fine, her mum says. They have to stay in hospital for a few days, but it's an actual miracle. Apparently, Jia Li called her mum before bed, and her mum said she just *knew* something wasn't right. Drove over to take her to A & E – and boom.'

Carlos pauses, tears welling in his eyes.

'But they're OK?' he repeats, his voice wavering. The sight of his concern melts Becca's heart: his wide, worried face, the size of his eyes.

'They're OK!' repeats Becca. 'It's a boy. Haoyu. A teeny tiny five pounds and two ounces.'

Carlos bursts into tears, his client watching on, helpless, and suddenly Becca finds herself wrapping her arms around him, rubbing his back and telling him it's all going to be fine.

'Her mum said it was all as good as it could be, Carlos. She's good! The baby is good!'

'I know.' Carlos sobs, wiping tears from his eyes with meaty knuckles. 'It's just so wild. Yesterday she was just Jia Li and now she's a mum?'

Becca bites on her lip and creases her face in sympathy. She nods. 'I know, it's mad. But she's OK. That's what her mum said. I repeat: she's OK. Obviously we need to cancel her clients, though, let everyone know what's happened.'

Carlos nods. 'OK, yeah. Urgh! Right. Carol, give me a moment, I just need to splash some water on my face. I don't know what came over me then, I just can't believe it! I'll be right back, OK?'

Carlos disappears to the bathroom and Becca puts her stuff in the staff room, reappearing to hear Carlos say: 'Sorry, Carol. Do carry on – so the sex club makes you send in a *full*-length photo as part of the criteria, I'm with you . . .'

Becca leaves Carlos to it and busies herself getting organised for the day. She heads over to Dana to see what her schedule looks like and they go through Jia Li's clients to figure out who can be moved, and who will need to be cancelled. Becca reaches out to a few hairdressing friends to see if they want to hire a chair at Trim for a while, too. Jia Li was going to drop down to two days a week for a few months, but

Becca has a feeling she might want to take some proper time off, after everything. A premature birth is no joke.

It's Dana that suggests they all club together for a baby gift. When Carlos leaves Carol's colour to develop, Becca fills him in.

'Dana had the very lovely idea of us all putting in for a baby basket or big present – or we could even organise the at-home beautician for her? That could be nice. Mani-pedi and a massage as the baby sleeps? Once they're home, I mean.'

'Cool, yeah,' says Carlos, checking out the rest of his day too. 'I'm going to need an extra twenty minutes for that one-thirty appointment,' he tells Dana, 'so can you call my three p.m. and ask if she's able to come in half an hour later? No worries if not, but just say it's for her own comfort and con-venience, and if she can't, we'll make it our problem, not hers.'

'Got it,' says Dana, already picking up the phone.

'I know Noah will want to pitch in. Do you want Noosh's name on the card as well, since apparently we're all grown up in our functioning relationships now? By the way – she's lovely, and I cannot believe you never mentioned her. You're such a dark horse!'

'Noosh and I broke up,' Carlos says, simply. He doesn't look away from the computer as he speaks.

'What?' asks Becca. 'When?'

'After the pub.'

'Last night?'

He lifts an insouciant shoulder, as though he's revealed he didn't have time to moisturise after his shower this morning, not that the longest relationship Becca has ever known him maintain has come to an end.

'Are you OK at least?'

'I'm fine.' Another weird half-shrug. 'Life goes on.'

'I know, but . . . I liked her. I could tell something was up but I thought it was drink, maybe, or . . . I don't know. That she was overwhelmed at the party? I'm sorry to hear it, Carlos. You seemed really happy with her.'

'Yeah, well,' he says. 'I suppose not everything is as it seems. We were only together a few weeks anyway. It . . . well, it wasn't *nothing*, but it wasn't a something yet. It's fine. Just my name on the card then. Obviously feel free to keep Noah on there.'

'Yeah,' Becca says, watching him head on over to check Carol's foils.

Later, as they tidy up for the day and Dana has gone, Becca is determined to circle back around to Carlos's break-up. Now it's just the two of them, she's hoping he'll be more amenable to giving her the details. They're friends – he can't keep this to himself. Becca hopes he isn't ashamed, that he hasn't done something stupid he doesn't want to own up to.

'Hey,' she asks him as they sweep up, her tone that of a woman very much not simply saying hey, but rather starting the beginning of a somewhat loaded sentence. 'Your break-up – it didn't have anything to do with Mike showing up and you helping, did it? You didn't seem to want to talk about it before but I can't stop thinking about it . . .'

Carlos stops tidying, just for half a beat, and then resumes his duties.

'I'll take that as a yes,' Becca probes, studying him for a reaction. He sighs.

'Kind of,' he says, eventually. 'Yeah.'

'Ohmygod, seriously? Why didn't you say? When we texted you just said he asked to go to a massive house in the rich part of town, and when you took him in the cab you were surprised he'd got in. And when I asked why you didn't come back you said you were over it . . . I knew she was mad you didn't come back, but she stayed for a bit, chatting with Noah and me.'

Carlos stands to attention at that. He stares at her through the mirrors and says: 'She stayed and chatted with you?'

'Yeah, she said that she'd told you she loved you but you wouldn't say it back . . . is that it? Because I know it's scary to take the leap, but—'

'She thinks I won't say it because I'm in love with you, Becca.'

He turns around, then, so they're looking at each other properly, not in the mirror.

'Me?' Becca laughs, waiting for the punchline. But the look on his face indicates there isn't one. 'Oh,' she adds, her voice small. 'That's . . .'

But she doesn't know how to conclude her thought.

'But you're my friend,' she says, after a beat. 'We're business partners. And Jia Li . . .'

'Jia Li?'

'I always thought you and Jia Li had a thing.'

'Seriously?'

'Seriously.'

Becca doesn't understand. Noosh thinks she and Carlos are a thing? She met Noah! Becca has talked to her about her wedding plans!

'So why didn't you set her straight?' Becca asks.

Carlos looks to the floor. 'I—' he starts, but before he can answer Noah knocks on the salon door, doing the through-the-glass-wave that he does, that's become his thing.

'Evening, all!' he says, when Becca lets him in, and he gives her a peck on the cheek.

Carlos nods. 'All right, mate?'

'Yeah, not bad, thanks. Not bad.' He turns to Becca. 'I've just come from the dog shelter – I don't smell like pitbull, do I? I thought we could grab dinner out tonight? There's some stuff I think we should finalise before the tour.'

'Finally got the support act gig for the Stones?' Carlos quips, and Becca can hear it, the edge to his voice, a tiny – seemingly insignificant – wobble, that she knows means way more than the sum of its parts.

'I'm off to America again,' says Noah. 'Sixteen dates in fourteen days – I'll be going all over the place. My stuff really took off during the pandemic, so they've got me over there to meet readers. I don't think anyone will turn up, like, but they're paying and I want to keep the publisher sweet.' He scrunches his nose up at Becca. 'Trust me to get a tour booked for the first time right as I'm getting married.'

Becca rolls her eyes playfully, but she feels so self-conscious, as if Carlos will be taking notes on her, somehow. She's sure she must have misunderstood what he was about to say, that she must have read too much into it. It's Carlos! Carlos could crush on a table if the legs curved in the right way! And OK, yeah, she's *thought* about him, on the odd occasion, but only because he's so overtly and obviously sexual. Over the years they've often been single at the same time, spending chunks of time as surrogate dates for each other on the weekends they needed a plus one for a wedding or birthday party, somebody to hang with at the pub. He's made it clear he thinks she's attractive, but then, she's made it clear she thinks he's attractive too. A spade is a spade. They've known each other for five years, had the salon together for five years. He's like a sibling. She knows everything about him. Noosh has got it wrong. They're close, but they're not in love.

'I forgive you,' she says, realising Noah is waiting for her to say something. It's a conversation they've had ten times already. No, it isn't ideal he's going away. Yes, she's going to miss him. No, she can't take the time off work. Yes, she wishes she could. Yes, they will both survive it – as long as he brings her back the supply of DayQuil and NyQuil she's requested. There's nothing quite like American cold medicine, she discovered on her first and only trip to New York.

'Although I hope this dinner comes with the news that you've been able to secure the venue? And the florist – that was you, too.' She's talking too fast. Noah is bound to spot that something is wrong, that she's being weird.

'I have done all that was delegated in my name,' he says, giving a wee 'Aye aye, captain' salute. 'You're not marrying a brute who thinks his only job is to show up. The question is, have you sorted the cake?'

Becca does a finger-gun point at him. 'No, but it's on my list for tomorrow.'

'Great. The Italian place then? I would ask if you want to join us, Carlos, but . . .'

Carlos waves a hand. 'No, no,' he says. 'Sounds like you've got a full agenda to plough through.' He turns to speak in Becca's direction then, but doesn't meet her eye. He's like a stage actor, trained to look up and out to the balcony seats. 'Why don't you get off? I'll lock up.'

Out on the street, Noah says, 'Is Carlos OK? He seemed . . . I don't know. Not very Carlos?'

'Yeah,' she answers. 'I think he's feeling a bit emotional after Jia Li's baby news.'

'It's so cool,' he replies, slinging his long arm over her shoulders. Becca had texted him at lunch to let him know. 'That will be us, soon enough.'

'Yeah?' Becca says, gazing up at him. But she's acting. She's not in the moment. She's been waiting years to talk about having babies with a husband-to-be and now she can't enjoy it because half her brain is back at the salon with Carlos, if only because he's her friend, her best friend, and Noah is right: he isn't himself. What the hell was he talking about back there?

'I'm thinking three. Three is a nice number. But spaced out, like three within ten years, say?'

'You think I'll still be fertile when I'm forty-five?' says Becca.

'Oh, yes, you're right. So three in . . . five years.'

'That's a lot of being pregnant.'

'Unless we lucked out with twins.'

'A two-for-the-price-of-one special. I wouldn't be mad at that.'

'No.' He smiles, kissing her forehead. 'Me neither.'

They order a bread basket and a glass of wine each as soon as they sit down, weighing up the pros and cons of the cacio e pepe versus carbonara, when Becca's phone bleeps. It's Carlos.

To clarify: I'm not in love with you. Noosh is way off the mark. I think she's just jealous of how close we are, and she'd never seen us together hanging out before last night. That's all xx.

Noah talks and talks, but Becca can't really concentrate. Carlos isn't in love with her. OK. That's good. Not that she thought he genuinely was, but in the twenty minutes since it all got suggested her tummy has churned and her skin has felt funny, as if it's too small for her body, and she might have to crawl out of it and find something bigger, like crabs do.

When Noah excuses himself for the loo Becca replies: *OK, phew! Is there any way you can fix it with her then? Also, I'm not in love with you either. To clarify! X.*

Excellent news. And no, not really. It's been a fun month, but she's not the one for me. It's OK: you win some, you lose some.

'Who's that?' Noah asks as he sits back down. Becca immediately flips her phone over so it's face down.

'Oh, just my mum.' The lie comes out quickly. It isn't intentional, it's just she knows there's no point ruffling any feathers, bringing up a non-event. Noah needed a lot of reassurance after the Mike incident last night; she doesn't want to spend another three hours doing it all over again because of Carlos.

'What's she after?'

'Wanted to know if she'll see you before you go. I told her we'll do a big Sunday lunch when you're back, welcome you home in proper English style.'

Noah takes her head, turning it over to trace the lines of her palm. 'It's going to be horrible without you,' he says. Again.

'Don't go then,' Becca jokes. Again.

'Bec . . .'

She pouts. 'Don't keep making me feel bad for not coming!' she insists. 'What am I supposed to do? My business is here as much as you say your business is over there!'

'Not *as much as I say* it's over there,' Noah corrects, scowling. 'Is that what you think? That I'm making up an excuse to be apart from you just weeks before our wedding? Because if you do . . .'

'No.' Becca pouts. 'Like you say. It's just bad timing. And, well – I suppose I have been dumped for America before, haven't I? So it's entirely possible I'm being mildly oversensitive to it.'

'Only mildly possible,' Noah teases. 'Got it.'

'Shut up.'

'I love you.'

'I love you too.'

They eat their food in happy silence and, once fuelled, Noah pulls out his laptop and they go over the wedding spreadsheet together.

'I'll keep it in Google Docs,' he tells her, 'so we can both work on it when we're apart. I'll email you the link, but you might want to download the app for your phone, too, so you can add notes on the move and all that.'

'Yes, chief,' Becca says, her voice mocking. He raises an eyebrow. 'Not the time for jokes,' she sing-songs when she clocks it. 'Got it. OK, moving on . . .'

'So, you've applied for the legal stuff, and we've got our guest list . . .'

'And it's a great list,' notes Becca. 'Small and perfectly formed.'

'Hard agree. Now let me see . . .' He squints at the screen. 'I suppose we should lock down the details for the invites, then? Send a save-the-date text to everyone like, yesterday?'

'Already done,' Becca tells him. 'With it being so close I figured we'd do a web page as an invite and send everyone the link with the details? Or are we supposed to put in a bit more effort?'

Noah bites his lip. 'Nah,' he says. 'That's our vibe, right? Small, intimate, and just a lot of fun? Very much like, hey, we love you, and we love each other, so we'd love to have you there as we make it official? It's on a Thursday lunchtime, after all. Some people might not make the vows, only the drinks afterwards.'

'The restaurant manager says that's all sorted. I gave him our budget, and he says we can do closed doors, loads of fresh flowers, endless trays of snacks floating around . . .'

'The perk of a two p.m. ceremony,' Noah notes. 'Done by three, and an informal gathering thereafter. People can either fill up on snacks, leave at five, or . . .'

'Pizzas?' supplies Becca. 'I mean, I guess we'll be hungry, won't we, so maybe the restaurant could do us something like that? If that's not too below them . . .'

Noah types into the spreadsheet, highlighting it in pink, to signify it's Becca's responsibility: *6 p.m. pizza? Discuss with manager.*

'Great,' says Becca. 'And we'll just play a wedding-day playlist off Spotify or whatever. I'm not especially keen to spend a day curating a special playlist nobody is going to be able to hear anyway. We don't even have "our" song, so.'

'Wait, we don't?' asks Noah. 'Not even "I Have Nothing"?'

Becca smiles. 'I can ask them to play that when we walk in?'

'Cool.'

'What about photography?'

'I'd like a professional there, yeah,' Becca tells him. 'I know everyone's a photographer with their camera phones, but some formal shots to show our grandkids would be nice, don't you think?'

'It's certainly in the budget,' Noah notes. 'Can that be you too? No. Actually. The time difference won't matter if I'm communicating via email. Me. I'll take that job.'

'So that leaves . . .' Becca starts. 'What we're going to wear, and if we want a wedding party. Do we want a wedding party?'

Noah scrunches up his face. 'If it was in a church,' he says, 'then maybe. But it feels a bit grand for the town hall, doesn't it?'

Becca nods. 'I feel the same.'

'Great! God, I don't know what people complain about. Planning a wedding is piss easy!'

Becca smiles. 'Bish, bash, bosh,' she says. 'Job done.'

'I'll say.' Noah grins. 'I can't wait to be married to you. Hook it up to my veins already!' He shakes a fist at the sky as if God himself might grant the wish.

'Me too,' says Becca, noticing how handsome he is all over again. She loves him. She does. This man she is going to marry.

32

She Texts Back

Delivering a baby with somebody bonds you, Becca understands, and binds you, too. She saw a whole other side to Carlos yesterday and finds herself excited for his arrival this morning. They're going to the retail park just outside of town to get baby stuff and decorations, then they're going back to Jia Li's to double check they got rid of all the mess yesterday and make it lovely for her first trip across the threshold as a mama. Jia Li was kept in hospital, and won't be back for a few days – though, miraculously, she and the baby are absolutely fine. It does give Carlos and Becca some additional time to get things sorted for their return though. Becca has been thinking of Carlos's face as he kept Jia Li calm, how he took off his shirt and his muscles rippled as he cradled the baby. He knew the baby needed to have skin-to-skin contact, and how he'd cried after – Becca had loved him more than she ever had in that moment, enveloped by tears and a thousand emotions herself.

'Man of the hour!' she hears Mike say as he opens the front door. She's tried to explain to him what it was like, the magnitude of the event, what it's like to hear a woman give birth, to see an actual baby come out of a body.

'I'll stay up by your head when that's us,' Mike joked, 'I've heard watching your baby mama give birth is like watching your favourite pub burn down,' and Becca had felt cross with him all night. He just didn't get it.

'Hey, you,' Becca says as she goes into the hallway where Carlos waits. 'Let me give you a hug. You were amazing yesterday, you know. I'm so proud of you.'

Becca isn't sure that Carlos has ever looked bashful in his whole life, but he does, right then, the tips of his ears colouring and his gaze shifting. *I could just kiss you!* Becca thinks, out of nowhere. She means it platonically, of course, like the feeling of wanting to eat a particularly cute and chubby baby.

'Come on,' he says, as way of reply, and it makes Becca's heart grow even more, seeing him let the compliment land.

'See you later,' Becca tells Mike, kissing his cheek. He's properly moved into her house, now. The London contract is up and he's looking for permanent work, deciding what to do next. 'I'll be back at about six, I reckon.'

'Shall I make a start on dinner then?' he asks.

'You're a darling,' she tells him. 'Carlos? Do you want dinner here too?'

Carlos is already out on the path, heading towards the gate. He turns, looks from Becca to Mike, and says, 'Nah, you're all right. Thanks, though.'

As Becca gives Mike one last kiss she swears she sees him look relieved. Huh. He's probably sick of hearing about what a hero Carlos is. That's fair enough.

'So,' Becca says as they set off, him driving, her the passenger.

'So,' Carlos echoes.

She takes off her gloves in the warmth of the car, and suddenly realises, as she sees the engagement ring, that Carlos doesn't yet know.

'Oh,' she says, out loud, sounding surprised enough that Carlos looks over at her, then down at her hand, which she's staring at.

'Bec – is that . . . ?'

'Yeah,' she says, sounding as shocked as he does.

'What!'

'I know,' she says, almost a squeal.

'Woah. You're engaged. Christ alive. Did that happen last night?'

'Last night?' she repeats. And then she remembers: she'd taken off the ring yesterday, when she was getting towels and flannels and making phone calls. She'd taken off all her rings, for hygiene purposes. 'No,' she says. 'In the Lakes. I suppose I had other things on my mind yesterday, I didn't think . . .'

'Of course,' Carlos says, and Becca gets the strangest feeling, as though she's disappointing him, somehow.

'Don't sound *too* excited for me,' she quips, watching the comment land: his eyebrow twitches, he takes a breath, and then his face is the picture of excitement and glee.

'Of course I'm excited for you!' he says, slowing down to wait at some traffic lights. 'I just wasn't expecting it so soon. You haven't even been properly back together . . .'

'I know,' says Becca, watching the folks meandering by on the pavement beside their stopped car. 'But when you know, you know.'

'So I've heard,' he says.

Neither of them speaks, then, and it takes everything Becca has in her not to apologise for blindsiding him. She hadn't meant to; it's just been the maddest twenty-four hours, that's all.

'Hey,' he adds, reaching out a hand to her knee. It is hot and heavy, and sends a jolt of something to her stomach. The lights turn green and he pulls it away again, to have his hands at ten and two on the steering wheel. 'It's amazing. I know how much you've wanted this. It was what you wished for on the summer solstice, wasn't it?'

'Yeah,' Becca says. 'It's funny, actually – I was telling Mike about that when it happened. That we'd done a ritual at the salon and he'd texted right after.'

'Right place, right time,' Carlos notes.

'Maybe.' Becca shrugs. 'Or maybe it was always meant to be. I never felt like we were truly over, you know?'

'Uh-huh,' he muses, indicating right for the entrance to the shops.

Becca can't detect what it means, this *uh-huh*. She's still all jumbled up from yesterday, not to mention the weekend, and all her feelings are jangling together in the pit of her tummy.

'You're such a closed book,' she tells him as they find a parking space. 'Here I am, freaking *engaged*, and I don't even really know anything about your love life. Is there anyone special in your life right now?

They climb out of the car and Carlos gestures to the baby superstore over in the far corner: three floors of everything a new parent and their offspring could ever need.

'No. Kind of,' he says, stuffing his hands into his pockets. 'I don't know. I don't want to talk about it.'

Becca doesn't know what to say to that piece of non-information.

'OK,' she settles on, and they walk into the store in a strange silence.

Inside, they snake through the aisles, trying not to get over-whelmed by the sheer vastness of what's for sale.

'That', Carlos says, pointing to a row of boxes on the end of an aisle, 'appears to be an actual stand-up urinal. Woah.'

Becca laughs. 'That's huge!' she says. 'Who would even put that in their house?'

Carlos squints to read the box. 'Speeds up potty training, apparently,' he says. 'Which can't be true. I was reading last night that boys do better peeing sat down because it empties more of their bladder and prevents accidents.'

'You were reading about potty training?'

He shrugs, unzipping his coat. 'It's cool, Jia Li having a kid. I fell down a Google hole.'

'I think that's very sweet,' Becca replies, genuinely touched.

He shrugs. 'I'm an onion,' he replies. 'I keep trying to tell you so.'

'I know you are,' Becca says softly, reaching out a hand to his arm. 'Hey, I just want to say . . . I know I give you a hard time. I mean' – she pulls a funny face and adopts a silly voice –'I think we give each other a hard time . . .' She's relieved to see Carlos soften at her words. OK. She can work with this. 'But you were incredible yesterday and I really do think you're amazing. I always have done. And I'm sorry if I'm bad at showing it. That's on me. You are, without a doubt, my favourite onion in the whole world.'

He narrows his eyes. 'You promise?' he says, voice low.

'I promise,' Becca assures him. 'And I'm sorry I forgot to tell you my news. That wasn't cool either.'

'No,' Carlos says. 'You're right, it was crazy yesterday. I suppose I just . . .'

'What?' Becca says, and she's suddenly stunned to see her hand is still on his arm, that somehow she's taken a step closer to him, close enough to smell the cedarwood in his cologne. Carlos looks at her hand, too.

'Nothing,' he says. 'Honestly. All I want is for you to be happy. And if you are, that's great. Truly.'

'Great.' She nods, releasing him from her grip. 'Yeah. I am. I'm happy.'

If either of them want to add anything else, they don't.

The alleyway, thinks Becca, recalling what happened. But then she forces herself to forget it, as she promised herself she would. No good will come from thinking any more about the size of his bicep and the feel of his breath on her cheek. The way his gaze made her own breath shallow. How his lips parted, just enough, as though with one second more he could have kissed her.

No.

She pushes it out of her head.

33

She Texts Back

Becca and Mike set the date of the wedding to be New Year's Eve so that they can enter the new year as a married couple. Jessie and Niall are pretty gung-ho about spending their money in whatever way everyone collectively sees fit – unsurprisingly, both of their mothers have a long list of wedding requirements, which Mike and Becca have decided to run with. They don't care – they just want to get on with having a life together, again. Everything else is bells and whistles.

Becca is, however, needed for one important aspect of the planning: the dress. Which is how, one Monday afternoon when the salon is closed, she finds herself trying on wedding dresses with Jessie, Regina, her mother *and* Betty in attendance, sipping champagne on the plush grey sofa as Carlos scowls, somewhat less enthused to have his day off hijacked by, essentially, clothes shopping.

'Thank you for this,' Becca whispers into his ear after he arrives. 'I don't mean to make you sound like a poor man's Jia Li, but as my best *male* friend it's your job to shoot straight with me, OK? These other bitches' – she gestures jokily to the row of women behind her – 'are already cooing and getting high-pitched and emotional. You need to steady this ship, OK, captain?'

Carlos puts a hand on her shoulder. 'Jia Li already called me this morning. I know she's gutted she couldn't be here. Apparently when you become a parent you have to prioritise the child? I don't know, something like that. She said I'm not even allowed to drink today. You never even mentioned that was part of the tradition! I've been deprived since even before knowing what was on offer!'

'Good!' Becca laughs. 'Jia Li is good for briefing you.'

'Oh, she briefed me all right,' he tells her. 'Twenty-five minutes she spent giving me instructions. At one point she even asked me if I wanted to write it all down.'

'Did you?'

'No, Becca, I didn't. It all boiled down to: don't drink like everyone else, tell your mum what a good job she did raising you, and make sure you balance your shoulders out with your hips? I'm less confident with that one, but I'm pretty sure I can tell you if you look hot or not. That's what we're after, I assume?'

Becca rolls her eyes good naturedly. 'Yes, a shagability score out of ten for every dress I try on. Only if you think the vicar himself would want to bend me over the font and have his holy way should you give me the thumbs up. OK?'

'Got it.' Carlos smiles. 'I'm ready.'

Becca looks at him. If she'd worried things were strange between them, she'd wasted her time. They were fine. As friendly and happy and normal as ever.

The women all coo over Carlos: *Isn't he handsome? Didn't he just deliver a baby? What a modern man! And a business owner too, what good manners, are you sure just a drop of champagne won't hurt, Carlos? Come on now, this is supposed to be fun!*

Becca goes through the dresses on display, making a mental note of how she likes the higher-necked styles over anything plunging or V-shaped, which surprises her in itself. She tells the assistant which ones she likes, and the assistant – one older woman, silk scarf tied elegantly at her neck, glasses ready on a string of pearls – looks her up and down and says, 'Excellent. But if I may, do consider this one.'

She holds up a one-shoulder beaded thing.

'A goddess-style neckline', Becca is told, 'will draw the eye up to your face, and you, my dear, have a beautiful face.'

Touched, Becca agrees, and proceeds to disappear behind the heavy velvet curtain to take off her clothes and be helped into various incantations of silk and tulle and beading. Carlos does his job impeccably, shaking his head at every offering, reinforcing exactly what Becca *feels* despite what her mother, Jessie, Regina and Betty tell her.

And then she puts on the goddess dress. It fits like a dream, with very little fussing required from the assistant. It's a long column, with a band across the waist that keeps things stiff, but not clingy. The full-length bodice underneath is tight, a raw silk, and over the top runs a dreamy beaded tulle with flowers, culminating in a big tulle bow at the shoulder. She's the Statue of Liberty, in the best possible way.

'Woah,' she says when she sees it, a sentiment echoed when the curtain is pulled back to the others.

She looks to her mother, first, and then Jessie, and then Regina and Betty. They're all speechless, a first for the afternoon.

'I'm liking this . . .' Becca begins, surprising herself with how much she needs them all to feel the same, even though She Knows.

Her mother is already crying, big heaving sobs with a tissue clutched in a balled-up fist at her mouth, nodding and nodding and nodding. Betty gives a big thumbs up, and then puts her arm around Becca's mum. Jessie stares, also nodding her head, her eyes filling with tears, her hand on Regina's leg, who is blinking back tears of her own and wafting a hand in front of her face like a fan. And Carlos is . . . dumbfounded. Becca cannot read his face *at all*.

'Carlos?'

His jaw is slack. Becca thinks she can just about make out the edges of a smile about to rise up on his face as she searches it for clues. The way he is looking at her – she hopes Mike will look at her like that, too, when she walks down the aisle to him. Carlos swallows hard and inhales so deeply that his chest could almost pop a button on his shirt. He sucks in his cheeks and Becca smiles, waiting for him to mirror her, to agree with everybody else, that this dress is it. She can feel the rise and fall of her own chest, is vaguely aware of the other women chatting between themselves, buzzing about, the assistant saying something to them. But still Becca looks at Carlos, and he at her, until the edges of her vision go fuzzy and everything stops.

'She needs water.'

'Please do be mindful of the dress, won't you?'

'Becca? Becca!'

Becca opens her eyes. Six concerned faces are frowning at her from above.

'Oh, thank goodness,' her mum says. Becca blinks.

'Ouch,' she says, aware of a vague feeling of hurt in her back and leg.

'You fainted,' Carlos says, and the crowd around her disperses as he bends down and looks at her to say, 'Are you OK? Can I lift you up?'

Becca nods, feeling helpless and frail just as she did as a girl on the playground after tumbling.

Carlos crouches down and hooks her arm over his solid muscle of a shoulder, then slips his other arm underneath her and hoists her up, as easily as an empty handbag. She nuzzles into his neck, wanting as much of the surface of herself as possible to be pressed against him, for safety. She closes her eyes. He deposits her into the large leather armchair to the right of the viewing sofa, so she's upright. She could almost be sad the moment is over, and as she drinks her water and takes a moment she realises: she wanted Carlos to keep going. To keep walking with her in his arms, out of the shop, all the way home, all the way to the moon.

Carlos follows her gaze to see what she sees: her mother flapping around; Betty following her; Jessie on her phone googling what to do when somebody has fainted; the assistant trying not to be too obvious about any damage that might have been done to the dress as she frets with a troubled Regina.

'Do you want to get out of here?' Carlos asks her, his voice low and discreet. Becca looks at him. She nods. He nods back, a confirmation. And then he launches into action, her hero.

'Ladies, would you mind awfully if I scoot away with the bride-to-be? I think we've found the winning dress, and I'd like my business partner to still be intact for her appointments this week – not to sound too callous, ha! – but I'm parked right outside so if there's no more business? Becca? Is that OK?'

Everyone looks to Becca and she nods, everyone understanding that the party has come to an abrupt but fair enough end. They've found the dress – apparently so fabulous she fainted in delight (or so she jokes to everyone).

'Do you mind if *we* still go to lunch?' Betty asks her. 'It's just that I'm starving, and it was a hard reservation to get . . .'

'Betty!' her mother scolds, hitting her girlfriend's arm. But then a beat passes and her mum looks at Becca and says, 'Actually, *do* you mind?'

Becca is taken out of the dress and slips on her own clothes, feeling fuzzy, as though Vaseline has been smeared across the lens of her life. People talk for her, at her, around her . . . but she, herself, doesn't have anything to say. She just wants to be home, in bed, preferably sleeping. There's a thought, somewhere at the very back of her mind, about weddings and Mike and Carlos, even? Murky questions that don't add up to make a proper answer. They only serve to make her exhausted. Absolutely, totally exhausted.

Carlos doesn't speak in the car on the way home. As they drive, the silence is deafening, his hands on the wheel and her eyes focused out of the window on the world passing by. *No matter what we do, the world keeps on turning*, Becca thinks to herself.

'Here we are,' Carlos says as they round the corner of her street and he stops his car outside her house. It's a dreary afternoon, and Mike has the lamps on in the living room already, illuminating her life inside, the collection of things she's curated for herself over her adult life, tastefully chosen, carefully collected. 'Home sweet home,' Carlos concludes.

They both look at the house. Becca can see the big, framed print she got a couple of years ago in Manchester, when she and Carlos had been to a training day and wandered around Salford Quays afterwards, talking about what they'd learned and weaving in and out of shops, not really stopping to look at anything until he saw the image and said it was 'very Becca'.

Carlos helped her to hang the curtains – Becca had moved in and thought herself quite handy with the old DIY . . . until the curtain pole she'd put up fell down, because she'd drilled directly into the plaster and hadn't used plugs with the screws.

How many nights have they sat – Jia Li there too, or not – drinking beer and ordering pizza and arguing over what to watch on Netflix? How many little Polaroids of them are on her fridge, or wedged into the bottom of photo frames and mirrors? Carlos helped her to paint her bedroom after she bribed him with tickets to a Foo Fighters gig at the NEC, gifted from a client. She would have taken him anyway. She suspected at the time he would have helped her regardless.

'Carlos . . .' she says, not brave enough to look at him.

'I know,' he says.

'What am I supposed to do?'

Carlos shakes his head. 'I can't tell you what to do,' he says, sadly, and when neither of them says anything else, time passes, and Mike eventually senses they're outside and looks out of the window to wave, and Becca gets out of the car without saying anything else.

34

She Texts Back

'Hey!' Mike says, opening the front door to her, backlit by the hall light so that his face falls into darkness. 'Are you OK? I've not heard from you all day but Jessie says you fainted? What happened? Here, come in, Bec.'

Mike holds out an arm to usher her inside. Becca doesn't turn around. She can't. This is all too confusing, too weird. She accepts a kiss from Mike on her cheek and moves past, kicking off her boots and taking off her jacket.

'Yeah,' she tells him, sliding on her slippers. 'I forgot to eat breakfast.' Her voice sounds hollow, tired.

'That's not like you.'

'I think I'm run down,' she says, standing up straight and watching him close the front door, sliding the safety latch across because that's them now, in for the night, locked away from the cold November evening, just the two of them.

'God, you sound awful. Come on, let me make you a tea.'

They go through into the kitchen, Becca pausing to adjust the blinds on their way through.

Carlos looks at her through the glass of the driver's car door, and Becca is aware of Mike asking her things, or telling her things. Eventually Carlos starts his engine, gives her one last look, and then pulls away from the kerb.

I can't tell you what to do.

'What did you say?' Becca asks, settling on to a stool at the breakfast bar and accepting a peppermint tea, honey on the side.

'I said,' Mike repeats, leaning on the opposite side of the counter before springing off and finding things to do: straightening the tea towels, clearing the dried-out and used tea bags from the tea-bag holder, 'if you don't feel well enough for a chat, that's OK, but I do have something I'd like to sound out with you.'

Becca sighs, casting a glance back over at the shut blinds in the living room. 'I have bandwidth,' she tells him. She'd rather hear Mike's thoughts than marinade in the confusing mulch of her own. He's handsome, Mike, in his marl-grey joggers with bare feet, his white T-shirt hugging his form. Isn't this what Becca always wanted? Her man, making her tea, asking about her day, looking after her? 'I'm just tired now, is all. I might go to bed early.'

Mike fishes about for new bin bags under the sink, coming up victorious and starting the messy endeavour of taking the full bag out, tying it, replacing it. He has an energy about him tonight, Becca thinks. Skittish. Something curdles in her stomach.

'So,' Mike presses, once he's done. Finally he stands still, the only tick betraying his outward demeanour a bobbing, excited leg. 'I have a whole PowerPoint presentation for you – I can give you the full kit and caboodle in terms of hard sell. But I'm . . . seventy-five per cent sure I won't need the hard sell.'

Becca drinks. It's warm and soothing, a reminder that she can do this. This will be OK.

But what is 'this'?

'I got a formal job offer today,' he says, raising his eyebrows as he waits for her to be impressed – which she is. She was impressed when he started putting himself back out there again full stop, proud that he got back up again after his proverbial fall.

'Oh, wow!' Becca says, genuinely thrilled. She thinks about what her dad said after they'd got engaged: a man needs to feel like a man. Is this what she has been holding her breath for? This last piece of the puzzle? 'I didn't even know you'd interviewed – I haven't wanted to breathe down your neck or anything. Oh, Mike, I'm so pleased for you!'

'Well,' Mike starts, and it's obviously what he is going to say before he says it, because the look on his face is familiar. Drummers tap on her temples, rhythmless but persistent. She rubs at them.

'It's a perfect role for me,' he says. 'The guy knows everything about me: everything about the business, how it started and how it ended, that it's been tough to bounce back. I met him through the consultancy gig. And he's gone out on his own and wants me to join him. He's passionate about having a team who have experienced failure to become better, which as a work culture is just great. There are two other people on the team who have had businesses end, for one reason or another, and as a team they go over the hows and whys as they build this new business – because it's a start-up. Again. The money is good enough and will only get better, the people are good, it feels like a really great fit . . . We're failing *up*, proving it's possible.'

'So what's the catch?' Becca asks.

'OK, well, I just want to say: this is probably the best offer I'll get. It's a coaching business: there's a website, an app, in-person and online events. It started from a place of grief for the founder, Jerry, and the ethos is based on how we have many losses in our lives, from our parents dying – which with Dad getting sick, it just so made me think, you know? – to the grief that comes from a smaller loss, like not getting a promotion or deciding not to have the second child you wanted, life events that we brush aside and don't properly examine. This coaching business encourages building in a grieving period for those things, too, in this really healthy and positive way, which is just . . .' He kisses his fingertips like a chef pleased with the meal they've just prepared. 'It's a contribution to undoing toxic masculinity, helping people embrace the lows as part of the highs, everything that I've been trying to do, personally, this year . . .'

Becca nods, letting him get his sales spiel out of his system. She loves him. She wants him to have the sparkle in his eye that she can see right now, plain as day.

'The thing is', he tells her, 'that it's in London, with some LA stuff needed to.'

'I see,' Becca says.

'And the culture is very face to face. Remote working is great for the right company, but for the stage these guys are at, we're talking being in the office at least three days a week, probably four.'

'Hm.'

She drinks the last of her tea as Mike watches her, then puts her mug down beside his untouched one.

'It feels like déjà vu, I know.' He holds up his hands, gesticulating with passion. 'This is exactly what happened last time. I get it. But London isn't New York, and we've already trialled what it's like for me to be away in the week and it worked, didn't it?'

Becca's shoulders slump. She runs a finger around the rim of her mug, around and around and around. Neither of them speak, and the air grows thick about them, like a crumbling house enveloped by rising weeds.

'I thought . . .' Mike says, eventually.

Becca looks at him. 'The past few months have worked because it was temporary, Mike,' she tells him. 'I've been so clear about what I need from you. So upfront from the start that I'm not interested in—'

'Me fulfilling my potential, like you fulfil yours?'

She remembers what he said, back in the summer, outside the café – that her certainty about what she wanted to do with her work life made him feel emasculated. Had she known then that this was ultimately where they'd end up, like a car crash in slow motion?

'It's only London, Bec.'

'How much time in LA?' she asks.

He looks at his feet. 'Fifty per cent,' he admits.

'Have you already accepted it?'

She refuses to look away from him as he avoids her gaze, staring at him until he gathers the courage to fleetingly look at her and say, in a small voice, 'Yes.'

Mike furrows his brow, frustrated, and closes his eyes as he cradles the back of his head, an exasperated coach whose team aren't playing their best.

'Look,' Becca presses, after taking a breath, knowing she has to say this now, that if they push it aside or agree to talk tomorrow she will never find the courage to say it and will somehow betray herself. Carlos's face pops into her mind, but this isn't about him. Not right now. This is about her and Mike. 'I'm not saying don't go.'

Mike looks at her. Oh my God,' he says. 'Is this an ultimatum?'

Becca shakes her head. 'No,' she tells him. 'And that *is* different from last time. I'm not angry that you're excited about this job, or that you want to take it. And if you want to move to London, or LA, I won't stop you. I haven't seen you this enthused in the whole time you've been back. I know you love me, and I love you too . . .'

'But what?'

'I don't know.' Becca shrugs. 'If your dad hadn't got ill would our reunion just have fizzled out? We got engaged under such *emotional* circumstances, and I wanted you, and us. But . . . are we sure we want to get married?'

Mike's jaw drops. 'Woah,' he says. 'So now you don't even want to get married? You're saying . . . what? What are you saying?'

'I'm saying . . . let's slow this down. Can we talk about it?'

'Talk about if we should get married?'

'Yes.'

Mike shakes his head. 'I honestly hoped you would say yes, you know. To moving. I thought we'd be husband and wife and start a brand-new life *together*. Not me just slotting back into the one you've made without me . . .'

'My life is here.'

'Even if I'm not?'

Becca bites her bottom lip. 'Mike, answer this honestly: is your life still going to be out there, even if I'm not?'

She knows what the answer is, because she's already seen it on his face. He wants the job more than he wants her. He *needs* the job more than he needs her – exactly as her dad said he would.

But.

She's . . . *relieved*. She can't fully articulate why, but there's an inescapability about the conversation, a sense of the other shoe dropping. They've finally got their final chapter. Their third act. Their conclusion.

'Ah, crap,' he says, again.

'I know,' she tells him, standing up and moving to give him a hug. This is it; this is their ending.

Should they ever have started?

Yeah, she thinks, hugging him. *I would always have wondered otherwise.*

They stand in the kitchen, holding on to one another in silence. Becca starts to cry. She loves him, she knows she loves him . . . but she isn't *in love* with him, not any more. They got carried away. And if Mike is really honest with himself, Becca knows he'll come to the same conclusion. She feels his love, but he isn't *in love* with her. He wouldn't happily move across the world without her if he was.

35

She Doesn't Text Back

'I can't believe you're two weeks out from getting *married*, Bec! Isn't it crazy to think how much has changed in only a few short months? Back in June all of this was just a wish and prayer and now here we are, only the middle of November, and . . . *getting married!*'

Becca sits opposite her best friend in the Italian deli, cradling baby Haoyu in her arms until he begins to squirm and cry, at which point she's grateful that Jia Li motions for him to be handed back. Jia Li has been flicking through the mirror selfies Becca took from the fitting rooms of John Lewis, where she found an incredibly chic Bianca Jaggeresque white suit for the wedding day, which she intends to pair with a red lip and a low chignon, and a bunch of yellow mimosa.

'You look very much like you, but on your wedding day, you know?' Jia Li declares. 'It's going to be amazing.'

'Yeah.' Becca smiles. 'That's the exact vibe that I want. I don't want to feel like I'm putting on a show, or a performance. And hopefully everything's been organised in a way that means all of you feel that way, too – the guests. I've been to a lot of weddings where I don't think I started having fun until after the dinner and speeches.'

Haoyu gurgles, a signal for Jia Li to flop her boob out. The first time she did it, Becca didn't know where to look, if she should leave, what was polite. She's seen Jia Li's boobs before, but to see her breastfeed felt so intimate, until Jia Li had waved a hand and said, 'I'm not gonna get any shier about it, so you may as well get used to it.'

'I know what you mean about this year being wild though – me engaged to a man I didn't know existed when we did those manifestations, you with a surprise baby. Which, I have to say, is less surprising than the fact that it's Dave's. I can't believe I never knew you guys hooked up . . .'

'I know,' Jia Li replies. 'But what can I say? When absolutely nobody knows, it makes it even hotter, and God, is that man hot in the sack. At the pub he's all conservative and formal but get him naked and *whoo*!'

Becca looks pointedly at Haoyu, as if he could understand any of it.

'He's two weeks old, Bec. I think he's too young to understand that he was conceived through my slutty declaration that I was DTF after one too many Bombay Sapphires.'

Becca laughs. 'Fair. Very fair.'

'I will say, though, I've had feelings for Dave pretty much this whole time. I don't know why I ever took him to the friend-of-a-friend party and actively encouraged him getting together with somebody else. When he left with Kaylee, I was gutted.'

Becca tuts. 'You idiot.'

'I know! I own that! Dave thinks so too! I was just so terrified to be so close to something that good. We'd sleep together every few weeks, and then every week . . . now I know I was so up for it because he'd already got me pregnant. I reckon it was the pregnancy hormones; I was gagging for it. I've googled it, and apparently in the first trimester all that blood flow can make your clitoris—'

Becca holds up a hand. 'I've got it,' she says with a chuckle. 'Thank you.'

Jia Li is nonplussed. 'Well. I tried to push him away, I suppose, and then he actually dated her – and I like her, you know? I'm just relieved they broke up for their own reasons and not because of me.'

'Didn't Dave say he always fancied you though?'

'Yeah.' She laughs. 'Intimidated, he reckons. My arse. The FBI couldn't intimidate that man.'

'And now you've given in to it. Given in to the something good . . .'

'Disgusting, I know,' Jia Li replies. 'It's like I didn't want to stare directly into the sun or something, and now I can't look away, even if it's blinding.'

'Blinded by love.'

'Who'd have thought?

The women smile; the baby feeds; their pastries are eaten.

'Don't kill me,' Becca says, and automatically Jia Li looks up and raises an eyebrow, like: *Oh here she goes, go on then* . . . 'But . . . I always thought that you maybe had a thing for Carlos . . . ?'

She lets the not-quite-question hang in the air. Jia Li shakes her head.

'You're an idiot,' she replies.

'I'm just asking!' defends Becca.

'I know you are! That's what makes you such an idiot!'

Becca shrugs and waits for a better answer, using the final bite of her croissant to mop up the last of the milk foam in her cup. When Jia Li doesn't offer any more information, Becca says, 'It's just – I know something happened. Years ago now . . .'

'It did,' says Jia Li. 'I tried to kiss him, he kissed me back for a split second, and then he said he didn't feel the same.'

'But you liked him?'

'For a heartbeat, when I first started, yeah. I think I mostly wanted to see if I stood a chance, really. And when I realised I didn't, I was upset for a week, maybe two, and then I was fine. I honestly don't think about it, except to occasionally give him shit for it. Have you thought I was secretly in love with Carlos all this time?'

Becca scrunches up her nose. 'Yeah,' she admits. 'I think I have.'

'I swear to God, the pair of you need your heads knocking together.'

'Who? Me and Carlos?'

'Yes!' cries Jia Li. 'Jesus Christ!'

Jia Li blinks at her, and Becca waits.

'Look,' Jia Li says, with a Tone. 'I'm not allowed to say any more because I am sworn to secrecy and *you*, my fair lady, have bigger things to worry about than Carlos. You're getting MARRIED.'

Becca wants to ask follow-up questions, and yet can't. His name turns over in the back of her mind: *CarlosCarlosCarlosCarlos*.

'Did you know Noosh broke up with Carlos because she thinks he's in love with *me*?'

'I did know that, yes.'

'Stupid, isn't it?'

Jia Li rolls her eyes so hard her head might fall off.

'You don't think . . .' Becca says.

'I said I'm not allowed to talk about it.'

'Talk about what?' Becca presses.

'Bec . . .' Jia Li says, warningly. 'If you open this box, you won't be able to close it . . .'

Becca searches Jia Li's eyes for clues, but only gets a warning.

'Fine,' Becca settles on, waving a hand. 'You win.' She mimics zipping her mouth and throwing away the key, because if she does that everything can stay the same and she doesn't have to know anything that might rock the boat. Then, getting back on conversational track, she muses: 'Did you ever think it might not happen? The happily ever after? You always seemed so relaxed that it would all work out and I've envied you for that, sometimes. All the years I tortured myself about where my guy is . . .'

'And he was in a bar, waiting for me to get his number for you.'

Becca grins. 'Yes, yes, my happily ever after is all because of you, the note-takers for today's deposition will be sure to write that bit in bold.'

353

'Thank you!'

Becca playfully hits her friend's shoulder, careful not to disturb the baby.

'And I did worry, for what it's worth,' says Jia Li. 'I put on a good show, but I have to admit that I feel a relief at the man, the baby. Like, I can exhale. Don't tell the other feminists I said that, though.'

'Your secret is safe with me.'

'And I'm happy you'll have that too. It's a new chapter, isn't it? Something more . . . stable.'

'I feel the same, yes. It's all I've ever wanted. My salon, my little group of friends and my family nearby, and a child and a husband.'

'But it is *this* man you want, isn't it? Not just any husband.'

Becca squints at the embedded almost-accusation within this, pouting her lips as she digests the question.

'I don't mean, like, you'd marry anyone . . .' Jia Li says. 'Don't get me wrong.'

'OK . . .'

'No, forget I even asked that, actually. Sorry. Baby brain.'

Jia Li fusses with Haoyu and Becca turns over the last ninety seconds of conversation in her mind. Of course she doesn't want just *any* husband. She wants Noah! If she'd met him in her twenties, or even any sooner, any closer to her break-up with Mike, would she have recognised him as somebody to spend the rest of her life with? No, not necessarily. But that isn't a comment on Noah, that's a comment on how she is in the right place herself, now, to take marriage and good guys and commitment seriously. They were at the right place at the right time, two people both ready for it and going all in. It's the love story she always wanted for herself.

'Tell me more about the wedding planning, anyway,' Jia Li presses, brightly, an obvious attempt to move the chat on and keep things light. 'Can I do anything?'

Becca looks at the baby, suckling away. 'I think you've got your hands full, don't you?'

Jia Li glances down, her eyes filled with love. 'Yes,' she agrees. 'But maybe I can get Dave on the case?'

'We're fine,' Becca insists. 'Town hall and the restaurant we got engaged at. Easy-peasy.'

'Good!' says Jia Li, keeping the brightness to her voice. 'That's good! Great. It's just all so amazing.'

'Yeah,' agrees Becca, but she knows there is more her friend wants to say. Jia Li won't push her agenda any further without Becca expressly inviting her to, and normally Becca wants to know everything Jia Li thinks, because Jia Li loves her and pushes her and challenges her, and, above all else, Becca trusts her. It would be so easy to say, *Jia Li, do you think I'm doing the right thing?* But doing so would mean admitting that somewhere, buried as deep as it is possible to stuff an errant, inconvenient thought, there is, indeed, a thought like that to be had. *And there isn't, is there?* Becca concludes, noticing the time. And so it remains unasked, neither woman bringing up the possibility of doubts, a game of chicken neither will name.

On the way home, Becca spots Mike before he spots her. She has a choice: she can hide from him, or she can approach. He looks up. They lock eyes. He raises a hand, slowly, as though he isn't sure what she'll do.

'I don't remember much from the other night,' he says when she reaches him. 'But I know enough to gather that I owe you an apology.'

'It was two weeks ago,' Becca says, wafting a hand to her shoulder as if that's where the past is.

'What if I said it's taken two weeks to gather my courage?'

Becca nods. 'I could believe that,' she replies.

He doesn't look well. Mike looks bloated, puffy, as if he's been drinking too much and sleeping too little.

'How's your dad?'

Mike nods. 'Yeah, OK. He's going to be fine. Just waiting for the latest bloods.'

'And Jessie? The baby?'

'They're good too, thanks.'

He scuffs his shoe on the ground, pulls his coat closer to his body.

'And how are you?' Becca asks, softly.

'Pretty low, to be honest,' he says with a hollow laugh. 'My business went under, I'm living in Jessie's spare room, I can't seem to . . . get a hold of myself.'

'Hmmmm,' says Becca. 'Is that why you came home? The business went under?'

He looks at her. 'I don't know what happened, Becca. I'm lost,' he sobs. 'I'm so lost.'

'Oh, Mike.'

Becca can't stand to see him this way. In her head he's this vibrant, larger-than-life, happy-go-lucky mirage of a man.

The person crying in front of her is a shadow of that. It hurts to see.

Becca opens her arms and Mike launches himself between them, wrapping his own arms around her and squeezing tight. They stand like that for a minute, which becomes two, Mike's crying getting worse before it eases off and peters out, until after ten minutes, maybe more, he finally pulls away.

'Sorry Bec,' he says. 'I don't mean to dump all over you.'

'Are you going to be all right?' she asks. 'You should speak to somebody – call your GP, explain what's going on.'

'Yeah,' he says, wiping his face with the sleeve of his coat. 'Urgh. Yeah. I know.'

Becca looks at him, weighing up what to do. She cares for him, but she can't be the person to help him through this. If he thinks she should be, Mike is living in the past – and, finally, Becca isn't. She hasn't been for a while, now. Noah has offered her a future, and she's taking it.

'I've got to go,' she says, and he nods sadly. 'Be well,' she tells him.

'Yeah,' he replies. 'You too.'

And yet, Becca cries when she gets home. There's only one thing for it: she needs her mum.

36

She Doesn't Text Back

Becca goes up and past the dog rescue centre, looping across the road and back down the other side of town, through the park, near the salon but not directly past it. She meanders out beyond the green and then knocks on her mum's front door, an unannounced visitor. Betty answers.

'Hello, you!' Betty says, smiling. 'What a nice surprise!'

Becca feels disloyal for the sinking feeling of disappointment that Betty is home. She wanted her mama to herself, not to have to share, but to have her mother's fullest attention so she could speak freely.

'Hey,' Becca says, trying to smile, and then Betty holds out her arms, wordless, and Becca sinks into them and she's trying not to cry but she doesn't know why, only that she's feeling a lot of feelings and would like to put a few of them down, so she doesn't have to carry them, so she doesn't have to bear their weight.

Still in the embrace, Betty says, her arms shockingly strong in their grip, 'It's just me here, kid, but I think you should come in anyway.'

Becca has never been alone with Betty without her mum in the other room, or on her way. Becca likes Betty, but she doesn't know her very well. It's strange, then, to cross the threshold of the flat with only her, to use the loo and come out to Betty holding two glasses of kombucha, because she happens to know Becca quite likes it. It's touching.

'We can just watch TV if you don't want to talk,' Betty offers, as Becca settles into a chair. 'Or I can be all ears, if you need a shoulder. Whatever you want.'

Becca looks at her glass. 'I don't know what I want,' she says. 'I feel a bit . . .' The words stick in her throat. 'A bit . . .' She can't finish the sentence. She doesn't know how.

'Hmmm,' says Betty, taking a long pull from her glass. 'It's not bad, is it? This stuff?'

Becca shakes her head. 'No,' she agrees, unsure if she's wrong to be emotional in front of her – Betty has never struck her as particularly sentimental. She's tough, a straight-shooter and a straight-talker. You always know where you are with Betty. That's what her mum loves, she'd told Becca once. She'd said Betty made it OK to be herself, because Betty is always, but always, *her*self.

'Nice to be surprised,' Betty continues. 'Try something new. I tend to like what I like now I'm seventy, but I can see how giving something a go can make a person feel young again. Remind them there's still so much up ahead.'

Becca doesn't know how to respond – it's a drink, not a newly invented position for the Kama Sutra – so she smiles.

'No time limit, I suppose is what I'm saying. Who told me I had to have everything set in stone by a certain age, a certain time in my life?'

And that's when Becca understands what she's doing. Betty is approaching her tears sideways-on. The kombucha is a metaphor for . . . well, actually, she can't figure that bit out. But Becca is certain that they're not just talking about kombucha.

'Have you felt that pressure before?' Becca asks, grappling to locate the exact direction the conversation is supposed to be going in.

'Sure,' Betty says. 'Why do you think I married a man in 1979?'

Becca nods. 'I got my hair cut into a bob the day before my twenty-first birthday because I thought grown-ups had short hair,' she confesses. 'I looked awful.'

'Yes.' Betty nods. 'Far better to do what we feel is right and go a little slower than rush over the finish line simply to be done.' Becca looks at her. Is she saying what Becca thinks she is saying? 'Plenty of time for bobbed hair,' Betty adds, her expression soft, her smile gentle.

Ah. Yes. She is.

'Am I getting married too fast?' she asks.

Betty shrugs. 'Who can say?' she replies.

'I think I'm supposed to have more conviction,' says Becca. 'Aren't I?'

Betty chews this over. 'Worries are normal,' she says. 'Doubts are normal. But what I would say is this: you know it's the right person when they're the one you can talk about those doubts with. And if you can't . . .'

Becca nods. 'I think you're right,' she says. Then: 'I saw my ex just now. He's not doing great.'

'Does that make you happy, or sad?'

'I don't feel smug, if that's what you mean,' she says. 'I feel more . . . sad that it isn't my job to help him. And I hope somebody does.'

'He's on his own timeline,' Betty says. 'He'll be OK. We've all got to paddle our own canoe.'

Becca nods. 'OK.'

Walking back to her house, Becca googles what time it is in Austin, where Noah is, according to the last text he sent her from the flight. Seven a.m. It's cold today, and she doesn't have her AirPods with her, so she holds the phone to her ear as it rings, old school. It rings and rings, her fingers already tingling from the chill, and after six or so high-pitched trills from FaceTime audio she assumes Noah won't answer, that it's too early. Right as she pulls the phone away from her ear the call connects, and she's hears an oddly enthusiastic, 'Hello!'

'Oh!' she says, noting how nice it is to hear his voice, how her blood surges with joy that he's there, that's he's answered. 'I thought it might be too early,' she says. 'I'm so glad you picked up!'

'Yeah!' he says, loudly, sing-songy. 'Of course! I was just about to take a shower, actually. Hi, babe!'

'Babe?' Becca smiles. 'Wow. You really must miss me. I don't think I've ever heard you call me babe, ever. Not since you once tried it and I took the piss.'

'What!' he says. Still loud. Still sing-song. Like, oddly so. 'No!' he says, poo-pooing her objections. 'I call you that all the time!'

Becca stops walking. *Spidey-Sense.*

'OK,' she says, letting it go. She looks around the park, the grey sky seemingly closer to the ground than a blue one, menacing. Ominous. A threat looming. 'Well. I've just been thinking about you,' she says. 'I've not heard from you much. I know you're busy, I just can't wait until you're back, is all. Is it going well?'

'Yeah, yeah,' Noah replies, quickly. 'Really well.'

And then she hears it. A door. Noah doesn't speak, and Becca finds she isn't able to. He just said he was about to take a shower. A door that thuds like that – it's a hotel door, not a bathroom door. He wouldn't be going out of his hotel door if he was about to shower. But somebody did, somebody either entered or left his room.

'Who's that?' Becca asks, holding her breath for the reply.

And when he tries to tell her it's nothing, no one, her Spidey-Sense goes aflame.

'It's Rachel,' he says. 'Just dropping something off for me.'

'Rachel . . .' His publicist, the person on tour with him, is a man called John. And then the penny drops. 'Rachel White? Your ex?'

Noah doesn't say anything for a very long time; all Becca can hear is his breathing. And then he says, his voice small, 'I'm so sorry, Bec. I've messed up.'

37

She Doesn't Text Back

Becca paces her living room, up and down, up and down. Noah sent his live location once he'd cleared baggage claim at Birmingham, and she can see him on the little map on her screen edging south to the M42 at a painstakingly slow speed, and then faster, hurtling towards King's Heath, the exit at junction 3, the left turn at Portway Island. She has no idea what she wants to say to him.

She's told nobody. The hurt she feels is so visceral, so searing, that she's worried that to open her mouth would be to scream and never stop. She's never felt pain like this. Three days ago she hung up the phone from where she stood in the park, walked home, showered, and stared at the wall until suddenly it was dark and she'd been there four hours. She didn't answer his calls, though he tried. He called and he called again, but her phone was on the sideboard of the kitchen, screen down, set to silent. She took off her Apple Watch so that didn't ring either.

She went into work as normal, slipping in and slipping out, even this morning, somehow managing to paste on a smile and do her work and keep putting one foot in front of the other. It took thirty-six hours to look at her phone – 54 texts, 19 missed calls, and an email that read: *Bec. I cannot lose you. I'm coming home on Friday. I'll come straight to yours. I don't think I can explain, but I can pledge to spend every single day of the rest of our lives making this up to you.*

He gets closer. She looks out of the window. A people carrier pulls up, the driver climbing out to help with the suitcase from the boot, a wan, tired-looking Noah getting wet from the rain approaching her front door.

'Becca,' he says when she opens it. She looks at him, trying to find clues about who he really is. He isn't the person she thought she knew. The Noah she thought she knew wouldn't be halfway across the world with another woman. The Noah she thought knew wouldn't even have come close to being so careless with her heart. So reckless.

She lets him in. They sit on opposite sofas.

'I love you,' Noah says. 'I don't know why I did what I did but I want *you*. I love *you*.'

Becca nods stoically. She doesn't feel anything. She is numb. Her voice is hollow when she asks, 'If you love me, why would you . . . Well. Actually. I'm not sure what you've done, exactly.'

Noah nods, schoolboy reprimanded. 'She was there,' he says, not using Rachel's name. 'At the first stop in New York. And she was persistent. She'd made it clear in Miami that she wanted . . . not that she wanted me back, we were never serious, but that she wanted to continue whatever it was we had.'

Becca bites her lip, processing. She should never have ignored her Spidey-Sense back on holiday, either. She *knew* Rachel was still into him, no matter what he'd said about her supposedly having a boyfriend.

'I said no – we were together, you and me, and I was happy. I *am* happy, Bec. But then she showed up on the first date of the tour as the interviewer, and somebody dropped out upstate so she came there too, and . . . and I know this isn't an excuse but I think I let it happen to prove that it shouldn't, you know? To prove to her, and myself, that there wasn't anything there any more, and . . .'

Becca feels tears in her eyes. Why would he do this? Why would he test their love? Because she does love him – or did. She doesn't know how she feels now. Everything she could say, or ask, is jammed in her throat and the quieter she is the more Noah just keeps talking. Knowing the details is a perverse, sickening pleasure. It hurts, and she asks him to stop.

'It was in my head about your ex, how he sent you flowers and you didn't tell me. I felt scared, Bec, that you were going to leave me for him.'

'So which is it?' Becca says. 'You did it to prove it was over between you and Rachel, or you did it to punish me for somebody sending me flowers and me trying to forget about it?'

'Why didn't you tell me he did that?'

'You hate knowing I even have an ex, Noah, let alone that he's tried to make contact with me. This isn't *my* fault. This is you!' Becca's voice is getting louder. '*You* made a choice to cheat. That's on YOU.'

'I take full responsibility,' he tells her. 'I don't know what I was thinking. I'm so messed up about it. Bec?'

He moves from his couch to hers, sits beside her, reaches for her hand. She lets him take it, observing it happen as an out-of-body experience.

'I need you to forgive me,' he tells her, and she tries to look at him, tries to focus, but it's like she can see through him, she can't make her eyes focus on his face, his body. She is only vaguely aware of the shape of him, his outline.

'I just don't understand how you could hurt me on purpose,' she says, finally. 'You didn't hurt me by accident. You made a choice to hurt me.'

He absorbs what she's said, looking to the ceiling, looking to the floor, looking at the hands in his lap.

'I know,' he says. 'And if I lose you because of it I am going to regret it for the rest of my life. Bec, listen. I am here, asking you to let me keep loving you. I need you to. I don't know what I'd do without you now I've found you . . . I know it's no excuse but my mum, I told you . . . it's made me so goddamn needy, and I hate that about myself. I hate needing anyone so I push them away before they can . . . before they can *abandon me*.'

And then he sobs, a big hiccup of a noise leaping out of his mouth, and it's a slap to the cheek, a way to drag Becca's consciousness back to the room to be where they are. She watches his face crumple, contort, so that he looks ugly almost, snot hanging from his nose, eyes screwed up, face red and blotchy. She doesn't hate him. She just doesn't understand what she did to deserve it. But then she has a thought.

It's all been too good to be true.

Meeting him, falling for him, getting engaged. That isn't real life. Real life is friction, and mistakes. People are fallible. They screw up. They even upset the people they love most in the world. Does that mean they should have the love once given them rescinded, a refund on a faulty product? Becca sighs. She's so tired. She hasn't slept since she found out, and now she could sleep for a hundred years. She reaches out a hand to his. She holds it.

'I'm not abandoning you,' she tells him, softly, crying herself now. 'I made a promise.'

His tears of relief leave wet patches on her shoulder, but Becca doesn't cry at all. She is stoic. Resolved. Searching for her courage to see this through because she hasn't come this far to only come this far. She has no choice. Everybody makes mistakes. She can still do this. Can't she? If he's sorry?

38

She Texts Back

The worst part of breaking up with Mike is telling her would-have-been in-laws, and her own mother. Everyone is disappointed and upset, had put so much faith in their love story.

'I can't un-know what I know now, though, Mum,' Becca had said when Shelley suggested they just postpone the wedding rather than break up altogether.

'But I don't understand, darling. He'd be back at weekends, and the job wouldn't be forever. Aren't you being a little heavy-handed?'

She'd tried to make her understand. She told her, 'He didn't even talk to me about the job, Mum. He accepted it without consultation precisely because he knew I'd be upset.'

Jia Li and Carlos have been more understanding. Becca has found solace in the salon, filling her diary with extra appointments. Work has been her refuge, chatting with people about their festive plans, what they've been up to. Monique from the manifestation ceremony came in, saying she'd finally left her husband. Carlos says he's seen Heidi, the food PR, praying for her sister, who has, indeed, made a full recovery. Becca might not have got the Mr Right she'd asked for, but so many of the people around her had their manifestations come true, and it stokes the fires of her hope.

'I admire your bravery,' Jia Li tells her when she stops by after closing one night; Haoyu is with Dave and so she is partaking in a newly rare night of freedom. 'It takes a strong person to go after what they want, but it takes an even stronger one to change their mind, or switch course.'

'Thank you,' Becca says. 'I do think it's for the best. I'm sad, but not . . . heartbroken, if that makes sense.'

'It makes sense,' agrees Carlos.

'And this year has definitely taught me some things. Mainly that I know, without a shadow of a doubt, that Mike isn't my guy. The last thread that had me holding on and held back, even without realising . . . it's gone.'

'You've purged the *what if*,' offers Jia Li, and Becca clicks her fingers and points because she's bang on the money.

'And me for him,' Becca adds. 'He knows for sure now too.'

'Yeah, but you nearly *married* him,' Carlos quips, and Becca looks at him, the truth hitting her like a ton of bricks.

'I don't think I would have done,' she says. 'It was never meant to be. Not in any universe.'

39

She Doesn't Text Back

The thirtieth of November fast approaches, the wedding only days away. Noah is sweet with Becca, attentive and careful, and Becca lets him try to make it up to her, try to get her trust back. That's what she tells herself: she owes it to love to try, Beyoncé and Jay-Z style. They can build back stronger.

'Bec? Hello? Earth to Becca?'

She blinks. Carlos is waving a hand in front of her face. It's just the two of them, after hours, clearing up.

'Sorry,' she says, coming to. 'I was miles away there.' She forces a smile. This is how it has been: distracted. 'I think a wine tasting is a great idea for the community calendar, yes. The sex workshop I'm less sure about but I could be persuaded. But wine, yes. Good.' She gives him two thumbs up and an approximation of enthusiasm, which feels more like a grimace, to be honest.

'Becca,' Carlos says, 'are you all right? I feel you've not been right, and I can't bear the thought of you in need of an ear and me not pushing the issue. I'm here for you, you know.'

She hates the tone of his voice. He's being all gentle and caring and it's unnerving. His jokes have stopped, his banter. She doesn't know what to say or how to pretend everything is fine and so the silences between them have become loaded, little bombs waiting to explode. Carlos has been asking what's going on and she's brushed it off but she can tell they're about to have a Chat because if she doesn't tell somebody, soon, she won't be able to get married. She needs to unburden her soul.

'No, I'm not OK,' Becca tells him, her voice coming from the other end of a long, dark tunnel. Then she self-corrects, 'Well, I am now. I haven't been.' Tears fill her eyes and she looks up to will them away. When that doesn't work and they spill over her waterline she uses two knuckles to wipe them, blinking fast. OK. It's coming out, whether she likes it or not. Crap.

'Sit,' Carlos says, in the most serious voice Becca has ever heard from him. He spins around a salon chair, locks the door, and pulls over another chair to sit knee to knee.

'You go slowly, from the beginning, and you don't stop talking until you've told me everything, OK?'

'Can you open a bottle of something?' she says, gesturing to the staff kitchen. 'Anything.'

She considers where the beginning of her story is, exactly how she wants to word it to Carlos. He locates a cold bottle of champagne and two mugs, orders a pizza for delivery from his phone, takes tissues from the front desk and gets a throw from the waiting area to drape over their knees.

Once Becca starts talking, she doesn't stop. She tells him everything. And as she speaks, Carlos's face gets darker and darker, until they've long eaten and drunk, and Becca has emptied her brain into the space between them, for Carlos's consideration.

She waits for his conclusion, for the special sentence that will help her get through this, to reconcile it all in her mind. Instead, Carlos stands up, gently folds the blanket into four, and tells her: 'I'm going to kill him.'

Carlos bolts for the back door, through the staff room, not even bothering to slow down enough for his coat. Becca thinks it's a sick joke at first, but his speed, his determination . . . the fact that he doesn't come back. He's not messing around.

Becca fumbles for her keys in her bag and leaps up to follow him. It's raining, awful November drizzle, the sort of rain that comes down fuzzy but leaves you wet to the bone. There are two routes a person can take back to Becca's if they go the back way, and she stands, looking left and right, trying to decide which way Carlos has gone. She looks one way, and then the other.

'Bugger,' she says, shaking her head, undecided – until she isn't, when she suddenly surges right and pegs it to the end of the back alley.

'Carlos!' she shouts when she sees him. He's striding to the park, his long-sleeved T-shirt stuck to his back, his head low. Becca can see every muscle of his shoulders and spine ripple as each foot thuds heavily to the ground. His fists are balled up. He's a video-game character, out for blood and vengeance. 'For crying out loud! Carlos!'

Becca breaks into a sprint, and it's actually not hard to catch up with him. 'Carlos!' she repeats. 'PLEASE!'

Becca manages to not only reach him, but to overtake him, so that she can slip in front and face him.

'Stop,' she implores him, dancing from side to side to block his path. They're at the edge of the park now, the rain coming down harder. She reaches out both hands to his shoulders and when he looks at her, water dripping from his eyelashes and chin, she says, 'This isn't your fight, Carlos.'

She's just as soaked as he is, the thin knit of her skinny polo neck a sponge, hair plastered in thick welts to the side of her face.

'Of course it's my fight,' Carlos says, his breathing heavy. His broad, generous shoulders rise and fall with his substantial breaths, his nostrils flaring. 'I'd do anything for you.'

Becca goes to speak, but doesn't, in the end.

'You just don't get it, do you?' he tells her, shaking his head, frustrated. 'I would climb the highest bloody mountain, and dive the deepest bloody sea for *you*. I can even play along and make-believe it's a good idea for you to marry a bloke you barely know, if it will make you happy. But that he would have you – have your heart – and treat it this way, so carelessly . . .'

Becca's vision blurs with tears, and as she blinks it makes them fall. Carlos is staring dead on at her. How many times has she looked into the handsome face of her friend? Except now, the way he's talking . . . he isn't her friend. Right now she's staring into the face of a man she loves more deeply than a friend. A man who loves her too.

She finally understands their truth – their truth that's been danced around for far too long.

'Becca . . . sod it.' Carlos throws up a hand, defeated by something, apparently. Becca suddenly senses what is coming and can't believe it, all at once. Carlos? Carlos. There's a lump in her throat, her breathing shallow and clipped. This is it. There's no going back now. It's happening. And she wants it to.

Carlos carries on, words flowing out of him like spilled water: 'I have known you a long time, now. And I have loved you for almost all of it. I *know* we are friends. I *know* we run a business together. I've tried to make it go away but it won't. And I always told myself that if you felt the same it would be worth the risk, and that if you felt the same you'd say something. And you never did. But lately, and you can tell me I'm imagining this if you want, because maybe I am, I don't know. But, Becca, I just can't shake the feeling that you're in love with me too. Despite how terrible an idea that might be. But whatever happens, you cannot marry a man who would do this to you. You don't have to love me back, but you cannot marry *him*.'

The rain continues to fall. Carlos stops, gulping for air. Becca looks at him, his familiar, annoying, perfect, friendly, everything-to-her face, and there's only one thing left to do. It doesn't need words. It needs action.

She launches herself at him, and Carlos catches her, his body solid, his grip precise. She loses herself in his mouth, feels his tongue against hers. She has so many thoughts, so many worries, but there, in this moment, finally surrendering to what she's never admitted to knowing, they fade away, blurring into nothing. It's just him, and her, and it is so, so right.

Becca has kissed many men in her time, but nothing – absolutely, categorically nothing – has ever felt more like a last first kiss than this. Carlos is purposeful and gentle, holding her tight so she can submit to his affection: he's confident not because he's cocky – he's confident because there's nowhere he'd rather be. She feels it in his tenderness as she holds the back of his thick neck, fingertips brushing the tattooed skin at the base of his hairline. He is savouring her, relishing the moment, and to know she is so special to him melts her so wholly that she lets out a little *uh*.

'Do *not* make a noise like that, Becca Calloway,' Carlos growls into her mouth. 'Or else I can't be responsible for what will happen next.'

She thinks of Carlos naked, what it will be like to have him inside her. It makes her throb, desire running wild through her. But this is beyond physical. Her heart has swollen eleven million sizes: it's love, true and proper. It always has been.

'I'm in love with you as well,' she says. 'In case that isn't clear.' She laughs, a gentle, self-conscious giggle, and Carlos smiles. She senses his relief: he's jumped, and she caught him.

'I am,' she presses, hands now in his hair, down his back, across his arms, exploring him, checking he's still there, that this is real. 'I have never, ever wanted to think I might love you because I can't lose you. But I do. I love you.'

'I've wanted to hear you say that for so bloody long.' He presses his forehead to hers and her whole being aches for him. Can they stay like this forever? Now they've got here, she doesn't want to let it go. She looks at him, drinking in his stubbled, tanned face, the laughter lines she knows so well, his eyes, his lips. God, his lips. They stand, touching, breathing, staring, and Becca can't stand it – she wants more. Her lips find his again. She is lost in him, and found.

Who knows how long they stay that way. It isn't long enough, that's for sure.

But, eventually, Becca becomes aware of the rain again, of being outside. The *whoosh* of a passing motorbike is strong enough to shock them both out of their trance, and Becca has to say the one thing she's worried about out loud, just to hear him say it's all going to work out just fine.

'I don't want to mess this up.'

He shakes his head, amused. 'We won't.'

'Are you sure?'

'Becca, I've never been more sure of anything.'

She goes in for another long, delicious kiss. She believes him. There's one last thing she has to do, though. She has to face the music with Noah.

And it's as if Carlos can read her mind, as if he knows exactly where her head has gone.

'Go,' he commands, his words strong but his voice soft. Becca can tell that he understands this next bit will be hard for her, even if the writing is on the wall. She feels a fleeting stab of guilt that she's given in to this with Carlos before properly ending things with her fiancé – even if he did cheat on her first. 'Go and finish it with that fool who has no idea what it is to treat you how you deserve to be treated. And then come back, and let me love you exactly how you should be loved.'

Becca nods, swallowing hard. 'I don't want this moment to end,' she says, and her honesty is rewarded with a kiss to the forehead, a wordless admission that Carlos wishes she didn't have to leave too.

It takes everything she has in her to untangle her hand from his, to do anything other than stand with him, finally able to enjoy what they are to each other. But she must. She walks away, knowing how good – how natural – it will feel to come back.

'Your arse looks incredible in those wet jeans!' Carlos hollers at her when she's almost at the edge of the park. She turns and looks at him across the soggy trees and dark tarmac. 'Truly phenomenal!'

She rolls her eyes playfully – this is the Carlos she's in love with: an idiot, but her idiot. His objectification is compensated with a faux-sexy wiggle, and he strides over, tugging her arm to spin her around, pressing her body to his. He uses both hands to grab her behind.

'Honestly,' he says. 'How I've managed to keep my hands off you all this time I'll never know. I'm all for the lovey-dovey stuff, but also . . .' He takes a dramatic inhale. 'Mmmmm, I swear.'

Becca tips her head back, delighted, exposing her neck so Carlos can kiss it. She gives his bum a little pat, and issues a simple instruction. 'Down, boy.'

Carlos paws at her again. 'Impossible,' he tells her. 'You've unleashed the beast.'

'Oh my God, stop it!' she squeals, wriggling out from his grasp. It'll be morning at this rate – she needs to go and sort out her life. 'You're distracting me! Let me go and . . .'

He nods. 'Yeah.' He releases his grip and holds up his hands. 'I'll behave,' he declares, smiling, but looking her up and down as if he could devour her right here, right now. Becca loves how his pupils have dilated, how it feels to receive this attention from him.

'I won't,' Becca retorts with a wink, and the look that passes across Carlos's face – love and lust, in equal measure – is something she wishes she could photograph and frame, a perfect reflection of everything that has come to pass, and everything that will be.

40

She Doesn't Text Back

Noah opens the door to her. She's sopping wet but resolved, now, as to what needs to happen next.

'Jesus,' he tells her. 'I could have sent a cab for you, Becca. Look at you! Where are your keys?'

She doesn't go inside. It's her house, and yet she doesn't want to go in.

'What happened?' Noah asks, his face falling in understanding. She searches his eyes, knowing this will be the last time she gets to look at him this way. Her fiancé. The man she fell in love with. She'd meant it. There's nothing about their romance she faked – she was unashamed in falling for him. Meeting him, getting to know him, taking him to bed that first time, and all the times after that. But she knew, in Miami, that she didn't have his full heart, and he lied to her about it. Noah might believe that he loves her, too, but even if he does, this isn't the kind of love she deserves.

Was she ever going to marry him? Did he mean it when he asked? Did she mean it when she said yes? She thinks so. She thinks they would have been happy.

But now Becca knows Noah is capable of betraying her. And the strength she feels in this moment tells her that there is a piece of her heart she withheld from him – a piece that was Carlos's, really, even if she couldn't admit it to herself. And she knows now that Carlos sees her, but that's not why she has to finish this. It has been finished for weeks, since it happened, and they've both been too cowardly to face it. Carlos is a separate thing to be thought about. For now, it's Becca and Noah, and in ten more seconds, it will simply be Becca, on her own again.

'It's over,' she tells him, and Noah nods.

'I knew it was,' he tells her. He packs his things and leaves. Becca doesn't sleep a wink.

41

She Doesn't Text Back

'Hey,' Becca says as she slips through the front door of the salon the next morning. Carlos is already there, Dana too.

'Hey,' Dana says.

'Hey,' Carlos says.

Becca takes in the sight of the place. The sky is bright and blue today, cleared by last night's storm. The sun is shining, so even though it's cold everything feels hopeful and possible. Christmas is in the air. Celebrations feel promised. She managed maybe an hour of sleep, finally, and woke up with a sense that everything is, finally, as it should be. Noah had texted: *I'm sorry.* She'd replied that she was too. What else was there to say?

'I put your bag and coat in the staff room,' Dana tells her, not looking up from the front-desk computer. 'Carlos said you left in a hurry last night. Is everything OK?'

Becca steals a shy glance at Carlos and says, 'Yes. Thank you. I'll just go and get it.'

In the back room she hears Carlos hand over his bank card for Dana to do a deli run.

'I'm feeling generous,' he tells her. 'Do you fancy picking up coffee and pastries for us all? Get whatever you want.'

If Dana has her suspicions they want to be alone, she doesn't let on.

'She's gone,' Carlos whispers as he appears in the doorway, his voice a low growl. He stands leaning against the wood, his face serious and brooding. Becca bites the inside of her cheek, an almost-smile that feels illicit. Carlos is her best friend – and yet here she is, looking at him through the eyes of something else, something more. His dark cropped hair, his neatly trimmed beard, the thick pulse of his gym-honed shoulders curving into the open neck of a shirt that she knows houses muscles and tattoos that she's teased him for, historically, made out like he's so not her type. The lad about town – that's how she labelled him to keep him at arm's length. But looking properly she sees the softness in his eyes, the gentle salt in the pepper of his temples. He's hot, and handsome, and beautiful – all of those things. And he told her last night that he wants her.

'I've been thinking,' he says, licking his lips as he looks at hers. She throbs between her legs, gets a sudden flash of her body pressed against his, the rain and the drama – will they laugh about that one day? Will that become the legendary story of how they came to be?

'I'm listening,' Becca says, her voice low too. 'What have you been thinking?' She says it as if she's teasing him, as if she's ready to hear a saucy dream or naughty idea. She's never spoken to him like that before – not without being tongue-in-cheek about it.

'We should date. You know. Do this . . . properly.'

'There's nothing proper about any of this,' Becca tells him. 'We already know each other.'

Carlos shakes his head. 'No,' he says. 'I don't think we do.'

He's opening himself wide for her, letting her see him vulnerable and scared. Becca realises she had better be more thoughtful. *This* is serious.

'OK . . .' she tells him. She can't look away. She wants him to kiss her again.

And that's how they end up sitting next to each other at a sushi restaurant in town that Sunday night, knees knocking and arms entwined, laughing and eating and drinking sake, everything changed, forever.

'Oh my GOD!' says Carlos, shaking his head as if even the memory is frustrating for him. 'That guy you brought to MADE Festival? God, he had the teeth, the little gerbil teeth . . .'

'Simon.' Becca nods. 'I *knew* you didn't like him. You kept calling him "mate", but, like, at the end of every. Single. Sentence. As if you were trying to be matey but by saying it so much you had the opposite effect, making it obvious you weren't mates at all.'

'I hold my hands up,' Carlos says, laughing. 'Half the time I'd want to be happy for you, and half the time I'd be thinking, *What does she see in these men? What have they got that I haven't?*'

Becca reaches out a hand to his knee and rubs it lightly. She pouts, as though she's sorry she ever made him feel bad. 'But you never even hinted . . .' she reminds him. 'Honestly, if at any point over the past few years somebody had said to me this would happen—'

'Well, yeah,' Carlos interrupts. 'I wouldn't have believed it either. I wanted it, but half the time had to pretend even to myself, I think. And I *did* date a couple of girls I thought I liked. Stephanie, you remember her?'

'Stephanie!' exclaims Becca, lifting the hand off his knee and accidentally hitting him with her emphasis. 'Oh, I liked Stephanie!'

'She liked you too. But she called me on it. She told me straight that she could see I loved you, exactly like Noosh did after less than an hour of seeing us together.'

'You know what it reminds me of?' Becca asks, and his hand is in hers now, their fingers dancing against one another's. It's weird, and awesome, and wild to Becca that this is happening. She's giddy and giggly. Like, oh, this is what it feels like when it is *exactly* right. Huh. 'I read somewhere that there are two ways to fall in love. Fireworks, an instant boom. And a sunrise, that slow dawning from night to day. You're my sunrise. In all the time I've known you . . .'

Neither of them is finishing sentences tonight. That must be what a true beginning feels like – everything lies unwritten.

'I remember the day I knew, though, with you,' Carlos counters. 'Sticking with the analogy, because obviously I thought you were fit. Facts are facts.' He laughs. 'But you were so calm and collected as we launched Trim. There wasn't a problem you couldn't fix, even if it was just knowing who to ask instead of fixing it yourself. The customers loved you, everyone did. And we went out to celebrate our first month trading.'

'To the Fox and Hound? I remember that, yeah,' Becca says.

'And we stayed until one a.m., just talking – about the business, but about our lives and our hopes as well. And I made you laugh, at one point, and you went from being fit to ... beautiful. The way you laughed with me, it was different to the laugh you give the clients. It was a proper belly laugh. I think I've been trying to make you belly laugh ever since.'

'Aww,' says Becca, smiling. 'And there I was thinking you just never took anything seriously.'

'I took you seriously,' he tells her.

They finish their food, sip their drinks.

'And so . . .' Becca says, feeling nervous all of a sudden, which keeps catching her off guard because since when is she nervous around Carlos? 'This, then . . .'

'You and me?'

'Yeah. What happens now?'

'You'd like a plan?'

'Yes, I think so.'

Carlos shakes his head, closing his eyes slowly, dramatically. 'Oh Becca. Becca, Becca, Becca.'

'What?'

He looks at her. 'Don't you see? There isn't a plan. In the summer, when you made us all do that mad manifestation and you declared to the universe that you wanted to meet your Mr Right? And everything after that was a sign of which plan was best?'

Becca can see where his point is going. She sighs. 'You can't plan for fate,' she says, concluding the thought for him.

Carlos shrugs. 'Well, you can make plans if you like, set little deadlines, trick yourself into thinking you've got some small semblance of control in this life . . .'

'But what will be will be,' Becca supplies.

'I think we both needed this past six months to finally make this happen,' he tells her. 'I'm not saying I needed you to get cheated on to build my courage, but that's the most now-or-never moment I've had in my life. It occurred to me that if I'd told you earlier – at that music festival, or at that night in the pub after our first month trading – you might not have been ready to hear it.'

'I think you're right,' Becca says. 'God, that's screwed up. I had to come so close to getting it wrong to know what was right.'

'And so now we . . . enjoy it. No rush, no time limits, no deadlines.'

'OK . . .' says Becca. 'Are we telling people?'

He shrugs. 'I feel like even if we didn't, people would know. Jia Li will only have to glance at us to call it. It's a good job she's still on maternity leave.'

'Jia Li!' exclaims Becca. 'Bloody Jia Li. She knew how you felt about me?'

'Ever since our little kiss-that-wasn't, all those years ago. I had to tell her. She's been my priest.'

'God,' observes Becca. 'Never let it be said that women can't be discreet when it suits. She honestly has never even come close to telling me, you know.'

'I think she knew you had to arrive to it in your own time.'

Becca asks the waiter for two more drinks, and when they come, they hold their glasses aloft in cheers.

'To taking it slow, then, and surrendering to what will be.'

Carlos leans in for a kiss. 'Or in my case,' he says, 'giving in to what always has been.'

42

She Texts Back

Becca walks through the park, the new year elbowing its way into spring with brighter sun and crisp blue skies. Coats and sunglasses weather, her favourite.

She thinks about all that has happened in the past few months. Mike has moved to London, his presence in Becca's life last year a hazy memory, fragments of a dream she isn't sure was real. New Year's Eve, what would have been their wedding day, came and went, and she was at work, busy, doing what she loves and nestled in amongst the people she loves to do it with: Jia Li coming in a few days here and there to get her out of the house, Carlos continuing to be Carlos: kind, abrasive, present. Dana has handed in her notice and is training to be a primary school teacher, but still wants to help organise their monthly evening events. They're her people, this is her life.

Maybe this year she'll go to a party and somehow get engaged to somebody else.

Maybe she'll spend the next twelve months meeting men who somehow miss the mark.

Maybe, in some other life, she's heartbroken too, because this was always going to be the year for it, despite her best intentions otherwise, because it's just not the time for love.

Regardless, she feels further from her happy ending than she ever has done, and on her thirty-sixth birthday she cried. She got gifts and cards and Carlos organised a delivery of sushi and sake in a very sweet gesture of friendship, but she still sobbed in the shower. Why is finding love harder for her than everybody else? Why hasn't it happened for her yet? Is it because she spends meandering walks to work having long internal monologues, imagining herself as the protagonist at the beginning of her own personal romcom, her thoughts the charming voiceover?

She decides to cheer herself up with a pastry from Clemants. She pushes through to the cool air conditioning, right as Coco – the manifestation mistress herself – is coming from the other direction.

'Becca!' Coco squeals, and Becca feels so special at the genuine delight spread across Coco's face. 'I was literally just thinking about you!'

The man at the back of the coffee queue turns his head halfway to look at them, and Becca thinks, *Oh! Handsome!*

'I didn't think this was your neck of the woods,' Becca notes.

Coco bats a hand. 'Smudging ceremony,' she explains and, looking at the clock on the wall of the café, adds, 'Which I am late for, as it happens. But I'll see if I can stop by the salon sometime – I need a trim.'

'Well, if you do it's on the house,' insists Becca. 'Just give us a call to let us know you're coming.'

'Deal.' Coco waits for Becca to speak, a patient pause as if to speak would be to simply fill silence, when clearing the way for confession is far more useful.

'My manifestation didn't materialise,' Becca says, assuming she's supposed to update her. 'But I'm still hopeful, so . . .'

Coco furrows her brow. 'Oh?' she responds. 'That's so odd – I could have sworn you've got the aura of somebody deeply loved. I can see it.'

Becca shrugs. 'Hopefully any day now,' she says, and Coco winks.

'Undoubtedly,' she tells her.

They say goodbye and Becca slips into the queue behind the man who quite obviously eavesdropped on her whole Coco exchange. He's in chinos and a baby-pink polo shirt, woollen coat over his arm, and as he senses her, he turns, forcing Becca to smile, shyly.

'Hey,' she says to the stranger, because he looks at her like he knows her, even though she doesn't recognise him.

Becca pulls out her phone as she waits, answering a text from her dad, who wants to know if it's OK to still see Paul, Mike's dad. They'd become close last year, two older men needing a friend. *Of course it is,* she writes. If something good came out of this past year, let it be that, she thinks.

The man in front of her turns around.

'I don't suppose you know much about kanelbullar,' he asks her, pointing to the selection on the other side of the glass cabinet. 'I appear to be suffering from a major case of decision fatigue.'

Becca smiles. He's handsome, this man: straight, white teeth and dark hair with a salt and pepper beard that frames his chiselled jaw. Just her type.

'Is that where there's too much choice and so you freeze up?' she asks him.

'Yeah.' He nods. 'I'm terrible for it. I should go through life just flipping a coin, letting the fates decide for me.'

'There are worse things you could do,' Becca points out, and it makes the man laugh.

'Have we met before?' he asks her. 'It sounds like a line, but I promise it's not. I'm Noah.'

'Becca,' says Becca. 'And no, I don't think we have. But it's a pleasure all the same.'

'Well,' says Noah. 'It's only a pleasure if you can actually help me choose. I've been cashless since the pandemic so I'm all out of coins for flipping.'

Becca is very charmed by him. He's got an easy way about him, an easy way of being. He exudes a confidence that Becca has always found sexy. Men who like themselves and the people around them are her kryptonite.

'How about this,' she challenges him. 'I'll put my phone behind my back, and if you guess which hand it's in, you get a kanelbulle. And if you don't, you get the raspberry tart – that's my favourite, for what it's worth. And if you feel disappointed with what the phone decides, you'll still have all the information you need.'

'Wise,' Noah says, clicking his fingers and ending with a single-finger point. He looks down at his hand, like he can't believe he did something so geeky. 'I have never done that before in my life, I swear.'

'Sure.' Becca laughs, and she likes this feeling. The little bubbling up in her tummy, the immediate joy of flirting. She's getting better at it.

It's technically Noah's turn next, so he gestures to the person behind Becca, saying, 'Mate, do you wanna go ahead? Big choices still being made here.'

'Ready?' asks Becca.

Noah closes his eyes, and she notices his lashes sit heavy and thick against his skin.

'Left,' he says, with a decisive nod. 'Side of the heart.'

Becca holds out her hand, phone between her fingers.

'Yes!' Noah cries, pumping his fist. 'That's the kanelbulle! I'm happy with that.'

The person he's let go up ahead finishes, and so Noah orders his kanelbulle and turns to Becca and says, 'Two? Do you want to join me?'

Becca doesn't know what to say. It's bold of him to ask such a thing with the audience of the barista. She looks at the screen of her phone: 8.23 a.m. She has an eight thirty.

'I actually have to get to work,' she says and, to his credit, Noah doesn't seem fazed. He takes the truth for what it is. He turns back to the barista.

'The man eats alone, then,' and he orders a tall black to drink in, too.

When Becca has ordered her skinny latte to go, she approaches Noah at his perch by the breakfast bar running along the glass front of the café. 'It was nice to meet you,' she says, with a smile.

'Likewise,' Noah nods. 'I hope we bump into each other again.'

'Yeah.' Becca smiles. 'In fact . . .' She holds up her phone. 'If you give me your number we could bump into each other on purpose? If you want?'

Noah smiles back. 'I want,' he says, and she unlocks her phone and puts it to contacts so he can add himself.

'OK then,' she says, pulling open the door to leave.

'OK then,' Noah repeats back.

43

She Texts Back

Becca works back to back all day, in her favourite kind of way: her clients all seem funny and interesting, wanting cuts and styles that make her proud of her skills. There's an energy to the day, and part of that is because of this morning, with this Noah guy. Isn't that just life? You're stuck in a rut until you're not, and sometimes it's as simple as being sad and then one day realising it would be easier to be happy. A switch has been flicked this morning, and Becca isn't mad about it.

'I don't know,' she explains later as she sits around a table at the Fox and Hound with Jia Li, Dave, Carlos, and baby Haoyu asleep in his pushchair. 'I always knew I'd be OK, it's just felt really hard to *be* OK since Mike. Maybe now is a time for setting some new intentions . . .'

'Oh God,' groans Carlos. 'Not this again. No more intentions!'

'Why!' exclaims Becca. 'It's nice! I know there's no use trying to change our whole lives, but a little energetic refresh doesn't go amiss. So if you'd like to support that, please, friends . . .'

Jia Li rolls her eyes playfully and explains to Dave: 'Summer solstice,' she says, her tone mocking. 'Last year at work we did a big manifestation ceremony to make our dreams come true or whatever.'

'That sounds quite nice to me,' Dave says pragmatically. 'What did you all manifest?'

All eyes fall to Becca, for some reason. She looks around at her little group, her eyebrows raised.

'What?' she asks. 'Because I'm the one who got engaged, I'm the bloody spokesperson?' She looks at Dave. 'It didn't work, obviously, because I tried to manifest Mr Right and a happy ending and . . . well. We all know how that turned out.'

Dave nods, digesting the information. 'And you two?' he asks Jia Li and Carlos.

Jia Li tries to remember. 'I think I said the same, actually,' she admits, coyly. 'So actually, it did work out. I mean, I was already pregnant when I did it so one could argue that *this little guy* is the love of my life . . .' She looks over to the sleeping bundle of cuteness. 'But, you know. You're definitely a close second.'

Dave pretends to be offended but can't for long, his fake gobsmacked expression giving way to a smile. 'Well, shame you can't marry your own kid,' he says, 'and you have to settle for me instead.'

Jia Li immediately hits Dave on the arm. 'Way to spill the beans!' she shrieks, shaking her head and looking between Carlos and Becca like: *Well! Now you know!*

'What?' Becca says, loudly, before Jia Li tells her to shush before she wakes the baby. 'Congratulations! You guys!'

'I know, I know,' Dave says, waving away the air with a bat of the hand. 'I'm the luckiest man alive. All this happiness from a secret friend-with-benefits. Who could have known?'

'Is that going in the speech?' Carlos jokes, standing up.

'Champagne?' Becca asks him, understanding exactly where he's going.

'But of course,' he says with a nod. 'I'm made up for you both, I really am. Grabbing hold of love. It's amazing. Really, really amazing. You're going to be so happy together. I can feel it.'

Jia Li holds a hand over her heart and Dave reaches for it and kisses her knuckles, Becca and Carlos watching, an audience bearing witness to two people grateful to have found each other.

As Becca and Carlos wait to be served, Carlos says, 'I think I'm jealous, you know.'

'What?' Becca asks, leaning against the bar next to him. 'That they're engaged?'

'Yeah.' He nods thoughtfully. 'There's a courage to it. I mean, sorry – I don't mean to be insensitive. I know, obviously, Mike and everything . . .'

She waves a hand. 'I've turned a corner,' she says, shrugging. 'Like I say, this guy, this morning . . . not that I think I went to buy latte and came back with the phone number of my husband, but it's reminded me that life goes on. I'm envious too, I think. Jia Li never made a fuss about finding the One, she just lived her life and it happened anyway. Proof it's possible. I think I'll try doing the same – not holding on so tight, not trying to steer the ship. Surrendering.'

Carlos laughs. 'Can't wait to see how that works out,' he says, and when Becca goes to admonish him for being mean he knocks his shoulder against hers and says, 'I'm kidding, Bec. You know I just want you to be happy.'

'Thank you,' Becca says. 'I just want you to be happy too.'

They grin at each other, and Becca almost reaches out to hug him – but then the champagne is out on the bar.

'Jia Li was just saying that your manifestation last year was for your friends to find what they wanted in love,' Dave says to Carlos, as Becca puts down the four flutes and Carlos pours the bottle.

'Was it?' he says, careful not to make the champagne fizz up and over the rims. 'Sounds like a very kind and generous thing to say. I mean, that makes sense, being the kind and generous man that I am.'

'You're joking,' Becca says, passing around the glasses he has filled. 'But you actually are those things, so.'

Carlos makes a gesture with his hand, wafting it about, and then says: 'Go on . . .' He looks conspiratorially at Dave and Jia Li. 'Keep it coming. It's not often you give me such glowing reviews. It's normally *Carlos, why can't you keep on top of the client colour records? Carlos, where's the sheet for the glasses hire? Carlos, why have you got so much holiday booked in?*'

'You do take a lot of holidays,' notes Dave, and Becca likes him more and more, with each passing evening she spends with him.

'Hey!' Carlos says. 'Blokes united, all right? New rule!'

Becca holds up a glass. 'Here's to you,' she tells Jia Li and Dave. 'For knowing love when you see it. And here's to

Carlos, who *does* take a lot of holidays, and who *does* forget to update his client records, but who is also funny and kind and entertaining and loyal.' She looks at him, Carlos's face impressed that she has indeed continued with her compliments. Why not? Why can't she tell her friends she loves them? The way he looks at her – eyes wide, genuinely touched – makes her want to continue. Can she make him cry? He looks emotional. OK, game on. She's going to ham it up to see if she can push him over the edge.

'Carlos, you're one of the most remarkable people in my life. You are.'

She can feel Jia Li's eyes on her and is vaguely aware that she's slipped her hand to Dave's knee, her knuckles turning white.

'I don't know how I would have done this past year without you. You cheer me on when I'm winning and run alongside me when I'm not, reminding me that there's only a good night's sleep between a bad day and a good one. We started as business partners and became best friends. And that is the triumph of my life. I miss you when you're not in the salon. I hear something funny and can't wait to tell you. You make my days better, simply by being who you are, even though who you are can sometimes be maddening because you need to take stuff just a tiny bit more seriously. But then, you remind me not to be so serious. I think you do that for all of us. So. Yeah, these two are getting married, yay for them.' Becca gestures at Jia Li and Dave, who are sitting in awestruck silence, their eyes flicking between Becca and Carlos, Carlos and Becca. 'But also cheers to you, the man every other man should strive to be more like. You're a marvel, Carlos Raverra, and knowing you makes me better.'

Carlos sits, his eyebrows raised, his features soft, and Becca thinks she's done it, that she has made him cry. Until, that is, she realises that she is the one who is actually crying. A fat, heavy tear lands on her hand and she looks down to examine it, surprised, and then quickly sits down, wiping her face, muttering, 'Sorry. Why the hell am I crying?' She looks at Dave and Jia Li. 'It's you two,' she insists. 'You're making me emotional!'

Carlos reaches out and snakes an arm around her shoulders, pulling her in and whispering, 'You little fucker. You almost made *me* cry!' and Becca laughs, and wants to explain that that was the point, but she can't.

'Jeez.' She scrambles in her bag for a tissue. 'I really am sorry! I don't know what's wrong with me!'

Dave coughs, as if he's trying to break through the tension. But there isn't *tension*, is there? Unless everyone is awkward about Becca's tears – if they are, they can join the club.

'Becca. You're killing me here,' Carlos announces, throwing a hand up for emphasis. He just clips a passing waiter, carrying a tray of empties.

'Watch out!' the waiter yelps, Carlos perilously close to knocking every single glass clean off. He snatches his hand back just in time.

'What is it about you and trays of glasses, Carlos! Crikey!'

I feel like I've just spoiled the moment.' He grins, impishly. Becca looks at him, shaking her head. Carlos – exactly as she knows him, and loves him.

'Is this a bad time to point out that it was actually *me* who wished for my friends and family to find love?' asks Jia Li. 'Now I think about it – Carlos wanted love, and it was me who said, *yes, and for the people I care about too.*'

'I can't give any more speeches,' laughs Becca. 'Sorry. I'm done.' Everyone else laughs with her.

'Well,' Dave says, tapping the table with his fingertips. 'At least you've already got a speech for when you two do finally get married,' he jokes, and everyone laughs again and Becca scrunches up her nose at Carlos, in on the joke, and it isn't until she gets home, later that night, make-up off and PJs on, staring at the ceiling in bed that she realises, the clarity suddenly startling . . .

44

She Texts Back

It's Carlos.

It's Carlos, and it always has been.

She picks up her phone and scrolls to his number.

No. She can't call him.

She needs to see him.

She *has* to see him.

With a wave of certainty so overpowering it makes her dizzy, Becca gets up, looks in the mirror, and decides she doesn't have time to do whatever she thought she might be about to sort out – her hair, piled high on her head, or her make-up, currently non-existent. She's in her pyjamas. At least her teeth are clean. She's going to go to him. She's about five and a half years too late, now she thinks of it. It has to be right now, this very second.

Every step she takes down the stairs mirrors a swelling in her chest, a summoning of her future, a leap of bravery and stupidity that makes her feel like a superhero. Carlos, Carlos, Carlos: it's him. It's him first thing in the morning, when it's just them in the salon and they sip coffee and he tells her some outrageous story from the night before. It's him chatting to a client in the next chair, prepping her work station when she's busy, asking after her parents and dragging her out to the pub after work. It's him on trips, on adventures, the person she wants to tell about the funny thing that happened, the sad thing she heard. She'd thought he was her best friend, and now the switch has been flicked, the light has come on, and she gets it. He's her soulmate. She wonders if he gets it too. She's about to find out.

Becca slips on the old trainers next to the doormat, grabs whatever coat she finds first, and swings open her front door in such a daze that she practically sees the man in question right in front of her, an apparition of her heart's desire.

'Hello,' he says, calmly, leaning against the outdoor porch frame with insouciant charm.

Becca blinks. It really *is* him. Her heart is about to leap out of her chest in . . . what? Excitement, or fear? She settles on both.

'Carlos,' she says, startled. He smiles, a half-grin that is at once shy and provocative. He has never been more handsome than he is in this moment. Her heart skips several beats.

'I had a feeling I might see you again tonight . . .' he says.

Becca's head swirls with thoughts, but she can't hold on to any of them long enough to let them fully form.

'You did?' Her voice is small. Is he saying he feels the same? Is she understanding this properly? Because if she says what she's feeling, she can't take it back – this is it. The freefall. There's time to change her mind, to say she'd forgotten to take out the bins or heard a fox. He holds her gaze, a challenge, daring her to pretend this is anything other than it is. She doesn't know he feels the same for sure, but she does, really. Peel back the stories she tells herself and, on some level, she knows not to be afraid. And yet. She'd love for him to say it first.

'I've been waiting for you,' he tells her. Becca doesn't trust herself to speak. 'Waiting for you to catch up,' he clarifies.

He's beautiful, Becca acknowledges, a thought finally coming to the fore. His dark, brooding eyes, his smooth, tanned skin, the tattoos she's joked about before but are so quintessentially Carlos . . . Everything about him is so comforting and familiar but looking at him – seeing how he is looking at her – feels new. Forbidden. Inevitable. The words stick in her throat.

'How long have you known?' she asks.

'Since the alleyway.'

She thinks back to that night, that night they almost kissed and brushed it off as if it was nothing. He says it as though it's obvious.

'Oh,' she says.

He adds, as if he may as well admit to eating the whole pack of biscuits and not just two: 'Maybe longer.'

It makes Becca smile. 'So what do we do now?' she asks. 'What happens next?'

Carlos laughs, and the distance between them – a few feet – feels like a continent. Becca licks her lips, anticipation swirling. Swallowing hard, holding his gaze, she's nodding without speaking, as if reassuring herself that yes, this really is happening. She holds out a hand, and, with that, she's answered her own question. This is what happens next.

Carlos takes it, steps inside, and closes the front door behind him. The house is in darkness – Becca had been rushing out in such a hurry. There's a beat as the lock clicks behind him, and then their bodies press together, his hands in her hair, her fingers on the base of his neck, and they kiss, and kiss, and kiss, hard and fast and furious, making up for all that lost time.

Becca can't say that sex with Carlos is exactly as she'd imagined it would be, because she'd never properly let herself wonder what he'd be like as a lover. It doesn't matter. Her imagination has limits, and what Carlos does to her goes way beyond them. Right up until the sun peeks through the curtains they lick and kiss and touch and laugh, all with a heavy dose of eye contact that feels so intense Becca comes in crashing waves of yearning. It's as if they've been preprogrammed with the exact specifications of their sexual preferences, understanding each other's bodies so intricately that their intimacy itself is the turn-on. Carlos bends her and moves her and is vocal about how sexy Becca is, how much he wants her, and she's just as vocal and appreciative in turn. They're two pieces who fit. It's hot. Becca has never experienced such a holy connection with somebody in bed. She didn't know it could be this delicious.

'Carlos,' she whispers as they lie naked and exhausted and boundlessly contented. Sex between friends can open up a million questions – or, in the case of Becca and Carlos, it can provide a million answers. Becca feels totally sated, thoroughly pleased.

'Hmmm?' he replies, the rise and fall of his muscular chest under her cheek, a hand cupping her arse as if he can't believe his luck.

'I think I forgot to say I love you,' she tells him. Their bodies have said it – their words haven't got there yet.

He pulls back his face so he can see her properly, a smile creeping up his cheeks. 'I figured you did,' he says. 'But just in case I haven't been clear: I love you too. Madly. In fact, I think you might be the love of my life.'

Becca sits up to look at him, head cocked to the side. 'So this is . . . happening?' she clarifies.

'Of course it's bloody happening,' Carlos hoots, pulling her naked body towards him. 'I love you, Becca Calloway.'

'I love you, Carlos Raverra.'

He strokes her hair, her back, and they let the moment land, two idiots smiling and in love, post-coital and drunk on one another. Then he adds: 'Shall we celebrate with breakfast? You've shagged the life out of me.'

Becca kisses him, smashing her face against his, her heart singing a thousand love songs.

'Let's make pancakes,' she says. They pad downstairs together, still unclothed, holding hands, stealing kisses every step of the way.

'Say it one more time,' he murmurs in her ear as she stands at the countertop mixing batter.

'That I love you?'

'Yeah,' he says, pressed up against her from behind. She stops mixing.

'I love you,' she sighs, cheerfully.

'I love you too,' he tells her, holding on to her hips, gripping tight. 'I love you so, so much. And now you know that, everything else can begin.'

They don't get around to making the pancakes.

It doesn't matter.

45

She Texts Back
She Doesn't Text Back

One spring day, Trim is closed. Inside, the hairdryers hang from their homes below each station, the kitchen remains unused, the back door locked shut. It's unusual, for a Saturday. It isn't Christmas, it isn't Easter. In fact, never before have they closed on a Saturday, their busiest day of the week. But this Saturday isn't like the others. Stuck on the front door in the lower left corner, there is a small, laminated sign. It says:

Salon Closed
If you didn't already know, we're getting married!
If you'd like to celebrate our love, we'll be at the Fox and
Hound for a drink from 6 p.m.
We will reopen in one week.
We love you! Almost as much as we love each other . . .
Thank you for being part of our story,
Carlos and Becca Raverra-Calloway x

The groom smiles wider than the moon in the wedding photographs. The bride's dress barely conceals her growing bump. They are phenomenally happy, together, a pair giddy and perfect, totally and utterly lovestruck.

Publishing Credits

If you add up all my novels, my novella, and my non-fiction work, *Lovestruck* is my tenth (tenth!) book. And you know what? I think it might also be my favourite.

That's in no small part because of the phenomenal team behind it. To everyone listed here: I am very, *very* grateful for everything that you have done to welcome me to Century and make this story what it is. You are powerhouses.

Editorial – Katie Loughnane, Coco Hagi, Laurie Ip Fung Chun
Copyediting and Proofreading – Richenda Todd, Gabriella Nemeth
Marketing – Hope Butler, Becca Wright
Publicity – Klara Zak
Sales – Claire Simmonds, Olivia Allen, Evie Kettlewell, Mat Watterson
International Sales – Richard Rowlands, Barbora Sabolova
International Rights – Amelia Evans, Monique Corless, Elizabeth Brandon, and the PRH Rights Team
Production – Annie Peacock
Design – Emma Grey Gelder, Holly Ovenden
Audio – Meredith Benson

Also, credit to:

Literary agent – Ella Kahn
Freelance Editor – Anna Barrett
Beta reader – Calum McSwiggan

And, of course, to the booksellers, book bloggers and readers who tell their customers, followers and friends about my books, and reach out to tell me they're reading too: you're the kindest, and I hope I've done you proud with this one.

Dear Reader,

I've just finished writing my next book, which is called *Enemies to Lovers* – a trope I'm obsessed with. Suffice to say, I had a lot of fun with it . . .

It's publishing in summer 2024 but I wanted to give you a sneak peak of what's to come. Please turn the page for an exclusive extract of the first chapter.

I hope you'll love Flo, love-to-hate Jamie, and pre-order the book so that their story lands on your doorstep or digital device right on publication day!

Thank you for reading, and for your support.

Love,
Laura x

1.

I am floating. I am floating on the crystal-clear water of whatever ocean laps around these sandy Greek shores. Is it the Aegean Sea? Hmmm. I should probably know that. I'll google it when I'm back near my phone. Obviously I don't have my phone in the water. It's just me, and presumably some fish, early-afternoon sun burning my skin and – if I wouldn't get laughed at by my ridiculous family for poetic hyperbole – I'd go as far as to say *bringing my very soul back to life* after four long years under grey Scottish skies. Actually, that's not strictly true. The university library was under grey Scottish skies, and so for the most part I was under strip lighting. Either way, this is the first time I've felt any semblance of hope, or freedom, or *possibility*, in ages. My friend Claire says that we're all solar-powered. I see what she means, now. It's like when the sun is out and the water glistens, everything that came before melts away. So much doesn't matter now I'm here, unmoored, bobbing about, the sound of my own beating heart surprisingly good company. Even last Christmas and The Thing That Haunts Me Most In This Life feels far away right now, and after my breakdown I didn't think anything could be any worse than that. Only I could hit rock bottom and then discover it has a basement. Classic.

Oh God. Thinking about last Christmas is setting off the wrong neurotransmitters in my head. I will myself to breathe, like the therapist taught me. *I'm okay. I'm okay. I'm okay.*

Standing up, the seabed squashing sand between my toes, the sun forcing me to squint, I notice a stranger up on the beach. There's Mum, Dad and my two brothers, Alex and Laurie, and there's Laurie's wife Kate, too. We got in an hour ago, the owners of the villa having kindly left us a picnic basket for an early supper, which we schlepped down here along with some beach chairs and our towels. Just the six of us.

Except, I'm here, so that should be five bodies up there on the sand.

I lower my body back into the warmth of the sea and swim as close to the shore as possible, staying submerged so I can surreptitiously dislodge a wedgie and do a little 'holiday wee'. I'm not embarrassed by that: *everybody* does it, and anyone who says they don't is lying. I turn to look again, now I'm closer. And it's then that I realise the sixth person up there with my family definitely isn't a passing local or a figment of my imagination. It's Jamie.

Those sneaky buggars – I'd bet a million and change on my family having withheld the information in case I didn't come. It's him! No warning, no foresight, no preparations to be had. Just BOOM. A hand grenade with nowhere to take cover.

Jamie Kramer – my nemesis – is on my family holiday.

And I am *furious* about it.

I can see, as I finally climb out of the ocean, that he's the colour of baked earth after four months sailing yachts across the seven seas for millionaires who like to leave their boats in one place, but pick them up in another. He's broad – broader than he deserves to be – and the thick dent of his spine looks like somebody has taken their thumb and smudged down the centre of his back, lumps and bumps and dents and pops all around it in places I didn't even know there could be lumps and bumps and dents and pops. His arms are as thick as my thighs. Jesus. What a show-off. I'm all for keeping fit, but Jamie takes it too far. That time could be spent on other things, like . . . reading . . . or . . . watching *The Real Housewives of Dubai*.

I take a breath, readying for *that look* he gives me: blank, unmoved, bored. But I have to say hello, because he's my brother's best friend, my parents treat him like a son, and I know everyone will be holding their breath to see if I'm going to be polite – which of course I will be, because as I keep trying to assert to my family, I'm not the little girl they continue to think I am. I might be the youngest, but when you've been through what I've been through, it makes you grow up. And I'm grown-up enough to wring out the seawater from my hair, shake the water off my arms, and make my approach to grab a beer and acknowledge his stupid arrival.

As I walk up to the cooler we stashed the drinks in, Jamie turns *just enough* that I *know* that he knows I'm here, but after an almost imperceptible beat he focuses his attention fully back on Mum without acknowledging me. Typical. Mum is in sickening rapture at whatever silly thing he's telling her. She's practically fawning, but I will do no such thing. This is how Jamie plays it with everyone. He lets people come to him, flexing his gravitational pull with that smile and that

3

easy laugh. I tried to bring it up with my mother, once, how he's stealthily manipulative, and she told me not to be so sensitive, that I was reading too much into it. The implication of that is *I do that because I am a bit unhinged* and so I never brought it up again. But I know I'm right.

I bypass them, getting my drink and popping the lid off, raising it in Jamie's direction as I make my way over to Kate.

'Hey, Jamie,' I say, not looking at him, acting as cool and indifferent as I can manage. I've already stridden off as he says my name in return.

'Flo.'

No hello, no hey. Just intoning my name as if we're lawyers in a B-list series and he's come to my deposition as a hostile witness. His timbre is low and gruff, like a country singer crooning about a broken heart. I hate that I notice.

'Christ alive, Flo,' Kate says to me as I flop down into the low beach chair beside her. My bum practically touches the sand through the low fabric of the seat. I misjudged the distance, and inelegantly flail about – careful not to spill my beer – trying to get comfy.

'What?' I ask, as I get settled. She looks at me, eyebrows raised in amusement.

'That's the holiday spirit,' she coos, taking the mick out of my sudden bad mood.

'Sorry,' I say, taking a long pull from my bottle. 'It's the 4 a.m. wake-up call to get to the airport. Blame Dad's obsession with arriving for flights four hours early.'

Kate sticks out her bottom lip and pulls a 'sad' face. It's a thing we do to sarcastically stop each other from ever moaning too much. 'Spoiled little rich girl upset that her daddy-waddy wanted to make sure there were no problems?' she teases, in a silly voice. 'How *horrible*.'

'You're right,' I nod, scrunching up my face. 'At least we had time for a beer and a full English. How many minutes did you and Laurie have to spare before you made it?'

'Ninety seconds,' Kate shoots back. 'But we did get to ride on the golf buggy thing after security, so silver linings.'

'Luck is *always* on your side,' I say, reaching over for my beach bag. I need my sunglasses. 'I have honestly never met somebody else for whom all traffic lights turn green, all doors open, free coffees are generously given . . .'

'Speaking of which,' she shrugs, noticing that I seem unable to find whatever I'm looking for, intuiting that it must be my sunglasses, and so pulling out a second pair from her beach bag, which I take gratefully. 'We did get complimentary croissants at Pret, to apologise for their stupidly long queue.'

'You almost missed the flight because you were in *Pret*?!' I shriek, and she motions for me to hush.

'Shut up!' she hisses, looking in my dad's direction to check he hasn't heard. She lowers her voice: 'I made Laurie swear he wouldn't dob me in for it. But I needed a ham and cheese croissant thing, and you know I can't function without a coffee in the morning.'

'You're preaching to the converted,' I say. 'Coffee is life.' I gulp down my beer and take in the perfection of our surroundings: powdery yellow sand stretching all the way around the cove, endless water, the sun lowering in the sky to envelop everything in its syrupy flame. With my back to

Jamie I can almost forget he's there – and then Mum titters at him yet again, and I'm reminded that he's here. Before Kate can ask me about it I say, 'Anyway, what was your "Christ alive" for? I fear I got you off track …'

'Oh,' she says, nodding. She's been taking in the view, too. She's already glowing, already looking relaxed and in the holiday mood. 'Yeah. I was just going to say that you look *ridiculous* in that bikini. Your waist, your boobs . . . if that's what almost getting sectioned does to a girl, I might need a breakdown myself.' I pull a face at her that's supposed to mean *are you seriously joking about what happened*, but it goes unnoticed. Unnoticed or ignored, which is quintessential Kate. Of course, I don't mind, not really, because she was one of the few people to keep treating me like normal when it was all happening. In fact, I think she was the only one, and the gallows humour is part of it. No special treatment for this basket case of a human, no kid gloves. 'Although,' she continues, 'I suspect that an episode of my own would involve a lot of comfort eating, thus thwarting my desire to get as snatched as you are.'

'You could arrange one of those happy breakdowns, put it in the contract between you and your brain.'

'Oh yes,' she agrees. 'Great idea. Dear brain, please refer to clause 3c, pertaining to getting my titties to sit as nice as Flo's in a teeny weeny string bikini.'

'This isn't tiny!' I squeal. 'This is a *family* holiday!'

'A family holiday in Greece, where the locals look like gods. Play your cards right and you could have a *fantastic* two weeks looking like that, baby.'

I arch an eyebrow. 'Sex hasn't been on my mind for quite some time,' I remind her.

'More's the pity,' she shoots back. I don't dignify that with a response. I've had bigger fish to fry, after all. 'By the way,' she says, lowering her voice and leaning in. 'How are we feeling about . . .' She nods her head in Jamie's direction, where he's now got not only Mum but Dad and my brother Alex eating out of the palm of his hand too. I was naïve to think she wouldn't ask.

'What?' I say, playing dumb, trying not to get drawn in. Kate is the only one who knows how much Jamie bothers me because she's got female intuition and had no sooner started seeing Laurie than had cornered me to demand explanations. But for everybody else's sake I do try to keep the peace. Jamie is around a lot, because a couple of years ago he lost both his parents in a car accident, and so Mum and Dad have unofficially made him their fourth child. I do actually have a heart, so he gets leeway for such painful trauma because God, I can't even imagine something that devastating happening. I feel for him for that. I do.

But then he's an arse to me, *again*, and suddenly the sympathy fades away.

'Okay,' Kate says. 'I see what game we're playing . . .'

'There's no game,' I tell her.

'Sure,' she says.

'There's not!' I insist, right as Laurie reappears from wherever he's been, asking, 'There's not what?'

He sits down on the sand in between Kate's legs, and she kisses the top of his head. They've been married for just over a year and are disgustingly in love. Kate tells him to mind his own business and I close my eyes to luxuriate in the heat on my skin and shut everybody else out.

'Shall we eat?' Laurie says, because ten minutes of silence from him is asking too much. 'I'm bloody starving. And did anyone think to bring down a speaker? We need to up the holiday vibe now that the whole crew is here!'

'I hadn't known we were waiting for anybody else to join the crew,' I say, without opening my eyes, trying to sound nonchalant.

I practically *hear* Laurie shrug, and peeking through one eye, see him already on his feet again, heading towards the hamper to start setting out the food. 'Flo, don't be ridiculous. It was all on the family email chain.'

I look at Kate. 'There's a family email chain?'

She pulls a face. 'Babe,' she tells me, pulling her sunglasses down to look over them dramatically. 'If you're not getting those emails, trust me: you're best off out of it. I love your mother as much as my own, but since she retired . . .'

'She's sending you *War and Peace* every day?' I supply.

'Like you wouldn't believe,' she replies with a sigh.

I scramble out of my seat to go help Laurie with the food – if you don't move fast in this family, you're only left with crumbs.

'Fine,' I say, waving a hand. 'I'll choose my ignorant bliss.'

But I try to push down the voice that quietly wonders: *If I'm not on that email chain, what else don't my family include me in?*

The sun begins its descent to meet the sea, and with the sunset comes a drop in temperature, so Jamie makes a fire. He creates a little circle with pebbles and stones, somehow manages to acquire driftwood, and genuinely gets it going by rubbing two sticks together, like a regular Robinson Crusoe. He's all massive hands and concentrated effort, and it's frustrating that he's even more handsome than usual, with his tan and his stubble and his grown-out hair. Mum applauds his masculine bravado, but the rest of us Greenbergs busy ourselves dishing out Greek salad and an array of crusty breads, olives and cheese, eating off our laps, the tinny notes of a summer beach playlist coming from the Bluetooth speakers Alex has thought to bring. All in all, it's not a bad little set-up – everything Jamie aside. I definitely do not look in his direction. We've still not spoken directly to one another. Let my mother have him. I'll keep my distance.

'Cor,' says Dad, helping himself to some more of the Greek wine we've been gifted. 'It's all right, all this, isn't it?'

'I'll say,' says Alex. 'I keep wanting to check my phone for urgent alerts that mean I've got to run down to A&E and put out another fire. But I don't. I can't believe I'm actually on holiday.'

'Same,' says Laurie. 'I don't remember the last time I've done less than a fifty-hour week.'

I sigh contentedly, in agreement, which Laurie deliberately misreads.

'All this a bit too much like hard work for you, Flo?' he teases. 'Bit more activity than you're used to, I'd imagine.'

I roll my eyes. Laurie thinks it's hilarious that not only did I get a degree in English, and then a master's, but I'm about to embark on a PhD, too. He was at uni for ages as well, but as a lawyer that was 'real studying' and not, as he loves to remind me, paying thousands to read books and 'wank off' about them.

9

'Laurie . . .' Mum warns, as if I'm six years old and might cry.

'It's okay, Mum,' I say. 'I know Laurie continues to be intimidated by anyone capable of the empathy it takes to put themselves in somebody else's shoes long enough to enjoy 80,000 words. Speaking of which, Laurie, how is it going with that book on the history of football that you got in your stocking? You were what, twelve pages in on the plane? That must be a whole word a day since Christmas.'

'I've been saving it, for your information,' Laurie bats back. 'I just needed a break from work. Work is a thing that grown-ups do, where—'

'Anyone want to play volleyball?' Jamie interjects, stuffing the last of the food from his plate into his mouth and patting his bare eight-pack of a stomach in satisfaction. 'I've got some energy to burn.'

Alex lets out an enormous beery belch.

'So that's a yes from Alex,' Dad chuckles, because for some reason Alex is allowed to be an absolute heathen and call it a laugh, whereas the rest of us get bound to a normal standard of manners.

'You in, old man?' Jamie asks, eyes alight with mischief in Dad's direction.

'Who are you calling an old man?' Dad counters, a glimmer in his eye. 'I could run circles around you and your . . . your . . . *abs*. With age comes experience, remember.' He drains his glass and gets up. 'And there's a six-pack hidden under here somewhere,' he adds, patting his own tum. 'Hidden deep, like, but definitely there.'

Jamie smiles. He doesn't do it often, even when he's charming Mum or bantering with Dad. He crinkles at the eyes a bit, sometimes even hints at a smirk, but a full-beam smile like the one he gives Dad now is a very rare occurrence indeed, at least when I've been around. His teeth are pearly white and in the three seconds I forget to be obtuse and look right at him, his tongue darts out over his lips and back again. I quickly look away.

'Michael,' Jamie says. 'You and me as the dream team, opposite Laurie and Alex, then?'

Of course, he isn't asking me to join in. *Of course*, he isn't! I think it's the indifference that makes me so mad. I have to work so hard to stay out of Jamie's way, but for Jamie, I don't even seem to cross his mind. How self-centred and mean do you have to be?

'There's life in this old dog too, I'll have you know,' Mum asserts, leaping up and going to stand with Alex and Laurie, her allegiance clear.

In unison, everyone turns to me and Kate, the expectation unspoken but written on their faces: one of us needs to make up the numbers because right now it's three versus two.

'I'll umpire,' smiles Kate, like butter wouldn't melt, reaching over for more bread and salad. I glare at her. I know I wanted to get invited to play, but I didn't want to be on a team as the consolation prize.

'Flo?' asks Dad.

I stand up. I might not have been anybody's first choice, but that doesn't mean I can't dominate the court.

11

'I play to win,' I warn my new teammates, wagging a finger. Dad winks at me, a subtle *that's my girl!* Jamie is already rigging up a makeshift court, drawing lines in the sand and hoisting up a very sorry-for-itself net that he must have found on his scavenger hunt for firewood.

'I wish I had a whistle!' Kate yells, in between mouthfuls of bread.

'Just shout loudly!' Laurie instructs.

'Okay!' she screams. Jamie grabs the ball Mum brought down from the villa, and commands Dad to keep left and he'll keep right. I stand behind them both, awaiting my orders from our self-appointed team captain, but they don't come. That would involve him acknowledging my existence, after all.

Kate screams, 'Go!', and Jamie throws up the ball confidently, the muscles in his shoulders rippling as if they've been told a joke, and he thwacks the ball over the net in Alex's direction, who bats it back with surprising grace.

'You're moving pretty fast for somebody who came last in Cross Country!' I rib him over the net.

He pretends a dagger has gone through his heart with a 'pouty' face.

'Long-distance running is for people with no brute strength,' he says. 'Your words don't hurt me, Florence.'

Beside him, Mum hits the ball towards Dad, who bats it back, and then Alex fouls out by pushing it into the net.

'Is that the brute strength you were talking about?' I ask, and he responds by lifting the ball and hitting it so hard that Dad doesn't see it coming, and it gets him square between the eyes.

'Michael!' Mum cries out, and Dad blinks several times as if he's trying to catch up with what's happened.

'Mike, you okay?' Jamie asks, shooting A Look at me, as if Dad's inability to stay focused on the ball is somehow *my* fault.

'You've got me at a disadvantage, I think,' Dad mutters. 'I might have had one glass of wine too many for the A-team.'

'You four play,' Mum says, coming around to take Dad by the hand and march him off to sit down. We loiter for a second, just to make sure he's okay, before Kate bellows, 'Get on with it then!'

It's me and Jamie now, a team of two. Except, Jamie obviously didn't get the memo because although Alex and Laurie work together irritatingly well, Jamie and I don't work well together at all, and he keeps getting in the way of all my attempts to hit the ball.

Alex and Laurie score another point. And another. I can tell it's bugging Jamie but *still* he doesn't speak to me. I'm going to have to break first, if there's any chance of getting the game back – and to wipe the smug looks off my brothers' faces, right now I'd rather sit down for a cup of tea and a chat with the Taliban.

'Stick left,' I say. 'And I'll stick right.'

Jamie flares his nostrils enough to let me know he heard me, and away we go again: I clobber the ball and get us a point. Jamie gets us another. I get us one more and now we're back even with the boys. But Jamie starts playing the whole court again, pushing me to one side; a couple of times we almost collide. I refuse to speak to him again, so instead I get aggressive with the ball, flying this way and that, flinging myself towards it so Jamie can't get it.

And that's how my bikini top ends up pinging off, over my head, so that yes, we score, but also, my tits are on full show to my entire family, because I've decided to do some sort of mid-air yoga in the semi-nude.

'Ewww!' cry Laurie and Alex, trying to decide who is more grossed out.

'Florence!' my father yells, right as Kate starts squealing with hysterical laughter.

I hold my arm across my boobs (they're just boobs!) and look for where my top has gone. I'm confronted with Jamie, inches from me, sweat on his tanned, furrowed brow, eyes dark with evident disgust for what he's just borne witness to. Standing this close, looking at him eye-to-eye this way, something jolts through me. My throat goes dry and my mouth flops open. I forget I'm topless as I try to catch the breath he's somehow stolen from me.

He hands me his T-shirt. His words are quiet but firm.

'Put this on,' he tells me. There's a tone to his voice, but I can't place it. He's mad, but also . . . maybe amused? Not *quite* mad?

But before I can figure it out, he walks back to the net.

'Let's play!' he shouts, his focus dead ahead.

His T-shirt smells like cedar and musk.

I hate that I notice that, too.